THE
HOURGLASS
DOOR

THE HOURGLASS DOOR

A Novel by

LISA MANGUM

SHADOW
MOUNTAIN

Quotation on pages 63–64: From *The Aeneid* by Virgil, translated by Robert Fitzgerald, translation copyright © 1980, 1982, 1983 by Robert Fitzgerald. Used by permission of Random House, Inc.

Quotations on pages 240–41, 262, and 263: From *The Divine Comedy of Dante Alighieri: Inferno* by Allen Mandelbaum, translation copyright © 1980 by Allen Mandelbaum. Used by permission of Bantam Books, a division of Random House, Inc.

Quotation on page 394: From *The Divine Comedy of Dante Alighieri: Paradiso* by Allen Mandelbaum, translation copyright © 1984 by Allen Mandelbaum. Used by permission of Bantam Books, a division of Random House, Inc.

First printing in hardbound 2009.
First printing in paperbound 2010.

Library of Congress Cataloging-in-Publication Data

Mangum, Lisa.
    The hourglass door / Lisa Mangum.
        p. cm.
    Summary: Dante, a prisoner sent from fifteenth-century Italy into the present time as punishment, meets and falls in love with Abby, a high school senior who may be the only one who can save him.
    ISBN 978-1-60641-093-6 (hardbound : alk. paper)
    ISBN 978-1-60641-679-2 (paperbound)
    [1. Time travel—Fiction.   2. High schools—Fiction.
3. Schools—Fiction.   4. Interpersonal relations—Fiction.   5. Good and evil—Fiction.]   I. Title.
    PZ7.M31266537Ho 2009
    [Fic]—dc22   2008053555

Printed in the United States of America
Worzalla Publishing Co., Stevens Point, WI

10   9   8   7   6   5

For Tracy
Presto—track 3

PROLOGUE

I t is the counting that saves him.

The darkness has robbed him of nearly all his senses; he fears his sanity is next. The fear is a suffocating weight on his chest, turning his limbs to lead, making his once-nimble fingers clumsy and useless. No, not entirely useless. He can still use them to count.

In the darkness, the space between the sounds he hears is filled with potential, pregnant with hidden life. He willingly chooses to live in this non-space if it will keep his sanity intact.

So he counts the drops of water falling from the rotting ceiling overhead . . . the number of times the prisoner next to him proclaims his innocence . . . the crumbs of the crust that the guards toss at him as if he were an animal . . . the steps it takes to circumvent his cramped cell.

He counts the days he lived before coming to this place— how many days in seventeen years? How many years in a lifetime?

It's hardest to keep track of the time. Without light, without variation, all the days blend into one seamless stretch of *now*. He longs for the uncertainty of the future.

The light hurts his eyes. The unexpected bustling of activity beyond the bars rattles through his ears like chains. He dares a glance, wills his eyes to focus.

Two guards run past his cell. One more trails behind them, a blanket clutched in his fist.

He knows he shouldn't be interested, shouldn't be curious. It will only make things worse, distract him from his counting. But he can't help himself. He stands on his toes, pressing his face to the cold bars.

And then he sees her. All the numbers run out of his head like sand through a sieve. All the images in his eyes fade until he can see only her. His heart beats in uncountable rhythms.

She is what he imagines the angels would envy. Her heart-shaped face frames brown eyes soft as newly turned earth, red lips full as blushing rosebuds, pale cheeks smooth as unmarked vellum. Dark brown curls tumble over her shoulders.

She stands on her toes too, her hand holding onto the door frame for balance. She scans the room, looking but not seeing. Her eyes touch his for a moment, move on, then return. Her rosebud lips bloom into a smile, and a wave of warmth rushes through him. He feels as though he is standing on the summer sun.

The guards stop her in the open doorway, wrap her in a blanket, rush her out of the dungeon. But not before the sight of her is burned into his mind. Hope lies thick on his tongue. He swallows it down, where it lodges, hard as a diamond, behind his heart. Against all reason, he holds onto that hope.

It is enough to keep the darkness at bay.

For a time.

❽

When they come for him, he counts the keys on their rings, the stars on their collars. These are the court's men.

Is it time for his trial so soon?

He counts the number of steps to the courtroom. The number of people clustered in small groups, whispering. Fewer than he thought there would be.

For a moment he dares to hope they will let him go.

He counts the seconds it takes for that hope to die. More than there should be.

The guards throw him to his knees. The judge speaks a string of words—too fast to count. Only one matters anyway. One word that changes him forever.

Guilty.

He shakes his head. How is it possible? There's been a mistake of some kind. Don't they know who he *is*?

The judge steps aside, gesturing to a black doorway that stands in the center of the room—tall as a man, but narrow, thin; it is a coffin, an open grave.

Crushing fear robs him of his sight, his breath.

Oh, yes. They know *exactly* who he is.

The guards strip off his shirt. It is only a rag; he is glad to be rid of it.

They spread his arms wide, bending them back as though

they are angel wings, primed for flight. But there is no escape. The guards pull him down, strap him down.

He can smell burning iron in the air. He can feel burning iron on his skin. He screams as fire rings his wrists, manacling him with pain.

He counts his screams, distantly, dispassionately. Fewer than he thought there would be.

It seems to take a long time to wrap the scorching, burning bands on his skin. Longer still for the fine detail work to be placed delicately on his inner wrists.

He counts the number of times he is grateful they didn't break his fingers or his hands instead.

❸

The fear is gone. Even the pain is gone, eventually. Numbness sets in like frost, like ice, moving through him like a glacier. Burning like banked coals.

Underneath his skin, he knows he will survive this. Vows to survive this.

They stand him on shaking legs, unsteady feet. They stand him before the door, a freestanding frame, unattached to anything. It's impossible to think it could lead anywhere, but he knows better. He knows very well what waits behind that door.

The judge speaks a few more words—meaningless gibberish.

His whole world has narrowed in focus to the black slab before him. There is no handle, no window. It is a door designed to swallow, to consume, to leave nothing behind. He notices that the polished brass hinges open only one way—*in*. He wonders why he notes this detail. It's not as though anyone will ever come *out*.

Now that he is closer, he can see the faint etchings—black on black—that cover the once-smooth surface: lines and angles folding in on themselves in a complicated labyrinth, whirling galaxies, a rising tide, a spiral shell, circles and crescents and stars. In the center of the mosaic is an hourglass, the top bulb filled with individual grains of sand just beginning to slide through the narrow neck.

He can almost hear the thrumming hum of trapped music straining to break free. Almost. Almost. The potential is suffocating him. The beauty brings tears to his eyes. Almost.

He reminds himself he must pay tribute to the creator of this door, this work of art, this machine that will transform him, transport him, translate him.

The judge asks him if he has any last words.

He thinks about that phrase for a long time. Last words. Does he even know any words that will last? Beyond time? Beyond that door?

He thinks about the last words he said to his mother. His brother. His lover. Distantly amused that they ended up all being the same words. He can still taste them in his mouth—sweet and exotic. He will not say them, he vows. Not here. Not in front of these men and this towering black door. Maybe not ever again.

But he has other, equally potent, equally powerful last words:

"Go to hell."

The men laugh. Even the judge hides a smile. "You first," he says as the door swings open, a silent yawning, a gaping hole. A hole cut into the very fabric of existence. A hole, waiting to be filled.

He takes a step forward into the darkness . . . and counts. *One.*

He keeps counting. *Twenty-two. Twenty-three.* The door closes behind him. *Eighty-four. Eighty-five.* The music fades. *One hundred six. One hundred seven.* Everything fades. *Two hundred forty-eight. Two hundred forty-nine.*

He keeps counting until he reaches the other door. The matching freestanding door with hinges that only swing *out.* The second door opens and he sees what waits for him beyond.

The door closes behind him, vanishing into the void. He is alone in a barren, flat wasteland with only the scorch marks of guilt on his wrists and the sharp diamond of hope in his heart.

There is nothing left to do but wait.

And count.

CHAPTER
1

"I s this a joke?"

I looked up from painting my toenails lime green to see my best friend Valerie stretched out across my bed, holding a piece of paper by its corner.

She sat up, crossed her legs, and read from the sheet in her hand. "'What's your favorite scent?' 'What would you do with a million dollars?' 'How would you achieve world peace?'" She hooked a strand of platinum-blonde hair behind her ear. "What kind of crazy college application is this?"

I screwed the nail-polish brush back into the bottle and blew lightly on my toes. I hoped Valerie couldn't see my hand shaking. "Mr. Bastian gave it to me. He thought I might be interested. I just took it to be polite."

"Mr. Bastian? The school counselor? He's a certifiable idiot; you know that, right? I mean, I once saw him stick a pencil up his *nose*. And it was one of those pencils with the little naked trolls with the wild pink hair stuck to the end. It was, seriously, ten different kinds of disgusting."

I shook my head. Leave it to Valerie to obsess about the details. "It's for Emery College." I tried to keep my voice casual, but my words sounded strained to my ears, forced through a suddenly tight throat.

"Where's that?"

I shrugged, not meeting Valerie's eye. I wasn't sure I was ready to have this conversation yet; I knew I wasn't ready to have it with Valerie. "Back east somewhere, I think."

Silence from the other side of the room.

"Back. East. Somewhere," Valerie repeated. "You. *Think?*" She shook her head. "Now I know this is a joke. What about our plans to go to State together and major in English and room together and have matching boxer terriers that we'd walk in the park every Saturday in order to meet guys and . . . and . . . and everything?"

I smiled weakly.

"No." Valerie shook her head and scrambled the length of my bed, clutching at the brass foot rail, the application for Emery College crumpled in her hand. "We had it all planned out. You can't do this to me. You *can't* go away to college *back east somewhere* without me!"

"Stop being so histrionic—"

"Don't use your AP English vocabulary words on me, Abby, I know what they mean better than you do."

"Val, calm down. It's just an application. I'm still planning on going to State with my very best friend in the whole world."

Valerie collapsed facedown in a heap, sighing with relief.

"It's true. I can't wait to room with Natalie at State," I said, laughing.

"I hate you so much it hurts," Valerie said, her voice muffled by my plaid comforter.

"I love you too," I replied.

Valerie sat up and threw a pillow at my head.

"Hey, careful—you'll smudge my toes."

"Green?" Valerie rolled onto her back and stretched her arms over the edge of my bed. "Why bother? It's too cold to wear sandals. No one will even see your toes."

I shrugged, grateful for the change in topic. "How long have we known each other?"

"Like, since forever."

"Like, since third grade."

"Whatever. It feels like forever."

I snatched the pillow off the floor and tossed it at Valerie's head. "Tomorrow's a big day. I want to look my best."

Valerie picked up the bottle of nail polish. "*Gangrene?* Someone actually named a shade of green nail polish *gangrene?* What's yellow called—*jaundice?*"

I snatched the bottle out of her hands. "It was on sale," I said a little stiffly.

"Ab, honestly, you shouldn't buy stuff like this just 'cause it's on sale." She examined my foot with a critical eye. "At least I know what to get you for your birthday—a pedicure."

"Better hurry, then. Only one more shopping day left," I reminded her.

Valerie dropped my foot. "How long have we known each other?" she mimicked my voice.

"Like, since forever," I mimicked back, my eyes wide and innocent.

A knock on my door interrupted Valerie's retort. My mom poked her head into my room. "Abby, time for dinner. Hi,

Valerie. You're welcome to join us if you'd like. Nothing fancy, it's just spaghetti and salad."

"Thanks, Mrs. Edmunds, but I should probably be heading home. Dad's trying a new recipe for his cookbook tonight and I promised I'd be his guinea pig."

"Mmmm, sounds exciting," Mom said, swinging the door wide. "C'mon, kiddos, time to move."

As Valerie gathered up her backpack and books, I slipped the crumpled Emery application into my desk drawer.

"See you tomorrow, Abby." Valerie pulled open the front door and skipped down the steps. "Good luck!" She waved from her car before peeling out of the driveway. Her cherry-red Lexus was a blur as she took the corner at full speed.

"She'll get herself killed one of these days," I said to my mom as I closed the front door.

"What's tomorrow?" Mom asked, following me into the dining room.

"Oh, nothing," I said, feeling myself blush a little. "It's just that Dave has a meeting with the district superintendent about some budget thing. He'll be late to rehearsal and he asked me to be in charge until he can get there." I sat down at the table and fussed with my silverware.

Hannah was already sitting at the dining-room table, her nose buried in a book.

Dad set the salad bowl down beside his plate. "Did I just hear you're going to be running the show tomorrow?"

"I guess so. I'm not exactly sure what I'm supposed to do. I hope Dave's not too late from his meeting."

"Shouldn't you call him 'Mr. Thompson' instead of 'Dave'? He *is* your drama teacher, after all," Hannah piped up.

Hannah was the stuffiest eleven-year-old I'd ever known. I blamed it on her recent obsession with Jane Austen novels.

I shrugged. "Everyone calls him Dave. He doesn't seem to mind."

"Still," Mom said, "maybe Hannah has a point—"

"So about Friday," I said, raising my voice just a little. It was a terrible segue and everyone knew it—Hannah shot me daggers from behind her book—but I was already nervous enough just thinking about filling in as assistant director for the school play that I really didn't want to spend the entire dinner discussing it or my drama teacher. Besides, I had something more important I wanted to talk about. "I was thinking—"

"Not to worry, sweetie," Mom said, passing the bowl of noodles to me. "Cindy called this morning to reserve four lanes at the bowling alley for Friday at five o'clock. Everything's all set."

My heart sank. "Oh. Thanks."

"Something wrong, Abs?" Dad asked.

"Well. It's just . . . I was thinking, maybe . . . we could skip the bowling this year?" I hated that my voice cracked, turning what should have been a declarative statement into a weak question.

"What?" Mom set down her silverware. "Why? I mean, Abby, sweetie, we've gone bowling for your birthday since you were four years old. I thought you liked it. Why would you want to change your plans?"

Maybe because I'm turning seventeen and I've gone bowling

for my birthday since I was four years old, I thought. I twirled spaghetti noodles into a knot around my fork.

"What about Jason?" Mom asked. "It's his birthday too, you know."

Jason. I'd only been three years old when my parents had moved next door to the Kimballs. And as the story went, Cindy Kimball had knocked on our door that same afternoon to say hello. When Cindy learned that I would be turning four on January eighth, and when Mom learned that Cindy's son Jason would be turning four on the *exact same day,* well, they took it as a sign. They'd been friends ever since. And it only stood to reason that Jason and I would be friends, too. We had celebrated every birthday together since then. For years, Cindy and Mom had spun themselves a fantasy in which Jason would marry "the girl next door"—me—and our families would be friends forever.

With a story like that, I supposed it was inevitable that Jason and I would end up dating. Which we had been doing for the last four months.

"I'm sure Jason wouldn't mind if we did something else," I said quietly, the words tasting like ashes in my mouth. The truth was, I knew Jason *would* mind. I knew he loved our bowling birthday parties. And I knew he'd been looking forward to this specific party since before Christmas.

"It's fine," I said at last. "Really. Bowling will be fun."

Mom and Dad exchanged a glance.

"Honest." Even I could hear the false note in my voice.

Hannah rolled her eyes, loudly turning a page in her book.

"Sweetie," Mom started, folding her hands on the table.

Dad shook his head. She frowned at him. Dad shook his head again. It was kind of cute that they still thought I couldn't read them both like a book: Mom wanted to argue her point; Dad wasn't going to let her.

"Well, let's see," Mom finally said, a little lamely. "Maybe it won't be so bad."

"And maybe this'll be the year you'll score more than a hundred points," Hannah said with an innocent grin, her eyes never leaving her book.

"Maybe," I said, tempted to stick my tongue out at Hannah. *And maybe someday I'll get to make my own choices about my own life, too.*

But I wasn't holding my breath.

The house was quiet. Mom and Dad had finished watching the evening news and I could hear the water running in the pipes. *That'll be Mom brushing her teeth.* A minute later I heard Dad's voice as a deep rumble through the wall followed by Mom's softer reply. As I lay in my bed, I was oddly comforted listening to my parents' bedtime routine. It was nice to know they felt so safe and comfortable together. That they were still happily married after so many years.

I thought about Jason. He would be like my parents. Jason liked a neat, predictable routine to his life. He wasn't much for spontaneity or acting on wild and crazy impulses. But his stability was one of the things I liked about him. I always knew exactly where I stood with Jason. He was unfailingly honest, even if that meant he wore his emotions on his sleeve.

On the other hand, if I was being completely honest with myself, I would have liked a little spontaneity. A surprise party, perhaps. Or even something other than a dinner-and-a-movie date on Friday night. Something to shake my life up a little. Something special.

Something no one was expecting. Something just for me.

I thought about the application for Emery College tucked away in my desk. I felt a little guilty for lying to Valerie about it. I hadn't taken it out of pity for Mr. Bastian; I had asked him specifically for information about the school. I had found Emery online while doing some research for a liberal arts college with a small student body and a high percentage of scholarship opportunities.

I switched on the lamp on my nightstand, blinking in the sudden flood of light. Slipping out from under my warm covers, I padded across to my desk. I hesitated, my fingers barely touching the drawer. I bit my lip. This was silly. Being a dutiful senior, I'd already filled out what seemed like hundreds of college applications. Why was this one so hard to finish?

Because I want this one, I finally admitted to myself. Emery looked to be everything I thought college should be. Located in a small college town, the school specialized in the liberal arts—specifically creative writing, theater, and every imaginable art medium possible. It had a thriving study-abroad program. Almost all the students lived on campus. A glance at the college schedule showed some kind of music, theater, or art show happening every week. It took my breath away. It was perfect.

It was also out of my budget.

My family wasn't poor by any means, but I'd always known I would have to apply for every scholarship opportunity that came my way—especially if I wanted to go to a small, expensive liberal arts college like Emery.

Everyone expected me to go to school at State or USC or somewhere else close to home. Maybe it was time to do something no one expected—not even me.

Quickly, before I could change my mind or talk myself out of it, I yanked open the drawer, grabbed the crumpled application, and flipped on my computer. I smoothed the paper with my hand, my heart beating wildly. I tucked my green-painted toes under my nightshirt to keep them warm as my Internet browser flashed to life. I took a deep breath and typed in the address for Emery College. Was I crazy for even trying this?

I clicked on the "Apply Now" link on Emery's home page and waited while the form loaded. Most college applications wanted to know your grades, your extracurricular activities, your service work, and your awards, but Emery wasn't like most colleges. Its application was like nothing I'd seen before.

NAME GIVEN TO YOU BY YOUR PARENT(S)
AND/OR GUARDIAN(S)?

That was easy. I carefully typed in "Abigail Beatrice Edmunds."

WHY WAS THIS NAME CHOSEN FOR YOU?

That, too, was easy. Abigail was my mother's grandmother's name. Beatrice was my father's grandmother's name. Family was important to my parents. Even Hannah's name was in honor of a great-aunt.

NAME YOU HAVE CHOSEN FOR YOURSELF?

Easy—Abby.

WHY DID YOU CHOOSE THAT NAME?

Because even as a first-grader, I knew going to school with a name like Abigail Beatrice was social suicide. Abby was easy to spell and easy to remember, but most of all, it was easier to *be* Abby.

Abigail was a girl with braids and braces. A girl who wore hand-me-downs. A girl who would never have friends, much less a good-looking boyfriend. Abigail wasn't going to be asked to Homecoming or try out for cheerleading or write for the school paper.

But Abby? Abby could be cute and bubbly. Popular. As Abby, I could do all those things and more. In fact, I had.

I grinned. As college applications went, this one was the easiest by far.

AGE OF YOUR BODY? AGE OF YOUR SOUL?

I shook my head, still smiling. "Curiouser and curiouser," I murmured. I clicked the box for *17* as the age of my body. It was almost true, I reasoned; my birthday was Friday. "Age of

my soul?" I tapped the mouse button with the tip of my fingernail, thinking.

What did the question even mean? What was the right answer? Was there one? I believed in souls—but how was I to
know how old mine was? I'd always felt older than my real age,
but did that mean anything? I left the question blank for the
moment and skimmed over the questions in the next section:
Goals.

WHERE DO YOU SEE YOURSELF IN FIVE YEARS?
WHAT IS YOUR GREATEST DREAM?
WHAT WOULD YOU DO WITH A MILLION DOLLARS?
WHAT DO YOU WANT TO BE WHEN YOU GROW UP?
HOW WOULD YOU ACHIEVE WORLD PEACE?

Maybe some of these questions weren't going to be so easy
after all.

My eye fell on the third question on the list. Bingo. I knew
exactly what I'd do with a million dollars.

My friend Natalie was a game-show fanatic, and she,
Valerie, and I had spent many a summer afternoon watching
reruns of *Greed, Who Wants to Be a Millionaire,* and *Deal or
No Deal,* debating what we would do with the winnings if we
had been on the show. We always laughed at the contestants
who claimed to want to spend their money on boring things
like paying bills, buying a house, or donating the money to
charity. Natalie's theory was that the way to win on a game
show was to have the most outlandish, amazing, impractical
dream possible. She believed the universe *wanted* to reward
people for dreaming big. So the bigger the dream, the more

likely it would come true. Her theory may not have been entirely sound, but she believed it to her core.

So what would I do with a million dollars? I'd charter a private jet and fly to Italy, where I would live for an entire month in the most expensive, luxurious penthouse suites I could find. I would hire some gorgeous, dark-haired, Italian male model to give me a private, personalized tour of the country's museums, restaurants, and shopping districts. Then, at the end of my million-dollar month, we would sail along the Mediterranean Sea, eating caviar and crackers, drinking something sweet and fruity, and feeding each other grapes and figs. At sunset, he would recite to me the most romantic Italian love poetry ever written.

Natalie thought it was an astoundingly fabulous use of a million dollars and swore that out of all of our dreams, mine was sure to come true.

But should I write that dream down on my college application? It was one thing to talk about it with your friends on a lazy August afternoon. It was something else to use it as evidence for why a college should accept you into its hallowed halls of academia.

I bit my lip. My glance fell on the masthead along the top of the Web site application: *Emery College. Established 1966. Live without Limits.*

If you say so, I thought. I took a deep breath and typed in my Natalie-approved, million-dollar, Italian dream. Every last detail.

It was almost two in the morning when I finished the last

question of the application, "What three words describe how you feel at this exact moment?"

Exhausted, I typed. *Nervous. Crazy.*

I clicked the "Send Application" button and leaned back in my chair. As the computer processed my information, sending my hopes and my dreams, my very soul, out into cyberspace, into the universe, I thought of a fourth word to describe how I felt.

Exhilarated.

CHAPTER
2

"Okay, people, let's not waste any time," I said into my headset. I cringed a little as I heard my voice amplified and broadcast through the auditorium. It didn't even sound like me.

The auditorium was crowded, noisy, and hectic. At the beginning of the semester, Dave had held rehearsals for Shakespeare's *Much Ado about Nothing* in small sections in the drama room. I had wanted to be involved somehow with the play since it was one of my favorites. As much as I loved the sweet, romantic love story between Hero and Claudio, I loved the comic interplay and quick wits of Benedick and Beatrice even more. Though I didn't get a speaking part in the play, I asked Dave if I could be the assistant director for the show. He had handed me the script with a grin and that had been that.

Today we were scheduled to run through all of Act One on the big stage—full costume, full props, full lighting—and everyone was excited for the chance to see the play start to come together. Everyone, that is, except maybe me. Today I was in charge of the play for the first time.

I swallowed hard and clutched my clipboard in my shaking hands. "Um . . . hello? I'd like to get started, please," I said. No one paid any attention to me. So much for painting my toenails lucky green. I scrubbed the back of my hand against my forehead. "Everyone, please, I need you to gather—" I tried again.

The heavy backstage double doors rocked open and then slammed shut as the stage crew walked onto the stage, talking loudly and laughing. Jason caught my eye and smiled.

My heart lifted at the sight of him. He slapped his friend Robert on the shoulder and then ambled over to where I was standing at the edge of the stage.

He brushed back my hair. "Hey, Abby. How're you doing?" Jason's voice always reminded me of butterscotch: smooth, golden, and sweet. Maybe it was because he was that same smooth golden color all over, from his wheat-blond curls falling over his hazel-gold eyes to the light tan on his skin that he managed to sustain even in the middle of January. When I had been younger I had read the myth of Jason and the Golden Fleece. I remember thinking how cool it would be if the Jason I knew turned out to be the same Jason as the hero of the story. I spent that whole summer calling him Fleece-Boy, and dreaming of a golden hero who would embark on a perilous quest to earn my love.

He certainly felt like my hero the moment he put his strong arms around me and hugged me on stage. I hadn't realized how frazzled I'd felt until this moment when I found someplace safe. No matter what happened, I knew I could always count on Jason to be there for me. I breathed in his familiar scent of sweat and sawdust, my rabbiting heartbeat speeding up for a reason other than nerves.

I stripped off my headset and pressed my face against his chest. "I'm better now that you're here," I said.

"Sorry we're late, Dave!" Robert called out as he knotted a red bandanna around his head and spun his hammer in his hands like a gunslinger.

"Dave's not here," Sarah said. She ran her fingers lightly over the piano, trailing up and down the scales. "No one's in charge, so I guess we're just supposed to do whatever until he comes."

What? No. *I* was supposed to be in charge. Dave had left me in charge. Why wasn't I in charge? This was not how I had envisioned rehearsal going. Frustration prickled under my skin. I had expected to be nervous, but why was I so *scared*? I hadn't been scared last year when I'd interviewed the principal for the school paper or when I'd tried out for the cheerleading squad. What was wrong with me?

"Dave said Abby was in charge," Jason said calmly, turning me in his arms so I was facing the crowd. Somehow his voice managed to carry through the room in a way my headset hadn't, and the noise died down as everyone turned to look at me. Sarah's fingers drew a minor chord from the piano. A couple of people laughed at the timing.

I felt myself teetering on the edge of the stage, held up only by Jason's strong hands. I held my clipboard like it was a shield in front of me. *Was it Jason? Had I been braver before we started dating?* It was a chilling idea, though it had the shiver of truth to it. I shelved the thought, unwilling to pursue the consequences at the moment.

I heard Jason's voice from behind me. It sounded a million miles away. "Abby, would you like us to work on the porch? I promise we'll stay out of your way until you need it for the end of Scene One."

I blinked myself back to the present. "That would be great, Jason. Thank you."

"No problem," he said. He leaned close to whisper in my ear, "Don't forget to count." His breath was warm against my skin. He hesitated for an instant, then his lips brushed a quick kiss across my cheek.

Jason's counting trick. The summer Jason and I were nine, our families had gone camping up in the mountains for the first time. We had followed a stream upriver, collecting rocks and pinecones. Night had fallen without us noticing, and the wind moaned through the high trees, rustling the leaves like bones. Disoriented in the dark, I stood frozen on the bank of the river. Part of me knew that if I just followed the river it would lead me home, but the rest of me was petrified, suffocating in the darkness. Jason had slipped his hand into mine and told me he knew a way to be brave. "Feel the fear 'til the count of ten, then count once more to be brave again," he had recited in a small, singsong voice. Together we had counted from one to ten and back again and together we had walked along the river back to camp.

I closed my eyes and counted as fast as I could under my breath, "onetwothreefourfivesixseveneightnineten." As I exhaled, I counted backwards from ten. When I hit "one" it was

23

like a switch suddenly flipped inside of me. My lingering fear evaporated. I could do this. I *would* do this.

Live without limits, I thought suddenly. If I was brave enough to apply for the school of my dreams, I was brave enough for this.

I straightened my headset and squared my shoulders.

"Dave will be here later. For now, let's set up for Act One, Scene One," I barked, surprising myself at how professional I sounded, how easily I slipped back into my familiar cloak of confidence. I consulted my clipboard, my hands steady and calm. "Rachel, turn up the stage lights, please. Sarah, are you ready with the intro? Good. I need Leonato, Hero, and Beatrice center stage." I pointed to the marks taped on the floor. "Allyson, where's the letter? We can't start the scene without it."

"Coming," Allyson called, dashing up the stairs, holding out a small white envelope. "Here it is."

"Perfect. Hand it off to Scott, please. Oh, and Allyson, if the rest of the props for Act One are set and ready, would you check with Jason to see if he needs any help with the porch before Scene Two?"

Allyson nodded, crossed to stage left where Scott the Messenger waited in the wings for his big entrance, and handed him the envelope.

I took a step back as the actors scurried to their places on stage and the crew assumed their roles behind the curtains. My heart beat faster with surprise and anticipation. It had worked. People were doing what I said. Maybe I couldn't sing or dance, but maybe I had finally found my hidden talent—

bossing actors around. I giggled, but when I heard it echo through my headset, I quickly covered it up with a cough.

"A glass of water for you, oh great-and-powerful director." Valerie held out a cup to me, curtseying as low as her costume would allow.

I pushed the headset mike away from my mouth and drank the water in two large gulps. "Thanks, Val. I needed this. You're the best."

"I cry your pardon, sweet gentlewoman. I know not of this 'Val' of whom you speak. 'Tis only simple Ursula, here to attend to your needs and to the needs of my mistress, Hero."

I laughed. "You're impossible."

Valerie shrugged, dropping her persona as quickly as she had assumed it. "Tell me something I don't know, darling." She gave me a quick hug. "Sorry I was late. This corset is beastly. I swear I'll hang Amanda up by her heels with her own sewing thread if she can't figure out a way to let me breathe in this thing."

"Please don't kill her. I still need her to finish Benedick's costume for the masquerade scene."

"As you wish," Valerie said with a deep sigh. "I've got to get back to my mark. I hear the assistant director is a positive *witch* if the actors don't do as they're told." She winked at me. "You're a natural, by the way."

"Thanks. I think I might like this directing gig."

"I meant at being a *witch*." Valerie danced out of my reach before I could whack her with my clipboard.

"I hate you so much it hurts," I called after her instead.

"I love you too," she sang back and blew me a kiss over her shoulder.

Grinning, I pulled the headset down to my mouth. "Okay, people, let's see how we do with Act One, Scene One. Action!"

I settled down in the front row to watch the play unfold.

Scott the Messenger stepped on stage and handed Leonato the letter.

"I learn in this letter that Don Pedro of Arragon comes this night to Messina," Leonato declared, brandishing the envelope like a flag.

I sighed and wrote a note on my clipboard for after rehearsal: *Remind Leonato to open the letter* before *announcing what's inside*.

❽

"Okay, everyone, take five," I said, gathering up my clipboard, notes, and headset. "So far so good, but I'd like to see Scene One again after the break."

I heard groans from the cast and smiled a little to myself.

Most of the cast pushed through the backstage doors, no doubt in search of cold water, fresh air, and some free time to check e-mail and text messages. A few cast members simply collapsed in the auditorium seats behind me. I saw Valerie corner Amanda and demand a looser corset. Amanda waved her hands in surrender and started rummaging in her sewing kit for a pair of scissors. I shook my head. Valerie always got her way; she was a daunting person to cross. It was the main reason I had been reluctant to tell her about my plans for Emery.

"Hey," Jason called softly. I turned to see him squatting on his haunches at the edge of the stage, his large hands resting on his knees. His eyes were in shadow, but the stage lights lined his hair with white fire. His shirt was open at the throat and I saw the glitter of sweat on his skin. I caught my breath at the sight of him. He looked like something primeval, something elemental. *And he's my boyfriend,* I thought with a secret thrill.

A smile curved his lips. "C'mere," he said, crooking a finger in my direction.

I set down my clipboard and headset. I pulled free the elastic that held my hair back and ran my fingers through my dark curls. I knew Jason liked my hair loose. He said when I wore it up, it made my face look pinched and stern. That was Jason, though—honest to a fault.

I sauntered over to the stage, leaned my elbows on the edge, and looked up at him, raising an eyebrow. "Are you sure we should be fraternizing like this? I mean . . . I *am* the assistant director, after all. And you're the"—I wrinkled my nose in mock disgust—"stage crew."

Now that I was closer I could see the stage lights reflected in his hazel eyes. He blinked in surprise. "I thought you liked it that I was on the stage crew."

I swallowed a sigh. That was Jason, too—impossible to tease. "I do. I was just kidding around."

"Oh," he said, standing up. "Anyway, I wanted to show you something. Do you have a minute?"

"For you? Absolutely." I reached up a hand and he bent down to pull me up on stage. "What is it?"

"It's back here." Jason kept hold of my hand as he led me backstage.

His hand was warm and slightly damp with sweat. His leather work gloves were tucked into the back pocket of his jeans. I suddenly felt a surge of irrational affection for those gloves. They looked like they had never been worn, but I knew that was just because Jason took such good care of them. The same way he took such good care of me.

I squeezed his hand, and when he looked back to smile at me, I felt a tingle of joy race along every nerve.

"Here." Jason pushed back a black curtain to reveal the porch he had been working on during rehearsal. "Do you like it?" he whispered, though we were alone in the half-lit area.

Leonato's house was the main set piece. The shop teacher, Mr. Frantz, had designed it to break into pieces and rotate so it could be used for both the interior and exterior scenes of the play. A partially finished porch ran along the entire front of the house, which had a simple roof of slanted slats in parallel rows. The design called for grapevines to be woven through the slats above the porch in honor of the play's Italian setting, but, until opening night, they would remain bare.

"Wow. I didn't think you guys were this far along. It looks great, Jas," I said.

"I wanted to show you this." Jason led me onto the porch. He pulled out a small flashlight from his tool belt and directed the white beam to a narrow corner of the wall.

I caught my breath. Carved into the wood a small butterfly floated next to the initials "AE." Reaching out, I traced the curved lines of the delicate wings. "Oh, it's beautiful."

"I know you like them." Jason ran his hand through his hair, exhaling with relief. "I know no one will see it, but I'll know it's there. And so will you. And we're the only ones who need to know."

My eyes couldn't stop tracing the initials Jason had carved into the wood. "Thank you. It's perfect." I turned toward him and held his face with my hands. I ran my fingers along his jawline, then traced his eyebrows and the slope of his nose. *"You're* perfect."

He grinned and clasped his hands around the small of my back. "I know it's early, but . . . happy birthday."

He rested his forehead against mine, our noses touching.

I swallowed, closing my eyes, breathing in his smell. The smallest part of me dared to hope that he would kiss me on the lips.

Before we had started dating, Jason had told me that he thought we should date at least four months before we kissed. Those months would be up this Friday, our seventeenth birthday. That was Jason to his core—scheduling everything, even romantic interludes.

But this small carving was a side of Jason I hadn't seen before. It was a side I liked.

I wanted to kiss him. I wanted him to kiss me back.

I shifted my weight forward ever so slightly, balancing on my toes, ready to close the distance between us and—

Jason stepped back. He hooked my hair behind my ears. "Tomorrow," he whispered. "Don't you want our first kiss to be special?"

This is special! I thought, leaning closer.

"We've made plans and everything."

I sighed. "I know." I leaned back on my heels and stepped out of the circle of his arms. "Listen, about tomorrow—"

"Where is everyone?" Dave's voice suddenly crashed through the auditorium speakers. "I thought we were rehearsing a play! Abby! Abby, where are you? I thought I'd left you in charge."

I grimaced. "Sounds like my cue."

Jason caught my hand as I turned to leave. "I'm sorry. It's just . . . see you tomorrow?"

"Yeah. Sure."

"Abby! Where are you?" Dave, never the most organized person, had an edge of panic in his voice.

"Sorry. I gotta go." I pulled free from Jason's hand. A cold, clammy sweat coated my skin and a wave of frustration coursed through me as I walked away from him.

I'd known Jason almost my entire life, and he was still living his life according to routines and schedules. So why did I still expect him to be someone different? Someone romantic and passionate and spontaneous? I had thought maybe the carved butterfly was a signal that our relationship was changing. But honestly—skipping the perfect kiss because it wasn't *scheduled?*

I sighed and pushed the troubling thoughts from my mind. What did it matter? Jason was my boyfriend. I'd known him forever. That had to count for something.

Didn't it?

CHAPTER
3

I ripped back the curtain with probably more force than necessary. The cast and crew had returned from the break and I saw Valerie as Ursula practicing her lines with Lily as Hero.

Dave was flipping through my notes on the clipboard, muttering to himself.

"Sorry, Dave. Were you looking for me?"

"Abby! Where were you?" He didn't wait for my reply; Dave never waited for anyone's reply. "It doesn't matter. I was just looking through your notes and, Abby, they are brilliant! You really have a gift. I am so impressed. I can't tell you what a relief it is to come back and see how much you've accomplished. I thought for sure I'd find the whole lot of you lounging around, but instead—"

Dave paused to catch his breath and I seized the moment. I had learned early on to interrupt if I wanted any kind of conversation at all with Dave. "I'm glad you're back. We were getting ready to run Scene One again. Do you want me to do it, or do you want to jump in?"

"Oh, you go right ahead. You're doing fabulous with Act

One. But maybe, if I could steal Benedick and Beatrice for a moment, we could rehearse the last scene in the play. We've been over it a thousand times but it's still missing something. And, Abby, you know, it's one of the most important scenes in the whole play. It's *the* kiss—the *ado* the whole play is based on—and it's just not working. I just don't know *what* I'm going to do—" Dave stepped up on stage and clapped his hands for attention. "Isaac. Cassie. You're with me. The rest of you—"

The main doors to the auditorium creaked open.

Dave whipped around, anger in his eyes. Everyone in the cast and crew knew how particular Dave was about his space. No one—and he meant *no one*—came to rehearsals without his permission. He claimed the invasion brought in a negative energy that interfered with the creative process.

A tall boy stood with one hand still on the door. He wore a heavy wool pea coat, a leather backpack slung casually over his shoulder. Snowflakes melted in his dark hair.

"This is a closed rehearsal," Dave shouted, striding up the aisle and flapping his hands as though brushing away flies. "You'll have to leave. Now."

The boy let the door swing shut with a clang. "I'm sorry?" he said, a trace of an accent underscoring his words. It sounded familiar but I couldn't quite place it.

"Closed rehearsal!" Dave said.

"I have a letter," the boy said, holding out a scrap of paper like a peace offering. "I am sorry I am late." His voice was low, sultry, and just the sound of it sparked a flash of heat at the base of my skull.

"What's that now?" Dave accepted the slim paper and

unfolded it with three sharp gestures. "Let's see. Let's see. Mmm-hmm. I see."

I stole a glance at Valerie. She raised her eyebrows and edged closer to me.

"Well, well, well," Dave said, all traces of annoyance gone from his voice. "This is unusual. But . . . come with me."

"Who is it?" Valerie asked.

I shrugged, trying to get a better look without seeming like I was trying to get a better look.

Dave led the boy down the aisle and to the stage, talking nonstop. "We're rehearsing *Much Ado about Nothing*. I assume you're familiar with the play? But we've already cast all the speaking parts, so you'll have to be one of the members of the court. Hmmm, we'll have to make sure Amanda starts on your masquerade costume." Dave snapped his fingers. "Though if you'd rather be on the crew, I suppose we could find a place for you there. Are you any good with your hands? Wood-working? Carpentry, perhaps? Or painting?"

The boy tugged at the sleeves of his coat, hiding his fingers from view. "I'm very good with my hands," he said, the smallest of smiles curving his mouth. "But I will be happy to help in any way I can." He avoided looking at all of us standing on stage and kept his attention focused on Dave. If he was uncomfortable with a crowd of strangers staring down at him, he didn't show it.

"Excellent! Perhaps I can find a place for you yet." Dave stopped, a frown furrowing his brow. "What did you say your name was?"

All the females in the cast seemed to lean forward to hear

his response. I heard Lily catch her breath behind me. The quiet in the auditorium stretched for several long seconds.

"Dan, did you say? Dan Alexander?"

"It's Dante, sir," the boy said. "Like the poet." That small smile made another appearance.

Dave swept his arm in a welcoming gesture over the cast. "Everyone, please meet Dante Alexander, foreign-exchange student from Italy." Dave consulted the letter in his hands. "How long will you be staying with us?"

Dante hesitated, brushing his long hair away from his face. "I . . . I'm not sure," he finally said.

"Well, let's not waste any more time, then." Dave clapped Dante on the back. "Drop your stuff and take your place. Abby, will you show our newest cast member his mark for Act One?"

Dante looked uncertain, but he obediently placed his backpack on a seat in the front row. He shrugged out of his heavy coat with one smooth, supple movement. I heard Lily murmur appreciatively to Sarah.

"Abby?" Dave asked again, Isaac and Cassie standing right behind him. "Can you handle Act One?"

Startled, I jumped, heat flooding my cheeks. I glanced at Jason, who frowned, and I felt another wave of embarrassment wash through me.

"Sorry." I consulted my notes, flipping through my few handwritten pages until I found the beginning of the script. Why was I so flustered? "Um, Dante"—his name felt strange in my mouth—"would you follow me, please?"

I climbed the stairs to the stage and directed him to stand behind Leonato with the other random members of the court.

"We'll get you a costume later," I told him. "For now, just stand there and pretend you're hearing the news for the first time."

"Grazie," he said softly. *"Farò il mio meglio."*

I didn't speak Italian, but I recognized *Thanks,* so I smiled and said, "You're welcome. If you need anything, I'll be right over there." I pointed to the backstage curtains, stage left, where Isaac and Cassie were rehearsing their last scene with Dave.

"Grazie."

"And . . . everyone ready?" I adjusted my headset. The cast snapped to attention. I scampered offstage. "Action!"

I'd seen Act One, Scene One, several times already today so I spent my time watching the new arrival instead: Dante Alexander from Italy. He wore his dark hair long, even in the front, and every few minutes or so, he had to reach up to sweep it away from his face with his long fingers. He had left his coat with his backpack but, oddly enough, he had kept his gloves on. They looked a little like motorcycle gloves, finger-less, but with longer cuffs. The sleek leather completely en-cased his wrists like bracers, the guards that archers sometimes wore.

He wore a fitted, plain white, long-sleeved shirt that not only complemented his olive skin but also showcased the lean muscles in his forearms and chest. He kept the sleeves of his shirt rolled down over his wrists despite the stuffiness of the auditorium.

But it was his eyes that I noticed the most. They were changeling gray—one moment they shimmered with the moon-white of reflected sunlight, the next they held the almost-blue edge of melting ice crystals, then they hardened to the shadowed gray of wet river stones. I wondered if they would stay gray in the sunshine, or if they would change color yet again.

But beyond his good looks and his amazing eyes, Dante had a stillness about him that I found intriguing.

He didn't just *watch* the play; he *paid attention*. He listened to the lines with a focused, fierce attentiveness, his whole body taut and alert. At first I thought it was because Shakespeare could be hard enough to understand if English was your *first* language, let alone your second, but as I watched him watch the play, I realized that it was more than that. It was as though he drank in the words, gained sustenance and strength from them. The look on his face as he walked along the stage behind Leonato made me think he was coming home.

I kept telling myself I should look away, I shouldn't be so obvious in my scrutiny, but then Dante turned and met my eyes as though he knew I had been watching him. Time seemed to slow down around me. I could taste the air on my tongue, stale and thick, as I inhaled. I could feel the touch of those gray eyes on my skin, like waves lapping at the shore, like dandelion seeds blown away at dusk. I felt like he looked right through me, right into me. Part of me wanted him to never look away.

That small smile curved his lips, slowly, so slowly, before he looked away again. Time seemed to snap back into place, rocking my senses. My heart tripped and stuttered for a few beats, stumbling as though I had run up a long flight of stairs.

Disoriented, I needed a moment to gain my bearings. A chill shivered just under my skin as I distinctly heard Dave say, "C'mon, people, it's just a stage kiss. What is the problem?"

I looked up in time to see Dave making a beeline stage left, heading straight for me. I tried to step back, but my heel hit the wall and I almost dropped my clipboard.

Dave reached out, grabbed my shoulders, and yanked me forward. He pressed his lips to mine, held them for a second, then pulled away. He looked over his shoulder at Isaac and Cassie, who were staring at us in shock. "See?" Dave demanded. "It's just a stage kiss. It doesn't mean anything." Dave released me and walked away without a second glance. "Now it's your turn." He waved his actors to step closer to each other.

The air in the auditorium pressed down on me. I couldn't breathe. The clipboard shook in my hands. My lips tingled, warm and dry.

What had just happened?

Had I just had my first kiss? With . . . with *Dave*? No, it wasn't supposed to be like this. First kisses were supposed to be special. They were supposed to mean something. They weren't supposed to be . . . *instructional*.

I looked around wildly: Valerie, doubled over as far as her corset would allow, laughing and gasping for air; Jason, frowning, his hazel eyes dark and unhappy; Dante, with that same small smile on his exotic face; everyone in the cast staring, pointing. The whispering hissed around me like insect wings.

I had to get away. Now.

I whirled around and ran for the doors, crashing through them blindly.

"Abby!" I heard Jason call my name, but the closing door cut his voice in two.

I stumbled to a halt in the hallway, leaning against the cool metal lockers. I cradled the clipboard to my chest.

Jason had followed me out. He caught up to me and touched my arm. Worry lines crossed his forehead. "Are you okay? You look a little—"

"Can you wait here with me a minute, please? I don't think I . . ."

"Of course," he said, gathering me in his arms. "As long as you need."

I listened to his steady heartbeat until I felt the heat subside from my cheeks. "I'm sorry," I whispered.

"What for?"

I shrugged. I didn't have to say anything more; Jason knew what I meant better than I did sometimes.

"It's okay, Abby. Dave may have been your first kiss," he said with a rumbling laugh, "but you'll be mine."

Annoyance flared as hot as my embarrassment. Sometimes Jason's unfailing honesty was more than I could take.

But then I tilted my head back to look at him. His face was as familiar to me as anything in my life. He hadn't meant to be arrogant or annoying. He had meant to tell me how special he wanted our first kiss to be. It was sweet, really, in a clumsy way. I felt my negative emotions drain away as the moment stretched out between us.

Ten-second rule, I thought distractedly, hope bubbling up in my chest. *If he kisses me now, it'll be close enough. It can count as my first kiss.* I closed my eyes and held my breath.

"Tomorrow," Jason whispered and pressed a kiss to my forehead.

The moment was over. Again.

I let my head fall forward onto his chest and swallowed a sigh. Hadn't we already been here today once before? Would this day never end?

Jason hugged me around the shoulders. "You okay?"

I nodded and stepped out of his embrace. "Thanks, Jas. Listen, I probably ought to get back. Rehearsal's almost over and Dave will want my notes."

"Do you need a ride home?"

"No, Valerie seems to think I won't be able to survive another day without a pedicure. We're supposed to go right after rehearsal." I wiggled my toes inside my boots. Stupid, unlucky nail polish.

"Okay," Jason said, tapping my nose with his finger. "In case I don't see you later—see you later."

I slipped back on stage, praying no one would notice me. Everyone did.

My face hot, I scurried to Dave's side. I shoved my clipboard at him, muttering something about the notes I'd written down, and was turning to leave when he caught my arm.

"Abby, would you do me a favor?" Dave said. "I told Dante you'd get him all set up with a script, costume, schedule—the works. I'll need him up to speed on the play by next week. We don't have any time to waste. I know he's just an extra, but even extras have to carry their weight in the show. I'm not having this production go down in flames because of a last-minute addition to the cast."

"Oh, okay," I stuttered, looking across the stage to where Dante stood surrounded by a flock of giggling girls. Valerie said something to him and he laughed. Dante caught my eyes with his and I felt that same strange sensation of time slowing down between us. He seemed relaxed, but in that one drawn-out moment I could see how tense he was in the way he held his body, how carefully he kept his hands from touching anyone. I could see the strain of maintaining his control reflected in the frost-white rims of his eyes.

"You're the best," Dave said, breaking the moment. "I knew I could count on you."

But long after Valerie and I had left rehearsal for the spa and our pedicures, I found myself thinking of the look in Dante's eyes, wondering what it was that had made him so tense, so careful, so afraid.

CHAPTER
4

The bowling alley was packed Friday night. Of course, since Willie's Bowling Bonanza had only eight lanes, our group with four lanes (reservations made, but ultimately not necessary) essentially had the run of the place. Besides my family of four, Jason had his entire family of ten (though that included several aunts, uncles, and at least one first cousin). Add in Valerie and Natalie, her brother, Robert, the rest of the stage crew, and one of Hannah's friends, and the party officially accounted for more than half of the people there.

Mom and Cindy must have gone over earlier in the afternoon to prepare because when Jason and I walked through the front doors at five o'clock sharp to the claps and cheers of our family and friends, I thought the place looked like a party store had decided to hide a bowling alley among its streamers and balloons. Cindy had even hung up her homemade "Happy Birthday" banner, which had made an appearance at every birthday party for every member of either family for the last five years. The blue butcher paper was torn and the silver letters faded, but Cindy insisted a birthday just wasn't a birthday without the banner.

"Oh, look, it's the birthday banner," I said to Jason, rolling my eyes a little.

But Jason grinned and swept his mom into a hug. "You found it! I thought we'd lost it after Kevin's birthday."

Cindy patted her son on the back. "I pulled out all the stops for you, sweetie. You only turn seventeen once, you know."

Jason looked around at the decorations littering the bowling lanes. "Thanks, Mom, it's just the way I like it."

"It's just like last year," I sighed under my breath.

"What's that, Abby?" Jason asked.

I plastered a smile on my face and shook my head. "Nothing, Jas. Let's go bowling!"

❽

"You, darling, are a better person than I am," Valerie said as she sat down next to me at the empty scoring table for Lane 5. She held a plate of birthday cake and two forks in her hand.

"Tell me something I don't know," I grinned, taking one of the forks and attacking a corner of the chocolate cake.

She shook her head. "Every year you invite me to your birthday party and every year I come and every year it's . . . this." She waved her fork in random circles, encompassing the chaotic festivities around us, the crowd of parents and siblings and friends happily bowling and cheering each other on. "How can you stand it?"

I shrugged, licking the frosting off my fork. "It's not so bad, I guess. I never have to plan the party. I never have to worry about what to get Jason for his birthday. I never have to worry about anyone forgetting my birthday." I ticked the points off on my fingers.

"You always do the same thing. You always invite the same people. You always get the same presents." Valerie listed her own points on her manicured nails.

"Not true." I nodded to the small pile of wrapped presents on the table behind Lane 1 where my parents were bowling with Hannah and her friend McKenna. "I don't know what's in that small gold box on the edge. Obviously, the flat pink box has a sweater from Aunt Marge—two sizes too big, but still, it's the thought that counts. The square one with the ribbon is from Hannah. She's trying to make me join the Cult of the Brontë Sisters, so my guess is it'll be either a giant volume of collected works or an illustrated edition of *Wuthering Heights*. No, wait. *Jane Eyre*. And you can take that to the bank." I grinned and ate another bite of cake.

"That's just what I mean. Where are the surprises in your life? Where is the unexpected hero arriving to sweep you off your feet and turn your world upside down?"

A loud cheer went up from Lane 2 where Jason, Natalie, Robert, Cindy, and Jason's brother Kevin were bowling. All ten pins were down and Jason had his hands raised in victory. Natalie squealed and hugged him tight.

"Jason can be surprising," I said, but it didn't come out as convincing as I wanted it to. I didn't look at Valerie; I could never slip a lie past Valerie.

"Ah, yes. Jason is full of surprises. Let me guess. He'll bowl a perfect 300 game tonight. He'll come over and kiss you on

43

the forehead and say something like, 'How's my best girl?' like you're some kind of pet. He'll get you what he always gets you for your birthday: a journal and a new pen, with a card that says, 'May all your dreams come true.' And then he'll take you home tonight and kiss you on the doorstep for the first time"—Valerie swept the back of her hand to her forehead, feigning a swoon, and then dropped her hand and looked me square in the eyes—"but instead of the fireworks you're expecting, Abby, it'll just be a kiss. A perfect, textbook, unsurprising kiss."

I toyed with my fork, scraping the last of the frosting from the plate.

"Jason's a great guy, Abby, don't get me wrong. He's got a good heart and he'll make some girl really happy. But let's face it. He's not making *you* happy. Ever since you guys switched from 'being friends' to 'dating,' you've lost something, Abby. You've lost the spark that kept you curious and daring and willing to branch out and try new things."

"I'm trying new things!"

"Like what?"

Like applying for Emery College, I thought. But I couldn't tell Valerie that. Not yet. I didn't want to jinx anything by saying it out loud. I pushed the empty plate away from me, worried that Valerie might be right.

"All I'm saying, Abby, is you need to take a hard look at your life, at your dreams, and decide if *this* is what you really want. Now, before you run out of time."

"Can we talk about something else, please? This *is* my birthday party, you know." I frowned. "Anyway, you already gave

44

me a present, you don't need to give me this dose of reality, too."

We watched Natalie bowl another frame, shaking her head and laughing as she scored two gutter balls in a row.

"Is Natalie dating anyone right now?" Valerie asked me.

I shrugged. "If she is, she hasn't mentioned it to me. Why?"

Valerie tapped her fingernails against the table. "I was thinking of setting her up on a date."

"Who with?"

"The new guy—"

"Dante?" I blurted. "You want to set her up with him?"

"What? No, not *him*. I was thinking of the new guy who just transferred to my math class." Valerie turned her piercing blue eyes on me. "But now why would you think of Dante Alexander so quickly? Has the Italian hunk been on your mind lately?"

I blushed. "It's not like that. Dave asked me to get him set up for the play, help him rehearse . . ." My voice trailed off as Valerie shook her head.

"No, you can't. Tell Dave to find someone else."

"What are you talking about?"

Valerie cut a glance right and left. I almost laughed; I didn't think anyone really did that outside of the movies. Valerie leaned close. "He's dangerous, Abby."

"Dante?" I thought back to the end of Thursday's rehearsal and the fear I had seen in his eyes. He hadn't seemed particularly dangerous. In fact, he had seemed desperately in need of help.

Valerie nodded. "He's not really an exchange student from

Italy at all. He's from New York and he's been living in Leo's apartment above the Dungeon for the last year. I think Leo is his uncle or some other relative. Anyway, I heard he was in some kind of trouble with the law in New York. Abby—they say he killed someone."

"Are you insane? Where are you getting this?"

Valerie sighed. "Honestly, Abby, it's all over the school."

"He arrived *yesterday*."

"I know. And Amanda's friend Ashlyn talked to James who heard it from Troy's girlfriend, Melinda Conner. As in *Officer* Conner. As in her *dad*."

"I know who Melinda Conner is," I said. "It's just gossip, Val. Besides, think about it: If *Officer* Conner knows that Dante has been hiding from the law for the past year in the Dungeon, why doesn't he just go over there and arrest him?"

"He's not 'hiding from the law.' He's on probation or something like that. As long as he doesn't commit any crimes, there's nothing the police can do about it."

"But—killing someone?"

Valerie shrugged and reached for her purse. "I'm just telling you what I heard."

"It's nonsense."

"Just be careful around him, okay? Please? For your very bestest friend?" Valerie batted her eyelashes innocently.

"Fine. I'll be careful. But I still have to help him with the play. I'm the assistant director. It's my job."

"Whatever. Here. I got you this." Valerie slid an envelope across the table with my name written on it in her looping, swirling handwriting. "It's a gift certificate to the spa." She smiled at me brightly. "It's like cash—only more restrictive."

I rolled my eyes. "Thanks, Val. You're the best."

"Tell me something I don't know, darling."

"How's my best girl?" Jason asked, reaching over to squeeze my hand before shifting his truck into third gear.

I shrugged, a flash of annoyance leaving a bitter taste in my mouth. "I'm okay."

"Really? You seem kind of quiet tonight."

It was after eleven; we'd been the last people out of the bowling alley and I was more than ready to go home.

"Sorry. No, I'm fine. Just tired."

Jason smiled over at me. "Well, I hope you're not too tired to open one more present."

I felt myself blush in the darkness. "You know you don't have to get me anything."

"I know. But I wanted to."

He turned onto our street. I could see lights glowing from both my front porch and his. Great. Looked like we'd have an audience for this kiss. I swallowed a sigh and tried to muster up some excitement, but all I ended up with was a twinge of a headache behind my left eye and a deep weariness in my whole body.

Jason pulled into my driveway and set the brake. He left the engine running, though, and the heater warmed up the truck's cab to the point where I could take off my gloves. The porch light hinted at a glint of gold around my wrist. I had truly been surprised at the gold watch my parents had given me and I hadn't taken it off all evening.

Jason reached into the backseat where he had stored the box of my other presents. He fished out a small, square gift from between the sweater from Aunt Marge and the illustrated edition of *Jane Eyre*. He gave it to me with hands that shook a little.

Some of my exhaustion vanished at the sight of Jason's trembling hands; I was flattered that he would be nervous.

I felt a swell of affection for him. Jason was a good guy—a good boyfriend. Valerie was wrong. Jason *did* make me happy. This kiss would be something special, something I would re-member forever. It had to be.

Smiling, my heart warm in my chest, I slid my finger under the envelope flap and pulled out the card. A pastel sunset cov-ered the top half of the card. Soft waves lapped at a golden beach. Written in raised, flowing script were the words "Happy Birthday." I opened the card and read the message inside: "May all your birthday wishes come true." No inscription. No personalized note. Just Jason's signature at the bottom.

I quickly unwrapped the present. A journal and a pen.

I felt my smile freeze on my face and my heart sink a little.

"Do you like it?" Jason rubbed the back of his arm with his hand.

"Y-yes," I stammered. "It's great. Thank you."

"I know I got you one last year, but I figured by now you'd have filled it up and might need a new one."

"It's really nice. Thanks," I said again, trying to inject some brightness into my voice. Didn't Jason know by now that I liked to keep my journal electronically instead of handwriting it in a book?

I coughed and swallowed hard. "I have something for you, too." I reached into my coat pocket and pulled out a slim CD jewel case. "I hope you like it." I had drawn "XVII 4 XVII" on the cover in dark blue ink and then written underneath it in block letters: "Seventeen for Seventeen."

Jason flipped the case over to read the playlist. He frowned and immediately flipped it back to the front. He popped it open and looked at the unlabeled CD. "What's on it?"

"That's the surprise," I said smiling. "You'll have to listen to it first. That way each song is like a mini-present you can un-wrap . . ." My voice trailed off at the slightly panicked look on Jason's face. "I'll e-mail you the set list," I sighed.

"Thanks," Jason said, his smile sincere. He popped out the CD from his truck's player and slipped in the one I'd made for him. "What's the first song?"

"It's a cover of 'Time after Time' by a singer named J. J. O'Hare. She's from Ireland and has this great jazzy-bluesy voice. Valerie downloaded a bunch of her songs for me, and when I heard this cover I thought of you."

"Leave it to Valerie to find the weirdest music on the Web."

"It's not weird," I protested, stung. I didn't mention that I had been the one to introduce Valerie to J. J. O'Hare's music.

"Hey, listen, I didn't mean it like that. I'm sorry."

"It's okay," I said, looking out the window. A swirling snow had started to fall, soft and silent. The heat in the cab was sti-fling. I wanted to open the door and lie on my back in the dark and let the snow fall onto my face, but the clock on the dash-board warned me that it was almost midnight and I knew Jason had other plans. I knew he was going to kiss me before midnight no matter what.

Sure enough, I heard Jason gently whisper my name. I felt his thumb stroking the back of my hand until I turned to look at him.

His nervousness was back. So was my annoyance. This was so obviously not the right time for a kiss. He had missed the perfect opportunity yesterday—twice!—waiting for this moment and now it was all wrong. The mood was all wrong—*my* mood was all wrong—and I felt frustrated that Jason couldn't see that, couldn't feel that.

Jason leaned closer. He closed his eyes.

Our lips met.

There were no fireworks.

At least not for me.

Jason pulled away and I saw the firework lights in his eyes, in the flush on his skin, in the tremulous curve of his smile. "You're my best girl, Abby. Thanks for the best birthday yet."

I felt so much older than seventeen. Cold and old and hollow.

I felt like crying.

CHAPTER
5

"A bby." Hannah's voice sounded loud right next to my ear. I started awake, rolling over and blinking at my sister who stood next to my bed, a smirk—there was no other word for it—on her face. Morning sun streamed through my curtains, turning my room a soft shade of white-yellow.

"There's someone here to see you."

I checked the time on my new watch: 8:12. Way too early on a Saturday morning for visitors.

"Whoizzit?" I mumbled, flopping my pillow over my face. "Jason? Tell him I'll call him later."

"It's not Jason," Hannah said. "It's some guy—Dan something?—from your drama class?"

My eyes flew open and I sat up in bed. "Dante? What's he doing here?" *How does he even know where I live?* I wondered.

Hannah shrugged. "I don't know, Abby. Why don't you go downstairs and ask him yourself?"

"You let him in the house?"

"Why wouldn't I?" Hannah asked. "It's the polite thing to do."

"It's the *insane* thing to do, Hannah," I growled. "Do you know what time it is?"

"I'll tell him you're coming right down." She smiled sweetly at me as she flounced out the door.

Grumbling at having to bear the burden of a younger sister, I crawled out of bed and shoved my feet into a pair of slippers. As I descended the stairs, I wrapped my robe around me and tried to smooth down my hair.

Dante was waiting for me in the front room. When I saw him, I stopped on the last step, feeling extremely frumpy and frazzled.

He had unbuttoned his navy blue pea coat, and I could see the long lines of his body underneath. He had brushed back his hair, though it still threatened to fall over his clear gray eyes at any time.

I caught my breath at the sight of those eyes. I had forgotten how beautiful they were. I felt like I could spend hours studying them.

"Abby?" That now-familiar small smile crossed his lips.

"What?" I startled back to the present moment. "Oh—" I hurried into the front room.

"Please accept my apologies, Abby. I didn't mean to wake you. I guess I didn't realize it was so early." Dante tugged at the gloves on his hands.

"No, no, it's okay," I said, trying furtively to pull my hair into a ponytail and out of my eyes. "What's up?"

Dante watched me curl up on the love seat and swallowed hard. He shoved his hands deep into his coat pockets. "I had hoped to speak with you about the play. But I could come back if now is not a good time . . ." He gestured to the front door and took a step away.

"No, it's fine." I didn't want to see him go. I was curious to find out why he'd come by. It couldn't just be to talk about the play, could it? I felt my breath quicken as I realized I hoped I was wrong. "It's a little early, but, knowing Dave, he'll want you ready to go by Monday's rehearsal. You may not have noticed, but he's a little *intense* about his work."

"I'd noticed," Dante said dryly.

I pulled a pillow to my chest and grinned.

Hannah appeared in the entryway, her attention immediately fixing on Dante. "Abby, Mom wants to know if your friend wants to stay for breakfast."

I looked at Dante. "Would you like to? It's okay to say no," I said in a stage whisper.

Dante's eyes flickered to the front door again and he looked so uncomfortable that an impromptu idea flashed through me. I turned to Hannah. "Tell Mom thanks, but no, we're going *out* for breakfast this morning."

I couldn't tell who was the most surprised at this statement, Hannah or Dante or me. I stood up from the love seat. "Just give me a minute to get ready, Dante, and we can go, okay?"

Dante nodded, naked relief in his eyes. "I'll wait for you outside." He slipped out the front door.

Hannah crossed her arms and frowned at me. "Mom's not gonna be happy about this."

"It's not a date," I said gruffly.

Hannah sniffed. "I'll say it right now, then—I told you so." She waltzed back to the kitchen.

I ran up the stairs, tossing my robe onto my bed the instant I closed the door behind me. My mind raced. What was I doing? I had just asked an almost complete stranger to go to breakfast with me. A potentially *dangerous* stranger, if Valerie was to be believed. A small laugh bubbled up. This was something the old Abby would have done—no schedules, no planning, just . . . seizing the moment, following where the day would take me. I hadn't realized how confined I'd been feeling until I realized how liberated I felt instead.

I changed out of my pajamas and pulled on a pair of jeans and a light green turtleneck sweater. I ran a brush through my hair and twisted it into a quick French knot at the base of my neck. On the way out of my bedroom, I grabbed my backpack, my jacket, and my keys.

I had just swung down from the stairs when Mom called my name.

"What's this about a breakfast date with someone?"

"It's not a *date,* Mom. Dante's in the play I'm directing. This is like a . . . a *working* breakfast. Look, I'll explain everything when I get home, okay?"

Mom crossed her arms and frowned; she looked just like Hannah. "I'm not happy about this, but—"

"Thanks, Mom, you're the best!" I kissed her cheek, pulled on my jacket, and slipped out the door.

I saw Dante straighten up from where he had been leaning against the porch railing. His breath plumed in the cold air.

"Ready?" I asked, jingling my keys.

Dante hesitated, looking down at the fuzzy blue slippers on my feet.

I laughed. "I guess this'll be a blue-slippers-and-breakfast kind of day. I'm surprised you didn't get the message."

"Perhaps it'll come later this afternoon," Dante replied with his small smile.

I cocked my head at Dante and felt another laugh bubble up inside me. Jason wouldn't have played along with me. Jason would have made me change into shoes. Of course, Jason wouldn't have shown up unexpectedly on a Saturday morning at all.

"Dante," I said, "I think we are going to be friends."

The rising sun changed Dante's eyes to silver, and the sudden tingle in my fingertips had nothing to do with the January cold.

"I'd like that very much."

"Shall we?" I gestured to my car parked at the curb.

I had taken only one step before Dante swept me off my feet, literally, and into his arms, cradling me to his chest.

I caught my breath as time seemed to coalesce around me. I had time enough to watch the sunlight slowly pool in the empty footsteps that led across the front yard, up the driveway, up the porch, and to my front door where Dante stood, holding me close. I had time enough to feel Dante's strong arms tighten around me, to hear the sharp intake of his breath. I could almost taste the dusty odor from his pea coat.

And then we were standing by my car. Dante lowered me to a clear spot on the curb and stepped back. I blinked, disoriented, my heart beating faster at Dante's nearness.

"I didn't want your slippers to get wet," he said quietly, tucking his hands back into his coat pockets. He looked a little pale.

"Th-thanks," I said. I opened the door, and the movement helped shake off the lingering sense of déjà vu.

Dante walked around the car and slid into the passenger seat.

"Where would you like to go?" I asked, turning the key in the ignition. My car rumbled, coughing and sputtering, to reluctant life. "The Dungeon's not open for breakfast, is it?"

Dante shook his head quickly. "No, let's not go there. Where's your favorite place? Someplace not too crowded," he added in a hurry.

"How much time do you have?" I turned the heater to full and breathed warm air into my cupped hands.

Dante's eyes were serious. "I have all the time in the world."

"Excellent. Helen's Café it is." I turned on my CD player and pulled out onto the street, the opening notes of "Stopping Time" by Darwin Glass trailing behind us like falling snow.

> *Only you can turn the time*
> *Only you can stop the tide*
> *Only you can turn and save me*
> *From tomorrow's bitter ride*

The parking lot for Helen's Café was empty. As usual. The service was so slow at Helen's that hardly anyone ever ate there anymore. But I didn't mind. In fact, on some days I liked the peace and quiet that Helen's offered.

The café was deserted when we walked in, and the sign by the hostess desk invited us to seat ourselves, so Dante and I selected a booth by the large picture-frame front window. The décor was classic kitsch—porcelain chickens nesting on high shelves; knockoff watercolors of limp water lilies; collections of spoons, shot glasses, and thimbles from around the world.

Dante looked around, seeming half interested, half appalled.

"Try not to look at anything directly," I suggested. "It makes it easier."

"This is your favorite place?"

I shrugged. "I admit the décor is terrible, and the service is worse, but the food is surprisingly good. Plus, with no one around, we can stay and talk as long as we'd like."

"Are we going to talk long?" Dante raised an eyebrow.

"Depends." I handed him one of the menus stacked on the side of the table.

"On?" He took the menu but didn't open it.

"On how much there is to say," I said lightly.

Dante regarded me with those clear eyes. "Then we might be here a long time."

I felt a flutter of anticipation and excitement. Quickly, I perused the menu even though I knew exactly what I wanted to order. I could still feel Dante's eyes on me. A thrill danced on my skin.

How long had it been since I'd had a getting-to-know-you

conversation? I knew everything about Jason; I knew nothing about Dante.

"Sorry for the wait." A waitress appeared at our table, notepad in hand, not sounding sorry at all. "What'll you have?"

Dante ordered pancakes (blueberry), eggs (over easy), and two slices of toast (rye). I ordered my favorite: a Belgian waffle with a custom raspberry, blackberry, and whipped cream puree, half an English muffin, toasted, and a tall glass of freshly squeezed orange juice. In January, a rare treat.

As the waitress left, I closed the menu and reached for my backpack. "Okay, here are the rules."

"Excuse me?" Dante frowned in confusion.

"The getting-to-know-Dante rules," I said, placing a notebook and a pen on the table. "Don't panic. There are only two rules to remember. First, you have to write down the first thing that comes to your mind when I say so. Second, you have to be completely honest. The game won't work if you lie about your answers." I ripped out a blank sheet of paper from my notebook and slid it across the table. "Ready?"

Dante looked from me to the paper and back again, a strange light in his eyes. "You are a dangerous woman, Abby," he said softly.

"Ha! No one's ever called me dangerous before." I felt myself blush under his gaze and thought that perhaps I shouldn't like so much the way my name sounded in his mouth.

"You are not afraid to ask for the truth. And you strike me as a person who is not afraid to *hear* the truth, either. That makes you dangerous." He picked up the pen and uncapped it. "I will play your game." He grinned at me. "I can be as dangerous as you."

He's dangerous, Valerie's voice reminded me. I pointedly ignored it. Dante had been the perfect gentleman so far this morning. I wiggled my newly pedicured, freshly repainted, lucky-green toes in my warm—and dry—fuzzy slippers.

"Number one: What do you think of when I say the word . . . breakfast?"

Dante wrote down two words and then looked up at me expectantly.

I blinked. "Um, that's it?" Usually when I played this game with one of my friends, it took hours because we all wrote such epic, rambling, convoluted responses. In fact, Valerie liked to see how much she could write before we forced her to the next word. Her record was a page and a half.

"You said to write down the first thing I thought of." Dante looked down at the paper in front of him. "Have I done something wrong?"

"No, no, it's fine. What about . . . Italy?" Surely that would spark a sentence or two.

Two words.

"Dream."

Another pair of words. *Okay,* I thought. *Interesting.*

I fired words at him faster and faster, some of the best ones I'd ever come up with for the game—*beauty, temptation, goal, wish, love, future, laughter, hope, heaven*—determined to get him to write a complete answer or sentence—something more than two words. But after each one, Dante wrote down just two simple words.

"Deadly."

Dante flinched, the pen hovering over the page.

"Hesitation!" I said as though I was calling a penalty. "Remember, you have to write down the *first* thing you think of. And you promised to be totally honest." I tapped the top of the paper.

The color drained from Dante's face. He didn't look at me. His hand trembled as he scrawled an answer across the page. Then he deliberately replaced the cap on the pen and folded the paper in half once, then in half again.

"What are you doing?" I asked.

Dante handed the pen to me. "I have revealed as much truth as I can. Perhaps we can finish this later."

I reached for the paper. "Let's see—"

Dante's hand slapped down on the folded square. "The rules said nothing about having to show you my answers." His voice had a hard edge to it that I hadn't heard before. In an instant, his eyes had changed from light gray to the dark gray of storm clouds.

I slowly withdrew my hand as though he had struck me, even though his hands remained flat on the tabletop. Shaken, I wondered what had brought on this sudden change in his attitude. Was it the game? It was supposed to have been innocent and fun.

I could feel the tension building between us, and that was the last thing I wanted to have happen.

The waitress finally returned with our food, plunking down the plates in front of us.

The interruption broke the tension. I could feel it draining away as we both fiddled with our silverware. As the waitress strolled away, I opened my mouth to apologize to Dante. He beat me to it.

"I'm sorry. I shouldn't have spoken to you that way."

"No, I'm sorry. You were a good sport to even play on such short notice."

Dante's storm-cloud eyes lightened a little. "Perhaps it's my turn to get to know you."

"Oh, I'm not that interesting," I waved off his words.

"You're the most interesting person I've met so far," he said.

"How many people could you have met since Thursday?"

"You might be surprised." Dante took a sip of water. "Leo has been a very good host."

"So you *are* staying with Leo?" I asked. "I heard he was, like, your uncle or something?"

Dante smiled crookedly. "Something like that. He's my . . . sponsor? Is that the right word?" He shook his head and tried again. "He's the person watching over me while I'm here."

"And how long will you be here?"

"Depends."

"On?"

"On how long you want me to stay," he said lightly.

Then you might be here a long time, I thought, a little surprised at my instant reaction. Before I could say anything, though, Dante nodded toward the waitress who was leaning against the door that opened into the back room.

"Is she the Helen of the Café?" Dante asked.

"Who, her?" I spread a thin coating of butter on my English muffin. "No, there is no Helen. It's just a name."

"Ah, but names are powerful. Telling," Dante observed. "*Abby*, for example, means *one who gives joy.*"

I smiled at the compliment. "What does your name mean?"

"*Lasting*," he said, a shadow crossing his features before he quickly segued with, "and Helen was the name of the most beautiful woman in the world."

"Helen of Troy."

"Helen of Troy." Dante nodded, taking a drink of water.

"Helen and Paris," I said, sighing a little. "It's kind of romantic, don't you think? Running away with the man of your dreams?"

Dante snorted. "What are you talking about? Helen's broken marriage vow was the downfall of the Trojans."

I shrugged. "Maybe, but the Greeks were going to win that war. I mean, have you read the *Iliad?* The Trojans were destined to fall—"

"Have you read the *Aeneid?*" Dante asked with a raised eyebrow. "There's always another side to the story. There's always more going on than you might imagine."

A slow smile crossed my face. How long had it been since I'd had a spirited discussion about something literary? About something other than Jason's shop class or his truck?

"The *Aeneid?* Never read it. I doubt it's as good as Homer, though." I set down my fork and leaned my elbows on the table, resting my chin on my laced fingers. "Convince me otherwise," I invited.

Dante glanced around at the empty café before regarding me with a bright light in his eyes.

"C'mon, Dante," I teased a little. "Convince me that Helen

was the true villain of the story." Watching the smooth lines of his throat moving as he swallowed a mouthful of water, I felt my own mouth grow dry.

Dante wadded up his napkin and tossed it on the table. He bowed his head for a moment, the stillness I'd noticed about him more pronounced. He seemed to gather up the nearby space, drawing it around him like a hurricane around an eye. "Helen brought war to Troy and left nothing but devastation in her wake. Aeneas has had to watch his friends and family die, his homeland be ravaged by war, his home burn to the ground. And as he stumbles into the smoking ruin of the temple, who does he find?"

Dante's countenance subtly shifted, his eyes growing distant and hard, his voice lowering in timbre and gaining in strength as the words poured out of him like smoky honey, like liquid fire.

> *That woman, terrified of the Trojans' hate*
> *For the city overthrown, terrified too*
> *Of Danaan vengeance, her abandoned husband's*
> *Anger after years—Helen, that Fury*
> *Both to her own homeland and Troy, had gone*
> *To earth, a hated thing, before the altars.*

He closed his eyes, sweeping his hands through his hair before continuing. Sweat beaded on his forehead and his chest rose and fell as he gulped in air.

> *Now fires blazed up in my own spirit—*
> *A passion to avenge my fallen town*
> *And punish Helen's whorishness.*

He leaned across the table. Heat seemed to radiate off him in waves.

> *"Shall this one,"* he hissed,
> *"Look untouched on Sparta and Mycenae*
> *After her triumph, going like a queen,*
> *And see her home and husband, kin and children,*
> *With Trojan girls for escort, Phrygian slaves?*
> *Must Priam perish by the sword for this?*
> *Troy burn, for this? Dardania's littoral*
> *Be soaked in blood, so many times, for this?"*

He looked at me from underneath lowered lids and his voice was deadly quiet.

> *"Not by my leave. I know*
> *No glory comes of punishing a woman,*
> *The feat can bring no honor. Still, I'll be*
> *Approved for snuffing out a monstrous life,*
> *For a just sentence carried out. My heart*
> *Will teem with joy in this avenging fire,*
> *And the ashes of my kin will be appeased."*

He slumped back against the booth and drained his water glass in one swallow. When he placed the glass back on the table, it was like a switch had been flipped: he was back from being Aeneas to being Dante. The transformation was startling.

Chills walked up and down my spine. "I'm convinced," I said. "Where did you learn to act like that? It was . . . incredible."

Dante smiled wanly across the table. *"Grazie."*

"Does Dave know you can act?" I asked, then quickly shook my head. "Maybe it's best if he doesn't know. He'd want to recast *Much Ado about Nothing* and then there would be much ado about everything. It's too bad you didn't transfer back in December when we held auditions. You would have sewn up Benedick's role, no doubt."

"I'm happy just being an extra," Dante said, toying with his toast.

"But to play Benedick? It's the best role in the play. He has all that great verbal sparring with Beatrice."

"I'm enjoying the verbal sparring with Abby at the moment," he said with a smile.

I felt myself blush, and a twinge of guilt wormed its way into me. Seriously, what was I doing? Not twelve hours ago I had kissed my boyfriend for the first time, and now I was having breakfast—and flirting?—with someone else? But this wasn't a date, I reminded myself. This was a *working* breakfast. Maybe it was time I started treating it as such before things got out of hand. At least more out of hand than they already were.

I cleared my throat and took a sip of my juice. "Speaking of the play . . ." I pulled open my backpack and fished out my tattered copy of *Much Ado about Nothing*. I set it on the table between us, a shield to deflect the growing attraction I knew we both felt. "I assume you've already read the play, but you can borrow my copy if you want to brush up on the story. You may be happy just being an extra, but Dave requires everyone to be familiar with the *entire* play. Even those of us without any lines." I pointed at Dante. "Even those of us backstage." I pointed at myself.

"Abby—"

"I think I've got a rehearsal schedule here somewhere." I dug in my backpack again.

"Abby." Dante cleared his throat.

I looked up. "Yes?"

"I . . . I'm sorry, but I'm not familiar with this play." Dante touched a finger to the copy on the table.

I blinked. "Really? Oh, well, it's one of Shakespeare's easier plays to read—not like *Hamlet* or *Richard the Third* . . ."

Dante looked down and aligned the edge of his fork with the place mat on the table.

"You haven't read *Hamlet,* either, have you?"

Dante moved his empty water glass a quarter of an inch to the left.

"Have you read any Shakespeare at all?"

Dante didn't say anything, embarrassment staining his skin like a dark shadow.

"Right. O-kay." I frowned, confused. "But you've read the *Aeneid* and Homer . . . how did you miss reading Shakespeare in your tour through the classics?"

Dante looked at his hands. "My education has been . . . uneven at times."

I nodded. "Well, that's easy enough to fix." I dug in my backpack again, withdrawing my drama notebook and slapping it down over the copy of the play. "Borrow my notes as well. I had to outline the whole play for Dave, plus do character analyses and plot summaries and identify the predominant themes of the play along with ideas of how to communicate those themes on stage." I grinned at Dante. "Dave can be a little *obsessive* about his plays." I tapped the cover of the notebook. "If you have any questions, just ask."

Dante gathered up the notebook and play. "*Grazie*, Abby. You are a good friend to help me."

I shrugged. "It's what friends do."

"I'm glad we can be friends," he said. He almost reached for my hand, but at the last minute he curled his fingers to his palm instead.

He kept his fist closed tight the entire drive home. We talked about school—I told him which teachers were the best and which days to avoid eating at the cafeteria. We talked about my family—Hannah's obsession with Victorian romance novels, Mom's latest cooking fiasco, Dad's love of bad puns. We talked about my friends—Valerie, Natalie, and Jason.

It wasn't until I had dropped Dante off at the Dungeon and watched him slip into the side door that led to what must be an upstairs apartment that I realized we had talked about everything—except him.

Tossing my backpack and jacket on the table next to the front door, I called, "I'm home."

"Abby, is that you?" Mom's voice came from the kitchen. "I thought you were going to breakfast with your friend."

"I did. I just got back." I walked into the kitchen and stood next to Hannah at the table.

Mom cocked her head. "But you just left . . ."

I felt a strange jolt, and my surroundings stuttered and jumped around me like a missed frame in a movie.

Time seemed to stop, and I had a chance to look around the table. Dad was still reading the sports page—the first section he liked to read in the morning. Mom was still in her bathrobe and slippers. Hannah was still in her pajamas. Breakfast was still hot—the bacon still crisp, the pancakes still steaming under puddles of sticky syrup, the juice glasses still full.

I glanced at my watch: 8:45. A wave of heat washed through me, followed by a splash of cold. It had been just over half an hour since Hannah had woken me up. Enough time to drive to Helen's Café and back—provided I hadn't stayed to eat. But I had. Hadn't I? I didn't feel hungry. If anything, I felt uneasy and disoriented. I sat down at the table.

My hand shook as I reached in my back pocket for the receipt from the café to check the time printed on the slip. My pocket was empty. How could that be? I clearly remembered paying for breakfast. But at the same time, I clearly remembered Dante picking up the check, paying for the meal, and pocketing the receipt. They couldn't have both happened. How could I remember two different things? I shook my head. Without the receipt, there was no proof of the hours I had spent with Dante at breakfast. Just my memories. How did I already have a morning's worth of memories if the morning had just started? What was going on?

"Abby, are you all right? You look a little pale." Mom

pressed the back of her wrist to my forehead. "Why don't you have something to eat?"

I shook off her hand and pushed away the plate of pancakes like it was poisoned. "I'm fine." Though I wasn't. "I guess I'm still a little tired from the party last night." Though I wasn't. "I'm sure I'll feel better by lunch." Though I wasn't sure of that, either.

CHAPTER
6

I slammed my hand against my locker. Stupid lock. Sighing, I shifted my backpack and tried the combination again. What was it again? 36–24–34? No, 34–24–36. That didn't sound right either. Why couldn't I remember three little numbers?

Crowds of people flowed up and down the hallway in a steady stream, eddying around chattering knots, parting, drifting, and re-forming in seamless currents. The constant motion around me was soothing and a little hypnotic. I felt like I could watch the patterns for hours.

C'mon, Abby. Think! I shook my head, studying my locker door and fiddling with the combination lock. But it was hard to focus. Hard to think. Grumbling, I dropped my backpack and hit the locker with the flat of my hand again.

Ever since Saturday's breakfast with Dante—days ago—my life had felt like it was one step behind and, as Hannah had so eloquently put it last night at dinner, I'd turned into a grouchy, grumpy mess.

And to top it all off, I'd been late to rehearsal every night this week and Dave hadn't been happy *at all*. I had a constant headache that no amount of aspirin could touch. I felt all twisted up inside like a Celtic knot; I couldn't even begin to figure out where to start unraveling the mess. I could feel the pressure weighing me down, slowing me down, keeping me down.

Leaning my forehead against the cool metal, I closed my eyes, feeling the rising pressure sliding through me like tentacles, sucking the energy and life from my limbs. I could still sense the ebb and flow of people moving—laughing, talking, jostling—all around me. I couldn't breathe. I felt like I was drowning.

A bright light flashed behind my eyes, stabbing into my brain like a hundred knives.

Not again, I thought wearily, my hands clammy with fear.

I'd been having these flashes every couple of hours, sometimes more frequently, for the last couple of days. And the terrifying thing was that they seemed to be flashes of the future. The first one had happened Sunday afternoon. A flash of white light and a glimpse of Mom cooking tuna casserole for dinner. I hadn't thought much about it until dinner: tuna casserole. Weird, but not that weird.

But then, when I woke up on Monday morning, I had another flash: Hannah wearing her blue shirt with the white lace trim. And that time I also heard the whisper of her complaint that her favorite red blouse still had a stain on the sleeve. When Hannah barged into the bathroom later that morning wearing that same blue shirt with that same complaint on her lips, I almost dropped the hair dryer in shock.

The flashes had grown more frequent, more intense, and

more accurate since then. It was like having some kind of a strange future déjà vu.

No, please, not now, I thought as the light grew brighter, the sharp pain lacerating my mind. Frantic, I spun the dial and the lock popped open. *Hallelujah!* I grabbed my books at random and shoved them into my already stuffed backpack. Maybe I could get to class before—

Natalie in a green shirt—

"Hey, Abby. What's up?" Natalie leaned against the bank of lockers, her green shirt the exact same shade as the one I saw in my mind's eye.

"Hey, Nat," I said, grateful that my voice still worked. In my vision I heard myself ask "What time is it?" a bare second before the words left my lips in reality. *A real-time flash? What was happening?* My eyes hurt from the double vision.

I saw two Natalies glance at the clock on her cell phone. "It's almost noon. Is your watch broken?" She nodded to—*a flash of gold on my wrist*—the gold watch on my wrist.

I shook it briskly, frowning. "I don't know. It hasn't been working right all week. It's been running fast, and then, I don't know, it'll just stop for a while and then start up again." My heart beat a double rhythm in my chest. Cold sweat covered my skin.

"Weird. Maybe it needs a new battery," Natalie said, waving the conversation away with her hand.

Now she'll say she's late for history—

"Listen, I'm late for history—what are you doing this weekend?"

I shrugged. "Unless Jason has plans, nothing, I guess." *Just slowly losing my mind is all.*

"Great. Then you're *both* coming to the Dungeon with us on Friday. If I don't see you later—see you later!" The surging crowds swallowed Natalie whole.

The double vision disappeared instantly. My constant headache roared with renewed strength. I blinked several times, my eyes dry and burning.

"Both?" I said, and then I felt Jason's hands slide over my shoulders. I hadn't noticed that he'd walked up behind me.

"You're not planning on doing your homework during lunch, are you?" he asked with a smile. He held up a brown paper lunch bag. "I thought we had a date."

"What?" I looked down at the books in my hand. "Oh. No. It's just . . . Is it lunchtime already?" I shoved my math book back into my locker.

Jason's forehead creased with worry. "Are you okay? You seem a little . . . distracted lately."

"No, really, I'm fine. Let's have lunch." Maybe some food would calm me down.

I followed Jason through the crowded cafeteria to our regular table. He pulled out the chair for me and I sat down gratefully. My limbs felt heavy and uncoordinated. The hands of my watch lurched into motion, sweeping in a swift circle around the dial. The edges of my vision blurred with a kaleidoscope of swirling colors. "I could use one of your mom's famous chicken salad sandwiches right now," I said, dropping my backpack on the chair next to me.

Jason looked at me quizzically. "How did you know Mom made chicken salad for lunch?"

My heart dropped in my chest. "Just lucky, I guess." I shivered despite the hot, crowded cafeteria. A sudden wave of nausea rushed through me and I grabbed the edge of the table and held on tight. The dizziness passed as quickly as it had come. When my vision cleared, I saw Dante standing across the table from us, concern in his stormy gray eyes.

I saw his mouth move, but I couldn't hear anything except a wild rush of wind in my ears.

"Abby?"

This time I heard my name clearly but I wasn't sure who had said it, let alone when. *What is happening to me?* Real fear gripped me, leaving a sour taste in my mouth.

I saw Dante hesitate a moment, then set his mouth in a thin line and walk straight for our table. "May I?" he asked, touching the back of the chair next to me.

"Sure," I said. With shaking hands, I lifted my backpack off the chair and pushed it out for Dante.

He sat down and clasped his gloved hand around my wrist. Time, already fractured, seemed to stop altogether. The roar of the cafeteria dulled to a distant murmur. I watched Jason turn toward me in slow motion, a frown on his face.

"I'm sorry, Abby," Dante said quickly. "I was careless on Saturday. I shouldn't have carried you to the car. I shouldn't have . . ." He shook his head. "If I had known you'd been suffering all this time . . ." A dark shadow crossed his face. "I thought I had it under control." He drew in a deep breath. I could almost see the flow of air into his body. "I know what you are going through and I will make things right," he said in a low voice. "I promise."

"What?" My mind struggled to keep up with the flood of his words. The pressure inside me flexed like a clenched fist.

"Meet me on the north side of the parking lot before rehearsal starts this afternoon. Alone." Dante leaned close enough to me that I could smell the dusty-sweet scent of his wool coat. "Promise me you'll be there, Abby. *Ti prego.*"

His fingers skimmed over the back of my hand like a summer breeze through leaves. Dante's eyes met mine and a feeling like a shower of cold water washed over me, leaving me clean, cool, and calm. My heart settled back into its normal rhythm. My eyes stopped seeing horrifying double visions of the present and the future. The tight knot in my chest loosened, unraveling enough for me to take a deep breath. I felt myself on solid ground for the first time all day, all week.

Dante removed his hand from my wrist and time snapped back into its regular rhythm. I could still feel the pressure in my bones, but now it was distant, tamed by Dante's touch. I hoped I could handle the remaining pressure on my own. I hoped the worst was over.

Dante leaned back in his chair as though we'd never had a whispered conversation in the middle of the cafeteria.

Without taking his eyes off Dante, Jason shifted his chair closer to mine.

"It's nice to finally meet you, Jason. Abby speaks quite highly of you." Dante tugged at the edge of his gloves, readjusting the fit of them over his strong hands.

"Thanks," Jason said with a curt nod of his head and a sharp glance at me. "When did you guys talk?"

"During breakfast on Saturday," I blurted and then immediately wished I hadn't said anything. I took a bite of my sandwich to prevent myself from saying anything else.

"Really?" Jason looked from me to Dante and back again, his hazel eyes hardening into amber.

"It was a working breakfast," Dante said smoothly, not looking at me. "Abby was helping me with the rehearsal schedule for the play."

"That's right," Jason said coolly. "I'd forgotten you were in the play. I haven't seen you at rehearsal the last couple of days."

"'I wasted time, and now doth time waste me,'" Dante said with a rueful grin. "You see, Abby, I have been studying."

I grinned. "*Hamlet,* no less. Good. You'll need it to charm your way back into Dave's good graces. He was set on cutting you from the play when you didn't show up Monday. Don't worry," I said as Dante frowned, "I talked him into giving you an extension. You're coming today, right?"

"Absolutely."

"Good. We're moving into Act Two and then jumping ahead to the scene at the masquerade ball. It's one of the best parts with Benedick and Beatrice."

"I told Abby she should have gotten the part of Beatrice," Jason interjected, draping his arm around my shoulders. "Dave was a fool to give it to Cassie."

"Cassie read the part better than I did," I said, not particularly eager to relive my failed audition in front of Dante.

"Yeah, but your middle name *is* Beatrice—Abigail Beatrice—"

"Jason!" I hissed, cutting a glance at Dante. "Don't."

"Abigail Beatrice," Dante mused. "One who *gives* joy. One who *brings* joy." He nodded slowly, the small smile curving his lips. "You are doubly blessed, then, to bear such a name."

I blushed.

The bell rang; Dante nodded to me and Jason and then slipped away in the crowds flowing down the hallway.

I pushed back my chair, but Jason gripped my wrist.

"I thought we'd agreed not to date other people."

Blinking, I frowned. "I'm not." Technically, *Jason* had made that decision, but I knew now wasn't the time to split hairs.

Jason glanced down the hallway.

"I'm certainly not dating *Dante,* if that's what you're thinking. We had *one* breakfast on *one* Saturday." My tone was sharper than I'd intended but I didn't apologize for it. My skin still tingled from the brush of Dante's fingertips.

"I don't want you seeing him."

I rolled my eyes. "Seriously, Jas, jealousy doesn't become you."

"I'm not jealous," he said stiffly. "It's just . . . I've been hearing things about him and I don't think you should be alone with him."

"Have you been talking to Melinda Conner too?" The pressure inside me that I had thought was gone flared up, and I felt the knot tightening around my heart again. "Valerie already told me all the rumors about him and frankly, I don't believe a word of it. Dante's been nothing but nice to me and I can't see him being a danger to anyone." I stood up, slinging my backpack over my shoulder. "Now, if you'll excuse me, I'm late for English."

Jason had the decency to look sheepish. "Abby—"

"I'll see you later, okay?" I walked away without looking back.

❽

As my English teacher droned on about the proper use of a semicolon in a sentence, I felt my attention drifting, floating away as effortlessly as the snow falling outside the second-story window. Usually English was my favorite class, but today I couldn't seem to concentrate on anything for more than a few moments. One thought had lodged in my mind like a stone in a river, and everything else circled around it like a whirlpool:

The sound of Dante's low voice, *Meet me.*

Dante said he knew what I was going through. Did he mean that he knew about the pressure I was feeling? The stress that kept me tied up in a knot? How could he? I hadn't seen him since Saturday.

My thoughts turned to lunch. He had apologized for being careless—that didn't make any sense at all. He hadn't done anything wrong. The only weird thing that had happened was that bizarre shift in time I'd experienced when I got home from breakfast. But that couldn't be his fault. I'd just misread the clock, that was all. It had all been in my imagination. It was still all in my imagination. It had to be. There was no other explanation for those strange white flashes, unless—

I felt the latent panic stirring and quickly averted that train of thought. I didn't want to be crazy.

He had promised he would make things right. I rubbed the back of my hand where he had touched me at lunch. I remembered the sensation of a soft breeze, a cool shower, and the instant lessening of the pressure behind my eyes, inside my heart. It'd been the first time all week I'd felt like myself. I wanted to feel that again. I needed to. I couldn't go on living with this monster suffocating me from the inside. Another day of it and I feared I'd crack under the pressure.

And Dante had said he could make things right.

But that meant meeting him in the parking lot before rehearsal like he asked me to. Did I dare go alone? I'd meant what I said about wanting to be friends with him. There was something interesting and mysterious about Dante Alexander from Italy.

Valerie had told me he was dangerous, but that was wild gossip. Jason had told me he was dangerous, but he was jealous. I couldn't deny that strange things seemed to happen to me when he was around, but did that mean I was in danger? Maybe it was something else. I remembered our flirtatious breakfast, the look in Dante's eye whenever he saw me, the small smile on his lips whenever he said my name. I bit my lower lip. Maybe the only danger was to my heart.

I heard again the sound of Dante's low voice, *Meet me.*

He had said he knew what I was going through . . .

After an eternity, the bell rang, releasing me from class but not from my endlessly circling thoughts.

I peeked around the corner. School had ended almost an hour ago and only a few scattered cars remained in the parking lot. Dante stood alone by the north edge of the lot, his hands buried deep in his pockets, his coat unbuttoned and open to the cold. He stood straight and still despite the brisk wind that ruffled his dark hair and the snow that settled on his shoulders. He might have been carved from stone for all that the elements affected him. I'd been watching him for almost ten minutes and he hadn't moved so much as a foot the entire time. The groups of people who walked past him parted and flowed around him like water around a rock, like he wasn't there at all. I was reminded of pictures I'd seen of ancient Egyptian ruins—the tall, dark obelisks frozen in time while all around them the world crumbled to dust.

I shivered in the chill wind and tried to rub some warmth into my arms. I'd left my coat and my backpack in the auditorium, thinking I would just quickly meet Dante to thank him for his offer of help but assure him that, really, I was fine, and then make it back to rehearsal before anyone noticed I was gone. But now that I was here, I couldn't seem to make myself take those few steps to him. I was afraid Dante would see right through my lies; I was more afraid that he wouldn't.

C'mon, Abby, if you're going to go, go! He's right there.

But I didn't move. I didn't know what to do. I tried Jason's counting trick, hoping it would ease my nerves.

You should go, I told myself. I rubbed at my forehead where my headache pounded like a hammer on the inside of my skull, making it hard to think. *If he can help, you* have *to go.*

I saw Jason and Robert exit the school's workshop that stood behind Dante and head for the main school building. Rehearsal would be starting in just a few minutes and I couldn't afford to be late again. Jason buckled his tool belt around his hips. He laughed at something Robert said, their breath steaming in the cold air.

As I watched them walk across the lot, I could almost hear Jason's voice urging me to follow the schedule, to go to rehearsal, to do the right thing and avoid contact with someone I barely knew, someone potentially dangerous. *Stupid Melinda Conner,* I thought. *Spreading stupid rumors.*

I took a deep breath and set my jaw. The old Abby wouldn't have stood around, listening to rumors and dithering and moaning about what to do.

Jason and Robert gave a wide berth around Dante; I wasn't sure they even saw him standing there. The door closed behind them, and then it was just me and Dante left in the parking lot. It was now or never.

Quickly, I darted across the parking lot and walked right up to him before my courage deserted me.

"Hi," I said breathlessly.

A smile crossed his face and a beautiful clear light sparked in his eyes. "Hello, Abby. I'm glad you came."

"Sorry I'm late." I brushed snow out of my hair and folded my arms against my chest, my teeth chattering.

"You're cold." Dante shrugged out of his coat and wrapped it around my shoulders.

"I'm okay," I said, though I slipped my arms into the long sleeves. His coat was already warm from his body heat and the wool carried that unique musky-sweet scent I had already come to associate with him. Pulling the coat around me felt like a hug. Inexplicably, I felt tears prickling in the corners of my eyes. Just being around him made the tight bands of pressure around my heart loosen. I drew in a deep breath, relishing the feeling of sharp, cold air flowing all the way to the bottom of my lungs.

"I have something for you. Will you walk with me?" He gestured with his hand.

I looked up at him, the snow frosting his dark lashes, and felt my heart constrict again, but this time with something soft and warm. I nodded and walked with him to the far corner of the lot where his car was parked.

"Nice ride." I whistled. Even under a thick coat of snow, the sleek lines of a vintage Mustang were obvious. I'd spent enough time with Jason to appreciate the beauty of a classic car.

"I borrowed it from Leo. He's out of town and doesn't know." Dante held a finger up to his lips. "Don't tell him, all right?"

"Thief," I accused with a smile.

"Once upon a time," he said, a strange melancholy in his voice. Quickly brushing the snow away from the car, he unlocked the trunk and grabbed a black bag. "This is for you." Opening the bag, he pulled out a small box wrapped in gold foil with a red ribbon tied in a bow across the top.

"Godiva chocolates?" I grinned. "My favorite. What's the occasion?"

"I wanted to thank you for the extra time you've spent with me. For helping me with the play and . . . and for being my friend. You have no idea how much you've helped me over these last few days. And I wanted to apologize for the extra stress I caused you. I know the pressure you've been under since Saturday."

I shrugged. "It's not been so bad."

"If I'm a thief, then you're a liar." Dante took the box from me and untied the bow. "Here. Close your eyes."

Obediently I closed my eyes.

"Keep them closed." Dante stepped close to me. I could feel the heat from his body and I wondered how he could be so warm standing in the snow when I was the one wearing a coat.

He pressed the edge of a chocolate to my lips and I opened my mouth. Sweet, dark chocolate with a hint of pineapple melted on my tongue.

I felt his hand gently cup my cheek, the leather of his gloves slick and cold against my skin, but when his bare fingertips touched me they were warm and soft.

"I promised I would make things right, Abby."

I heard him take a deep breath and then release it slowly, whispering a string of Italian words into the wind.

For a flickering moment of time, the wind that had been swirling snow around us cut off into nothing. In its place, I heard what sounded like the echo of water rushing past in the distance.

"Keep your eyes closed," Dante said again, his voice strained.

I squeezed my eyes shut tighter, acutely aware of the taste of pineapple and chocolate coating my tongue. Stars sparkled in the darkness behind my eyes. The pressure I had been living with all week returned in full force, its edges as hard as rock, as sharp as glass. I couldn't breathe.

I opened my mouth to gasp in a last breath when the pressure suddenly disappeared like a popped balloon. I felt the tension drain out of my body, flowing away from me in waves. In its place was a sweeping feeling of openness and light, of wind and sky. My mind was clear, razor-sharp. I felt wonderful.

Dante's voice came to me from a million miles away, "Open your eyes."

I did and saw Dante's quicksilver gray eyes looking back at me with a mixture of fear and hope. "How do you feel?" he asked quietly.

"Better," I said, surprised at the truth. The ache in my head, my bones, my whole body was gone. I felt unaccountably happy. I hadn't realized how dark my life had become until all the shadows had been burned away.

"Chocolate can have that effect," he said, handing me the box again.

My mouth twisted in a half-smile. "I guess I hadn't realized how much stress I was under. Can I tell you something and you promise you won't laugh?"

Dante nodded.

"I thought I was going crazy."

"I know how you feel."

And somehow I knew that he did. Buoyed up by my good mood, I impulsively took the step that separated us and hugged him tightly. "Thank you," I whispered into his chest. "Thank you for keeping your promise." Hot tears of relief and gratitude left tracks of fire on my cold cheeks.

I felt a jolt of surprise run through him, but after a moment, he wrapped his arms around my shoulders. I felt his hands on my back, gently soothing.

"Abby, no, *non piangere,*" he murmured. "Don't cry."

He held me until my tears stopped. "I'm sorry. I'm not usually like this." I gulped down a lungful of icy air and attempted a laugh. "Natalie's the one who usually gives out random hugs." I wiped my eyes and shyly stepped out of his embrace, my heartbeat surprisingly swift. "So where have you been the last couple of days?"

"I had some personal business to attend to—"

"Abby? There you are."

I whirled around to see Jason standing behind us, darkness clouding his eyes. I hoped his face was red from the cold wind, but when his eyes never once flicked to Dante, I knew I was wrong.

"Dave asked me to find out if you were 'at all willing to come to rehearsal today, because if not, he'll need to find another assistant director.' His words."

"No, no, I'm coming." I turned to Dante. "Thanks again for the chocolates. And for everything. You're coming to rehearsal, right?"

Dante nodded. "I'll be there."

"Okay, I'll see you inside." As I trotted across the snow to

Jason, I tucked the box of chocolates into my coat pocket. Jason grabbed hold of my hand, shooting a dark look back at Dante, and we headed for the school.

"It's not like you to forget your coat," Jason said quietly.

"What? Oh," I stammered, realizing too late that I was still wearing Dante's coat. "It was cold, and Dante was just being nice."

Jason tightened his grip on my hand. "And the hug? Were you just being nice back?"

My temper flared a little, burning away my good mood. I shook my hand free of Jason's. "Yes, actually, I was. Being nice is what *friends* do."

Jason stopped in the snow and looked at me for a long moment, an unreadable expression on his face. "Maybe someday you'll be that nice to me." He turned and walked into the school.

"Jason!" I called, but he didn't turn around. I balled up my hand into a fist. What was wrong with me? I hadn't meant to make him unhappy or upset.

As soon as I entered the auditorium, Jason saw me and turned away. I started to follow him, but he disappeared backstage and out of sight. Dave called my name and waved me over. I sighed. I'd have to apologize later. If he'd let me.

I took off Dante's coat and laid it on one of the chairs. I transferred the chocolates to my backpack. A few minutes later, I saw Dante slip through the door, and he gave me a quick wave before he took his place on stage.

I slouched in my seat, my notebook open on my lap, but I wasn't taking notes on the play. Instead I was doodling random designs in the margins and thinking. Without a doubt the last few days had been some of the strangest I'd experienced. In fact, ever since Dante had walked into the auditorium last Thursday, my life had felt a little off-kilter, a step behind everyone else's.

I watched Dante walk across the stage, following his blocking for the play. He scratched at his neck with one gloved hand. *What is the deal with those gloves?* I wondered. He wore them all the time, but he didn't seem comfortable with them on, like they didn't fit. I wondered why he didn't just take them off. Maybe he was covering a rash, or a birthmark.

Or maybe he wears them for protection, I thought absently. *Like motorcycle gloves.* Protection from what, though? I thought of how careful he was not to touch anyone. I remembered how, on Saturday, he'd almost touched me at Helen's Café, but then hadn't. *Could that be it?* No. *He carried me to the car that same day,* I argued with myself, *and he touched me at lunch today. And just now, in the parking lot.*

But that brought up another question: Why had he apologized for carrying me to the car? He'd made it sound like he'd done something wrong. Of course, that was silly. He hadn't wanted me to ruin my slippers in the snow, that was all.

I doodled a pair of fuzzy bunny slippers in my notebook. I remembered how I'd felt that strange sense of time slowing down when he'd held me in his arms. It had been the same feeling I'd had when I'd gotten home after breakfast—of time being out of whack—but it was then that time had seemed to snap back into place for me. And after that, the horrible white flashes of the future had started.

LISA MANGUM

Idly I wrote down *white flashes* in the middle of my paper. On the left side I jotted down a short list—the befores: *Dante carried me to the car; weird thing with time; breakfast at Helen's; breakfast at home.* I tapped the pen against my lip, wondering where my wandering thoughts were taking me. On the right side of my paper I wrote another short list—the afters: *glimpses of the future; horrible pressure; Dante's touch at lunch; chocolates in the parking lot.*

Since our meeting in the parking lot, the tight pressure that had been lodged in my heart all week had been exorcised completely. And somehow I knew the white flashes were gone and wouldn't be coming back.

I circled Dante's name where it appeared on both lists and then drew a line connecting them directly through the words *white flashes.* It was like Dante had healed a rip in time itself. And how exactly had he done that? I wondered.

I was starting to realize that when it came to Dante, there were a lot of questions I just didn't have the answers to. *Curiouser and curiouser . . .*

I drew a rabbit standing in the bunny slippers and holding a watch. *I'm late for a very important date,* I wrote in a thought bubble above his head. That reminded me: Natalie had said something about going to the Dungeon on Friday with her and Valerie and Jason. I hoped I could smooth things over with Jason before then.

I looked up in time to see him walking up the far aisle of the auditorium with Robert and exiting out the back doors. He didn't look at me once. I sighed. It seemed like lately I could never get my timing quite right.

I closed my notebook over my fractured thoughts and tried to concentrate on the end of rehearsal, though without much success.

❂

After dinner, I fished out my chocolates for a late-night treat and noticed a slip of paper stuck to the bottom of the box. Unfolding it, I saw a list of words written in a bold, slanted script running along the left-hand margin: *breakfast, Italy, dream, beauty, temptation, goal, wish, love, future, laughter, hope, heaven*. Next to each word my name had been written in the same bold script.

Confused, I flipped the paper over but it was blank. What was this? And then I knew.

It was Dante's getting-to-know-you list. Apparently he had thought about me and, following the rules, he'd written down my name every time.

Every time except for the last one.

I read the last line and felt a chill run a finger along my spine. There in black and white were two words:

Deadly. Me.

CHAPTER
7

"You remembered the tickets, right?" Valerie asked Natalie. Parking at the Dungeon was always at a premium, but it was even worse on show nights, so all four of us had squeezed into Valerie's convertible Lexus. It was a tight fit for me at five-six; it was almost impossible for Jason's six-foot frame.

After finding me with Dante in the parking lot, Jason had barely spoken to me. But I knew he wasn't one to hold a grudge, so on Thursday I had apologized and said all the right things and smoothed everything over. There was still a slight strain in our relationship, and I hoped a date at the Dungeon would help put us back on even footing.

"Right here," Natalie said, flipping through the tickets like playing cards before passing two of them to me and Jason in the backseat.

"Zero Hour?" Jason read the name on the ticket. "Never heard of them. Are they any good?"

"Never heard of them?" Valerie almost choked on her Diet Coke, and the Lexus veered alarmingly to the left. "They're only the hottest rock band right now."

"If they're so hot, why are they playing the Dungeon?" Jason asked, trying to shift his legs into a more comfortable position in the limited space.

"Because this is where they got their start," Natalie explained quickly before Valerie could open her mouth. "A couple of years ago, these three guys showed up and started playing gigs at the Dungeon. Leo managed to get some big-time music producer to come to a show, and he signed the band that same night. They've been touring for almost a year promoting their first album—*Ten to Midnight*."

"Honestly, Abby, has your boyfriend been living in a cave?" Valerie demanded as she pulled into the parking lot of the Dungeon.

"Well—" I said, but Valerie braked hard and swerved to the right, sliding her Lexus into a narrow space between a green Jeep Cherokee and a white Honda, saving me from having to respond.

"Um, Valerie, I don't think this is a parking space," Natalie said, looking out her window.

"Nonsense. My car fits, doesn't it?"

"Well, yes, but I can't open my door."

Valerie sighed dramatically and pushed a button on the dashboard. The top of her convertible peeled back. A light snow fell from the dark sky. "Everybody out before the snow ruins the leather."

I shot Jason a grin, which thankfully he returned, and we scrambled out the back of the car, sliding down over the trunk.

"And don't you dare scratch the paint job," Valerie called over her shoulder without looking at us.

Leo's Dungeon was a simple two-story building with a hand-painted sign over the front door. Tonight there was also a single poster for Zero Hour next to the door. As boring as the outside of the building was, though, the inside more than made up for it. Posters from bands that had played there covered one entire wall: the Zombie Heads, Complicated Shoes, Swedish Bitters, even Darwin Glass. The Dungeon was open every night but Sunday, and every Friday night was live music night, where Leo invited anyone with a band to come play at his place. Leo believed that kids needed a place to hang out, but he had three strict rules: no drugs, no drinking, no smoking. Breaking one of his rules meant lifetime banishment from the club. Even the rowdiest kids behaved themselves under Leo's watchful eye.

A festival atmosphere settled over the crowds of people who were milling around the parking lot and wandering in and out of the Dungeon. Everyone was talking or dancing to the music that poured through the open door. I waved to Sarah and Lily, who were hanging out with a couple of the guys from the football team. Jason took my hand and we followed a trail of footprints in the snow that led to the door.

If the Dungeon was the hottest club in town, the Signature Wall was the coolest place inside. When Leo first opened his club, he had started an unusual tradition: you come in, you sign your name on the wall. Now, decades later, the wall was covered with names and messages from his customers. There was one signature that looked eerily like Jimi Hendrix, and another that Valerie swore was from Kurt Cobain, but Leo would never confirm or deny any of the rumors.

When we finally made our way inside, we headed straight for the wall to sign our names. Since Valerie always dotted the "i" in her name with a heart, and since she was at the Dungeon almost every Friday, I saw her heart all over the wall. Natalie's signature was a narrow scrawl of pink. I signed my name beneath Jason's. He hesitated, then quickly drew a plus sign between our names. I slipped my hand into his and gave it a quick squeeze. It was nice to know he wasn't mad at me anymore.

Because I knew they were playing tonight, I scanned the wall for the signatures of the band. I saw the bold, blocky letters of Zero Hour almost immediately. Both the "o's" in *Zero* and in *Hour* held two arrows pointing to where midnight would have been on a traditional clock face. The only numbers on these blank clocks, though, were the Roman numerals MDVI that crawled along the bottom curve. A thick black chain with three links connected the two clocks, and inside each link was a name: Tony. Zo. V.

The band certainly knew how to make a statement, I'd give them that.

Across from the Signature Wall was the bar where Leo usually held court, overseeing his customers like a benevolent deity. Tonight, though, I was surprised to see Dante behind the bar instead of Leo. He wore a crisp white shirt, unbuttoned at the throat, sleeves rolled up to his elbows. His black gloves were shadowed blurs as he poured drinks for the steady stream of customers crowding around.

"What'll you have tonight?" he asked us as we slid onto the stools lining the bar.

"Strawberry soda," I said.

"Make that two," Jason chimed in, leaning against the bar next to me.

"Make that three," Natalie said.

"Diet Coke," Valerie said, breaking the rhythm.

Dante nodded. He flipped a bottle of Diet Coke from underneath the bar, resting it on the back of his right hand. With his left hand, he quickly slapped a glass down, filling it with a scoop of ice. Gripping the bottle in his left hand and then passing it to his right, he spun the glass in a tight spiral, pouring the soda into the center of the glass. Bubbles fizzed and spat. Dante splashed a slice of lemon into the drink and the glass came to a stop in front of Valerie's hand.

"Show-off," she said with a wink as we all applauded his flair.

Dante grinned, showing his teeth in a flash of white. "I can't help it if I'm good with my hands," he said. "Three strawberry sodas?"

Quicker than my eye could follow, Dante had placed three tall, narrow glasses on the bar and filled each with a rich red liquid, a splash of soda water, and a paper umbrella. A split berry on the rim completed each drink.

"Wow," I said, taking a sip. "This is better than Leo's."

"Where is Leo?" Jason asked, reaching past me for his drink.

Dante fussed with spinning an empty glass on the bar. "Leo's . . . on vacation for a time. I'm filling in for him."

I had just opened my mouth to ask another question when

Julia, farther down the bar, signaled for a refill. Dante nodded to us and walked away to help the other customers.

Jason ate his strawberry in one bite, then leaned down to kiss me on the top of my head. "Be right back." Jason pointed across the room at Robert, who was waving him over to his table near the front of the stage. Robert had his arm around a girl I didn't know.

Valerie and Natalie were having a conversation, so I took my strawberry soda and wandered past the pool tables at the back of the Dungeon to the glass cabinet standing next to a door marked "Employees Only." In addition to owning the Dungeon, Leo also collected antiques and curios. He kept his treasures on display, and there was always something new to see.

Like tonight. A complicated-looking machine rested on the top shelf of the cabinet. The machine was roughly square in shape, but it had three notches carved into the side so it looked a little like a giant brass *E*. Buttons and dials covered the face of the machine and each notch had been engraved with a different design: a spiral shell; a half-sun, half-moon circle; and a staff of music with five notes placed in a rising scale.

"Beautiful, isn't it?" Dante asked softly beside me.

I watched his reflection in the glass. He wasn't looking at the machine. I blushed. "What is it?" I didn't really care; Dante had a way of really *seeing* me that sometimes made me uncomfortable.

Dante hesitated. "You'd have to ask Leo."

"It's amazing, whatever it is."

Dante looked out across the crowded floor. "Are you a fan of Zero Hour?"

I shrugged. "They're okay. Valerie really likes them, though."

An awkward silence fell between us. "Dante . . ." I started, even though I didn't know what I was going to say next. I wanted to ask him about his getting-to-know-you list. I wanted to ask him how he'd healed me from the white flashes I'd had. I wanted to ask him to touch me again.

"It looks like they're about to start," he said. "I hope you enjoy the show." He slipped away into the crowd.

Frustrated with Dante's seeming uncanny ability to appear and disappear at will, I joined my friends at a table with Robert and the girl who turned out to be his new girlfriend, Heather. Just then the lights went down and the show began.

The sound of a ticking clock pulsated through the speakers. Spots of different colored lights flickered across the stage like a rainbow torn from a fractured prism. From out of the swirling darkness came the sound of one, two, three, four sharp staccato beats of V's drumsticks. The drums rumbled to life with a deep, growling bass beat. The sound crested like a rising wave before crashing down with a splash of golden cymbals and a single white beam of light split the darkness on the stage like a sword.

Zo stood at the microphone, wrenching a single note like a wailing banshee from the silver guitar in his hands, his eyes closed, his head back, his face fiercely beautiful with primal intensity. As the harsh note faded away, swallowed up by the dark, tribal heartbeat of the drums, by the endless rhythm of the ticking clock, Zo opened his dark eyes and leaned close to the microphone. He whispered four simple words.

"It's time, my children . . ."

A spotlight flashed on Tony standing to Zo's right. Tony pulled a high note screaming from his guitar and then danced his fingers down the frets, the sound rising, falling, diving, washing over the crowd.

Zo caressed the microphone with his hand and spoke four more words.

"Zero Hour has come!"

As the band launched into the riffs and fills of their hit single "Into the River," I jumped to my feet, barely aware that everyone else in the club had done the same. It was instinctive. It was inevitable. The music demanded it of us, pulling at us, holding us captive to the driving rhythms of drum and bass. And over it all, Zo's voice rose like an avenging angel.

> *It's time, my children*
> *When the waves rise high*
> *When the waters run deep*
> *When the clock strikes midnight*
> *You'll feel the mark of Zero Hour*
> *And you'll never be the same again*

I joined my voice to the chorus swelling from the crowd, feeling the past week's stress wash away from me. The music swept me along like the river's current the band sang about, a fast and dangerous current, but refreshing and sustaining as well. I closed my eyes and danced to the music, feeling the possibilities spiraling around me, feeling the energy of the crowd, feeling alive like never before.

As I clapped and cheered at the end of the song, I caught sight of Dante standing behind the bar. His eyes were black pools of shadowed night. His whole body quivered with coiled tension. I watched him gasp for air as though he were drowning, his chest heaving with the strain. His eyes whipped to me across the room and I felt a flash of panic shoot through me. He *was* drowning—somehow he was being washed downriver in the midst of this crowded dance floor and I was the only one who could throw him a line, could save him from oblivion. He needed me. Now. Right now.

I took a step in his direction, confused by the intensity of my emotions but wanting to help somehow.

And then I heard Zo's voice start another song—*"The world is older than we imagine / Time more fluid than we think"*—and then I felt Jason touch my arm and then I broke eye contact with Dante for just a second and then and then . . . and then the moment was gone. I shook my head, trying to clear my thoughts. I realized how thirsty I was. That must have been why I was thinking of drowning, why my thoughts were filled with images of rushing water, of crashing waves.

I grabbed Jason's strawberry soda and drained the rest of it in a single swallow. Revived, I turned my attention back to the show, singing and clapping along with the crowd.

But in the back of my mind, I could still see the image of a shadowy figure, standing alone on a bleak and barren shore, his hand extended to me as I was swept away on a wave of light and sound.

"Abby? Are you asleep?" I felt Jason's hand on my back and I abruptly jerked upright from where I had been resting my head on the bar.

"No. No, I wasn't asleep," I slurred, rubbing at my eyes. "What time is it?"

"Almost two," Jason said. "The show's been over for nearly an hour. C'mon, it's time to go home."

The wild, dancing, singing crowds had thinned, dispersing like fog at dawn, and the Dungeon was nearly empty. Zero Hour had finished packing up their gear, but a few knots of people were still talking to the band, unwilling to let the amazing evening come to a close. I saw Valerie talking to V, her hand on her hip in full flirt mode.

"Where's Natalie?" I asked, looking around the room.

"She got tired of waiting for Valerie and went home with Robert."

"Must be nice to have a brother to hitch a ride with in a pinch," I said.

"It can come in handy. Wait here. I'll be right back," Jason said. He tousled my hair before heading in the direction of the bathrooms.

Pleasantly exhausted, I yawned and stretched my back, my ears ringing a little from the show. I felt remarkably alert and refreshed, considering the late hour. I saw Dante and Zo talking to the right of the stage. I found myself grinning and, seized by a sudden impulse, I hopped down from the bar stool and walked over to them.

"Hey, Dante," I said, leaning on one of the large black boxes marked with Zero Hour's numberless clock faces.

"Hello, Abby," he said with that small smile I only seemed to see when he said my name.

I flicked a glance at Zo. He was taller than Dante. Older, too, but probably not by much. The frosted white tips in his dark black hair glimmered in the stage lights. A dark black chain had been tattooed around both of his wrists.

Zo caught me looking at his hands and he pushed up his sleeves so I could see them more clearly. "Do you like them?"

"Sorry," I said. "I didn't mean to stare." I narrowed my eyes. "They look like the chains in your band's logo."

He rotated his wrists outward, and I saw the familiar numberless clock logo marked on the inside of each wrist. The same arrows pointed to a nonexistent midnight hour. One wrist held the letters MDVI while the other changed to MMVI.

"I've felt the mark of Zero Hour," Zo said, pulling his sleeves back down, cutting a glance at Dante. "And I've never been the same."

I recognized the reference to "Into the River." Even his speaking voice managed to evoke the same angelic tones of his music. "That's dedication," I observed. "But which came first— the band? or the tattoo?"

A smile tugged at the corners of Zo's full mouth. *"Il tempo è più fluido che tu pensi."*

My eyebrows rose in happy surprise. "You're Italian?" I looked to Dante. "So do you guys know each other?"

"We know some of the same people," Zo said, a strange look in his eyes.

"We lived in the same neighborhood. Before. In Italy," Dante said curtly. He clasped his hands behind his back and I saw the muscles on his arms tighten.

"Cool. It must be nice to see a familiar face, Dante. Or at least hear Italian spoken properly once in a while."

"It certainly is nice to see your face, Abby," he said, his voice low, and I felt a blush cross my cheeks.

"So, Abby," Zo cut in, "did you enjoy the show?"

"Very much. I hadn't really heard a lot of your music so it was exciting to hear it for the first time live. You're really talented."

"Thank you." Zo lifted my hand and breathed a kiss along the inside of my wrist, his lips not quite touching my skin. His hand was strong, the calluses on his fingertips rough. He inhaled deeply. "Ah, yes, I recognize you. You were quite active during the show. Enthusiasm such as yours is . . . refreshing."

"*Fermati*, Lorenzo," Dante snapped, yanking my hand away from Zo's mouth. "*Lasciale stare.*"

"*Appartiene a te?*" Zo asked, an amused glint in his dark eyes.

Dante's jaw clenched and he looked away.

I frowned, confused at the byplay. I'd have to ask Dante later what he had said. Either that or start learning Italian.

"You see, Abby," Zo turned to me smoothly, "a good performance requires a certain amount of give and take. If the crowd is active and energetic, willing to accept what we are offering, then it makes my life so much easier." He inclined his head in a formal bow. "So I thank you, Abby, for your acceptance of me tonight."

Zo's smile curved his lips but it never reached his eyes.

The euphoria I had been feeling shriveled inside me. I shivered and stepped back, bumping into a solid body behind me.

"Hey, great show, man," Jason said. "Do you guys have any CDs left?"

Zo nodded and pointed him in Tony's direction. "Tell him it's on the house. A willing gift for a willing fan."

"Thanks," Jason said brightly. "So where are you guys headed next?"

"Oh, I think we might stay around town for a little while." Zo's eyes never left mine. "Take some time to reconnect with our roots before starting up another tour."

"Cool. Maybe we'll see you around, then," Jason said.

Dante made a small, inarticulate noise deep in his throat.

I stumbled after Jason, my exhaustion finally catching up to me. As Jason slipped the CD into his jacket pocket, as he helped me into my coat, as Valerie found her keys, as we finally left the Dungeon, I was acutely conscious of Zo's eyes on me, watching my every move, and his feral smile remained sharp in my memory, even after I had fallen asleep.

CHAPTER
8

Zo's smile stayed with me over the next few days. I saw it in the curve of the moon at night, in the teeth of Jason's circular saw blade that he used in the shop garage. At those times I would hear again the whisper of his angelic voice, *Thank you, Abby, for your acceptance of me,* and feel again the shiver along the inside of my wrist where he'd almost kissed me.

More than once I thought about talking to Dante about it, but every time someone mentioned Zo or Zero Hour around him, his face closed and his eyes grew dark. I didn't dare bring it up. Plus, I hadn't had a spare moment alone with Dante since he'd given me the box of chocolates. I would see him at school, and we talked every day after rehearsal, but he was careful never to be alone with me. I sometimes wondered if I'd made a mistake, if maybe he wasn't interested in me after all, but then I'd see that small smile cross his lips when he said my name and a certain spark in his eyes as they changed from gray to blue when I walked past him and the countless almost-times he reached out his hand for mine before pulling back, tugging on the edge of his gloves instead.

No, I didn't think I was mistaken.

I stayed busy with rehearsals, school, and my friends. There was some general excitement about a week later when someone broke into the Special Collection section at the university library and stole some documents. The police weren't saying exactly what was stolen or if they had any suspects, and the story was quickly relegated to "old news."

Likewise, Zo's smile was relegated to the back of my mind, and before I knew it, two weeks had passed in a blink and suddenly it was the end of January.

❽

"Abby, Jason's here." Mom knocked three times before opening the door. "He's in the front room."

"Thanks, Mom," I said, checking my reflection before running a brush through my hair one last time. "Would you tell him I'll be right down?"

"Sure thing, sweetie."

Jason and I were long past making formal plans for Friday night dates. I just expected him to show up and he did, every week, at 7:30 for dinner and a movie. I glanced at my watch. Right on time, as usual.

Skipping lightly down the stairs, I tugged at the hem of my blue sweater and brushed nonexistent wrinkles from my jeans. "Jason, we'll have to hurry if we want to make the 8:15 show—"

Jason stood up as I entered the front room. A box of pizza sat on the low coffee table next to a six-pack of soda. "I thought maybe we'd stay in tonight instead of going out. Is that okay?"

I spied the DVD in his hand: *Roman Holiday*. "I thought you hated that movie."

Jason held the case by the corners and spun it in his hands. "I know you like it."

"You're too good to me." I grinned. "What else did you bring?"

"Hand-tossed, thin crust, half black olive and pepperoni, half pineapple and ham, extra sauce," Jason rattled in a single breath. "A West End Pizza original."

"Best pizza there is," I grinned, grabbing the box and the soda. "C'mon downstairs."

Hannah and her friends had already claimed the family room and were sprawled out around a large poster board that was covered with pictures cut out from magazines.

"Hannah, out," I barked, jerking my head toward the door. "We want to watch a movie."

"No." Hannah glared at me over the tops of the cards in her hand. "We're not done with our game yet."

"Yeah, and I'm gonna win," McKenna said, shifting some of her cards around in her hand.

"You are not," Cori said. "I already know the Who *and* the Where."

"What are you guys playing, anyway?" I set the soda and pizza on top of the TV.

"A&B Clue," Hannah said proudly. "The A is for Austen and the B is for Brontë. See, we made our own board and we cut pictures out of magazines for the different places and people and weapons. Here's the ballroom in Netherfield Park from *Pride and Prejudice,* and here's the attic from *Jane Eyre,* and the moors from *Wuthering Heights* run along this whole side."

I snorted back a laugh and glanced at Jason.

"That's really creative, Hannah," he said with a straight face, stretching his long legs out on the couch.

Hannah glowed with the praise. "Thanks. Would you like to play?"

"Sorry, we'll pass." I flipped on the DVD player. "You can finish your game, but then you guys have got to head upstairs, okay?"

Hannah held a brief council with her friends. "Okay, but we want two slices of pizza and a soda. *Each.*"

"No way."

Hannah shrugged. "Okay." She picked up the die and rattled it in her hand for a solid minute, her eyes never leaving mine.

"Fine, you can have one slice and two sodas. To *share.*"

"Two slices and three sodas."

"Three sodas and half the breadsticks."

"Deal." Hannah spun the die onto the board and moved her bottle cap into the Attic. Quickly consulting her notes, she declared, "It was Mr. Darcy, in the Attic, with his devastatingly good looks."

McKenna groaned and Cori threw her cards down in disgust.

Triumphant, Hannah flipped over the mystery cards, winning the game.

"Gives 'if looks could kill' a whole new meaning, doesn't it?" I said to Jason. "Okay, here are your sodas and here are your breadsticks and there is the door."

After they had left, we set up camp on the couch, the pizza box serving as a makeshift table and the remaining sodas nestled in the cushions between us. As the opening credits played, I tucked my feet under a blanket to keep them warm. "This was a good idea."

"No problem," he said, saluting me with his can of soda.

We watched the movie in companionable silence. I rested my head on Jason's shoulder, enjoying the feeling of calm contentment that welled up inside me as he gently stroked my hair.

As the end credits rolled on the screen, I yawned and stretched, wiggling my toes to get the circulation flowing again. "You're a good sport. You really could have picked a different movie."

"I'm glad you still liked it."

"I'm glad you did too," I teased, standing and picking up the empty pizza box. "You didn't fall asleep once this time."

"Well, just once. There near the end."

"The end is the best part!"

Jason locked his hands behind his head. He watched me for a moment before speaking again. "I was afraid you might be tired of all things Italian."

"What do you mean?"

"You've been spending a lot of time with Dante lately, and I—"

"Jason, how many times do I have to tell you—I'm not dating Dante."

"I know. It's just . . . I think you might want to be careful around him. He's been hanging out with that Zo character a lot and—"

"Dante and Zo? I don't think so. Dante doesn't even like Zo." I shoved the pizza box into the trash can with probably more force than necessary.

"Still. You know the break-in at the library a couple of weeks ago? Melinda said her dad said he suspects Zo was behind it. Zo and his band."

"Melinda needs to learn to keep her mouth shut," I muttered. "I bet she thinks Zo is also behind the bank robbery last week and yesterday's carjacking, doesn't she? And since Zo is Italian and Dante is Italian, Dante must be in on it too, right? I know—maybe they're all members of the Mafia!"

"You have to admit, strange things have been happening around town ever since they showed up."

"Strange things happen all the time, Jason, if you're looking for them."

"All I'm saying is that I'm worried about you. I want you to be safe, that's all."

I sighed. "I know. I'm sorry. I didn't mean to snap like that."

"It's okay," he said, crossing the room to stand behind me. His strong hands rubbed at my shoulders and neck.

Instead of relaxing me, his massage merely pinched at my nerves. Stepping away from him, I busied myself with ejecting the DVD from the player and gathering up the empty soda cans so I wouldn't have to see the hurt on his face.

I told myself Dante and Zo could do whatever they wanted in their spare time. It wasn't any concern of mine. And yet, I couldn't deny that I felt the tiniest bit unsettled at what Jason had said. The truth was, I could easily believe Zo was at fault for the recent crimes in town. I'd seen his smile; I'd felt his breath on my skin. But Dante? No. I'd also seen Dante's smile, felt his breath on my skin, and there was no way Dante was a criminal.

"Abby?" Jason said quietly. "What's wrong? Can I help?"

Jason, for all his size and strength, looked lost and small. I set down the DVD and walked back to him. He didn't deserve to bear the brunt of my frustration and unease. He was doing the best he could. I stepped close and wrapped my arms around him. After a moment he hugged me back.

"*This* helps," I murmured.

"I'm glad," he said. "Abby, can I ask you something?" He paused. "Would you like to go to the Valentine's Dance with me?"

I leaned back to look him in the face. "You're asking me?"

"Well, you are my girlfriend—"

I shook my head. "Of course I'll go. I was already planning on it. Dad's taking Mom out to dinner and Hannah's sleeping over at McKenna's house so I don't have to baby-sit that night. I'm surprised you felt like you had to ask."

"I want it to be special. It's Valentine's Day, after all, and I know you girls care about that a lot."

"It will be special."

Jason smiled. "I was hoping you'd say yes. Well, I knew you would, but . . . anyway, I got you something. Hang on." He ran back upstairs and returned holding his coat in one hand, rummaging through the pockets with the other. "I know it's here somewhere. Ah!" He pulled out a small black box and held it out to me.

I took it warily. "You're not proposing, are you?" I joked.

"Open it."

I cracked the lid back and caught my breath. It wasn't a ring. It was a delicate gold necklace, the chain shimmering like gossamer thread. A golden butterfly flew from the necklace, its wings spread wide to catch the light. "Jason, it's lovely."

"I saw it and thought you might like it."

"I love it."

Beaming, Jason reached his hand into his pocket again. "I saw something else I thought you might like." He handed me a slip of paper.

"What's this?"

"It's a claim ticket for a dress at Harrod's. I know you and Valerie like to shop there. The dance is only a couple of weeks away; I didn't want anyone else buying it, so I went ahead and paid for it. You just have to go pick it up."

"Jason, I . . . I don't know what to say." It was the truth. As touched as I was by the butterfly necklace, having Jason not only pick out my Valentine's dress before officially asking me to the dance but then buy it without me took some of the excitement out of the whole thing. "I'm sure it'll be beautiful. I can't wait to see it." I tried to muster up some enthusiasm but fell flat.

"I can't wait to see you in it," Jason said, bending down to kiss me.

I closed my eyes. We'd kissed a few times since that first

kiss on our birthday, but sadly, I'd never felt the same fireworks he did. I wanted to. I wanted to be swept away. I wanted to feel a tingle all the way down to my toes. I wanted my breath to be stolen and time to stop . . .

With a shock, I realized I wanted to be kissing Dante.

I broke off the kiss.

Jason grinned and brushed my hair back from my face. "So it's a date?"

"I'll pick up the dress tomorrow," I promised. "I'm sure I can convince Valerie and Natalie to go shopping with me."

"I'll plan on it."

I knew he would.

❽

"Ugh, this dress makes me look enormous. It's like two hippos are camping out on my thighs." Valerie tossed a blue dress over the top of the dressing room door. "I can't wear this one either. And which one of you picked out this green thing? Do you *want* me to look like Godzilla?" Two more dresses flopped over the door frame.

I stifled a laugh as Natalie grabbed the hangers and pulled the mass of colored, silky fabric into her hands. "Do you want me to grab you a different size?" she asked sweetly.

Valerie flung the door open, stalking from the dressing room like an angered queen. "Shopping is not about the *size*, Natalie, darling, it's about the *dress*. Abby knows what I'm talking about."

I held up my hands. "Don't drag me into this. My dress is

all picked out and paid for." I patted the bag draped over my arm. Smiling, I slid past Valerie into the dressing room. "All that's left is to try it on."

I hung the dress bag on the hook of the dressing-room wall. Kicking off my shoes, I pulled off my shirt and jeans. My breath quickened just a little. I wondered what the dress would look like. Jason wasn't big into surprises. I hoped this one was a good one.

I unzipped the bag in one quick motion.

A spill of dark fabric billowed out. My mouth dropped open. The dress was brown. And plain. And there was a bow.

Gingerly, I lifted the dress off the hanger and held it up to my body. I shook my head in disbelief. I slipped the dress over my head, feeling the slightly rough fabric rub against my skin. It wasn't much better on me than it had been on the hanger.

It was loose around my chest and tight across my hips. The sleeves were almost long enough to reach my elbows, but certainly not long enough to reach my wrists. The neckline dipped to a point where a hint of cleavage could be seen—provided I'd had some cleavage, which I didn't. At least the skirt was long enough—the hem touched the floor—and I knew that with heels it would be the perfect length. I was relieved to see the skirt had some fullness to it, too, a little swish and swirl. Maybe it would be enough to save me at the dance.

I closed my eyes, silently wishing that when I opened them, I would be wearing a different dress. A dress that fit me, one that I could be comfortable in.

But no.

I could imagine so clearly Jason wandering through the

store, looking for something he thought I might like. I knew he didn't have that much extra cash to spend, so he must have stopped by the sale rack first. Knowing Jason, he probably found everything in his price range and then everything in what he guessed would be my size and then picked the best of what was left. For Jason, shopping wasn't about the size or the dress, it was about efficiency. He had probably picked this dress because he thought it would match my eyes. Too bad it didn't match anything else.

And to be fair, the dress wasn't exactly *ugly*, it just wasn't *pretty*.

And it was *brown*. The tag on the sleeve said "Cocoa Foam," and maybe it did look a little like chocolate, but did Jason seriously expect me to wear this to the dance?

"It must be nice to have a boyfriend who can shop for you," Natalie said. I could hear the clink of metal hangers as she hung Valerie's discarded dresses on the return rack.

"It might be nicer if said boyfriend had better taste in clothes," Valerie quipped.

"Jason's taste is just fine," I protested weakly. I clutched at the skirt with numb fingers.

I could hear Valerie rolling her eyes, even from behind the door.

"Don't mind her," Natalie said. "I think it's romantic."

"Thanks, Nat," I said, though privately I had my doubts.

"Enough chitchat." Valerie knocked on the door. "Come out and let us see."

I blew out my breath and squared my shoulders. There was

no way out of it now. I might as well get it over with. I closed my eyes and opened the door.

I heard simultaneous "Ohs" from my friends, and even with my eyes closed I could tell they were horribly underwhelmed.

"Ta-da." I tried to inject some enthusiasm into my voice.

When silence met my words, I dared a peek. Natalie looked like she might cry. Valerie's face was impassive, her lips barely bowing in a frown.

"It's not that bad, is it?" It was true I didn't love the dress, but Jason was my boyfriend and he had tried to do something nice for me. I suddenly felt a little protective of Jason and his thoughtfulness. "It was on sale," I said lamely.

Valerie nodded once, briskly. "Well. That's it, then. Abby has her dress. C'mon, Natalie, let's find something for you."

"Wait. What? That's it?" I grabbed Valerie's arm as she turned away. "What about my dress?"

Valerie patted my hand. "What about it? It's brown. It was out of season *last* season. I don't know anyone who would willingly wear it. But it was a gift. You have to wear it, no matter how much you'd rather not."

"We can pretend to like it if that will help," Natalie volunteered.

I smiled crookedly. "Thanks, Nat, it might."

She grinned back at me. "Then I love it!" She hugged me, then held me at arm's length before pulling me into another hug. "You look so great in it!"

I couldn't help myself. I laughed and hugged her back.

Leave it to Natalie to see the silver lining in this particular storm cloud.

"Now put that back in the bag before it gets all wrinkled and ruined," Natalie said, shooing me back inside the dressing room.

I caught up with my friends, who were browsing through another rack of dresses. I tried to keep my dress bag from bumping into anything.

"Tell me again why you're shopping for a dress to wear to a dance that no one's asked you to yet?" I asked Valerie.

Valerie thumbed through the hangers like a Vegas blackjack dealer. "Because if I wait until V asks me to the dance, it'll be too late to go shopping. Do you think this dress would look nice with my black hair?" She held up a silver-white sheath dress draped in lace organza.

"It would look great," I said, "if you *had* black hair."

Valerie held the dress away from her, examining it with a critical eye. "Well, obviously I can't go to two dances in a row as a blonde."

"Obviously."

"*Did* V ask you to the dance?" Natalie asked, idly checking the size of a yellow sequined dress.

"Not yet, but he will; he just doesn't know it yet," Valerie said. She paused, a sly smile on her face. "The poor boy won't know what hit him."

"Why V? I would have thought you'd set your sights on Zo. You know, lead singer, guitar player." I lingered at a simple, pale blue A-line dress with capped sleeves and a sweetheart neckline. The color reminded me of Dante's eyes when he was thinking intently about something. I awkwardly shifted my dress bag to my other arm.

"Because V's the drummer."

"So?"

"So the drummer is the heart of any rock band." Valerie held up a tangled web of red-and-white straps bound together with silver links.

"You'd look like a peppermint stick rolled in razor blades," I pointed out, and she put the dress back.

"A good drummer," she continued as though I hadn't spoken, "can transform some sappy ballad into a passionate anthem. Zo's got a good voice, but without V keeping time, he'd be nothing but a guy with a guitar singing some lame song about how he can't live without you."

"Sometimes a love ballad can be nice," Natalie chimed in from across the rack.

"She's right. 'Out of My Mind' is just Zo and a guitar, and I think it's one of the best songs on the album."

"Absolutely," Valerie agreed, flicking past a trio of identical pink gowns. "But 'Into the River' *is* their best song. Period. Hands down. And it's all because of V's drumming."

"Maybe," I said.

"What do you guys think about this dress?" Natalie held up a light yellow dress covered with small flowers.

"I think you'd look like a flower garden threw up on you," Valerie said, taking the dress from her and shoving it back on the rack. "Come with me." She scanned the room and then grabbed Natalie by the hand and made a beeline for the corner. Her hand hovered over the hangers, her fingers twitching like a magician's. She struck, withdrawing a single dress. "Here," she said. "Wear this."

Natalie's mouth made a round O as she looked at the dress Valerie held out for her. It was a beautiful, soft burgundy velvet dress; the color brought out the auburn highlights in her brown hair. The elegant skirt fell from a high empire waist and was covered with delicately embroidered gold-and-burgundy patterns. The hem, trimmed in dark golden ribbon, skimmed the tops of Natalie's shoes.

"You can borrow my fire opal necklace and Abby's earrings."

"Oh, it's beautiful." Natalie checked the tag. "And it's on sale!" She kissed Valerie on the cheek and flew into the dressing room.

I shook my head in amazement. "How do you do it?"

"It's a gift," Valerie grinned. "And speaking of gifts, what's this I see around your neck? Something I'm going to want to borrow?" She hooked her finger under the gold chain around my neck and pulled out the butterfly pendant.

"Jason gave it to me when he asked me to the dance."

Valerie sighed and let the pendant flutter through her fingers. "What were you thinking, Abby?"

"What? I like it. I think it's pretty." I slipped the butterfly under my collar.

"Of course it is, but by accepting it, you're giving Jason more false hope."

"What are you talking about?"

"Jason's feeling threatened by your obvious and continued interest in one Italian foreign-exchange student, Mr. Dante

Alexander, and this whole thing—going to the dance, picking out the dress, giving you the necklace—it's Jason's way of reminding you that *he's* your boyfriend."

"I know he's my boyfriend. Dante's just a *friend*. I'm not interested in dating him."

"You're such a liar, Abby."

"What!"

"We go to the Dungeon and your eyes immediately go to wherever Dante is. During rehearsal, you pay the most attention to the scenes he's in, even though he's just standing in the background. And on no less than three separate occasions over the last month, you have chosen to take Dante's call when his name showed up on your caller ID instead of finishing our conversation."

I opened my mouth to protest, but closed it immediately. Was she right? Of course she was. Valerie was always right when it came to relationships.

"It's okay," Valerie said softly. "It'll be good for you to be friends with and date a guy other than Jason. Just—let him down easy, okay? For all his faults"—she rattled the dress bag I held in my arms—"he really is a good guy."

"Break up with Jason?" I swallowed down a dry throat. "I couldn't do that. Not so close to Valentine's Day. I mean, he's already made plans and everything . . ." I trailed off at the look of pity in Valerie's eyes.

"You're breaking up with Jason?" Natalie said from behind me, an odd catch to her voice.

"What? No," I said, whirling around to face her. "No,

Valerie and I were just talking about . . . about something else," I finished lamely.

"Oh." Natalie looked down and absently ran her hand over the velvet fabric. She gave a sad half-smile and then shook her head. "I just thought . . ."

"That dress looks perfect on you, Nat," Valerie said gently into the awkward silence that had fallen between us.

Natalie twirled for us. "I really love it," she said.

"Excellent. You should buy it. Now, if I could just find the right dress for me . . ." Valerie swept Natalie away with her, shooting me a pointed look over her shoulder.

What—? And then the penny dropped.

The strange note in Natalie's voice had been thinly disguised *hope*.

Natalie—and Jason? My *best friend*—and my *boyfriend*?

I waited for a surge of some kind of hot emotion—jealousy, perhaps, or anger—but instead all I felt was a strange mixture of sadness and joy. And relief.

CHAPTER
9

I thought about Natalie's almost-confession all week. I didn't mention it to her or to Jason, but I watched how they were together, amazed that I hadn't seen it before. The looks. The quick touches. The bright laughter. Through it all, I knew Natalie didn't want to ruin my relationship with Jason and I was touched that she had taken such pains to keep her feelings secret.

I also thought about my feelings all week. I would randomly check my emotional pulse to see if jealousy had reared its ugly green head, or if anger had lashed out with its red-hot tongue, but the only constant emotion I felt was relief.

I was still looking forward to going to the dance with Jason. Despite my shifting feelings, Jason was my friend and I didn't want to disappoint him after he had worked so hard to prepare a special night for us.

But Valerie had been right—as usual—and I could tell Jason was feeling anxious about my friendship with Dante because he kept wanting to do things I liked and deferring to my every whim. He even suggested we go to the Dungeon's first-ever Poetry Slam on the Friday before the dance because he knew I'd been interested in it. We made plans to go together, but at the last minute, he came down with a nasty head cold, so Valerie and I went instead.

The Dungeon was as busy as on a concert night, people milling in front of the door, crowding around the bar, squeezing into the booths. Valerie and I were lucky to find an empty table near the bar and immediately claimed it for our own.

"Can you believe this crowd?" I asked, draping my coat over the back of my chair. "All this? For a Poetry Slam?"

"I'm not surprised," Valerie said. "Rumor has it Zo is unveiling some original work tonight. New lyrics for Zero Hour's next album."

"Really?"

"I hope they're here. I need to be *accessible* for when V asks me to the dance." She pursed her lips. "I don't see him, though."

I scanned the crowd with her. "He's over there." I pointed toward Leo's glass cabinet of curios.

Zo, Tony, and V huddled around the case, arguing about something. Zo leaned forward intently, shooting a glance over his shoulder at Leo and Dante, who were busy behind the bar. Tony and V followed his gaze. Tony shook his head at something Zo said and folded his arms across his chest. V tapped the glass cabinet, his eyebrows drawn together in a frown.

I wondered what they were talking about and wished the noise in the Dungeon wasn't quite so loud.

"So you're still hoping V will ask you out?"

"Hope, nothing. I'll make sure he does or die trying."

Valerie attempted to catch V's eye, but he turned his back to us, his attention fixed on the strange brass object in the cabinet.

"I'll come to your funeral," I assured Valerie.

"I hate you so much it hurts."

"I love you too."

The lights dimmed, cutting our conversation short. Leo stepped up to the microphone. I hadn't seen Leo around the Dungeon for a while; Dante said he'd been on vacation. The time off must have agreed with him because Leo looked younger than I remembered, the lines around his mouth and eyes softer and less noticeable.

"Thank you all for coming out tonight. A few ground rules and then we'll open the stage. First, anyone can come up to the microphone. Remember to introduce yourself and your poem. Second, you can share an original piece of work or one from a published poet. And last, but most important, no heckling, booing, or snide comments. We're all adults here, let's act like it." Leo looked out over the crowd. "Now. Who's first?"

We all tried to look at each other while not looking at anyone.

"No one?" Leo grinned. "Then I'll start. My name is Leo and I'll be reciting an original poem." He cleared his throat. "Roses are red, violets are blue, everyone's a poet, let's hear one from you."

We all laughed with him and, the ice broken, a few people nervously made their way to the stage. Leo graciously yielded the microphone, returning to the bar, a spring in his step.

As the crowd grew braver and more and more people

stepped up to the microphone, Valerie leaned over, nudging me with her shoulder. "You ready?" she asked.

I nodded, surprised to realize that my nerves tingled with anticipation, not fear.

The girl on stage finished an Emily Dickinson poem to scattered applause and darted into the darkness.

I pushed back my chair before I could change my mind.

My heart pounding, I took the stage. The Dungeon looked different from up here, the room longer and wider, filled with more people. The hot lights burned my skin, drying my eyes and my throat. I swallowed once, twice. I wished I'd brought my soda with me.

"Hi," I said into the microphone, wincing at the sound of my amplified voice. I saw Dante, his eyes glittering in the dim shadows behind the lights. "My name is Abby Edmunds and I'll be reciting an original poem. I call it 'The Sands of Grief.'"

I pulled a square of paper out of my pocket and unfolded it with trembling fingers. I'd written the poem a month or so ago after a particularly vivid dream. I'd been lost in a dark fog and it was hard to breathe. I was looking for something important and if I didn't find it, terrible things would happen. But I couldn't remember what it was; I could only hope that I would recognize it when I saw it. And then the fog parted and I saw a figure standing on a hill in the distance. In the fluid logic of dreams, I recognized him without seeing his face. He was a stranger, yet somehow I knew and loved him. The words had seemed to come from everywhere and nowhere, filling my dream to the edges. When I woke, I wrote them down before they disappeared with the dawn. I hadn't shown the poem to anyone. Part of me couldn't believe I was going to present it in public; the rest of me couldn't wait to begin.

> In the darkness of night,
> Demons strut, taunting, goading.
> In the light of day,
> Angels sing glorious songs.
> In the time in between,
> We live our lives alone and searching.
> And sometimes, softly,
> You understand damnation.
> All is forgotten, all is lost,
> All but forgiveness
> And the memory of her kiss.

The sound of my blood pounding in my ears drowned out the applause from the crowd. I caught a glimpse of Valerie's grin as she stood up and cheered. Dante leaned against the bar, a thoughtful expression on his face. Leo turned away, his shoulders hunched and guarded. In the back, Zo clapped lazily, his dark eyes watchful and hungry.

I nodded my thanks to the crowd and hurried off stage.

"That was great," Valerie gushed.

I wiped the sweat off my forehead. "Your turn."

"I think I'll have to wait my turn," Valerie said, nodding to the stage.

Turning in my seat, I saw Dante stride onto the stage, the white lights lining his body in silver.

He stood at the microphone, his stillness spreading out from him over the stage and the audience until it filled the

Dungeon completely, demanding our attention. The silence breathed with him.

Dante brushed his hair out of his eyes, his gaze sweeping the crowd, starting with Leo standing behind the bar, lingering for a moment over Zo and his friends, and coming to rest at the table where I sat with Valerie. I felt that familiar slowing down of time, the strange thickening in the air, the heightening of all my senses.

"Ciao," he said, his accent thicker than usual, richer and deeper. "My name is Dante Alexander and I'd like to share an original work this evening. I call it 'The Angel's Envy.'"

He shifted his weight and his fingers tugged at the backs of his gloves, restlessly, incessantly. I wondered if he was even aware of his actions.

Then he opened his mouth and all my wonders and worries were carried away by the sound of his voice.

I didn't understand a word of his poem, but the music of his native tongue wove its way into my heart. I felt the rolling vowels along the edges of my fingertips; I resonated with the thrum and throb of the rhythm of his words. Sharp consonants prickled under my skin. Liquid vowels dripped over me like honey. I closed my eyes, surrendering to the emotions Dante summoned inside me.

It reminded me a little of how I had felt after Zero Hour played, but with the band's music my emotions seemed to run wild, a tsunami of energy crashing through me. Tonight Dante's words filled me with a gentle ebb and flow, like a midnight tide rising under the moon.

I looked around the room, seeing the same emotions

reflected on the faces around me. Valerie cradled her chin in her hands, her eyes half closed, utterly relaxed.

Dante's last word lingered in the room, holding us captive. It wasn't until he stepped back from the microphone and out of the spotlight that the spell was broken and I was able to catch my breath.

We didn't applaud. It seemed wrong somehow to break the spun silence with something so crass as clapping or cheering. Dante didn't seem to mind, though, and as he stepped off the stage, he caught my eye and inclined his head in a formal bow, a ghost of a smile on his lips.

"Wow," Valerie breathed, tracking Dante's progress through the crowd. "I can see what you see in him. Oh, he's coming this way."

Indeed, Dante had changed direction, veering away from the bar and heading for our table.

"May I join you?" he asked, his deep voice ringing through the silence that swirled around him like a cloak. If he was aware of the number of eyes trained on his every move, he gave no indication of it.

"Of course," I said.

As he sat down, I heard a ripple of disappointed sighs run through the room. I had to suppress a happy grin at the thought that of all the tables in the Dungeon, he'd chosen to sit at ours.

No one dared take the stage after Dante's performance. After a few moments, Leo flipped the spotlight off and the house lights on. He watched Dante, a troubled look on his face.

"I loved your poem," Valerie said to Dante, reaching out to touch his forearm.

"Thank you." Dante deftly moved his arm away, clasping his hands under the table. "I enjoyed your poem as well, Abby. I especially enjoyed the middle lines—'Sometimes, softly, you understand damnation,'" he murmured. "A powerful truth."

Somehow the lines sounded even better coming from him, deeper and more melancholy.

"I'm glad you ended it with a kiss, though. It's important to hold on to your memories. Sometimes they are all you have left." Dante's eyes drifted out of focus as he looked into the distance between us. He licked his lips, placed his hands back on the table, and pressed the palms flat against the wood.

"Are you okay?" I asked. I'd never seen him this twitchy, this anxious and unsettled.

"Yes, I'm fine." He offered me a smile I didn't believe. "It's been a long week. I just need some time alone." A tick jumped along his jaw. He curled his hands into fists and swept them under the table again.

I exchanged a glance with Valerie.

"Would you excuse me?" Dante said, suddenly standing up, almost knocking over his chair. The feverish look in his eyes worried me. Without waiting for a reply, he turned and walked away, his steps awkward and lacking his usual grace.

"What was that all about?" Valerie wondered out loud.

"I don't know," I said. I watched Dante weave his way through the crowd, not back to the bar, but to the door marked "Employees Only." He disappeared into the darkness. "I hope he's okay."

"He'll be fine," Zo said, sitting down in the chair Dante had recently vacated. "He's probably just under some pressure and needs to blow off some steam. It happens to everyone, right?"

Tony sat down next to me, and V pulled a chair from an adjacent table to sit next to Valerie, who immediately leaned closer to her chosen target.

"It seemed a shame for two lovely ladies to remain unaccompanied; I hope you don't mind." Zo's presence filled the space between us, his grin sharp and angular. He had folded back the cuffs of his shirt, displaying his black chain tattoos proudly.

"We don't mind, do we, Abby?" Valerie purred, smiling at V.

He smiled back hesitantly. V was shorter than Zo, stockier and thicker through the chest. Dark eyes dominated his narrow, serious face. He scratched at the back of his arm and I noticed the same tattoos chained around his wrists. Glancing at Tony, I saw he wore them as well.

"No, of course not," I said, though I couldn't stop myself from glancing again at the closed "Employees Only" door.

"So tell me, Zo," Valerie said, "when are we going to hear the new lyrics you promised? I thought for sure tonight was the night."

"They're not ready yet. Soon, though. I promise. It's been a while since we've played a live show. Maybe we'll debut the new song next Friday."

"You won't have much of a crowd next Friday," I said. "It's the Valentine's Dance and we'll all be at the school. At least, those of us with dates," I added under my breath for Valerie's ears only.

She glared at me before turning her attention back to V.

"Is that so?" Zo said, arching an eyebrow, a lazy smile playing around his mouth.

Tony grinned. "Maybe *we* should go to the dance, Zo. What do you think? I could use a night out." If V was shadow, then Tony was sunshine with his blond hair, fair complexion, and a bright gold lining his chestnut-brown eyes.

I saw my chance. Valerie would owe me big-time for this. I took a deep breath and dove in. "You can't go to the dance unless you're a student." I looked from V to Valerie and smiled. "Or unless you're dating a student."

Tony was the first to pick up the hint. "But certainly you both have been snatched up long ago, no?" he asked, his eyes dancing.

"Well, *I'm* going with Jason, but Valerie . . ." I shrugged eloquently.

"I understand," Zo said, playing his part. "You've merely been waiting for the right man to come along." He patted the back of Valerie's hand, looking pointedly at V.

Valerie blushed, glancing under her lowered lids at V. I had to swallow a giggle. She was a natural.

"I *was* hoping," Valerie said, trailing her fingers along V's arm. "I mean, if you aren't doing anything else . . . ?"

When V finally realized we all were staring at him, his eyes darted around the table from Zo to Tony to me, looking for some kind of support or escape.

"V, are you going to be a gentleman and ask the lovely lady to the dance, or not?" Zo murmured.

V cleared his throat. "Um," he said.

"I'd love to." Valerie squeezed V's arm, leaning her head on his shoulder.

"Well, I'm glad that's settled." Zo clapped his hands and rubbed them together briskly. "V and Valerie will go to the Valentine's Dance—how appropriate. Do you think anyone would mind if we offered a free concert that night? What do you say, boys? Are you both up for a dip into the river?"

The three members of the band looked at each other, an electric current charging the air between them. Tony laughed out loud. Even V's normally stony face cracked into a grin.

"You'd really play at the dance? That would be fabulous!" Valerie said. "I'll talk to Lily tomorrow—she's on the committee—and we'll get it all arranged. Just think, Abby, Zero Hour playing at our dance!"

"Fabulous," I agreed as a chill shivered on my skin and a small headache wormed its way into the base of my skull. I felt like something important had just happened but that I'd missed it. "I need another soda." I grabbed my empty glass and turned to the bar. "Would you excuse me?"

As I left the table, I couldn't help but think to myself that Valerie had been right yet again—V still didn't know what had hit him.

❽

It was close to closing time at the Dungeon and Valerie still sat with V and the band. I sighed, stirring my straw through the melting ice in my glass and leaning my elbows heavily on the bar top, bored and alone. Valerie was my ride home and it didn't look like she was in any hurry to leave.

"Can I get you another soda?" Leo asked, whisking away my empty glass and wiping down the countertop with a white towel.

I shook my head. "No, thanks."

Leo smiled, showing all his teeth. A mane of white hair framed his round face and his blue eyes were the color of faded denim. There was something about Leo that made me feel comfortable and safe around him.

"It looks like you could use a Midnight Kiss." He laughed at my expression. "No, no, *mia donna di luce*, it is nothing like that. It is a special drink. I'll make it for you."

"Oh, no, I couldn't—"

"On the house. For a good friend of Dante's." Leo flipped the towel over his shoulder and, as he did so, his sleeve pulled up a little over his wrist.

I blinked. I could have sworn I saw the faded pale lines of what looked like a chain circling his wrist. I rubbed my eyes. It must have been later than I'd thought.

"How do you know I'm a friend of Dante's?"

"I know all of Dante's friends," Leo said, shrugging. "He speaks very highly of you, Abby Edmunds. You have made quite an impression on him."

I blushed, wrapping the straw around my finger.

Leo caught me looking at the "Employees Only" door. "Perhaps he has made an impression on you too, yes?"

"I wish I knew more about him," I said, the late hour leading me to the truth. "He's not very talkative about himself or his past. I mean, he hardly ever talks about Italy or his family or anything personal at all."

"Dante's past is his own. It's not my place to tell another man's secrets."

"But you're his family, aren't you? Isn't that why he's staying with you and not someone else?"

Leo paused, and I sensed he was choosing his words with care. "I care for Dante like a son. I have vowed to watch over him and protect him while he is here. He is staying with me so I can teach him what he needs to know about this world and his place in it." Leo absently cleaned a glass with the edge of his towel. "Dante can be stubborn and headstrong. Sometimes I worry that he is taking unnecessary risks. Dangerous risks." He flashed a smile at me. "I know he borrowed my car without permission, for example. And that he kept the Dungeon open while I was gone despite my specific instructions otherwise."

"He said you were on vacation," I said, surprised that Dante had been selective with the truth. From behind me, I heard Zo's voice rise up in angelic laughter, the deeper timbre of V's and Tony's voices murmuring in harmonious conversation.

Leo's blue eyes clouded over and a small muscle clenched in his jaw. "It would have been better had he followed the rules, but what is done is done."

"He did a good job, if that makes you feel better," I said.

Leo shook his head, a smile returning to his eyes. "I know he did. Dante is the kind of man who will do his best at whatever task is placed before him. He is conscientious and kind.

He cares deeply for others and feels emotions strongly. I believe that is why he has been keeping parts of himself to himself. He will tell you what he can, Abby, in his own time. I'm sure of it.

"And now, *mia donna di luce*—your drink." Leo hummed low in his throat, a musical growl that rumbled in his wake as he methodically selected a round goblet with a thick pedestal and set it in front of me. It was the size of a small fishbowl. He draped his towel over the mouth of the glass, his actions measured as though he were performing a ritual or a magic trick. "This is a special drink because it is made with a story and a song."

Folding my arms on the bar, I sat up straighter, intrigued.

Leo nodded his approval at my interest. His low voice whispered like a passing secret and I had to lean forward to catch his words.

"Before the beginning, there was a void. A darkness. Then, from out of the darkness came a sound." With a quick flick of his wrist, he snapped the towel off the glass, a shivery chime ringing deep in the glass bowl. Before the sound had completely escaped the round bell of the glass, Leo tipped a bottle of dark black liquid into the goblet, thick and viscous. "The sound resonated through the darkness of the void, reaching . . . searching. And then, in the darkness, the sound met another of its kind and"—he deftly tipped some smoky amber liquid like a splash of bottled sunshine into the glass— "Harmony was born."

Leo flicked the rim of the glass with his thumb and forefinger. The note that rose was deeper than before, shimmering in the air before fracturing into two notes. He withdrew a long glass tube from underneath the bar and, inserting it into the black and amber liquid, gently stirred the contents into a golden blend. As glass struck glass, the rising notes it produced danced around each other.

"Melody came next." With his free hand, Leo tipped in a handful of ice cubes. The small splashes trilled like rising scales.

"And the music of the spheres spread throughout the darkness, infusing it with magic."

Leo added bubbles to the drink, each one a tiny jewel of light and air in the swirling liquid.

"The darkness felt the magic and heard the music and dreamed of sloughing off the shadows and dancing in the light. From out of the depths of those dark dreams, Time was born."

A colorless river of clear liquid spilled into the glass, filling it to the brim. The golden bubbles churned, fizzing and jumping like sparks.

"And when Melody saw Time dancing in the dark spaces, she saw the future unspooling in his wake. She reached out for Time, gathered him to her rhythms, and in the darkness . . ."— Leo covered the glass with his towel again—"they kissed a midnight kiss. And thus was born the first Dawn of creation."

Leo slipped the towel off the glass one last time and I gasped. The bright golden liquid had transformed to the softest pink blush of the rising sun.

"Make a wish. They say those who drink down the Dawn will have a wish come true before the next sunrise." Smiling,

Leo pushed the goblet into my unresisting hands. "Enjoy your Midnight Kiss, Abby."

Caught up in the story, I swallowed down the drink without stopping. It was pure poetry going down my throat and tasted of the clear, crisp air of an autumn morning, of the velvety shadows of a winter night, of the tickling green summer grass on bare feet, of the scent of the first springtime rose.

Gasping, I set the goblet back down on the counter, my head spinning, a grin spreading across my face. "That was amazing. What exactly did you put in it?"

"I told you—a story and a song."

"And a wish," I reminded him.

Leo smiled, drying his hands with his towel and gathering up the empty goblet. "Good night, Abby. And good wishing."

I swiveled on the bar stool, leaning back against the cool railing. As I felt the Midnight Kiss tingle through my veins, I thought about stories and songs. I glanced once more at the "Employees Only" door and thought about wishes and Dante.

I closed my eyes, and wished.

CHAPTER
10

The cold night air felt like silk on my hot skin. I leaned against the wall and imagined that I could feel the throb and pulse of the music through the bricks. I could certainly hear it blaring through the doors even though I was out in the school's courtyard. I sipped at my glass of punch and closed my eyes, wondering why I wasn't having as much fun as I had hoped.

Jason looked fabulous in his suit and he had made sure his tie matched my dress, which, he said, matched the color of my eyes. My parents had held us captive to the camera, taking countless pictures before finally releasing us with a final hug and a kiss. Mom even kissed Jason on the cheek, saying how handsome he looked.

Personally, I thought I looked drab and outdated in my dark brown dress. Under the flashing lights of the dance floor, my "Cocoa Foam" dress looked more like a "Dirt Brown" knockoff. All the other girls were wearing delicate pastels of blue or green or shades of pink or white as befitted a Valentine's Dance, and then there was me—a chocolate kiss among all the shiny silver wrappers. I brushed my hand over the giant ruffled bow attached to the hip of my skirt and tossed back the remainder of my punch, wishing it was something fizzy and sparkling. I could have used some bubbles in my stomach, if only to approximate the excitement I was missing.

Absently, I ran my fingers over the butterfly necklace at my throat and idly wondered what Dante was doing tonight. I knew he hadn't asked anyone to the dance; in fact, I hadn't seen him much since the Poetry Slam at the Dungeon a week ago. He'd been like a ghost at rehearsal—coming late, leaving early. I indulged myself for a moment, imagining that Dante had picked me up instead of Jason (even though I knew Leo had forbidden Dante to drive) and that we had gone to Helen's Café to pick up a to-go order of strawberry scones and cream (even though I knew Helen's didn't have takeout) and that we'd spent the evening at Phillips Park, eating scones with our fingers and playing connect-the-dots with the stars overhead (even though I knew it was much too cold to stay outside for long).

Even as the thought occurred to me, I shivered and rubbed my arm with my free hand. I sighed. *Once more into the breach,* I quoted to myself, steeling myself to take the plunge back into the heat and whirling lights of the dance.

"Stop."

Startled, I turned around, thinking someone was speaking to me. But the courtyard held only a few couples, none of whom were paying any attention to me.

"I can't let you go in there. *Fermati!*"

It was Dante's voice, crystal clear in the cold night air.

What was he doing here? I peeked around the corner of the school and saw him standing by the workshop a few paces away from the building. He shoved his hand against Zo's chest. Bright beams of moonlight puddled on the snow around them.

"In English, Dante," Zo tsked. "Have you been neglecting your lessons? Leo will be most unhappy."

"You have to leave."

"You can't stop me." Zo grinned, showing all his teeth. "Besides V and Tony are already inside. You don't want to break up the band, do you?"

"What you're doing, Zo . . . it's dangerous. It's not right. I can't let you go in there."

Zo raked a hand through his dark hair. "What *we're* doing . . . ? What about the stunt you pulled last week? After all your talk about keeping the balance and staying in control, you go and do something like that?" He shook his head. "You're unbelievable."

"It was a mistake. I've paid for it all week. I'm not going to let it happen again."

"Yes. You will. You'll have to. Don't you understand, Dante? It's the only way to truly survive. Give it a year, or two, or three, or a hundred, and you'll see that I'm right."

"For you, maybe. But what about them—?"

"What *about* them?" Zo snapped. "Don't tell me you feel sorry for them? They're nothing." He laughed, the sound like shattering glass. "You're weak, Dante. You always have been. Apparently, you always will be."

"It doesn't have to be like this."

Zo barked out a harsh laugh. "Right, right. I forgot. We

could always end up cracked and drooling, our minds shattered while our bodies live on indefinitely. Such an appealing option."

I saw Dante stiffen at Zo's mocking tone. His voice was as dark as the night. "Leo says that as long as we keep the balance—"

"You can't trust Leo. Haven't you figured that out by now?" Zo sighed. "I can see that it's pointless to argue with you, so I'll just ask you one final question: Why? Why do we have to follow the rules? Keep the balance? Why—when we can have it all?" Zo took a step back, spreading his arms wide, embracing the night. "We have all the time in the world, my friend. And we can have all the *life* that goes with it, too."

I didn't see where the switchblade came from, but suddenly Zo held a thin blade in his long-fingered hand. With one motion, he cut through the shadows, slicing Dante's arm from shoulder to elbow.

A ringing roared through my ears. I felt a scream stick to the roof of my mouth. My glass felt like a rock in my frozen hand.

Dante groaned, clutching his arm and falling to his knees like a supplicant in front of Zo.

"We're not like them," he said softly, gazing down at Dante with something like pity, or maybe disgust, on his face. He squatted in front of Dante to look him in the eye. "We'll *never* be like them ever again, and the sooner you realize that, the better off you'll be."

Zo stepped over Dante's hunched form and sauntered

toward the school. I watched him pull open the side door and slip inside without a backward glance.

I tossed my glass to the ground and grabbed my skirts in the same motion. I was at Dante's side before the door had finished swinging closed. "Are you okay?"

I reached out for him, but he recoiled, hissing through his teeth. "No, please, Abby, don't." His eyes were black and flat with pain. The moonlight traced the grimace on his pale face. He held his left arm awkwardly with his right hand, his shoulders hunched inward. Sweat covered his face like a transparent mask.

"Don't be stupid," I said. "Let me help you."

His eyes roamed aimlessly over the schoolyard as though he were looking at something else entirely. He lapsed into Italian, speaking quickly, urgently.

"Slow down. I can't understand you." I touched his curved back with one hand and his wrist with the other, trying to be careful of the wound on his arm.

He cut off midword. I could feel the strong muscles of his arm quivering with strain. He looked even paler, though I hadn't thought it was possible.

"Please. Abby." He forced each word through clenched teeth. He looked from my face to my hand on his wrist. "Not. Now."

I pulled my hand away. "Sorry." I felt something sticky and warm on my fingers and absently brushed my hand on my dress.

"No—" Dante choked.

I looked down and saw a smear of dark red blood on my hand, my dress.

The edges of my vision blurred. I felt myself tilting. *Don't faint,* I told myself sharply. *Don't be one of those girls who faints at the sight of blood.*

I drew in a deep breath and focused on keeping my hands from shaking. My skin seemed to burn where the blood was drying on it. *No time for that now.*

I set my jaw and ruthlessly forced the growing panic into a locked corner of my mind. Distantly, I could hear the music cut short, and in the lull I could hear the ebb and flow of chattering conversation from inside the school. Then the opening drum riff of "Into the River" hammered through the doors and Zo's voice rose into the night. Shivers crawled on my skin. I couldn't take Dante inside the school. Not with Zo there.

"Right. Come with me," I said, helping Dante stand up.

I felt like I was swimming in deep currents with dangerous rocks lurking just under the water. If I didn't keep moving forward, I'd sink below the surface and drown. Somewhere in the back of my mind, I thought that Melinda had gotten the rumors all wrong. Dante wasn't the dangerous one; Zo was.

I slipped under Dante's right arm so I could support him on his uninjured side. His body was fever-hot next to mine and he kept his left arm pressed tight across his stomach. I could feel his chest rise and fall with each labored breath. Together we stumbled the few yards to the door of the workshop adjacent to the parking lot.

I stood on my toes and managed to retrieve the spare key from the lintel of the door frame. I bounced the key in my palm. "Thank you, Jason," I murmured, unlocking the door with a click.

The building was part workshop, part garage. The air smelled heavily of steel and oil. Huge, misshapen lumps of metal hunkered under dark tarps like sleeping dragons. I ushered Dante in and closed the door behind us. The moonlight filtering in through the row of narrow windows set high on the wall provided the only illumination. Luckily, I had spent more than one afternoon in the garage with Jason, watching him repair his truck or tinker with a new bit of machinery. Even in the dark, I knew my way to the office, where there was a first-aid kit. I had also spent more than one afternoon bandaging up Jason after he'd banged his finger with a hammer or cut himself on a sharp metal edge.

"Abby?" Dante's voice cracked along the edges. A shiver ran through his body. It wasn't much warmer inside the garage. I was cold, and I was wearing a full-length velvet dress. Dante must have been close to freezing in his thin, long-sleeved T-shirt.

"It's okay," I murmured. "Trust me." I reached up to squeeze his hand that draped over my shoulder. The leather gloves he wore were cold and slick with what I hoped was only sweat. He clutched at my hand like a lifeline.

Deftly I maneuvered us through the maze of cars and machines to the back corner office. Once inside, I felt it was safe to flip on the light. No one from the school would be able to see the office light unless they were standing behind the building.

Dante blinked in the sudden light, his eyes still black and

distant. "I told him . . . I warned him . . ." he murmured. "I was too late."

I helped him sit on the edge of the desk. "Okay, let's take a look."

Dante didn't resist as I gently lifted his left arm away from his chest and turned it toward the light. It was worse than I had feared. Zo's cut had sliced through the fabric of Dante's shirt and deep into the skin beneath. Blood stains bloomed on his shoulder and encased his forearm in solid red.

Shock ran through me like lightning.

"Not right . . ." he muttered, not looking at me. "Dangerous . . ." He clenched his fist, and I saw that his fingers were coated in red. He wouldn't stop shivering.

I bit my lip. "This is bad, Dante. You need to go to the hospital. You'll probably need stitches." I moved past him, reaching for the phone on the desk.

Dante's right hand flashed out, gripping my wrist. His lips skinned back over his teeth in a snarl of pain. "No hospital. No doctors. No police."

Though my hands shook, my voice was steady. "What about Leo, then? You need help."

His face softened. "*You* can help me." Some of the pain left his eyes, changing them from black to gray. He tugged me closer to him, groaning as the movement jostled his injured arm. "Please. I'll be all right, I promise. I just need you to bandage my arm. I don't need to go to the hospital. Please. I know you can help me."

I hesitated. The truth was, he couldn't wait for Leo, he

couldn't wait for me to drive him to the hospital. He needed attention now. And I was the only one who could help.

I swallowed, my heart beating hard and fast. "Okay," I said quietly. "I'll try."

"*Grazie,*" he said, letting go of my wrist.

I focused on opening up the first-aid kit, concentrated on finding a clean towel in the stack of rags, telling myself that washing my hands in the sink was the most important thing I could do.

I turned off the water and took a deep breath. "We'll need to take off your shirt," I said.

Dante looked at his blood-soaked arm lying limp in his lap and then reached into the first-aid kit with his right hand. Plucking the small scissors from the kit, he handed them to me. "It's an old shirt."

I stepped in front of him, detecting his familiar scent even under the copper-sweet smell of blood. Time seemed to slow down, as it always did when I was with him. The night stretched around us in a silent, protective cocoon. Being so close to him made me a little dizzy. *Not now,* I told myself. Still, my mouth felt dry and I had to swallow twice before I dared open the scissor blades in my hand.

I gently slid the blade underneath the cuff of his sleeve. "I'll try to be careful, but tell me if I get too close."

He reached out and brushed my cheek with the back of his hand. "*Grazie, bella. Grazie, il mio angelo.*"

I smiled swiftly and then looked down, concentrating on my task. The scissors ate at his sleeve with tiny, precise bites.

As the fabric peeled away, revealing more of Dante's wound, I felt a wash of hot anger flood through me.

I shook my head. "Tell me why Zo did this to you."

Dante watched the scissors move steadily up his arm. "You heard," he said quietly; it wasn't a question.

Embarrassment burned in my cheeks. "I didn't mean to."

"Zo was—is—doing something dangerous tonight. I tried to talk him out of it." He looked out the office window at the darkened garage. "This was his way of making his point."

"What were you guys talking about, anyway? Something about keeping the balance? Zo kept talking about 'us' and 'them'—what was that about?"

"It's an old philosophical disagreement."

I stopped cutting and looked up at him in disbelief. "A philosophical disagreement," I repeated. "What kind of *philosophical disagreement* leads to . . . to this?" I gestured to the narrow slash on his arm that was slowly weeping blood.

"Oh, just the existence of the soul, the concept of time, the meaning of life itself—you know, the usual philosophical conversations that always seem to end in violence." He tried to grin, but on his pale, drawn face it looked more horrific than humorous.

I didn't smile.

Dante's grin faded into a straight line. He looked away.

"You'll have to tell the police, you know," I said. "You can't let him get away with this."

"No!" Dante's head whipped around. "No police. I told you that. This is between me and Zo. I can handle it. He won't try anything like this again."

"You're the victim here. What have you got to lose?"

Dante flinched and I almost stabbed him in the shoulder
with the scissors. "Hold still," I said, snipping the last threads
connecting sleeve to collar. "I'll vouch for what happened. Just
tell them the truth."

Dante looked a little sad. "The truth, *cara,* is more complicated than I can explain."

"And what is the truth?"

"Ah, yet another philosophical discussion that could lead
to violence." He gestured to his wounded arm. "I fear I have
already shed enough blood for one evening. Perhaps we could
discuss it another day?"

"This is serious. Why are you making a joke out of it?"

His eyes found mine. "Because the truth is dangerous and
I promised myself I wouldn't put you at risk again."

"Again?" I remembered the white flashes of future time, the
dark pressure in my chest. Maybe that had been Dante's doing,
but so had been the healing, the sweet taste of chocolate.

Dante was silent.

"So, what, you're going to lie to me? To keep me safe?" I
looked up at his face. "Safe from what?"

Instead of answering, Dante pulled his shirt off, effectively
distracting me from further questions.

I didn't want to stare, but it was too late. I couldn't help it.
My eyes drank in the sight of his long, lean body sitting on the
desk before me. He wore a gray tank top, jeans, and gloves. I
felt my heart slip inside my chest. The light did amazing things
to his skin, turning it a deep shade of olive brown. Distractedly
I thought that I had finally found something that matched the

color of my dress perfectly. I could see the rhythmic pulse of his heart in the dark shadow nestled in the hollow of his throat.

He reached up with his right hand and brushed his dark hair away from his eyes. His beautiful gray eyes. His eyes that were smiling at me.

I blinked, coughing to cover my embarrassment at being caught staring. I dropped my gaze, my heart working to settle back into its normal rhythm.

Dante chuckled low in his throat at my awkwardness.

I tried to keep my hands steady as I wiped the blood away from his arm. Now that I had cleaned the wound, I realized it wasn't as bad as I had first thought. There was still a little blood oozing from the puncture wound in his shoulder, but even that seemed to be closing up. The cut along his arm was shallower than I expected and ended well above the elbow. He probably wouldn't need stitches after all.

I fixed a square of gauze over his shoulder, taping the edges down. Then I unrolled a strip of gauze and began wrapping it around his bicep. The bone-white cloth made a sharp contrast against the dark olive of his skin. I brushed at the fine hairs on his forearm with my fingertips and felt his skin pebble with goose bumps. I wondered if the shiver on his skin was from the chill in the air or from something else. I hoped it was from something else.

I cut the gauze and taped it down. "There. No stitches, but you'll probably have a nice scar to show the ladies." I laughed a little breathlessly. "I'll admit, when I first saw your shirt, I thought Zo must've nicked a major vein to have spilled that much blood."

"I'm a fast healer," Dante said, a strange catch in his voice.

I turned around to finish repacking the first-aid kit. When I rinsed my hands in the sink, the cold water felt oddly warm on my skin.

Dante's hands were oddly warm on my skin as well. He slipped his hands over my shoulders and I jumped, whirling to face him in the tight enclosure of his arms. I hadn't even heard him stand up from the desk, much less move behind me.

"You're an amazing woman, Abby. I hope you know that." He gently tucked an errant curl behind my ear, his fingertips sliding down the curve of my neck. "Thank you for saving me tonight. May I give you a gift in return?" he asked, his voice smooth and low. He ran his palms down my arms, cradling my cold fingers in his warm hands.

I swallowed. My heart did its sliding trick, this time adding a flip at the end. I felt a lift in my stomach. He was going to kiss me; I was sure of it.

"Okay," I whispered.

He rubbed his thumbs along the inside curve of my palms. "Three gifts, actually—a secret, a question, and a truth."

"Okay," I whispered again.

"The secret," he said softly in my ear, "is that today is *my* birthday."

"Really? Why didn't you tell anyone? Happy birth—"

Dante pressed a finger to my lips. "It's a secret, remember? Now for the question: You may ask me how old I am."

I raised my eyebrows. "But I know how old you are. You're seventeen. Eighteen now, I guess."

Dante didn't smile. His eyes searched mine, intense and unflinching. "Ask," he said firmly.

"How old are you?" I said, feeling a little silly.

"*È così*—the third part of your gift: a truth." His eyes were the color of frost at dawn. "I was born in 1484."

I opened my mouth, but Dante looked so serious that my laugh came out as a dry gasp instead. I shook my head, sure I had misheard him.

"I gave you this last gift because you asked for the truth tonight. And because you are someone who is brave enough to hear the truth." He touched his forehead to mine and closed his eyes. "And because it is all I can give you right now." His voice was a hair's breath above a whisper.

A sudden flash of insight raced through me. He knew I wanted him to kiss me. Hard on the heels of that realization was another one: He wanted to kiss me too.

With a soft moan, Dante pulled away from me.

Before I could say anything, he bolted through the office door, leaving me in the empty garage, alone except for his ruined, bloody shirt on the desk and the heat of his hands on my skin.

CHAPTER
11

Ilocked the door behind me and replaced the workshop key on the lintel. The air seemed colder now than it had before, cutting like a knife across my skin. I involuntarily rubbed my hand over my hip where Dante's blood had dried on my dress. The fabric felt stiff and scratchy under my palm. I saw Dante's footprints in the snow, leading away from the school, the gaps between the steps wide and uneven. He must have been running there at the end.

I sighed, torn between wanting to follow his footsteps and knowing I needed to get back to Jason and the dance. I glanced at my watch and tapped the face with my fingernail. The hands had frozen in place, pointing to midnight. There was no telling how long I'd been gone. Jason would be worried about me.

I gathered up my skirt and carefully picked my way over the icy parking lot to the courtyard in front of the school doors. I navigated through my thoughts just as carefully.

What had Dante meant about today being his birthday? Had he really said he'd been born in 1484? It would mean he was more than five hundred and twenty years old. That was impossible. Completely and totally impossible.

But then why had he chosen his words so carefully? He had treated the information like it was fragile. A truth that could break apart as soon as he spoke the words. A truth that could shatter our friendship.

But . . . five hundred and twenty-five years old? My mind shied away from the number.

My thoughts felt jumbled up in my head, everything unraveling the moment I tried to follow a single thought to its logical conclusion. I couldn't make sense of anything.

The one thing I was sure of, though, was that my lips tingled as though Dante *had* kissed me. I ran the tip of my tongue across the edge of my lip and the tingling intensified. I tasted again the ghostly sweet pink flavor of the Midnight Kiss I'd swallowed at the Dungeon. I guessed I would have to wait a while longer for my wish to come true.

Valerie and V were kissing in the courtyard. He had her pressed against the school wall, his strong drummer's hands curling around her hips. Valerie's arms twined around his neck.

Embarrassed to have caught them in such an intimate embrace, I tried to slip past them into the school, but Valerie chose that moment to come up for air and she saw me.

"Hi, Abby. Where have you been? You missed everything!" Her eyes were dreamy and unfocused, fever-bright in the darkness of the night. V leaned closer, nibbling on her earlobe. "Jason's looking for you, by the way." She waved her hand in the general direction of the door before closing her eyes, succumbing to V's attention once more.

Seeing them together made me even more uncomfortable and confused. Valerie *never* kissed on the first date. It was one of her unbreakable, unbendable, unbreachable rules. If Zo was not to be trusted—and after what he had done to Dante tonight, I was sure he couldn't be—then could his band mates be any better? I bit my lip, worried. I'd have to talk to Valerie. Soon.

I pushed through the door and stopped in shock, frowning. Valerie had been right: I *had* missed everything. The dance was practically over. A few couples still lingered in front of the empty stage, but other than that, the only people in sight were the janitors, pulling down the torn pink and red streamers that dangled from the ceiling like tattered clouds. The harsh fluorescent lights reflected off the limp white balloons that drifted across the floor in some unseen breeze. The air seemed to hold the echo of Zero Hour's music, and I thought I could hear the whisper of Zo's voice haunting the almost empty room. *It's time, my children . . .*

Ingrained reflex made me look at my watch even though I knew it was broken. Startled, I saw that the hands had jumped from midnight to ten minutes past two. Could it really be that late?

I scanned the room once more and spotted Jason sitting on the far side of the dance floor. He was hunched over in his chair, his head resting in the palms of his hands. My heart clenched to see him so forlorn and alone.

I wove my way through the remains of the Valentine decorations, stepping over the torn banners and silver confetti scattered across the floor. "Jason?" I brushed my hand across his shoulder as I sat down in the chair next to him. "Are you okay?"

Jason looked at me with red-rimmed, bleary eyes. "No. I'm not."

I withdrew my hand at the sharp tone in his voice. "I'm sorry—"

"You should be," he snapped. "I can't believe you would do this to me."

"Do what?" I curled my hands into fists around my skirt. "What are you talking about?"

Jason's mouth dropped open in honest surprise. "You left the dance over *four hours* ago. I looked everywhere for you. I was worried about you." He shook his head. "If you didn't want to come to the dance with me, you should have said so instead of just ditching me." His bow tie hung around his neck in loose ribbons. He'd unbuttoned his collar and his cuffs. He looked like a wrinkled shadow of the Jason who had picked me up a lifetime ago.

"I did want to come to the dance with you. It's why I'm here—"

"Now." Jason's mouth thinned as though he tasted something bitter.

"I'm sorry I was gone so long. I honestly didn't know it was so late. I guess I lost track of time."

"That seems to happen a lot when you're with *him*."

I blinked in surprise, too stunned by the acid in Jason's voice to say anything.

"Isn't that where you were? With *him?* With Dante?"

I pressed my lips together, wishing they would stop tingling. "Yes, I was with Dante. But it's not what you think—"

Jason snorted.

"It's *not* what you think," I repeated firmly.

Jason looked down at his hands clenched into fists on his knees. "I wanted this to be a special night for us, Abby."

"The night's not over." I tried to keep my voice light even though my heart thumped heavily in my chest. After a brittle silence, I finally said, "Do you want to get some hot chocolate or something?"

Jason ran a hand through his golden curls.

His silence hurt more than his curt words.

"Valerie said Zero Hour played. Were they good?" I asked, not really caring, but wanting to say something.

"Oh, yeah, they were great. They really know how to work a room. It was incredible. The highlight of the evening. The whole crowd got up and danced." Jason pinned me with dark golden eyes. "Too bad I didn't have anyone to dance with."

"Don't be like that."

"Like what?"

I pursed my lips. "Do you want to hear my side of the story or are you just going to sit there passing judgment without all the facts?"

"Fine." Jason leaned back in his chair, folding his arms across his chest.

"Fine," I repeated. I took a deep breath. "I went outside for some fresh air and I saw Dante and Zo get into a fight. Dante got hurt and I took him to the workshop office so I could bandage him up. We talked and then I came back to the dance. That's it."

Jason's eyes narrowed in blatant disbelief. "That's it? That's the story?"

"That's the *truth*."

He shook his head, a dry laugh escaping his lips. "You're amazing, Abby, I really mean that. I thought we were better friends than this. Zo was here all night playing with Zero Hour. How could he have gotten into a fight with Dante? When?"

"You don't believe me," I said, stung. "You think I'm lying." Cold anger filled me. I covered the dried blood on my dress with my hand, tangible proof of the fight that would wipe the righteous anger from Jason's face. I wanted to put his hand on the stain, make him feel the rough edges where the blood had soaked into the fabric, make him believe me, but I didn't. I heard Dante's voice, low and fierce in my memory—*This is between me and Zo.* Dante hadn't wanted anyone else to know; whatever it was that had happened between them, well, it wasn't my secret to tell.

"I'm not a liar, Jason," I said hotly.

"I saw you, Abby," he shouted. "I saw you with him. I saw him *kissing* you."

"He didn't—"

"Right. I know what I saw. It was worse than watching Valerie and V slobbering all over each other all night." Jason shook his head. "I thought you were my best girl. I thought . . ."

I couldn't speak. I couldn't move. I'd never seen Jason this angry, this hurt. Tears tickled the back of my tongue. I swallowed them down. They tasted like salt, desiccating my throat.

"I waited for you for a long time. When you didn't come back, I went looking for you. I walked around the whole school looking for you. And then I saw the light on in the workshop."

My heart stuttered in my chest, threatening to stop beating.

"I was so relieved to find you." Jason's pale face looked like chalk. "And then I saw him standing behind you, his hands on you . . . your hands on him . . ."

"Jason . . ." My voice didn't seem to want to leave my throat.

"I saw him lean over you and . . . and . . ."

"He didn't kiss me," I tried to whisper again.

Jason shrugged, a mere twitch of his shoulder. "Maybe not. But I bet you wanted him to."

Now my heart stopped.

"You know what hurts the most?" Jason asked. All the anger, all the hurt, had drained from his voice, leaving it flat and hollow. "That you never told me you were unhappy."

"I wasn't," I protested, but we both heard the false note in my voice.

"I guess I knew this was coming. I guess I've known it since our birthday." Jason pulled off his tie and shoved it into his pocket. "It's why I wanted to wait to have our first kiss. So maybe you would kiss me like I was your boyfriend, and not like I was your brother."

"Jason . . ."

"It's okay," he said, but we both heard the false note in his voice.

"Please." I touched his hand. His skin was colder than

snow. I looked into his hazel eyes and saw in their liquid golden depths the fading hope that maybe we could still be friends, and the firm knowledge that we certainly couldn't be *dating* friends. I felt a sliver of my heart shiver with pain, shooting icy needles into the nerves of my fingers and thumbs. My fingers spasmed, clutching, desperately trying to hold onto something I knew I'd already lost. "I don't want it to be like this."

"It already is," Jason said sadly, moving his hand out from under my fingers. His eyes held mine for a long time. They were the eyes of a stranger. "You look really beautiful tonight, Abby. I don't know if I told you that yet."

A lump lodged in my throat. "Thanks. You look nice in your tux too."

He stood up stiffly. "It's late. I should take you home."

I wanted to say all the words that people usually said at times like this—*I'm sorry. I never meant to hurt you. I still want to be friends*—but Jason and I had been so close for so long, the words were there without either one of us saying anything. I didn't know if I was glad of that or not.

Instead, I rose and followed him silently across the floor. The tears I had swallowed finally spilled over my cheeks.

I looked over my shoulder, sure I would see a shadow-Abby and shadow-Jason still sitting in their chairs, holding hands and happy, the ghosts of who we used to be now that we were someone else. But the chairs were empty, adrift in a sea of broken paper hearts.

CHAPTER
12

It took exactly three hours and thirteen minutes for the news of Jason's breakup with me to race through the school on Tuesday morning. I had hoped the Monday holiday would give me a little bit of protection from the gossip-mongers in the school. No such luck. I cowered at the back table of fourth-period world history, chewing on a hangnail, terrified of what the next two minutes would bring. The seat next to me—the seat that had been Jason's all year—was empty, and I kept darting glances from his seat to the door. Jason hadn't picked me up for school earlier—not that I had really expected him to—and we'd been careful to avoid each other in the hallways all morning. It was like some complicated dance that only couples who had broken up with each other could perform. I wondered if all couples, happy or not, were slowly dancing their way around each other toward this kind of inevitable, horrible, awkward end. It was a depressing thought.

History was the first class we had together. We couldn't avoid each other anymore. The dance led to here, to now.

The door opened and Jason walked into the classroom. My heart chattered inside my cold chest. He glanced around the room, his eyes skipping right over me. He walked down the aisle between the black tables; for a moment I thought he was going to take his regular seat next to me, a grin on his face, and ask to borrow my notes. For one brief shining moment I thought everything could go back to the way it had been. I thought I could have my best friend back.

Jason pulled out a chair at a table two places in front of me and sat down without even looking at me.

Everyone else in the class, though, looked from Jason sitting next to Melinda Conner back to the empty seat next to me.

The whispers rustled through the room like dead autumn leaves skittering across cement. The sound made the hairs on my arm stand up.

I let my head fall on my crossed arms on the table. *Don't cry,* I told myself sternly. *It's only one class. You can hold out for fifty-five minutes.* I deliberately didn't think about the agony the lunch hour was sure to bring.

A dull thump sounded next to my ear. Peeking out of the corner of my right eye, I saw a black leather backpack blocking my view. The empty chair squealed in protest as someone pulled it back sharply across the waxed linoleum floor. A familiar musky-sweet scent reached my nose.

I sat up straight in my chair, my mouth dropping open in amazement as Dante sat down in the chair next to me. He raked his hair out of his eyes with one gloved hand and then flipped open his notebook, copying down the notes written on the board.

The whispers rose in the room like high tide. I felt the eyes jumping from me to Jason to Dante back to Jason and back to me, around and around in ever-tightening spirals until I could almost hear the instant the realization clicked for everyone in class: I wasn't with Jason anymore; I was with Dante.

Knowing how fast the gossip would spread, I felt torn between wanting to make some kind of announcement that no, everyone had it all wrong, and feeling a secret thrill that maybe, yes, everyone was exactly right.

Did that make me a bad person? A bad friend? I chewed on my hangnail. Why couldn't these things be painless? Why did someone always have to get hurt?

Melinda inched her chair closer to Jason, grinning.

On opposite sides of the room, Lily and Sarah both flipped open their cell phones, fingers flying over the tiny keys.

Robert turned around in his chair, muttering to Jason, flicking glances past Jason's shoulder to me and Dante. I saw Jason shake his head once, then twice, cutting across Robert's words with an angry gesture of his hand.

"What are you doing here?" I whispered to Dante.

He paused in writing down his notes. His changeling eyes were the color of clear white-blue water. "Transferring." A small smile played around his lips. "I'm sorry, Abby, have I taken someone's seat? Would you like me to sit somewhere else?"

"No, it's fine. It's just . . . I mean, I thought after Friday . . ." Flustered, I sighed, trying to organize my thoughts, trying to ignore the gossip and speculation churning around me. "How's your arm?" I finally said.

A rim of frost hardened around Dante's eyes. "It's fine."

"Good," I sighed with relief. "Did you talk to Leo about what happened? I know you said you didn't want to but—"

"Abby, it's fine," he said firmly, turning to a clean page in his notebook.

"Oh. Okay." I fumbled my history book out of my backpack, plunking it down on the table between us. "Sorry I asked."

He leaned close to whisper in my ear, "Thank you for your concern, but honestly, my arm is fine." And to prove it, he reached around my shoulders with his left hand and pulled my chair closer to his. The squeak of the chair and the stares of the class only made his smile wider. For the first time, I noticed a dimple hiding in the corner of his grin.

I shook my head. What was I doing, noticing his smile at a time like this? What was *he* doing, flirting with me at all? Didn't he know Jason had broken up with me mere hours ago? What game was he playing? He couldn't get away from me fast enough on Friday night, and today, he couldn't get close enough?

"*Rilassati,* Abby," he continued to whisper into the shell of my ear, his breath sweet on my skin. "With any luck, Zo's performance will have worked its way through the school in a few days. Don't worry—things will be back to normal soon enough."

Before I could respond to this confusing statement, Ms. McGreevey rapped her ruler against her desk, calling the class to order.

Dante scrawled a note, angling his notebook so I could

read his perfectly flowing script: *Meet me before rehearsal?* The bottom of his "t" tilted up with a little hook.

I pulled the page closer and wrote a reply: *Sorry—Mtg Valerie.*

Dante nodded his understanding. *After?* The tail of his "f" reached all the way to the next line; it looked like an "s" sliding across the page.

I hesitated, wondering what I was getting myself into, then wrote: *OK.*

"I have a couple of announcements before we begin today," Ms. McGreevey said. "First, Mr. Thompson has asked us to remind all students that tickets for the school play, *Much Ado about Nothing,* will be on sale beginning next Monday. Opening night tickets for February 27 are buy one, get one free, so make sure you purchase your tickets early."

Butterflies beat their slow wings in my stomach. I wasn't ready to think about opening night so soon.

"Second, Principal Adams has been receiving reports of suspicious activity on school grounds—fights, graffiti, and the like. There have also been some thefts from the school library *and* the workshop on campus. He is urging us all to keep a sharp eye out for individuals who are not students enrolled in the school who may be hanging about the building or grounds. I hope it goes without saying that if any of you see anything suspicious, you will report it to me or to Principal Adams." Ms. McGreevey peered at us over her long nose.

I glanced at Dante, who had grown still and thoughtful next to me. On an impulse, I jotted a name on his paper: *Zo?* I bumped his elbow, flicking my eyes to the paper.

He followed my gaze, saw what I had written, and his gray eyes clouded over. He drew a thick X over Zo's name and then closed his notebook, resting his hand on the cover.

Curiouser and curiouser, I thought, tapping my pen against my finger. What was going on between those two? I would have thought they'd be good friends since they had a shared history, but instead, they had clashed almost every time I'd seen them together.

"Pop quiz," Ms. McGreevey announced, and I, along with the rest of the class, groaned, but pulled out a sheet of paper.

During the quiz, Dante hummed a lilting, haunting melody under his breath, and before I knew it, class was over.

Maybe sitting next to Dante wouldn't be so bad after all.

I sat alone at the lunch table, not sure who, if anyone, would be joining me. I wasn't betting on Jason—not after history—and sure enough, he walked past me to sit down two tables away with Robert and his other friends. I tried not to show my hurt. I didn't even have my hopes up that Dante would join me. Ms. McGreevey had asked him to stay after class. As long-winded as she was in class, she was generally even worse *after* class. There was no telling when Dante would be released.

I hadn't seen Valerie all day, which was bad since we'd planned to meet before rehearsal. I set my sandwich down as I spied Natalie strolling into the lunchroom, a pair of dark sunglasses banded across her eyes. I half-stood and waved my hand to get her attention. She picked her way carefully through the crowd, wincing and flinching at every loud laugh, every bang of the trays on the tables.

Collapsing in the seat across from me, she dropped her head in her hands and proclaimed in tones of profound hurt, "Ugh."

"Ugh, indeed," I agreed.

"Oof, not so loud." Natalie pulled off her sunglasses and pressed her hands to her closed eyes. "I keep thinking this headache will go away, but I can't seem to shake it."

"Do you need some aspirin?" I reached for my purse but Natalie waved it away.

"I've got so much Extra-Strength Excedrin in me, I don't dare take anything else."

"How long—"

"Friday." Natalie folded her arms and rested her head on the table. "If this is what a hangover feels like, I'm glad I've never gotten drunk."

"Are you going to make it the rest of the day?"

"I have to." Natalie roused herself from the table and scraped her hair back with her hands. "I have a test in math I can't miss."

"But if you're sick . . ."

"I'll be fine," she said unconvincingly. She pasted on a crooked smile. "Tell me what's going on with you, Abs."

"You mean before or after my life ended?"

"What do you mean?" she asked.

"What do you mean what do I mean? I figured it would be

all over school by now. Jason broke up with me. On Valentine's."

Natalie waved away my words. "Yeah, you and the rest of the school."

"What do you mean?"

"What do you mean what do I mean?" she parroted back. "*Everyone* broke up on Valentine's. Ben and Sarah. Lizzy and Chandler. Eve and Will." She ticked the names off on her fingers. She made a face. "Natalie and Chris."

"What? It was your first date!"

"First and last, apparently." She shrugged.

"So what *did* happen?"

"Valentine's happened." She stole the cookie from my lunch, crumbling it between her fingers.

"Hey—" I swiped the cookie back and stuffed it in my lunch bag. "Now talk. Tell me everything."

"What's to tell? Chris picked me up Friday night. I looked *stunning,* by the way. We were having a great time at the dance. Zero Hour played and we danced to every song. Then Chris took me home and as we pulled into my driveway— bam—he told me he didn't want to see me again. Said he'd been thinking about one of the songs Zero Hour played—you know the one: '*The world is older than we imagine, Time more fluid than we think.*'" She sang the lyrics in her low alto voice and I felt the hairs stand up on my arms. She shook her head. "Anyway, Chris made up something about how he didn't want to waste what little time he had left dating just one girl. How he wanted to branch out and live life to the fullest. I swear it's like he was going through a midlife crisis. He's only seventeen,

Abby!" She jammed her sunglasses back on. "That's when this killer headache started and it hasn't left yet."

I sat stunned for a minute. I didn't know what to say. Finally, I managed, "Oh, Nat, I'm sorry," but it came out sounding as helpless as I felt.

"Maybe it was for the best, you know? I mean, I just said yes to the dance to be nice. I don't know if I really saw a future with Chris."

I couldn't help it. My glance darted to where Jason sat with Robert. He ran his hand through his curls, and I felt my skin prickle. How many times had I seen him do that casual gesture? Hundreds, if not thousands. I knew so much about Jason—his habits, his quirks—could things really be over between us? I couldn't quite believe it. Yes, we'd still be friends, but I knew it wouldn't really be the same. What had happened to my future with Jason?

Dante walked through my field of vision, heading for the doors. Hunched down in his dark coat, he flipped up his collar with a snap and pushed out into the afternoon light. I thought I saw him favoring his left arm, but maybe it was my imagination. The cut Zo had inflicted had been deep. I worried I hadn't patched Dante up well enough, despite his demonstration in history.

Natalie followed my gaze. "So he *is* still alive."

I startled, the feel of Dante's hot blood and hotter skin a tangible memory on my fingers. "What? Why do you say that?"

"Oh, just that no one has seen him around school much lately. Rumor was he'd had a run-in with an old enemy"—Natalie lowered her voice dramatically—"who was looking for vengeance." She laughed. "How do these stupid rumors get started anyway?"

In my memory, I could see clearly the white-hot slice of Zo's blade as it cut through shadows and skin. I managed a smile for Natalie, grateful I didn't need to formulate a reply. Apparently the news of our breakup wasn't the only story Jason had been telling over the long weekend. I was relieved that the tale had quickly devolved into rumor. I just hoped Dante didn't think I'd been the one telling his secrets.

"Rumors or not, he's a strange one, isn't he?" Natalie continued, stealing a swallow from my water bottle.

"What do you mean?"

"Well, he seems so secretive. He's unpredictable—never where you think he's supposed to be. And he's always wearing those strange gloves." Natalie rubbed her own hands together. "I don't know. There's just something—odd—about him. Janey tried to talk to him every day in biology for a whole week but he just ignored her. I would think he was being rude, but he ignores everyone. Well, everyone but you. He must really like you."

"And that makes him odd?"

"No, no," Natalie stammered. "I didn't mean it like that. It's just that you're the only person he talks to or spends any time with."

"I'm sure he has other friends . . ." I started to say, trailing off as Natalie shook her head.

"If he does, they're not from around here. Haven't you noticed, Abby? Practically the entire female population of the school would kill for the chance to get close to him, but every time they see him, he's with you."

"And that's a bad thing?"

"Yes!"

"Because . . . ?"

"Because you're Jason's girl. You're off the market. Dante should be up for grabs, but he's not playing by the rules. I personally know of at least four girls who asked him to Valentine's—Holly even asked him back in January!—but he turned down every single one of them."

"Maybe he's not into dances . . ." I said lamely.

"And maybe he wanted to go with you," Natalie finished.

"He didn't, though," I said quietly. Yes, he had come to the dance, but it hadn't been to see me. He'd been there to stop Zo from doing something dangerous.

I remembered what he had said in history: *Zo's performance will have worked its way through the school in a few days.* Had Dante been there to stop Zo from performing at the dance? But why? How could singing a song be dangerous?

I shook my head, dislodging a string of unanswerable questions.

Natalie finished off my water. "I bet he would have if you hadn't been going with Jason."

"But I'm not Jason's girl anymore," I said softly, watching my one-time boyfriend crumple up his lunch sack in his hands.

"I know," Natalie said just as softly, her eyes on him as well, a strange mix of emotions crossing her face.

I felt a catch in my throat. My friend was in love with my ex-boyfriend. I knew I should be willing to step aside for her, but I wasn't sure I could do that. My past was filled with memories of Jason. Letting him go would be like letting go of myself. And then there was Dante. I counted him as a friend—and maybe as something more—but did pursuing a relationship with him mean I'd have to cut Jason out of my life entirely? Couldn't I have both? Couldn't I find some balance between them?

The bell rang. I watched Jason stand up from the table and walk away, surrounded by his pack of friends. Natalie grabbed her sunglasses and followed him down the hall.

I felt myself teetering on the edge of tears. Everything was such a mess. I waited until the cafeteria was empty before I slowly got to my feet and made my way to class, my steps filled with uncertainty.

❸

"Valerie! Wait up!" I hitched my backpack higher on my shoulder and jogged across the courtyard toward her. She was standing by the edge of the parking lot talking to someone—V. I missed a step when I recognized him.

I saw her lean forward, give him a quick kiss, and then shoo him away. He disappeared in the maze of cars before I reached Valerie's side.

"What are you doing? Didn't you hear the announcements this morning? You know he's not supposed to be on school grounds."

"What? He stopped by to see me." Valerie tossed her jet-black hair over her shoulder. She hadn't dyed it again after the dance and it looked almost purple in the afternoon light. "Some of us have *nice* boyfriends."

I cocked my head, confused by the harsh remark. "Principal Adams said—"

"Oh, please, Abby, I thought you didn't pay attention to *rumors*." Valerie headed back to the school and I walked in her wake.

"It's not a rumor if it's the truth."

She stopped, turning on me. "What are you talking about?"

"The bad stuff that's been going on? I think V has had a hand in it. V and Zo and Tony."

Valerie arched an eyebrow with deadly precision. "Really."

I squirmed a little under her piercing regard. "Yeah, I think—"

"*I* think you're jealous."

"What?"

She nodded. "It's obvious, isn't it? You wanted to be the only one with a good-looking Italian for a boyfriend, and now that I'm seeing V, you're jealous."

"That's not it at all!" Anger and surprise snaked through me, making my hands shake. "Since when have I cared about the guys you date? But I don't trust Zo and I don't trust his friends, either. I'm worried about you, Valerie. I don't want to see you get hurt."

She shrugged, which only made me angrier.

"Why are you acting like this? I had a really hard weekend and I don't want to fight with you—"

"Whatever, Abby. Listen, I'm meeting V after rehearsal so

can we talk about this some other time—like never?" She turned on her heel.

The words poured out of me without a chance of me stopping them: "I hate you so much it hurts." For the first time I realized I meant them. My fingernails dug half-moons into the palms of my hands. My whole body shook with emotion.

Valerie waved at me over her shoulder. "I love you too." Her voice was venomous-sweet.

Speechless, I watched her walk away from me. What was happening? First Jason. Now Valerie? Where was all this anger coming from? Had everyone around me gone crazy? For a moment I wished I could have those strange white flashes of the future again. At least then I might have some warning. At least then I might not get hurt.

❽

I stumbled into rehearsal a few minutes late, but Dave didn't notice. I was pretty sure no one noticed. I blotted my eyes with a wadded-up tissue, making a mental note to have more on hand. I would need a steady supply if breaking down at school was going to become a regular habit.

"Okay, people, let's run that scene one more time. And with feeling, please!" Dave's voice crashed through the speakers.

Taking a deep breath, I grabbed my clipboard and a pen. I marched up to Dave, tapping him on the shoulder. "Hi."

"Oh, Abby. You're here. Good. I'm trying to convince Claudio and Hero that they really *are* in love with each other, but it's impossible. And don't get me started on Benedick and Beatrice! I don't understand it. You'd think we were running the show for the first time instead of practically being at dress rehearsals—"

"What would you like me to do?"

"Dante's been helping Jason put the finishing touches on Leonato's house. Would you check on their work, please? I swear, I don't know what I'd do without Dante today. He's about the only person besides you willing to work. At this point, I'm willing to forgive him for missing the last few rehearsals."

"I'm on it," I said, though my heart didn't want to play along. Dante? Working with Jason? This should be fun. I sighed and trudged up the stage stairs.

Slipping behind the back curtains, I crept up on Leonato's house. Maybe I could check on them without being seen . . .

I peeked through the curtains. Jason and Robert were hanging the shutters on the side windows of the house. I could hear the rise and fall of their voices, asking for tools and discussing the basketball team's chances for a win on Thursday. A few other crew members bustled around the building, weaving the plastic grapevines through the lattice-work roof and painting the inside of the house light blue.

Dante sat on the floor of the porch, a screwdriver in his gloved hand, affixing the railing to the banister poles. Everyone gave him a wide berth, and he seemed happy to be left alone with his work. He wore a simple gray tank top and jeans, and was scrubbing the sweat off his forehead with a bare arm. I realized with a start that the deep slash that Zo's blade had left on his arm was gone. No bandage. No gauze. Nothing but smooth skin.

"Not even a scar to show the ladies," I said to myself. I thought I was quiet, but Dante's head perked up and he looked straight at me.

"Abby?" Dante's voice, full of happy surprise, reached out to me through the darkness.

I parted the curtains and stepped lightly onto the porch. I saw Jason see me and then turn away.

"Don't mind him," Dante said, motioning me closer. "He's angry."

I grimaced. "Popular emotion today." I sat down on the floor next to him. It was cool in the shadows backstage. I wondered how long I could hide out back here before Dave would need me again.

Dante glanced at me. "I told you—don't worry. Things will be better tomorrow."

"How can you be sure?"

Instead of answering me, Dante smoothed a soft cloth over the portion of the railing in front of him. "What do you think? It's been a while since I've done any freehand woodwork. Do you like it?"

The banister was at eye level. As my eyes adjusted to the dimmer light, I could see a thick pattern of flowers carved into the curved wood. Blossoms blended into ribbons, which flowed around stems and leaves, which bloomed into more petals. Following the lines soothed my tired eyes and lifted my heart. I felt like I could almost smell the rich roses, touch the petals. I gasped when I realized that the delicate carvings covered the entire length of the banister railing.

"You did this?" I couldn't take my eyes off the beautiful work. "By hand?"

I sensed Dante shrugging next to me. "I keep telling people I'm good with my hands, but no one seems to believe me."

"It's . . . it's amazing," I said, feeling the utter inadequacy of the word to describe what I saw.

A mischievous grin touched his lips. "Look here." He pointed to the bottom of the railing where it curved into the banister pole. I thought I saw letters hidden in the labyrinth of vines in the dark wood. A name. *Beatrice.*

My eyes spelled out the letters, noting the small hook at the bottom of the "t."

"Is that . . . ?"

"She's an interesting character, wouldn't you agree? Feisty and headstrong. Vibrant. I was imagining her as a young girl, lazing away a summer afternoon, bored with waiting for her life to begin, and then . . . daring to leave her mark." Dante ran the ball of his thumb along the hidden name. "Declaring to the world, *'Questo è chi sono. Ero qui. Sono importante.'*"

"In English, please."

"'This is who I am. I was here. I matter.'"

The passion in Dante's voice tugged at my weary heart. I regarded him for a moment. "That's my middle name, you know," I whispered.

He turned his gray eyes to me, soft as a rain cloud. "I know." He reached out his hand and almost touched mine. "If anyone sees this, they'll think I did it for the play. But I did it for you."

A stone fist clenched my heart. I didn't have to look behind me to know exactly where Jason's small carved butterfly hung frozen in the wood, quietly floating next to my initials. Had it been only a few weeks since Jason had given me that gift? Why did it feel like forever ago? It seemed impossible that just a couple of days ago Jason had dropped me off at my house in my Valentine's dress and driven away, and yet here I was with someone else. Everything was happening too fast. I wanted to be friends with Dante but I didn't think I had the strength to try dating him just yet.

Tears welled up in my eyes. "I have to go. Thank you for showing me your work. It's perfect."

I stumbled through the curtains and across the stage, falling into the first available seat in the auditorium. Through tear-filled eyes I saw my whole life spread out in a tableau on stage: Dante, pushing aside the curtain, a concerned line creasing his forehead. Jason, standing behind Dante, a jumble of emotions on his face: seething anger, bewildering loss. Valerie, chatting with Lily, pointedly ignoring me.

What in the world was I supposed to do now? *Just hang on until opening night,* I told myself. *Just play your part until then.*

Maybe if everyone could just play their parts and leave me alone, I'd figure out a way to survive the intervening weeks. Somehow.

CHAPTER
13

S urviving the next week turned out to be the least of my worries. Surviving the afternoon was going to be hard enough on its own.

Rehearsal proved to be the worst we'd had since day number one. Afterward, as I walked toward the parking lot, Valerie sped by me in her cherry-red Lexus. So much for my ride home.

"Great," I muttered, though after our earlier fight and an entire afternoon of frosty non-communication, I wasn't particularly surprised that she had ditched me.

I *was* surprised, however, to see Jason drive past a moment later with Natalie in the passenger's seat.

"Double great," I sighed, slinging my backpack off my shoulder and unzipping the top. Fishing out my cell phone, I flipped it on, only to see a fat red line bisecting the battery icon.

"Triple great!"

"What's great?" Dante asked from behind me.

I shoved my phone into my backpack again, turning

around. "Oh, just my stupid sister drained my stupid cell phone battery and now I'm stranded here without a car or a phone or a way home since my stupid friends are either mad at me or—in one special case—dating my extremely recent ex-boyfriend." My voice cut off as I felt the familiar prickling of tears in the back of my throat. No. I wasn't going to cry. Not now. Not in front of Dante.

"I'm sorry." I gulped down the icy air. "I just remembered—you wanted to talk to me after rehearsal. What's up?"

"It's not important right now." He brushed back his hair with a casual gesture. "Would you like me to walk you home?"

I shook my head, undone by his gentle voice. Mom and Dad had spent all weekend obviously not noticing either my reluctance to talk about the dance or the conspicuous lack of Jason's visits over the weekend. Instead, I had spent the whole time playing endless rounds of A&B Clue with Hannah and her friends, trying to avoid awkward questions. No, I didn't want to go home just yet.

"Walk *me* home, then?" he asked with a small smile, the humor in his voice eliciting a return smile from me.

Suddenly, spending the afternoon with Dante seemed like the best idea in the world.

I wound my scarf tighter around my neck and we walked across the parking lot together.

"It must be nice living at the Dungeon," I said after a few minutes of comfortable silence.

"It's not too bad," he said, slipping his hands into his pockets. "Leo is like a father to me."

"You don't talk about your family very much. How long has it been since you've been home?"

"Sometimes it feels like a long time," Dante said quietly. "Other times . . ." He shrugged. "Other times it feels like it was just yesterday."

"I know how that is. Last summer I spent a week in Albuquerque for a yearbook and school newspaper convention. I was homesick the very first night, but by the end of the week, it felt like I was a native Albuquerquian." I breathed out a laugh in a wreath of cold air. I hadn't thought about that trip in ages. "The whole time I was gone, though, I missed my family—even my sister Hannah, if you can believe it." I tugged at the end of my scarf. "I can't imagine being away from my family for a whole year."

"It *has* been an unusually difficult year," Dante said.

"What about your family? Do you have any brothers or sisters?"

"I had an older brother."

"Had?" I sensed we were skirting a sensitive topic and tried to choose my words carefully. "Is he . . . ?"

Dante nodded.

"I'm sorry."

"It was a long time ago," he said, a peculiar strain to his voice. We walked quietly together for several steps before he spoke again. "I wanted to be just like him once."

"What was he like?"

"He was a hero," Dante said firmly.

I could tell by the set of his jaw that he was done talking about his brother and I wasn't going to force the conversation.

"Thanks for keeping me company this afternoon," I said finally.

"*Mio piacere.*"

His accent slipped off his tongue like water.

We stopped at the corner, waiting for the light to change. It was surprisingly nice just being with Dante, at once exciting and comfortable. The "walk" light flashed and Dante placed his hand beneath my elbow as we crossed the street. I could feel the warmth of his fingers through the sleeve of my coat. He helped me onto the curb and then slipped his hand back into his pocket.

"Here are the rules," he said suddenly, sliding a crooked half-smile my way. "The getting-to-know-Abby rules."

I grinned at him in anticipation.

"We're three blocks away from home. I'll ask you a question at the start of each block and you have until the next block to answer."

"These are pretty long blocks," I observed.

"I have some pretty good questions. Ready?"

"Is that your first question?"

"No, my first question is this: What do you think the future holds for you?"

"That *is* a good question." I rocked back on the heels of my boots, knocking my toes together, thinking. I wondered how much hedging Dante would let me get away with. Probably not much. He was a stickler for the truth.

"No stalling," Dante said, slipping his hand underneath my elbow again, turning me in the direction of the sidewalk. He gave me a gentle push. "Answer."

"My future, huh?" I stumbled into a fairly brisk walk. "You sound like a college application."

"Are you going to college?" he asked, raising an eyebrow.

"Is that your second question?"

"Follow-up questions don't count. Neither do questions that clarify, support, or expand on the original question."

"Man, there are a lot of rules to this game."

"*Life* has a lot of rules," he said ruefully.

"Don't I know it," I nodded in agreement. "That's why I think there will be some rule-breaking in my future."

"How so?" Catching the look I threw him, he quickly added, "Clarification."

"Yes, I'm going to college. No, I'm not going where anyone expects me to. At least I *hope* I'm going somewhere unexpected." My steps slowed; Dante matched his pace to mine. "I sent in an application for Emery College ages ago and I haven't heard back from them yet. The Web site said it could take six to eight weeks to process the application and I know it's only been five, but . . ."

"But you're still checking the mail every day?" Dante suggested.

I felt a faint blush in my cheeks and nodded. "It's hard to wait for something you really want, you know?"

Dante regarded me with clear eyes for a moment before echoing my words back to me: "Don't I know it."

"What are *you* waiting for?" I asked, hoping to surprise him into answering one of my questions. I should have known better.

"What's so special about Emery College?"

So I told him what I'd learned about it from the brochure and the Web site. I told him how much I wanted to go someplace new, someplace where *I* was new. At Emery, no one would know me or my past. It would be a fresh start, a clean slate. It would be a chance to branch out in new directions without any of my old baggage weighing me down. It would be like being reborn.

"There are no expectations of me at Emery," I said. "Emery's motto is 'Live without Limits,' you know, and I want that so bad. I've grown up in this little town and sometimes I feel like there are limits everywhere I turn. I feel like there's this preset path all laid out for me and all this pressure to walk from point A to point B without any detours or places to stop to enjoy the scenery." I blew a sigh through my teeth. "So I'm doing what everyone *expects* of me—good grades, extracurricular activities, the works—but someday . . . someday I'll do something *unexpected*." I surprised myself with the fierceness in my voice.

"I believe you will, Abby," Dante said. "I hope I'm there to see it."

"Thanks," I said. I laughed under my breath. "You know, you're the only person I've told that I've even applied to Emery. Don't tell anyone, okay?"

"I'm good at keeping secrets." Dante flipped up the collar of his coat, tucking his chin behind the fabric as the winter wind picked up its pace.

"Thanks," I said again. Glancing up I saw the familiar two-story building of the Dungeon a few yards away. "Hey, we're here. What about the other questions?"

Dante's mischievous smile appeared. "I guess I'll have to ask them another time."

I liked the promise inherent in his words and felt warmth bubble through my veins; I was already looking forward to the next time.

We stopped outside the side door, hesitating, both of us wanting to continue the conversation, both of us waiting for the other person to say something.

"Do you want—?" he started.

"I should—" I said at the same time.

Dante brushed the snow from his hair. "Please. You first."

"Oh, I was just going to say I should be getting home." I didn't want to, though. I wanted to stay with Dante, even if it meant standing in the snow and cold for another hour.

"Come inside for something warm to drink first," he suggested, opening the door behind him. "I'll ask Leo to drive you home afterward."

The warm air wafted out, enveloping me. I hadn't realized how cold I was. I slipped into the Dungeon without any more encouragement.

"Can't you drive me home?"

Dante shook his head. "Leo has revoked my driving privileges for the moment."

"Bummer."

Dante smiled wryly, then helped me off with my coat, laying it on the bar top.

I sat on one of the stools at the bar, touched by Dante's old-fashioned courtesy.

He took his coat off as well as he hopped lightly up the one step behind the bar. He looked at me expectantly. "What would you like?"

I ruthlessly squashed the blush rising in my face. Now was *not* the time for total honesty. I grinned instead. "Something . . . unexpected."

"As you wish." Dante's hand hovered over the rows of glittering bottles behind the bar. When he struck, it was swift and sure. Turning around to face me, I saw he had chosen a small box with worn and bent corners. I could make out the picture of a sun rising over a beautiful green pasture dotted with roses and guessed that the faded yellow Italian words that marched along the bottom of the box promised some kind of summer-warm tea inside. Just the thing for a cold winter's day.

Dante flipped a white ceramic mug up onto the counter and filled it with hot water. From the box, Dante withdrew a single packet, wrapped in a delicate web of white netting. "You're expecting this to be tea, aren't you?"

I nodded.

"But you asked for something unexpected, didn't you?"

I nodded again.

"Then watch closely." Dante dropped the packet into the mug and placed his hand over the top. Steam rose from between his fingers. When he removed his hand from the mug, the delicate scent of roses filled the air. He slid the drink to me.

I wrapped my hands around the mug, feeling the heat from the drink warm my frozen fingers. Inhaling the steam, I could smell lilacs along with the roses. I lifted the mug and took a small sip. "It's chocolate!"

Dante leaned over the bar, resting his weight on his elbows. "I told you it would be something unexpected."

"But . . . how . . . ?" I took another swallow of the delicious, deceptive liquid. It should have been tea. It looked like it. It smelled like it. But it wasn't. The rich chocolate flavor filled my mouth.

"It's an old family secret—"

"And you can keep a secret," I finished. "I know." A gentle heat flooded through me with every swallow of Dante's drink. "Can you at least tell me what you call it?"

Dante shook his head.

"Figures. Mmmm, this is way better than Leo's Midnight Kiss."

"Leo made you a Midnight Kiss?"

"Mm-hmm. He said he mixed a wish into it for me. Why? Doesn't he make them for everyone?"

"No. No, Leo hasn't made that drink in a long time." Dante flashed a smile at me. "He must like you."

"I bet you make *this* drink for everyone, though, right?"

"No," he said softly and his voice sent chills chasing the waves of warmth along my skin. "No, I haven't made this drink for anyone in a long time either."

"Does that mean you like me?" I asked lightly, teasingly, but my heart pounded hard in anticipation of his answer.

It seemed like Dante looked at me for a long time before he pushed himself away from the bar, tugging at his gloves. He cleared his throat. "I need to talk to Leo about something. Then I'll see you home."

Dante pushed through the door behind the bar and I

mentally cursed my clumsiness. Valerie made flirting look so easy; she should have warned me how disastrous it could be in the wrong hands. At least he hadn't said no. That was something. But his mood certainly had shifted. One minute he was smiling and happy. The next minute he was withdrawn and cold. What was he thinking?

"Dante," I heard Leo say in surprise. "I wasn't expecting you until later. How was school today?"

Glancing up from my musings, I noticed the door had swung closed, but the latch hadn't caught. With the Dungeon empty, I could hear the conversation in the back room even though I tried not to.

"Things are worse than we thought."

Leo sighed. "I was afraid you'd say that."

"The whole school is still suffering from the emotional hangover. It could be another two, maybe three days before people are back to normal. I'm sorry, Leo. Zo was unhappy with my interference and unleashed it on the crowd. It's my fault as much as anyone's."

Emotional hangover. It was an apt description. I'd thought I had been the only one suffering, but now that Dante mentioned it, there had been a general miasma of misery hanging about the school ever since Valentine's Day. Plus, according to Natalie, the breakup rate had been unusually high lately. And somehow it was Zo's fault. Maybe my hunch about Zero Hour was right after all.

"Three more days?" Leo sounded shaken. He sat down heavily, a chair creaking under his weight. "And everyone was affected?"

"No, not everyone," Dante said. "Most of the teachers are fine, though they are struggling to maintain order in class. And the people who didn't attend the dance are fine. Abby's fine, thankfully."

My ears pricked up at the sound of my name. I knew I shouldn't be eavesdropping, but I couldn't help it.

"You took a risk with her—"

"What was I supposed to do, Leo? I couldn't let her go back to the dance until it was over." I heard Dante pacing across the floor. "I needed her to stay with me."

"I know, *figlio,* I know. I'm grateful she was there to help. I'm just sorry she's involved."

Involved? What was I involved in? Was Leo saying that I *shouldn't* have helped Dante at the dance?

"What are we going to do about Zo? He's getting worse. Reckless."

"Leave Lorenzo to me, Dante. After what he did to you . . . I don't want something like that to happen again." Leo paused for a long time. When he finally spoke, his voice was quiet, uncertain. "What have you seen lately?"

Frustration weighed down Dante's words. "Nothing. It's all a jumbled mess. It has been every time I've gone. I'm trying, *Papà,* I'm looking. But trying to pick out Zo or Tony or V is like trying to isolate a single raindrop in a hurricane. I don't like being blind when it comes to him. The clearest thing I've seen all month was the three of them at the dance, but I couldn't see downstream enough to know what kind of long-term repercussions were in store. Maybe trying to *stop* him was the worst thing I could have done."

"What are you seeing now? Anything?"

"Just Abby."

"Abby?"

I slipped off the bar stool and crept closer to the door. I didn't understand half of what Dante and Leo were talking about, but the way Dante said my name . . . I had to hear the end of this part of the conversation.

Dante's voice took on a new quality: urgency. "She's everywhere, Leo. In all the paths I'm walking, she's right there." Dante's footsteps stopped. I heard him take a deep breath. "I think I need to tell her—"

"No!" Leo's voice cracked through Dante's words. Even I flinched out in the other room and scampered back to my seat. "You know the rules, Dante. You must not break them. Ever. It was bad enough you bent them as far as you did at the poetry reading."

"But when *Zo* does it, it's within the rules?"

"Lorenzo is still angry, still unwilling to accept his circumstances—"

"And I'm not? I have more reason to be angry than any of them. At least he and his friends have had four years to get used to this."

"I know it takes time—"

Dante's harsh laugh felt like sandpaper on my skin.

"—and I'm not discounting your feelings. You have acclimated amazingly well," Leo continued, "and I trust you in ways I'd never trust Lorenzo or Antonio or Vincenzio."

"Do you approve of what they're doing?"

"Of course not," Leo snapped. "Of course not," he repeated

more softly. "I had hoped that by encouraging them to stay in town for a while, I would be able to reach them. Show them the error of their ways. Help them find a balance they can live with." He sighed. "Maybe I was wrong to think I could help."

"Maybe you're wrong about Abby, too," Dante said, a thin edge to his voice. "Maybe she can help."

"Dante," Leo warned. "No one can know."

Silence from the back room.

Leo's voice was kind but firm. "I know you want to. I know she means something special to you. But telling her will only endanger her more. Trust me; nothing good can come from it. Promise me you won't tell her anything."

Deeper silence.

"I know you don't want to hurt her, Dante."

I held my breath.

Then Dante's voice, resigned and bitter, slid through the crack in the door: *"Lo prometto."*

❧

Dante crashed through the door, scooping up his coat with one hand.

"Is everything okay?" I stumbled over the words.

"Fine." Dante grabbed a set of keys from underneath the bar. "I'll take you home now."

"But I thought Leo—" I stopped. A cold mask descended over Dante's face. Now was not the time to mention Leo or his rules. "Thanks," I mumbled.

For being as angry as he was, Dante's control was impressive.

The Mustang growled, eager for speed, but Dante didn't push it even a mile over the speed limit. He flipped the blinker at every lane change and crossroad. He checked the mirrors and his blind spot.

"Worried about getting a ticket?" I tried to lighten the mood with a small joke.

"I'm trying to keep you safe," he said.

"I'm tough. I can take it."

A muscle jumped in Dante's jaw.

Pulling into my driveway, he got out, intending, I guessed, to open the door for me, but I'd already stepped out of the car. We stared at each other for an awkward moment; Dante's eyes were metallic silver, a barrier as thick as steel. Then he got back into the car and drove away.

I raised my hand to wave, though he was already too far away to see it. Instead, I saw Jason standing by the mailbox on the corner of the sidewalk. He held a handful of envelopes up to his eyes, shading his face from the setting sun. He was far enough away that I couldn't read his expression, but I knew he had seen the whole thing.

I sighed, feeling the slow roil of anxiety boil through me. I felt terrible at the way we had left our relationship after the dance. I felt like part of me was torn and jagged along one edge and I couldn't figure out how to smooth it out or knit it back together even if I wanted to. Dante seemed to think everyone would be back to normal in a couple of days. If Jason's anger at me was somehow Zo's doing, then what would Jason be like at that time? Would he feel bad about what had happened at the dance? Would he want to get back together? Would I?

I glanced down the empty road, looking for the ghost of Leo's Mustang.

Maybe what I wanted was to just slice all the ragged ends off—a clean break, a clean slate. A new beginning. Not for the first time I wished my acceptance letter from Emery had already arrived.

I watched Jason walk into his house.

I felt the edges of my heart tear a little more. Maybe all I really wanted was a friend I could count on.

I walked into the house, dropping my backpack and my jacket on the couch. I was exhausted, worn out and weary. I could hear my mom on the phone in the kitchen.

"Oh, Cindy, that's wonderful!" Mom's cheerful voice scraped my nerves raw. My stomach rumbled; I hadn't eaten since lunch but I wasn't sure I could face Mom and her boundless energy and good humor just then. Absently, I flipped through the stack of mail on the side table by the stairs, half-listening to Mom's one-sided conversation, half-remembering the look on Dante's face as he drove away.

My eyes fell on a slim, white envelope addressed to me. A quick glance at the return address: University of Southern California. I inhaled sharply, tasting the sweet hint of cocoa and roses, all that remained from Dante's hot chocolate surprise. Somehow I knew this next surprise wouldn't be quite so sweet.

"It's no bother. I'm making cookies anyway. I'll send Abby

over with some in a little bit. I'm sure she'll want to talk to Jason in person. I'm surprised she's not over there already, actually."

I paused, my fingers brushing the flap of the envelope. Talk to Jason about what? I thought we'd said it all on Valentine's Day.

"No, Abby hasn't heard back yet, but I'm sure something will come soon. She applied just about everywhere, after all."

Crushing the letter in my fist, I dropped the rest of the mail on the table and darted upstairs. I didn't want to be in the hallway when Mom finished her phone call. And the last thing I wanted to do was go over to Jason's house. Not before I'd read the letter from USC. Maybe not after, either, come to think of it.

I pushed open the door to my room. The door had barely closed before I'd torn open the envelope, allowing a single sheet of paper to flutter into my trembling hands. I knew what it said without even reading it. Fat envelopes contained letters of welcome acceptance, glossy photographs of campus and students, pages and pages of class schedules and calendars; thin envelopes contained a meager handful of painful words: *sorry, apologize, regret.*

When I finished reading the letter, a hard rock thunked in my belly, sending shock waves through my fingers and toes. They didn't want me. I didn't get in. I'd been denied. Rejected. Turned away. Passed over. The rock rumbled through my hollow insides. How was it possible? What was wrong with me that USC didn't want me? And if USC didn't want me, would

Emery? I sat down on my bed. Would any college? What would I do then?

A knock rattled my door.

"Go away," I called, crumpling the letter into a jagged ball.

Hannah opened the door and leaned against the doorjamb. She tilted her head to one side as though considering an important decision. "Mmmm, no." She waltzed inside and sat down at my vanity table.

Groaning, I dropped my head in my hands. "Not in the mood, Hannah," I warned.

"That's okay. You don't have to be." Her fingers danced lightly over the rows of nail polish lined up by the mirror. "Ah-ha!" She selected a bottle of bright pink polish and settled in to paint her nails.

"Hannah!" I snapped. "I'd like to be alone, okay?"

She barely glanced at me, lifting her hand and blowing on her nails. "What's wrong with you?"

"Take your pick. Right now it's because my bratty little sister can't seem to take a hint."

"I'm not little. I'm almost as tall as you."

I sighed through gritted teeth. "Get. Out."

Hannah's pout deepened to a wounded frown. "Fine." She rose to her feet like a queen, gliding toward the door.

I cleared my throat. "My polish?"

She scowled and dropped the bottle onto the tabletop. "I don't see why you're so upset. It's not like you even wanted to go to USC."

"What are you talking about?" Cold stabbed through my heart. I shoved the horrible rejection letter under my pillow.

How did Hannah know already? Had she told Mom or Dad yet? I couldn't bear the thought that everyone knew of my failure.

"So Jason goes to USC without you. Big deal. I thought you were holding out for Emery College anyway."

"Jason? At USC?" I stumbled over my thoughts, trying to arrange them into some semblance of order or meaning. "And what do you know about Emery?"

She shrugged.

Pressing my lips together, I crossed the room in three short strides and shut the door. I pointed to the chair.

She wavered. "My polish?" She held out her hand with a small grin.

I slapped the bottle in her palm. "Now sit down and start talking."

"There's not much to say. Jason got his acceptance letter from USC today. Apparently there was some mention of a scholarship, too." Hannah regarded her nails objectively, then brushed on another layer of pink.

"How do you know I didn't get *my* acceptance letter today too?" I was proud that my voice held steady over the dangerous words.

"Because I got the mail." Her voice softened a little and she suddenly looked younger than eleven.

I felt tears pool in my eyes and furiously blinked them away. It seemed like I was spending most of my time lately trying not to cry. "Do Mom and Dad know?"

Hannah shook her head. "Not until you tell them."

"Thanks," I croaked, the tears thick in my throat. "Thanks for not telling."

She shrugged again, a sly smile flashing across her pixie-thin face. "I can keep a secret. I haven't told them about the fact you applied to Emery College, or that you broke up with Jason on Valentine's, or that you're dating Dante from your drama class, have I?" She ticked the points on freshly painted nails.

My jaw dropped open. "How do you know about all that?"

Hannah looked at me with pity. "I may be eleven, Abby, but I'm not stupid."

CHAPTER
14

I managed to avoid delivering a plate of celebration cookies to Jason that night. In fact, I managed to avoid Jason altogether for almost ten days. I tried valiantly to keep my life as normal as possible. School. Rehearsal. Homework. Repeat.

I should have known better. I should have known chaos would catch up with me eventually.

Jason caught up with me one night during rehearsal. Dave had been in a bad mood since the beginning of rehearsal when he announced he had a pounding migraine. I offered to take over, but Dave wouldn't hear of it. Tomorrow was opening night; this would be our last full run-through. Dave micromanaged every detail, so thankfully all I had to do was sit halfway back in the auditorium and watch the play.

By the end of Act Two, I had flipped off the spare headset mike and tossed it onto the chair next to me. Doodling on the clipboard, I watched as Hero and Claudio fell in love. I scowled. They made it look so easy. Lately my relationships seemed more like Beatrice and Benedick: all spar and spat. I drew a lopsided heart and struck a jagged lightning bolt through it.

Lately, I'd been avoiding Valerie as studiously as I'd been avoiding Jason, but for different reasons. The guys from Zero Hour seemed to be everywhere. They had invited Valerie into their inner circle, and she spent all her time making out with V or laughing at one of Tony's stories or listening rapturously to Zo's latest lyrics. I saw her at the Dungeon a couple of times and I thought she looked different—older somehow. There seemed to be a sharper edge around her now. Groupie-Valerie hardly resembled friend-Valerie anymore. I missed hanging out with my friend, but it was clear she wasn't missing me. Zero Hour had written some new songs, and she obviously preferred to stay with them during their practices rather than do any-thing else.

Poor Natalie spent her time shuttling between me and Valerie, trying to convince both of us that the other one wanted to make amends, neither one of us believing her. What made it worse was that I could tell Natalie really wanted to spend her time with Jason. It was proving hard to avoid him when he kept hanging around whenever Natalie was with me.

And then there was Dante. He was everywhere too—pouring me drinks at the Dungeon, writing me notes in history, walking me home after school—but unlike Zo and his friends, Dante had an unsettling habit of disappearing. It seemed like every couple of days he'd be late to school, or ask to cut our evening short. Sometimes he'd be gone for the whole day. Leo didn't seem bothered by Dante's unpredictable schedule, so I tried not to let it bother me either.

It bothered Dave, though. He didn't say anything to Dante directly, but instead lectured the entire cast on the virtue of punctuality. It might have had more effect if Dave hadn't been late to his own rehearsal that day.

"Hey, Abby."

Jason sat down in the seat next to me. Panicked, I glanced up at the action on stage. We were deep into Act Four and there was plenty of time before Dave would call for a break. Jason had timed his ambush well.

"Hey." Part of me didn't know what to say to him, but another part of me wanted to tell him everything, just like the old days.

"Play looks good."

"Thanks." I turned my pen over in my fingers. "Leonato's house looks great."

"Thanks. Your boyfr—I mean Dante did a nice job on the railing."

I nodded, noticing Jason's verbal slip but choosing to let it slide for now. I wasn't sure if Dante was my boyfriend just yet, though he was lobbying hard for the role.

"How have you been?"

I shrugged. "Busy. You know how it is."

After a few moments of silence, Jason took the pen from my grasp, laying his strong hand over my fidgeting fingers. "I'm sorry for what happened. At the Valentine's Dance." He held my gaze. "I'll be honest, that night is mostly a blur—actually, I don't remember much of the next week, either—but I must have done something to make you mad at me. Whatever it was, I was hoping you'd forgive me and that we could go back to being friends." He rubbed his fingers along the back of my hand. "I've missed being friends with you, Abby."

I'd missed him too. This was the Jason I'd grown up with and been friends with for all those years. "Emotional hang-over," I murmured, remembering Dante's strange conversation with Leo at the Dungeon. Whatever Zo had done seemed to have finally run its course. Maybe this was the signal that things had returned to normal.

I looked at Jason straight on for what felt like the first time in a long time. Shadows tangled in his golden curls, eclipsed his hazel eyes, softened the chiseled planes of his face and his jaw. I could see behind the man's face to the boy I knew so well. Was I really willing to throw away all that shared past? Could I really shut Jason out of my heart, out of my life? Did I really plan to hold onto the anger and hurt from our breakup? Especially if he hadn't really meant it? No, on all counts. I couldn't stay mad at Jason. What's more, I didn't want to.

"I remember what happened," I said gently. "I lost my *boyfriend* that night." I covered his hand with mine. "But don't worry, my *best friend* is still here."

Jason's golden smile appeared on his boyish face. "Hey, you know you'll always be my best girl, Abby." When I grimaced slightly, he continued, stretching his smile into a grin. "My best *girl* friend—as in 'friend-who-is-a-girl.'"

I answered his grin with one of my own, my heart feeling lighter than it had in weeks. I slugged him on the shoulder. "Don't you forget it."

"Promise," Jason said, crossing his heart with his index finger.

"You better not. I know it'll be hard when all those beautiful USC coeds are throwing themselves at your feet."

Now it was Jason's turn to fidget with the pen. "About that—"

"Don't tell me the girls are already fighting over you?"

Jason's honey-colored skin turned cinnamon. "I'm sorry I didn't tell you myself. I really didn't think I'd get in—the admission rate is crazy—"

My heart skipped a step.

"And then when the packet came in the mail and there was a scholarship, too . . ."

My heart fell down an entire flight of steps.

"I know we'd planned on going to State together, but I . . . I couldn't say no."

I scraped my tongue off the roof of my mouth and managed to string a couple of words together. "Of course not. You'd be a fool to pass up a scholarship to USC."

Jason ran a hand through his curls. "Um, Abby?" He stared down at his fingernails. "Natalie got in too," he blurted.

I felt the words fly right out of my head. I managed to hold onto one letter, though: "Oh." It didn't seem big enough to express everything I was feeling.

"She found out yesterday. She wanted to tell you, honest, but she didn't want you to think she was rubbing it in. I mean, since you hadn't heard back from a college yet and . . . and everything."

"It's okay." I tried to keep my voice light. I still had a week before the all-important six-to-eight-week time frame was up for my Emery application. I hadn't given up hope completely.

"I'm sure you'll hear something soon. Hey, maybe you'll get into USC too and then we can all still go to college together."

"Yeah," I croaked. "Maybe."

For a while we watched the actors onstage circle each other, their bright costumes fluttering like butterfly wings. I concentrated on my breathing, my lungs feeling tight as a cocoon.

"Hey. You okay?" he asked.

I looked down at his hand covering mine, thinking hard about his question. Was I okay? Would I be okay watching my friends go off to USC without me? Would I be okay if Emery said no?

Even if Emery said no, I still believed in their motto, "Live without Limits." Maybe that meant letting other people live their lives without the limits I placed on them. Nothing I could say or do would stop Jason and Natalie from going to USC. So instead of feeling left behind and abandoned, maybe I could be happy for them, for breaking beyond their own limits.

Slowly, I nodded. "Yes. Yes, I think I'm okay." I smiled, and it didn't feel fake or forced at all. "If you see Natalie before I do, tell her I'm happy for her. USC is lucky to have her." I bumped his shoulder. "You too."

Jason bumped me back. "Thanks. I know I need to start planning my class schedule, reserving a dorm room, moving—there's so much to do—but the whole thing is a little over-whelming. I'm not sure it's sunk in yet, you know?" He laughed a little. "How am I supposed to think about my future when I'm having a hard time thinking about a date for the Spring Fling, and that's only in a couple of weeks?"

"You're not asking me to the dance, are you?" I grinned. "Because we both know how our *last* dance turned out."

I was surprised to see Jason blush a little. "No, actually, I'm thinking of asking Natalie."

"Well, you don't need my permission. I'm not your girl-friend, remember?" I teased.

"I know," Jason said. "But you're *her* friend too. What do you think she'd say if I asked her?"

My eyes found Dante onstage without any effort. I felt the pull of him from all the way across the auditorium. It was automatic, irresistible.

"I think she'd say yes. In a heartbeat."

Jason brightened. He leaned back in his seat, a wide smile across his face. "Thanks. You're a great friend; you know that, right?"

Silence fell between us as we watched the closing scene of the act. The best thing, though, was that, even though we'd talked about some hard things, it wasn't a painful, awkward silence. It was the calm, contented silence of two people who know each other well enough to know that sometimes silence can say everything that needs to be said.

"Okay, everyone," Dave said into the headset mike, "I'm starting to think we might just pull this off. See you all tomorrow. Don't be late!" As the crew and cast dispersed into the wings to change and clean up, I caught a glimpse of Valerie cornering Amanda, her eyes flashing with anger, her hands balled into fists on her hips.

I rushed onstage, arriving in time to hear Valerie say, "I don't care. You have to fix it."

"I'm sorry," Amanda said, "but there's no time left—"

"And how is that my fault?" Valerie snapped.

Amanda blinked. "It's not, but—"

"Then stop making excuses and *fix* it."

"What's the problem?" I asked.

Valerie turned on me and I had to force myself to resist retreating a step. I'd noticed some changes in her appearance over the past few weeks, but since we'd both been avoiding each other, I guess I hadn't been prepared to see those changes up close.

Dark circles ringed her foggy, clouded eyes. Her hair hung straight and flat down her back, stripped of its usual bounce and curl. The stage lights cut harsh angles along her face, making her look older, harder, meaner.

"Amanda's says I'm too fat to wear her blasted costume."

"I didn't say that," Amanda stammered.

Valerie withered her with a look.

"It's okay, Amanda," I said, touching her arm.

She took the hint and ran with it as I had hoped. Literally. She was gone before the door finished swinging shut.

"What's your problem, Valerie?" I demanded.

"Why is everything suddenly *my* problem?" she snapped. "Amanda must have done something to my costume because it doesn't fit right anymore and she's refusing to fix it. It's like she *wants* me to look terrible on opening night. I bet she and all her stupid friends are looking forward to laughing at me when I have to waddle out on stage in this costume that's too small for me. I bet—"

"Stop," I said, holding up my hand. "Just . . . stop, okay? You're not fat and Amanda didn't do anything to your costume."

Valerie flung her hair back over her shoulder, crossing her arms and tapping her long fingernails on her elbow. "I should have known you'd take her side. I thought we were friends, Abby. I guess I was wrong." She shook her head. "And to think of the *years* I've wasted on you."

I felt like I'd been punched in the stomach. Where was this venom coming from? Where had my best friend gone? Was she even still *in* there underneath all that paranoia and suspicion?

"You've changed," I said, my voice steady and firm. "This isn't you. I'll talk to you later." I turned to walk away, my hands shaking.

Valerie laughed harshly. "You think *I've* changed?" She grabbed my arm and spun me around. "Take a good look at *yourself*, Abby."

"What do you mean? I haven't changed."

"That's my point. You're still meek little Abby, dutifully following the rules like a good girl. You've never had any drive or ambition or dreams. Honestly, Abby, what did we ever have in common? If I've changed, it's simply because I've finally decided to reach out and take what's mine instead of being like you—content to let life pass me by."

I felt a wave of rage sweep up my legs, crashing hot and

hard into my belly. "I have dreams," I said, tasting the iron behind my words.

Valerie rolled her eyes. "What? College?" She spat out the word as though it was poison. "Let's see, your ex-boyfriend gets into USC. Natalie gets into USC. Even *I* got into USC. But what about you, Abby? If you're the perfect one, where's your acceptance letter?"

I bit my lip. I hadn't heard about Valerie's acceptance. It didn't matter, though. My newly found resolve to be happy for other people's successes carried me through whatever awkwardness or pain I might have felt. "Congratulations," I managed to force through my teeth. "I'm sure you'll enjoy USC."

She laughed. "Oh, I'm not going to USC. I'm not going to college at all. When Zero Hour is finished writing the new album, they're heading back to New York and I'm going with them."

"What? Are you crazy? Do you really think your parents will let you ditch college so you can be a groupie for some band?"

"Like I'm going to listen to my parents."

"The Valerie I knew would have. The Valerie I knew wouldn't be making such a stupid decision about her life."

"Then I guess you've never really known me at all." She swept past me, almost knocking me down.

As I watched her leave, a bitter lump lodged in my throat. What was going on? Jason seemed to have snapped out of whatever emotional trauma Zo had inflicted on the school; why hadn't Valerie?

Because she is still seeing Zo every day, I realized as a white flash of certainty settled into my bones. *Zo and Tony and V.* This was their doing. Somehow they and their music had transformed the Valerie I knew into this Valerie I didn't. This was their fault. They had to be stopped. I had to make them stop. But in my memory I could see Zo's predatory eyes, his wicked, teasing grin, and I wondered if he could be stopped at all.

The hot stage lights burned like fire on my suddenly cold skin.

❽

Dante was waiting for me at my car in the parking lot. He was leaning against the side of the door, his head tilted back, watching the stars twinkle into life in the twilight sky. I slowed my pace so I had time to appreciate the long lines of his body. Just seeing him standing there in his wool coat and leather gloves made me feel calmer. Dante had a knack for stillness. A quietness I appreciated. As crazy as my life got, I knew I could always count on Dante to be the eye in my storm.

And after my argument with Valerie, I needed some relief from the storm raging inside me.

"Ready?" Dante asked, reaching to open the door for me.

"Absolutely," I sighed, grateful for his attention.

Dante looked in my face and then held his hand against the door, preventing me from getting into my car. "Tell me what's wrong, Abby." It wasn't a question. It wasn't even a demand. It was a tender invitation, and I broke down at the gentleness of his voice.

With tears streaming down my face I told him about what Valerie had said to Amanda and then to me and about my suspicions that Zo was somehow behind it—even though it sounded absurd when I said it out loud—and about my frustration over not getting into USC when all my friends had and about how afraid I was that I wasn't going to get into Emery either and then what would I do? How could I live without limits if everywhere I turned I was faced with impossible obstacles?

Dante listened to the entire emotional eruption without a single word. He simply handed me a handkerchief from his coat pocket. He almost brushed back my hair, but at the last moment rested his arm on the roof of my car instead, close enough for comfort, but not quite close enough to touch me. He nodded in all the right places and waited until I had run out of words and breath. The tears were endless, though. Weeks of stress and worry had built up inside me. I hated crying in front of him, but once I'd started, I couldn't seem to stop.

"It seems like you're the only person I can talk to anymore." I hiccupped through my tears. "My parents don't know that Jason and I broke up or that I didn't get into USC, so I can't talk to them about anything. Jason and Natalie are dating and Valerie hates me." I felt a fresh wave of tears rise up and bit my lip to keep from crying again.

"Valerie doesn't hate you," Dante finally said. "You are right to suspect Zo's involvement in her . . . transformation."

"Do you know what he's done to her?"

Dante thinned his lips and looked away. "It's complicated.

Don't worry. I'll take care of it." He shook his head slightly before turning back to me. "You should talk to your parents about Jason, about college. I'm sure they would help if they knew."

"I know, Dante, I will." I wiped at my eyes with his handkerchief, which was now streaked all over with my makeup. "Lousy, cheap, non-waterproof mascara," I complained, attempting a laugh. "I must look a wreck."

"I've seen you look better," Dante said.

"Gee, thanks." I covered my face with my hands.

"I thought you were brave enough to hear the truth," Dante said, a note of amusement in his deep voice.

"And I thought you were smart enough to know when a girl *wants* to be lied to," I retorted.

"In that case . . ." Dante pulled the handkerchief from my hands and used it to dab at my eyes. "You look beautiful. *Molto bella.*"

I saw the sincerity in his clear eyes and felt myself blush. How did he always manage to make me feel this way with just a look and some Italian? Maybe I was a hopeless romantic after all. *Hannah would be so proud of me,* I thought, amused.

"Here are the rules," Dante announced, finally opening the car door for me. "The cheering-up-Abby rules. You drive where I tell you to and no questions allowed."

"What? Where are we going?"

"No questions. Just drive."

I slid into the front seat and Dante joined me, sitting in the passenger's seat. I moved to toss my bag in the back when Dante plucked it from my hand. "First, call your parents. Tell them you're with me and you'll be home before curfew." He paused. "When is your curfew?"

"I thought you said no questions."

"Not from you."

"Midnight, on the weekends."

"Excellent."

So I called home as instructed. Mom told me to have a good time and to check in with her after my date.

"It's not a date, Mom," I insisted. I covered the phone with my hand and whispered to Dante, "It isn't, is it?"

Dante simply arched an eyebrow and smiled.

I felt the butterflies wake in my stomach and a grin tug at my lips. "Sorry, Mom," I said, "it's totally a date." I flipped the phone shut and dropped it in my bag. "Now what?"

"So many questions. You're not very good at following the rules, are you?"

"It's cheering me up."

"Then let's not stop."

I started the car. While the heater warmed up, Dante opened the glove compartment and pulled out my Preston Bus CD. He handed it to me and instructed me to play track one. I did as I was told. "Rosemary, That's for Remembrance" bloomed from my speakers.

We pulled out of the parking lot and headed away from school, away from home, away from the stress. I didn't know where we were going, and I didn't want to know. I just wanted to enjoy the moment of uncertainty, of unpredictability, of possibility.

The chorus of the song kept us company as we drove off into the night:

> Rosemary, that's for remembrance
> Pansies, that's for thoughts
> Fennel, columbine, and rue
> Pray, love, remember—
> And forget-me-not, forget-me-not, forget-me-not . . .

I felt like Cinderella. Almost. Only in this story, the pumpkin coach was just my rumbling old car and both the prince *and* the princess had to be home before midnight.

As I drove home alone through the dark, quiet streets, I couldn't help but think that Dante had been true to his word. He had cheered me up—no question about it. First, he'd taken me to Helen's Café for a late-night breakfast. Then, after a long conversation about nothing and everything, he had directed me to the Wise Old Owl bookstore, where we'd walked up and down the cramped and curving aisles talking about the books we'd read (mostly classics for Dante) and the books we wished we'd read (mostly classics for me). The small bookstore café offered hot chocolate with peppermint-flavored marshmallows, and Dante ordered us two. One with extra whipped cream for me.

The entire night passed in a blur of comfortable conversation and company. Before I knew it, the clock had chimed eleven, the bookstore was closing, and it was time to head for home. Sometimes, when I was with Dante, I felt like we had all the time in the world. Other times, it seemed like if I blinked, I would miss the whole evening. I tried hard not to blink all night.

Outside the Dungeon, I turned the car off and we sat for a minute in the dark, listening to the hissing and ticking as the car caught its breath.

"Thank you for a wonderful evening," I said.

"*Mio piacere,*" Dante murmured. In the dim glow of the streetlight, I could see him studying my face. "Was it a good date?"

I rubbed my hands along the curve of the steering wheel, fidgeting but unable to stop. "So far."

"I'm glad." Dante unbuckled his seat belt and turned to face me. "I don't know how you do it, Abby."

"Do what?" I ran my fingers along the key chain dangling from the ignition.

"Keep your balance. I've watched you juggle school and rehearsal and your family. Jason. Natalie. Valerie."

I frowned at the mention of her name.

"You make it look effortless."

I barked a laugh. "Did you miss my meltdown a couple of hours ago? *That* was effortless. The rest . . ." I closed my eyes and leaned back against the headrest. "Sometimes it's really, really hard."

"Then you make it look like it's worth it."

I smiled slightly. "How does the saying go, 'If it's worth doing, it's worth doing well'?"

"'Screw your courage to the sticking place, and we'll not fail,'" Dante quoted back to me.

"*Macbeth*," I identified. "You've been studying." I opened my eyes and turned to look at Dante.

The light brushed star fire along his profile; I could see the slope of his nose, the shape of his lips. The air in the car felt heavy and warm. I swallowed. I wondered if he would kiss me, if his lips would match mine.

"Abby." Dante's voice was a breath in the shadows. "Abby, I—"

I could smell the musky-sweet scent of his coat as he moved closer to me. I could hear his body shifting inside his clothes, the creak of leather as he adjusted his gloves. I wondered if he was finally taking them off, if he would finally touch my skin with the bare palm of his hand. He was so careful not to touch me that on those rare occasions when he did, I'd feel it on my skin for hours afterwards. I felt the hairs on my arms lift in anticipation.

Dante leaned over, drawing close enough that our coats almost touched. I could feel his breath on the curve of my neck. "I'm glad I could make you happy," he whispered into the shell of my ear.

"Me too," I whispered back. I knew if I turned my head, I'd be close enough to kiss him. The space between us felt alive, charged with promises. If I moved, would he kiss me? Would he let me kiss him?

I would never know.

A heartbeat later, Dante had pulled away, returning to his seat, gathering up the bag of books he'd purchased at the Wise Old Owl. It was hard to see in the dim light, but I thought his hands were trembling slightly.

He paused before opening the door, looking back at me over his shoulder. "Good night, Abby," he said, though I was sure he had wanted to say something else.

"Night, Dante."

He closed the car door and I immediately exhaled a long-held breath. My heart beat swiftly in my chest, pulsing in my wrists. I could taste a mix of frustration and excitement in the back of my throat. He'd been so close. Why hadn't he kissed me? Why hadn't *I* kissed *him?*

The clock on the dashboard ticked closer to midnight. I thought about the last time I'd been in a car with a boy and the wish of a kiss at midnight. I experienced a strange sense of déjà vu as I compared that night in January with Jason to the moments I had just spent with Dante. The circumstances were eerily similar—a cold evening, a warm car, the air thick with nerves and barely checked emotions. But this time I hadn't been frustrated at being kissed and not wanting it, but by wanting the kiss—and not getting one. This time I could feel the fireworks sizzling inside me, and I couldn't wait for Dante's kiss to set them free.

I watched as he walked toward the Dungeon, the last stragglers from whatever live show had played earlier passing him in the dark. I swallowed hard at the sight of his measured pace. He moved gracefully, as if he had all the time in the world to get where he was going.

I felt younger than seventeen. Warm and young and full of life.

I felt like flying.

My house was quiet as I unlocked the door. I checked in with my parents; I had to wake them up to let them know I was home. It was nice to have parents who trusted me enough that they felt comfortable falling asleep instead of waiting up for me to come home.

I peeked in on Hannah as I passed her room. Curled up on her side with her hands folded under her cheek, she looked like an angel. I shook my head. If only she were an angel when she was awake, too!

Closing my bedroom door behind me, I changed into my pajamas and brushed my hair out. I could still feel Dante's nearness and the almost-kiss we'd almost shared. I was too keyed up to sleep so I turned on my computer to check my e-mail.

The ding of new mail in my inbox sounded loud in the sleeping house. I quickly turned the speakers off. As I scanned down the list of incoming messages, my eyes found one from Admin@EmeryCollege.edu. Subject line: Application for A. B. Edmunds. Suddenly the hum of the computer was the loudest sound in my room. I think I stopped breathing.

I clicked on the message. *Please, please, please . . .*

The e-mail opened and I read it in less than a second. There wasn't much to read. But this time, the short letter wasn't bad news.

Dear Ms. Abigail B. Edmunds,
Yes.
Please contact me to discuss scholarship opportunities.

Sincerely,
Mr. Wilson Cooke
Admissions
www.EmeryCollege.edu/Orientation/FreshmanClass.htm

I clicked on the link, unable to believe what I was seeing. Images and information filled screen after screen. Class schedules. Maps of the campus. Dorm room layouts. Calendars of events. Everything I wanted. My future unfurled before me like a banner, freeing me from who I had been, leading the way into who I would become.

I wanted to get up and dance. I wanted to wake up my parents—even Hannah—and shout the news from the rooftop. I wanted to call Dante and tell him. I even picked up the phone before I happened to glance at the clock. It was after one in the morning. Where had the time gone?

I hung up the phone, savoring the future moment when I could tell him in person.

As I lay in bed that night, watching the moon drift through the sky, I thought about midnight kisses and wishes. I thought about fireworks and friends. I thought about how short a journey it was between feeling like crying . . . and feeling like flying.

CHAPTER
15

"How many more posters do we have?" Natalie asked, scraping her hair back into a rough ponytail. "It feels like we've hung up a hundred."

"A hundred and five," I reported, stapling the last corner to the store's bulletin board and standing back to check my work.

Four months ago, Dave had designed posters advertising *Much Ado about Nothing*. Three months ago, they had arrived in large boxes that he'd stacked in the drama room. Two months ago, he'd started hanging them up around town, despite my warnings that it was too soon and that they would just be taken down in a month's time. I'd been right, and when Dave had discovered the disaster, he'd ordered the entire drama class to spend an entire Saturday morning rehanging the posters.

"Don't worry, Nat, we only have a dozen or so left."

"Good, my fingers are killing me." Natalie shook her hands out, rubbing her palms on her jeans. "Tell me again why we're hanging up posters instead of celebrating your good news about Emery? Shouldn't these posters have been up weeks ago? I mean, why bother advertising a play *the day* it opens?"

"Because Dave's an idiot," Jason said, shifting the remaining posters from one hand to the next.

"Because Dave's not very organized," I corrected. "And because it's my job. At least you guys will be off the hook soon." I grabbed a poster from Jason's stack. "*I* still have to help stage the play tonight."

"That's what you get for being the assistant director," Jason said, grinning. "All I had to do was build the sets. No worries. No stress. Nothing to do opening night but sit back and relax."

"Yeah, don't remind me. I am so not looking forward to dealing with Dave tonight. He'll be so wired and stressed, I just know it's going to rub off on me." I shook my head.

"So about this celebration . . ." Natalie hinted. "We really should be doing something wonderful for you, Abby. It's not every day you find out your dreams are coming true."

"I still have to call about the scholarship thing," I said, but Natalie waved away my words.

"Yeah, but you're *in*. They said yes. That counts."

A secret thrill ran through me. They *had* said yes. To me. I had managed to wait all the way until six in the morning before I couldn't stand it anymore and had to wake up my parents with my good news.

Mom's happy scream woke up Hannah, and Dad managed to placate her Saturday-morning grouchiness with the promise of breakfast at Helen's Café to celebrate my acceptance to Emery.

I'd called the Dungeon on our way there, but no one had

answered. When I'd called after breakfast, Leo had picked up. No, Dante wasn't there just now. No, he wasn't sure when he would be back. Yes, it would be before the curtain rose for the play tonight.

Leo gave me the same speech all day, every time I called. I couldn't help it, though, I was filled with nervous energy and desperate to tell Dante my good news. I couldn't understand why he had disappeared today of all days, or why Leo wouldn't tell me where Dante had gone.

"Done," Jason said, jamming the stapler into his back pocket. "It's almost two. That should be enough time to have lunch before Abby has to be to the school for the play."

"It's almost two?" I grabbed Jason's wrist, twisting it to look at his watch. "I was supposed to be at the school a half hour ago. Dave is probably flipping out."

"I thought you didn't have to be there until four." Jason extracted his arm from my grip.

I shook my head. "The *cast* doesn't have to be there until four. *I* have to be there early." I groaned. "Dave's going to kill me."

"But what about lunch?" Natalie frowned. "What about our party?"

I shrugged, grabbing my bag and digging for my keys. "I'm sorry, Nat. You guys go without me. We'll do something after the play, okay?"

"Break a leg!" Jason called out after me as I ran through the parking lot toward my car.

I pulled into traffic in a move worthy of Valerie at her

wildest and sped down the street. If I didn't get to the school soon, I feared Dave would break more than just my leg.

❽

Thankfully, Dave had bitten only three of his nails to the quick and I'd arrived before he could start on the fourth. Amanda was already there, sewing kit in hand, hemming the last of the masquerade costumes.

The rest of the afternoon passed in a blur, but the closer the clock inched toward four, the more hectic things became. There was a tense moment when Valerie arrived with V in tow to pick up her costume from Amanda.

I wanted to say something, but my mouth was dry, so I just tried to smile as she swept past me, knocking my shoulder with hers.

"She'll come around," Amanda said to me, a dark red velvet dress draped over her arm. "It's just the stress of the play that's making her crazy."

"I hope so," I said. But as I watched V wrap his arms around Valerie, kissing her by the backstage door, I had my doubts.

"Here." Amanda nudged my arm. "Dave wanted me to give this to you. I hope it fits."

I looked down as Amanda held out the red dress to me. "What's this for?"

She shrugged. "Dave says everyone has to be in costume for the play."

"But I'll be backstage. No one will even see me."

"Hey, if you want to tell Dave, be my guest." She pointed across the room to where Dave had collapsed in a heap, a dark cloth pressed across his eyes in classic migraine misery.

"Oh. Right." I held up the dress. The square neckline was low but not too low and a delicate lace hem peeked out from beneath the edge of the full velvet skirt. The bodice of the dress was made entirely of woven silver-white ribbons criss-crossing each other in tight, overlapping layers like the feathers on a bird's wing. It must have taken Amanda hours, but the effect was stunning. I felt like I was holding folded angel wings in my hands. "It's beautiful. Thank you."

She smiled at the compliment. "Let me know if it doesn't fit. There's still a little time to make some adjustments before six."

Adjustments weren't necessary, though. The dress fit perfectly. Anticipating my unique duties as assistant director, Amanda had sewn a dress that I could move in easily without tripping over the skirt's hem. She'd even cunningly hidden a small pocket that was the perfect size for stowing the battery pack of my microphone.

As I pinned up my hair, donned my headset, and switched on the battery, I took a deep breath and squared my shoulders. This was it. All our long months of practice came down to this. Opening night. A thousand things could still go wrong—probably *would* go wrong—but we had done the best we could.

I surveyed the backstage chaos, mentally noting who was here and who was missing.

Lily and Ethan (Hero and Claudio—check) were chatting by the curtain. Valerie (Ursula—check) stood sullenly next to

Jill (Margaret—check), who was already in character, tending to Cassie's needs. (Beatrice—check.) Don Pedro, Don John, Benedick—check, check, check. Groups of messengers, watchmen, and attendants milled around backstage, burning off extra nervous energy before the curtain rose.

One person was noticeably missing, however—Dante. I scanned the crowd a second time, keenly aware of the absence of his tall, lean frame, his dark hair, his glittering snowfall-shaded eyes. A faint note of panic sounded inside me. Where was he? Where had he been all day? Had he somehow forgotten?

Dave appeared at my side, checked his watch, and then called for the cast to assemble one last time.

"Okay." He drew in a deep breath, looking intently at each person in turn. "Don't screw this up." We all waited for him to say something more, but he simply turned away, grabbing my elbow and walking me to the stage door.

"Great pep talk," I muttered. Dave's uninspiring pre-performance speeches were legendary in the drama department, but this one was beyond belief.

"Thanks," he said absently. "Are the props set for the first scene? Have you checked on Benedick? He was looking a little sick this afternoon. What about Beatrice's mask for the ball? Did Amanda finish it? Is Amanda even here? I haven't seen her—"

"Yes. Yes. It's fine. Yes, she did. Yes, she's here." I answered his questions almost as fast as he asked them.

"Oh, good," Dave sighed. "I'll need you to manage stage right tonight. I'll take care of stage left. That's where most of the entrances and exits are and I want to be there in case someone misses a cue."

I nodded my understanding. I could hear a low, scratchy hum in the earpiece of my headset. I jiggled the battery and the static went away. I hoped it would stay away. If Dave was going to stay stage left, then the headset would be his only means of communicating with me while the play was running. I couldn't afford to spend tonight with a broken headset.

"I'm counting on you," Dave said.

"I can do it," I said.

He put his headset on and walked quickly into the shadows of stage left.

I resumed my place in the wings, where I could see the action onstage as well as behind the curtain. With the bright stage lights shining down, all I could see was a large, faceless mass of people filling the auditorium. Excited butterflies filled my stomach. It looked like a sold-out crowd.

"Places, please." I heard Dave's low voice in my headset. I repeated his words to the cluster of actors who surrounded me. They scattered in a rustle of fabric and footsteps.

I flipped open my script to Act One, Scene One, and watched as Leonato, Hero, and Beatrice took their places around Leonato's house. Scott the Messenger stood next to me, the all-important letter gripped tightly in his hand. A handful of extras stood on the porch, filling in the stage with their presence. Dante's spot by the banister remained empty. I felt my excitement for the evening drop a little. He hadn't come. Even though no one in the audience would notice his absence, I had, and I knew the play wouldn't be the same without him.

"Everyone ready?" I could see Dave's mouth move and I heard his voice in my ear. I took a quick survey around me. Everything looked good to me. I nodded to Dave from across the stage. "Then let's go," he said.

I gestured to Richard to open the curtain.

Grinning, he pulled on the cord, drawing the curtains open in one smooth motion.

The audience quieted as Scott strode on stage—a little fast, but not too bad—and handed the letter to Leonato.

I practically mouthed the words with the actor: "I learn in this letter that Don Pedro of Arragon comes this night to Messina."

I breathed a silent sigh. We were off. For better or worse, the play was under way.

Glancing over my shoulder, I checked to make sure everyone was in place for their next entrance. Don Pedro and Don John straightened under my gaze, tugging at their jackets. I could see Claudio silently practicing his opening lines. Benedick stood next to him, nervous and twitching. He looked horrible. The dim light backstage turned his skin a waxy yellow-green. Even at a distance, I could see the sweat pouring off him.

Frowning, I gathered up my skirt and had taken exactly one step toward him when Benedick vomited all over the stage floor.

Claudio and the Dons managed to scramble away, thankfully avoiding the worst of the mess. The rest of the cast gave Benedick a wide berth, edging away, rustling and whispering.

I grabbed my headset and hissed, "Dave! Help! Benedick's

sick and—" The only answer I heard was the heavy weight of silence that pressed on my ear. Numbly I looked down at my battery. The bright red eye of life had dimmed and faded to black.

Cold fear clutched at my spine, paralyzing me for a moment. A snatch of dialogue reached me from onstage—"How much better it is to weep at joy than to joy at weeping!"—and I groaned. We were almost to Benedick's cue. But he wasn't going onstage anytime soon. He'd collapsed into a ball on the floor.

My paralysis snapped and I ran to his side. Ruth was there with a glass of cold water and Amanda was cleaning up the mess with some of her fabric scraps. Claudio tried to help as best he could without ruining his costume.

"Thanks, guys," I whispered, kneeling down and stripping off my headset. I glanced up at the horrified faces that ringed us. "Sherri," I barked. "Run stage left and get Dave." She vanished before I'd finished. I leaned over Benedick. "Isaac? Can you hear me?" I touched his arm, feeling the fiery touch of fever under his skin.

"Don't feel good," he slurred. "'Msorry, Abby."

"It's okay." I risked a glance at the action onstage. The Dons were gathered in the wings, waiting for their cue.

"What are we going to do?" Claudio hissed. "We need him for the scene. He has, like, half the lines—"

"I know." I cut him off with a gesture. "Let me think." But that was easier said than done. Isaac was in no shape to perform tonight, that was a given. I bit my lip, wondering if I dared order someone to step in as Isaac's unofficial understudy.

The problem was that, while we all knew some of each other's lines, no one but Isaac knew the entire part.

"Abby—" Claudio tugged at his jacket. "We gotta go on."

"Then go!" I waved him to join the other actors, poised in the wings. "I—" But I didn't have a clue as to what to say next. Maybe Dave would know what to do. But Sherri hadn't returned with him, and even if he *had* been here instead of me, the harsh truth was that we were out of time. Maybe . . .

A pair of polished black boots stopped in front of me. My eyes darted up to meet Dante's clear gray eyes. Dressed in his costume—black pants and a tight white shirt—he took in the situation with one glance and then a small smile crossed his lips.

I heard Scott announce the cue: "Don Pedro is approached." My heart beat triple-time and my mind raced, trying to think of a way out of the problem. Time spun out in painfully slow ripples. It seemed like the agony would never end.

"I would apologize for being late," Dante said, "but it appears I have arrived just in time."

My mouth dropped open as Dante strode past me and the rest of the silent cast, directly into the bright lights.

Don Pedro and his company looked to me for instructions. Should they go on? Should they stay backstage?

"Go! Go!" I hissed, waving them onstage in Dante's wake.

Don Pedro nodded and darted from the wings, smoothly overtaking Dante so that he was the first to reach Leonato and deliver his line: "Good Signior Leonato, you are come to meet your trouble."

Dave silently skidded around the curtains, arriving breathless at my side. "Abby, what happened? What's wrong?"

"Isaac's sick and Dante's onstage in his place," I said in one breath, gathering up my skirts and stepping past Dave to the edge of the curtain, almost unable to believe what I was seeing. Dave followed, speechless.

Dante assumed Benedick's place in the action seamlessly, as though he had been rehearsing it every single day. Leonato and Beatrice kept glancing at him, thrown off balance by the sudden change in the casting. Dante, though, was relaxed and confident, with a smile bordering on arrogance. It was perfect for Benedick's role. I dared a sigh of relief; maybe we were going to make it after all.

"Abby!" Ruth hissed from behind me. "No microphone!"

The sigh caught in my throat. My gaze jumped to Dante's ear—no mike—and then to the small of his back—no battery pack. Claudio hadn't been lying—Benedick had the most lines in this scene. If the audience couldn't hear him, we were sunk until near the end of the act. Ruth pushed Isaac's mike pack into my trembling hands and padded away to take her place for her cue.

I watched in silent desperation as Don Pedro gestured to Beatrice, "I think this is your daughter."

Leonato smiled and inclined his head, "Her mother hath many times told me so."

I held my breath, a wordless prayer frozen on my tongue.

"Were you in doubt, sir, that you asked her?" Dante's voice rang out clear and strong through the auditorium.

I gasped in relief. Dizzy stars filled my vision, sparkling and vivid. I leaned against the backstage wall, gulping in air until the stars disappeared.

Amanda slipped up next to me, offering a glass of cold water and my headset, which was alive again with a fresh battery. "Are you okay?"

I nodded. "So far." I downed the water in two large swallows. "How's Isaac?"

"Okay. We moved him to the drama room."

"Thanks," I said, slipping my headset on again. "Maybe you should have been assistant director."

"I should go tell his parents," Dave stammered, obviously torn between needing to see to Isaac and wanting to see Dante's unexpected performance. Responsibility won out, and he slipped out the backstage door.

Returning my attention to the action onstage, I watched in amazement as Dante's Benedick traded verbal barbs with Cassie's Beatrice. To Cassie's credit, she played off Dante as easily as she had Isaac. The audience laughed in all the right places, and I started to breathe easier. Somehow we'd managed a complete switch of the main character of the play midscene and no one in the audience seemed to even suspect.

When Dante exited the stage near the end of Scene One, I grabbed his sleeve as soon as I could. I could feel the heat of the stage lights on his clothes and the deeper heat of his body beneath. He fairly crackled with energy.

"I hope you don't mind my stepping in for Isaac." He brushed his hair away from his sweaty forehead. A wild and slightly reckless look burned in his eyes.

"No . . . How . . . ?" I stumbled over my words, my

thoughts scattered by his intense gaze. I swallowed and tried again. "When did you learn Benedick's part?"

Dante's smile sparkled in the shadows. "I've been studying."

I couldn't help but return his smile. "It shows."

"I guess I'll finish the role for Isaac, then?"

"You're the only one who can," I said. "Check in with Dave in case he has any instructions for you. Then check with Amanda to see if his costumes will fit you. Quick—you'll be on again before you know it."

Dante raised an eyebrow. "Not until Act Two. I've got plenty of time."

"Not that much. Just go already!" I laughed as Dante sauntered away.

Weeks of rehearsal kicked in and the play ran practically on autopilot. Scene flowed into scene and act flowed into act, seamlessly, effortlessly, beautifully. The lights flooding the stage felt dizzying, intoxicating. The energy rose with each scene that passed.

And Dante . . .

Dante commanded the stage whenever he stepped in front of the lights. I could feel the charge in the audience, the almost imperceptible snap of attention from the crowd as Dante delivered his lines. He had declined the use of a microphone, and after his opening performance I hadn't argued his decision. His voice filled the stage, reaching to the edges of the auditorium. His Italian accent was audible but somehow never interfered with his lines. If anything, it was the last little detail that made

LISA MANGUM

us all believe that he *was* Benedick, courting the prickly
Beatrice with his quick wit and pointed comments.

And instead of overshadowing the other actors, his performance seemed to elevate everyone else. No one missed a
cue, no one missed a mark, no one missed a line.

Finally it was time for the masquerade scene at the end of
the play. I could hear an audible gasp from the audience when
the lights came up on Amanda's meticulously sewn costumes.
They glittered like jewels spun with gold, like butterflies' wings
fluttering on a summer's breeze, like prisms split into rainbows.
The actors danced and glided through the scene: Hero and
Claudio, finally unmasked, proclaimed their love; Benedick
and Beatrice were tamed at last by each other's words.

As with any good Shakespeare comedy, the script called for
a kiss to end the play. As the scene marched toward the inevitable moment, I couldn't help but smile at the memory of
my first rehearsal when I'd been in charge. It had been the day
of my disastrous first kiss, and the day I'd first met Dante.

From my viewpoint in the wings, I could see Dante's face
clearly as the revelers were unmasked, as Benedick's feelings
were unfolded in a tattered note to Beatrice. Through the entire play, Dante had seemed so confident, so at ease, but now,
at this moment of emotional vulnerability—at the crucial moment of the kiss—I saw the hesitation tighten his face, the fear
frost the rims of his eyes. His fingers curled against his dark
gloves.

The tension in Dante's voice was clear to me, though I
hoped no one else heard the awkwardness of his delivery: "A

228

miracle! Here's our own hands against our hearts. Come, I will have thee; but, by this light, I take thee for pity."

As the audience laughed, Cassie swished her skirts flirtatiously. "I would not deny you; but, by this good day, I yield upon great persuasion; and partly to save your life, for I was told you were in a consumption." Cassie leaned in toward Dante, obviously anticipating the kiss written into the script.

Dante's gaze flicked past Cassie's shoulder to meet my eyes directly. I felt a tingle speed down my spine, and time seemed suspended between us, a tenuous, trembling moment that bound the two of us with an unseen, unbreakable connection.

I knew in that moment that I didn't want to watch Dante kiss Cassie, even in a play. But I also knew Benedick *had* to kiss Beatrice—the play couldn't end without their kiss—so I swallowed the "Don't" that threatened to escape my lips, feeling it lodge in my throat, jagged and rough.

Time skipped over my skin like a falling leaf. I saw every moment pass by with crystal clarity.

Dante inhaled, uncurling his long fingers. He turned his head ever so slightly toward the audience, his lips curving upward in order to include the crowd in his plan. But it was a stage smile because I never saw it touch his frosted eyes. As his smile grew into a full-fledged grin, Dante reached up to grasp Beatrice's feathered mask, which she had pushed up to her forehead.

I couldn't see Cassie's face, but in the drawn-out moment of time, I saw her almost take a step back and knew she was trying to cover her confusion at Dante's unscripted action.

"Peace," Dante said, lifting the mask and twisting it around

Cassie's head. "I will stop your mouth." But he didn't stop it with a kiss like he was supposed to. The scarf that had secured Cassie's mask now covered her lips, effectively silencing her. She raised a hand, unsure whether to strip the scarf from her face or to slap Dante for his radical departure from the script. Dante caught her hand, bowed low, and pressed his lips to the cuff of her sleeve.

The audience erupted with laughter, cheering and clapping.

Don Pedro was the first to recover, stumbling over his last line, "How dost thou, Benedick, the married man?"

As Dante finished his final speech, I felt time lose its strange elasticity and return to normal. My heart felt like I'd run a race.

Dante held tight to Cassie's hand and they danced along with the rest of the cast as the play came to a close. Even though I knew the steps were choreographed down to the inch, he managed to make them look natural, spontaneous. When Richard pulled the curtain closed, Sarah hit the final chords of the lively reel with her usual flair.

Backstage, Cassie yanked her hand away from Dante's grip and pulled the mask from her face. "Don't you *ever* do that again!" she hissed, turning her back on him.

The applause was deafening. Dave barely gave the cast time to assume their places for the curtain call before Richard pulled them open again. Impossibly, the applause seemed to increase in volume. One after another, the cast stepped forward to take their bows until only the two couples were left. Lily and Ethan smiled and waved to the crowd. Cassie curtseyed low, trailing her feathered mask from her hand. When Dante stepped forward to take his bow, the audience surged to its feet, cheering and whistling. The noise crashed over the stage like a wave.

Dante didn't seem to hear any of it. He bowed a second time and then, without a backward glance at the rest of the cast, walked offstage.

Richard quickly yanked the curtains closed for the final time. The cast held their emotions in check for all of one second before they too erupted in clapping and cheering. It had been our best performance ever and everyone knew it. I pulled off my headset and joined in the celebration, laughing with relief.

Dante closed his hand around my elbow.

"You were incredible," I said. "The audience loved you."

He never broke stride, and, ignoring the rest of the swarming cast, pulled me along with him through the stage doors.

"Hey, Abby, great show!" Jason called from down the hallway where the audience was pouring out of the auditorium.

"Thanks!" I waved.

He and Natalie moved to intercept us, but Dante deftly sidestepped the crowd, maneuvering me toward the outside doors.

Laughing, I called back over my shoulder, "Guess we're going this way. We'll talk at the party later, okay?" I stumbled a step or two in my dress as I tried to keep up with Dante's long legs. "Slow down a little, would ya?"

He did, but only until we had cleared the crowds in front of the school. Once we hit the parking lot, he quickened his step as though he couldn't wait to leave the building and the crowds behind.

"What's your rush?" I panted, still breathless with adrenaline. "Don't you want to bask in the adoration of your fans?"

"No."

I noted the tightness of his mouth, the tension between his shoulders, and thought better of asking any more questions.

When we reached my car, he flipped down my visor, catching my spare key in his fist. He held it out to me. "Drive."

I turned the key in the ignition. "A bunch of the cast is heading over to the Dungeon—"

A shudder ran through Dante's body. He wouldn't look at me, turning instead to rest his forehead against the window. "Anywhere but there."

"Okay," I murmured. My adrenaline high from the play drained away, replaced with a chill brittleness that filled the space between us.

I drove aimlessly through the town, circling familiar streets, slowly making my way farther and farther away from the heart of the city. At one point I flipped on the CD player, eager for a little music to break the silence in the car, but Dante stopped it before the first notes sounded.

Dante didn't want to talk, either. He sat rigid in the passenger's seat, his eyes locked straight ahead. In his hands he held his mask from the play. Amanda had gone all out for the leads, and Benedick's mask was a shimmering silver-green marvel with gray goose feathers arching above the dark and empty eyes.

I watched from the corner of my eye as he methodically

stripped the feathers from the frame, then the gray fibers from the quills. When he started on the green metallic sequins rimming the bottom edge, I knew where I should take him.

I flipped a U-turn at the next light and made a beeline for Phillips Park.

We pulled into the deserted park and I turned off the car. We sat for a few minutes in the dark, listening to each other breathe.

"I like to come here when I need to get away from it all," I said, unbuckling my seat belt. "Sometimes I sit on the swings. Or go to the playground. Sometimes I just sit on the grass and look up at the stars." My voice trailed off, and for the first time all night I didn't mind the silence that filled the car.

Dante looked down at the ruined mask in his hands, seemingly surprised at what he'd done without thinking. He closed his long fingers around the now-blank mask, crushing the edges in his hands. His own face was blank, drawn and pale in the shadows.

I heard his breath catch as he murmured something in Italian. I thought it might have been "I'm sorry." I leaned closer to hear his next words.

"I'm not who you think I am, Abby," he said in English.

I almost smiled. It was the kind of melodramatic line people said in bad made-for-TV movies, but then I saw his eyes, bleak and distant, and I knew he was telling the truth.

"I thought you were Dante Alexander, foreign-exchange student visiting from Italy."

He shook his head slowly, sadly. "Not exactly."

A touch of fear brushed through me. "Then who are you?"

CHAPTER
16

Dante flung open the car door and stumbled outside into the night. Starlight bathed his body. Shadows layered his dark hair. His shoulders rounded under some unspeakable weight. His hands were bunched into tight fists at his side.

I gathered up my heavy skirts and opened my door. Circling the car, I approached him slowly, cautiously, like he was some kind of wild animal.

"Dante?"

He leaned against the car, tipping his head back, his beautiful gray eyes closed against the brightly burning stars.

"Tonight was a revelation, Abby," he said, his voice ragged with strain. "Being onstage . . ." He shook his head and ran his hands through his hair. "Being onstage tonight was a revelation. It's easy to be someone else. It's easy to pretend. To say the lines someone has scripted for you. It's harder to be yourself. It's harder to speak from the heart. Harder to speak the truth." He drew in a shuddering breath. "And the truth will be harder yet to hear. But I'm tired of pretending, Abby."

My heart broke at how jagged my name sounded in his mouth. "Dante—"

He moved to me then, suddenly and without warning. His hands slid up my bare arms, curled around my shoulders, came to rest at the base of my neck. His body was close enough to mine that I could feel his heart beating swiftly in his chest. His eyes searched my face. "I'm tired of pretending to be someone else, Abby. I'm tired of no one knowing the truth."

The gentlest of pressure from his hands—and he tilted my face to his—

"I'm tired of *you* not knowing the truth."

His lips came down on mine, soft as the starlight, hot as the sun.

He tasted like cinnamon—both bitter and sweet. He trembled like a flickering candle flame in my arms, his skin hot and sweaty under my fingers. Warmth filled my blood, my heart, my mind. A wild rushing sounded in my ears, like wind in the trees, like water falling into foam, like a note quivering on the edge of sound. It was the kiss I had dreamed of. A kiss that opened inside me like a flower, blooming into sweet life. A kiss that carried inside it all the words and emotions that could never be voiced.

Dante cradled my head in his hands and drifted kisses along my jaw, down my neck. "Abby," he breathed into my skin, his hands unfastening the pins holding my hair in place. "I've been waiting to do this since the moment I first saw you."

"Why didn't you?" I asked, my own voice unsteady. Valerie had been right; it was impossible to breathe in a corset. I felt his fingers combing through my curls as they tumbled free. I ran my hands along the smooth muscles of his back.

"I didn't want to hurt you," he said.

"Trust me," I breathed out in a smile. "This doesn't hurt."

Dante pulled back, his face serious, his gray eyes dark with some unnamed emotion. "That's because I'm being very careful." He slipped his hands from my hair and rested them on my shoulders. "I'm as dangerous as Zo in my own way. Maybe, to you, even more dangerous than to anyone else."

"What are you talking about? You're nothing like Zo."

He brushed his thumb along the curve of my neck, across my collarbone, to the hollow of my throat. "Oh, no, Abby," he murmured sadly. "I'm exactly like Zo."

Dante dropped his hands from my neck. He unbuttoned the cuffs of his sleeves and folded up the fabric with three sharp, precise motions. Then he stripped his gloves from his hands, letting them fall to the ground like empty husks.

There on the backs of his wrists twined two heavy black chains branded on his skin. And on the inside of his wrists, two circles with arrows pointing at nothing and the letters: MDI. MMIX.

Cold fear leached the heat from my body. I brushed a finger along one of the chains around his wrist. I narrowed my eyes. "What is this?" My voice sounded harsher than I intended it to. "When did you become such a big fan of Zo's band? Was it before or after he stabbed you—?" The words stuck in my throat.

"No, you don't understand. I've had these a long time. . . . This was done to me long before . . ." Dante groaned and pulled his hands out of my grasp. "I'm not explaining this very well. It wasn't supposed to be like this."

"Then explain it to me. Is this why you always wear those gloves? So people won't see these marks?"

He nodded.

"So what do they mean?"

Dante hesitated. "Do you remember what I told you that night at the dance? When you bandaged me up?"

I nodded cautiously. How could I forget that night?

Dante seemed to be waiting for me to say something.

I didn't want to say it. I didn't want it to be true. It *couldn't* be true. "You told me it was your birthday," I hedged.

"And?"

Dante was right. Speaking the truth was hard. I found I couldn't do it. I bit my lip and looked down.

"And I said I was born in 1484. Five hundred and twenty-five years ago," he said in a low voice. A ring of white-frost ice edged his gray eyes.

"How . . . ?" I shook my head. "I don't understand."

Dante unclasped his masquerade cloak from his throat and spread the gray-green cloth on a nearby patch of prickly winter grass. "Don't tell Amanda," he said with a crooked smile. "She'll kill me." He sank to his knees and gestured for me to join him.

I didn't know what to do. What was he talking about? Five hundred and twenty-five years old? It hadn't been possible the first time he'd said it; it wasn't any more possible now. Only this time I was sure I hadn't misheard him.

He looked up at me. "I promise I'm telling you the truth."

I bit my lip, then sat beside him, spreading my skirts over my knees. "I'm listening."

Dante chafed at the chains around his wrists. "I was born Dante di Alessandro Casella in the year 1484 in a small village outside of Florence, Italy. I was the second, and youngest, child of Alessandro and Caterina. My older brother, Orlando, had gone to war. I had wanted to go with him. But I was too young. And I had different talents."

I remained quiet, uneasy but intrigued.

"I was apprenticed to Leonardo da Vinci as one of his scribes and messengers."

My eyes opened wide. "*The* Leonardo da Vinci?"

"Yes," Dante said. "*The* famous da Vinci. He was famous even in my time. It was an incredible honor to work for him. Those were amazing days, living and working with the Master. Days I'll never forget."

He fell silent, his eyes wistful and distant.

"But . . . ?" I prompted. "In stories like this it seems like there's always a 'but.'"

He smiled a little. "Indeed. *But.* But the job was incredibly difficult. Da Vinci always had a new invention, a new idea, a new way of looking at the world, and all of those new ideas had to be written down, copied out, documented, and annotated. It helped that I had a near-perfect memory and a near-perfect hand for writing and drawing. I think it was because of those two things that da Vinci shared with me the secret of his most terrible invention."

I leaned forward, twisting the hem of my dress in my hands.

"A machine that could break through the barriers of time itself," Dante said delicately, as though he feared the words would disappear before he had a chance to say them.

I blinked. "You're telling me Leonardo da Vinci invented . . . a time machine?"

"He invented all sorts of things that you take for granted in this day—helicopters, tanks, calculators, musical instruments. Is a time machine so hard to believe?" Dante's voice turned sharp in the darkness.

"Well, yes. Because time travel isn't possible."

His lips thinned into a hard-edged grimace. "Yes, Abby, I assure you that it is. It's how I came here. It's why I received these." He held up his hands, revealing the chain brands around his wrists.

"Tony and Zo and V have the same marks. Well, almost the same. Theirs are darker."

"I think they've enhanced their marks with tattoos. But trust me, underneath, they are branded just as I am."

"Are you telling me that they came through the time machine too?"

Dante nodded. "They came through shortly before I did. Leo helped them make the transition. He's helped all of us."

I frowned. "Leo has these same marks too?" A faint memory stirred: the sound of glass ringing on glass and a pale pink drink. "How many of you are there?" I couldn't believe we were even talking about this. It was crazy. But as crazy as it was, I had to acknowledge the fact that maybe, just maybe, he was telling me the truth. Dante had never lied to me before.

Dante hesitated, sensing my confusion. "I know of at least a dozen besides the five of us."

"And you all came through this machine?" I struggled with the flood of information. "Why brand you with chains?"

Dante swallowed, looking down at his hands, away at the empty swings. Anywhere but at me. "We're chained like this because we're criminals. It's a mark of our guilt. A brand we must wear the rest of our long, endless lives. The time machine was our punishment, our sentence, and our execution."

In my memory I heard Valerie's voice from all those months ago: *He's dangerous. . . . He killed someone.*

No. Not Dante.

But in my memory I also saw Dante's explosive anger at Zo—Dante's quickness, his strength, his temper—his hands becoming fists.

The night wind slipped through the high trees as though fearing to come too close.

"What . . . what did you do?" I had to force the words past numb lips.

Dante didn't say anything for a long, long time. He clamped one hand around his wrist, hiding the black mark. I could almost see the white bones of his knuckles moving beneath his dark skin. He squeezed so tightly I wondered if he was trying to erase the mark through sheer pressure.

"Dante?" My fingers twitched in my lap. I swallowed. I reached out to touch his arm, but his words stayed my hand.

"'As soon as any soul becomes a traitor,'" he muttered, his Italian accent so thick it almost obscured his words. "'As I was, then a demon takes its body away—and keeps that body in his power until its years have run their course completely.'"

My forehead furrowed in confusion. "What are you talking about?"

He shook his head. "Dante's *Inferno*. The ninth circle of hell. Where traitors to kin and country are forever locked in a frozen lake, endlessly tormented by Lucifer himself."

Misery etched harsh lines along his mouth, shadowed his clouded eyes.

My heart stood still in my chest. Traitors to kin and country? What had Dante done? "Who did you betray?" The words slipped out soft as a breath.

He shook his head, digging his nails into his wrist. "Everyone. No one. Does it matter?" Dante asked, his voice low and hoarse. He displayed his red-and-black wrists for my inspection. "They marked me guilty."

"But that doesn't mean you are, does it?"

He wouldn't meet my eyes.

I reached out and gently tilted his chin up, forcing him to face me. "You wanted to tell me the truth," I reminded him gently. "So tell me." I let my hand drop from his face to his wrist. I could feel his swift heartbeat through his marked skin. "I can take it." Though I didn't know if that was true at all. Dante's behavior tonight had been erratic and confusing and it had turned all my emotions upside down. One minute he'd been distant and silent, one minute passionate and wild, one minute angry and frustrated.

Dante looked down at my hand on his wrist. Hesitantly, he covered it with his own. I felt that almost-familiar tingle of his skin on mine, and the world around us sharpened, crystallized into focus.

"You remember I told you my brother had gone to war?" Dante traced the delicate rivers of my veins as they snaked across the plains of my hand, through the valleys of my knuckles. "There was a note. Delivered to the enemy." His finger trembled on my skin. "Countless people died. Including my brother."

"You didn't give the note to the enemy, did you?"

Dante's finger stilled for a moment before resuming its aimless wanderings. "No. Zo gave the note to the enemy."

I caught my breath. If Dante blamed Zo for Orlando's death, then it was no wonder there was bad blood between the two of them.

One detail remained clear, though.

"Then you're not guilty. I mean if it was Zo who—"

"It was Zo who implicated me in the conspiracy. Zo who told the authorities where to find me. Zo who testified of my guilt."

"But he lied, didn't he? You were innocent!"

Dante's smile was bitter. "The laws of guilt and innocence were a little different in sixteenth-century Italy."

"Didn't you tell them the truth?"

"Of course I did. But they were looking to capture all the traitors—everyone involved in the betrayal. By then they knew Zo was the leader. Why wouldn't they believe him if he told them where to find the last member of the conspiracy?"

"But why would he do that? What had you done to him that would make him hate you that much?"

Dante shook his head. "I don't know," he said softly. "But he hates me. And I don't trust him."

"And they sent you through the time machine anyway? Even though you were innocent? That seems a little extreme."

"What better place to keep dangerous criminals than the future? We'd automatically be someone else's problem. Besides, we'd all be far enough into the future that we couldn't negatively affect the flow of time." Dante shook his head, his eyes focusing far away from the here and now. "We were all reported dead, you know. To our friends. Our families. It was all very clean and efficient. If not exactly merciful."

My head pounded with the unfairness of it all. Dante had been plucked from his life, falsely accused of treason, and then sentenced to the most cruel and unusual punishment possible.

I turned my face away so Dante wouldn't see my tears of helpless rage. How could someone do that to him, to anyone? I brushed the tears from my cheeks.

I wished he hadn't told me any of it. I wished I had gone to the Dungeon to celebrate opening night with my friends. I wished . . .

I looked back at Dante, who was sitting quietly in the moonlight, his hands resting loosely in his lap like they belonged to someone else. Tension covered him like a shroud.

I wished I believed him.

He needed me to believe him. I could see it in the tight set of his shoulders, in the pinched skin around his eyes and his mouth.

I drew in a deep breath, as though Dante's words still

lingered in the air, words that I could hold in my mouth and weigh the truth of on my tongue.

Born in Italy more than five hundred years ago . . .

Italy tasted like truth; he sounded too much like a native to think otherwise.

But five hundred and twenty-five years old?

Sent through a time machine as punishment for a crime he didn't commit . . .

I couldn't imagine Dante as a criminal; I shook the thought away.

But a time machine?

"What was it like?" I asked suddenly. "Going through the time machine, I mean."

"Does that mean you believe me?" A grim humor crept into Dante's voice.

I shook my head. "You have to admit, the whole thing sounds pretty crazy. Terrible and horrible, maybe, but still crazy."

"I know. But it's the truth."

I locked my gaze with Dante. "Then tell me the whole truth," I said. "Tell me what it was like."

He was silent for a long time. So long, in fact, I wondered if he would say anything at all. Maybe I'd finally pushed him too far.

Then he did speak. As his voice spilled out into the night, he kept his gaze on me, steady and heavy, holding me captive to his words.

"The truth is, it didn't look like a time machine at all. That was part of the beauty—and the horror—of it. It was just a door. A tall, narrow, dark black door covered with symbols and images that opened into shadow. The construction was ingeniously designed, elegantly simple. In theory, you simply walked through the door, through the shadows, and through another door on the other side. In practice, though . . ." A tremor ran through his body. I could see his muscles clenching with remembered tension. The starlight slid along his jaw like the blade of a knife.

I shivered, trying to imagine opening a door and walking, not into another room, but into another time.

"I thought I'd gone blind," Dante said quietly. "It was so dark. Dark and cold. I hadn't expected the cold.

"Even the air smelled old. Charred. Though that may just have been my skin." Dante rubbed at the marks on his wrists. "I could barely feel my hands because of the pain. I had been so grateful they hadn't broken my fingers, my hands, that the pain from them branding me hadn't registered until that moment. The moment the door closed, I knew . . . I knew I couldn't go back. I had no choice but to go forward.

"I remember hearing the creak of the hinges as the door closed behind me. I kept waiting to hear the click of the latch as well, but it never seemed to come. And then I heard the music. Music like I'd never heard before. It seemed almost tangible in the darkness. I could almost feel it resonating in my bones, could almost pinpoint exactly when the sound became harmony, became melody."

Something about his words sounded familiar. I couldn't help but think of the story Leo had told me once about magic and music and the dawn of creation. "The music of the spheres," I murmured.

Dante nodded solemnly. "And then, when the music had faded . . . all I could hear was the sound of my breathing in that narrow darkness between the doors. I don't know how long I stood there, trying to summon up my courage."

"What did you do?" I asked, swallowed up in Dante's eyes, feeling claustrophobic even under the clear night sky.

"Eventually, I started walking. And I counted. I counted every step until I had left everything behind. The door, the music, the past. I didn't know what else to do." He finally closed his eyes, breaking our contact, releasing me from the weight of his words, from the truth of his past. "One hundred eighty-five thousand, four hundred twenty steps."

"You remember the exact number?" I felt the night's dark air tingling in my veins from the deep breath I was holding.

"How could I forget? Every step forward was another day I walked into the future."

"More than five hundred years?"

Dante opened his eyes and I felt the air rush out of my lungs. His mouth curved like a scythe, sharp and angular in the moonlight. "It goes by faster than you think."

CHAPTER
17

I sat up on the cloak, wrapping my arms around me for warmth, tucking my feet under the hem of my heavy skirt. I wasn't sure if I believed Dante, but he sounded like *he* believed it. "Then what? Assuming I believe you—then what? You traveled more than five hundred years in the future. To here. To now. What was the plan? What were you supposed to do? Just live your life?"

Dante ran a hand through his hair. "It's hard to explain. I'm not sure I have the right words." He plucked at the edge of the cloak. "Traveling through time . . . it changed me. It put me beyond the reach of time."

"Beyond the reach of time? What does that mean? You're not going to age? You'll be eighteen forever?" I smiled to take the sting from the skepticism in my voice.

But Dante didn't return my smile.

I swallowed. "What about . . . what about dying? You're telling me you're not going to die?" I couldn't help but glance at his shoulder. I'd seen his unnaturally quick healing firsthand. But certainly he couldn't mean . . .

Dante kept his gaze level with mine.

A chill swept over me. I started to shake. What was I doing here? This was insanity. This wasn't real. None of this could be real. I stumbled to my feet and began walking away.

Dante rose to his knees, grabbing my cold hands in his, preventing me from leaving. His skin felt feverish against mine. "No, Abby, don't leave. Please." The moonlight burned in his eyes. "Just, let me try to explain. And then . . . and then, if you want to leave . . . I won't stop you."

I looked at those changeling, quicksilver eyes that were filled with such desperate need. I remembered the night at the Dungeon when Zero Hour had played. I remembered the night in the garage when I had bandaged up Dante from Zo's blade. I remembered how both times I'd felt like I might be the only person who could save him. I remembered how much I had wanted to help him then, if only in some small way. I felt the same way right now. Maybe just listening a little longer would help. Maybe it would be enough. Certainly I could do that much.

"Okay," I said, my voice quieter than I felt. "Okay. I'll stay."

He exhaled slowly. *"Grazie."*

I sat back down at the edge of the cloak. I still needed some distance between us.

"This is the way Leo explained it to me. Time is a river. The river bends and loops and meanders, but it always, only, flows one way—away from the past, toward the future. And all of us are carried through our lives on the current of that river. We live and love—and age—immersed in the all-encompassing waters of the river of time."

Dante's voice rose and fell in a mesmerizing, languid rhythm. I felt my breathing and my heartbeat match that same rhythm.

"And like the fish that swim in deep water, you are unaware of what is all around you, all the *time* that permeates through you. It's invisible—but without it . . . you would never survive."

Dante reached for my hand, pressing his palm fast against mine, twining our fingers together. I could feel the heat of his skin, the faint pulse of his blood rushing through his wrist so close to mine.

"The river is *now*. This moment. This breath between us. The space between your heartbeats. The moment before you blink. The instant a thought flashes through your mind. It is everything that is around us. Life. Energy. Flowing, endlessly flowing, carrying you effortlessly from then . . . to now . . . to tomorrow. Listen: you can hear the music of it. Of the passage of time."

I could hear it. I could feel it, too—in the rise and fall of my breath, the ebb and flow of the air as it moved from my mouth to my lungs and back again. I could feel a tingle of energy, as though I had caught a snowflake made of pure light on my tongue and let it melt through my whole body.

"Do you feel it?"

I nodded, unable to speak, lost in the new layer of the world unfolding before my eyes.

I thought I saw a faint golden shimmer around our clasped hands, rippling in the air like a mirage on a hot day. But the shimmer didn't extend to Dante's hand. It was like a thick, black line had been drawn around his fingers, around his whole body, a second skin that breathed when he did, constantly flexing and adjusting to his movements. I blinked and it was gone.

He untangled his fingers from mine, drawing back until our skin was almost touching, but not quite. I could still feel his heat, the tension taut in the space between our hands. The hairs on the back of my arm stood up.

Dante reached into his shirt pocket, withdrawing the silk handkerchief Benedick used as a prop in the play.

"As I said—I'm beyond the reach of time. Passing through the time machine lifted me from the river, but I'm not dead. It left me—to complete the metaphor—stranded on the riverbank." He draped the sheer fabric over his hand, hiding his long fingers, his branded wrist. "I am cut off. Exiled."

I shivered at the bleak tones in his voice. I edged a little closer to him, wanting to feel his warm hand on mine again. "But it can't be all bad, right? You're still alive, aren't you?" I attempted a smile.

His lips thinned humorlessly. "I wonder sometimes." He crushed the cloth in his fist. "Part of being human—of being truly alive—requires you to recognize and to experience the passing of time. The time machine stole from me my past, my present, and my future, abandoning me on a desolate, barren, *timeless* bank. I can no longer feel the passage of time. At all. There is nothing." He swallowed away the quaver in his voice before he continued. "There is no time to age me, so, in a sense, I'm immortal. Invincible, even—it's why I didn't bleed to death when Zo cut me. But if I'm not careful, if I succumb to the pressure, I'll go insane."

A frown furrowed my forehead. "Pressure? What pressure?"

Dante frayed the edge of the handkerchief with restless fingers. "Leo said if we are careful, we can return to the river—to visit, not to stay. When we're here, we are constantly surrounded by life but eternally separated from it as well. We need that connection, however tenuous, to have any hope of survival. But if we stay too long, then the pressure of being in what is now, for us, an unnatural environment, can kill us."

"But I thought you couldn't die?" I hoped Dante hadn't noticed I stumbled over the words a little.

"Some things are worse than death. Leo had a friend, Giovonni, who thought he was strong enough to handle the pressure. Strong enough to stay in the river, in the flow of time. When Leo eventually found him, the prolonged exposure had washed his mind clean. He had lost all his memories. Worse, he had lost the ability to create new memories. No language. No comprehension. Nothing. He was alive—he's still alive, in fact—but what made him Giovonni is . . . gone. Erased. He is a blank slate—forever."

I shivered and rubbed my hands together. "So, how do you keep that from happening to you?"

"By keeping the balance," Dante said firmly. "I come here"—he pressed his bare palm to mine again and I shivered at the contact—"to the river, because I have to in order to avoid going insane, and I stay as long as I can. I stay until the pressure of time becomes too intense. Then, to avoid having my mind washed clean"—he draped the cloth over his hand again—"I return *there,* to the bank, to release the pressure."

A thought occurred to me, a piece of the complex puzzle he'd presented to me. "So those times you missed school and rehearsal? The days when I can't seem to find you? Are those the times you're . . . on the bank?"

Dante nodded.

"And where is that, exactly?"

He looked away into the darkness. The stars were glittering pinpricks in his fathomless eyes. "It's . . . not here."

"You talk about it like it's a real place," I said.

"It is a real place. At least as real as it has to be."

"I don't understand."

Dante chafed at his wrists absently, endlessly, choosing his words carefully. "The bank is a space—an existence—that runs parallel to *now* but is entirely separate from it. It's like a mirrored reflection of this life—only here, life flourishes. Here, time flows along its measured course. On the bank, there is only emptiness. A barren wasteland. A nothingness . . ."

"It sounds awful," I murmured.

Dante shrugged. "It's my life now. I have to keep the balance. If I falter too far either way . . ." He leaned forward, his words falling like stones between us, his shrouded hand pressed hard against mine. "Do you know what it's like, Abby? To be so close to life—and not be able to touch it? To not be able to dive in and let the water close over you and have the current carry you away? To be forever denied the one thing that you long for most of all? The one thing that will save you—" His voice sheered off into silence.

Tears filled my eyes and I brushed them away with the back of my hand. I wondered if the same rules applied to Leo, to Zo and his friends. And if so, I wondered if they coped with keeping the balance the same way. I could have been wrong, but they never seemed to be gone as long or as often as Dante. It was a long moment before either of us spoke again.

"Do you believe me, Abby?" He handed me his silk hand-kerchief, crumpled from his efforts to explain an impossible story. "Please. I need you to believe me."

I hesitated. I wanted to believe him, but everything he had told me seemed so unbelievable. So far-fetched, so crazy. And yet . . .

And yet the longer he spoke, the more it sounded like the truth. And what if it was? What would that mean?

"Can you show me?" The words were out of my mouth before I knew I was going to say them. "The bank? I think I could believe you if you could show me."

His eyes searched mine with a dark intensity. "It's a dangerous thing to ask. I'm not sure. . . ." He shook his head and drew in a deep breath. "Do you trust me, Abigail Beatrice Edmunds?"

I opened my mouth, but Dante covered my lips with his fingers.

"Be sure of your heart before you speak."

I closed my mouth underneath his fingers. *Did* I trust him? I'd only known him since January. Yes, we'd spent time together rehearsing for the play—we'd even been on what could only be properly defined as a date—but was that all that was required for trust: spending time together?

Or was trust based on more than that? On character? On experience?

I'd felt his blood on my hands. Was that enough?

I closed my eyes and concentrated on my breathing, on the feelings in my heart, on recapturing that moment of golden light. Was Dante the kind of person I could trust—possibly with my life? I had seen his temper, but it had never been directed at me. I had heard his quick wit cut others like a razor, but his words to me had always been kind and gentle. I had witnessed his moodiness, but, honestly, it hadn't been any worse than Valerie's mood swings or Hannah's snarky comments.

It was clear *he* trusted *me*. Who had he asked for help at the Valentine's Dance? Who had he confided in with his deepest secrets? Who had he kissed with all the passion of his wild and fierce soul?

Wasn't trust ultimately a decision of the heart?

I opened my eyes. I took the silk scarf, smoothed it over my fingers.

Dante looked at me with apprehension.

"I trust you," I said simply.

He cupped my face in his hands and kissed me, hard and insistent. His mouth moved on mine and electricity shot through my veins.

"*Grazie*, Abby. *Sei una bellissima donna, e ti ringrazio per avermi creduto dal fondo della mia anima.*"

His murmuring voice sent shivers down my spine.

"So, what do we do?" I asked, once he had let me catch my breath.

"*We* don't do anything. *You* hold tight to me"—Dante suited action to words and intertwined his fingers with mine— "and *I* . . . do this."

CHAPTER
18

The transition was instantaneous. For a moment, I wondered if anything had even changed at all. I was opening my mouth to ask Dante a question when I realized how dramatically my surroundings had, in fact, altered.

There was no air. I couldn't breathe. I was drowning in an ocean of nothingness.

Pressure squeezed my lungs like a vise. I was acutely aware of the flow of blood in my body, the sound of it roaring in my ears. My heartbeat hurt inside my chest. Darkness feathered the edges of my vision. I tried not to look at the landscape around me. The world shimmered drunkenly, tilting just enough off center to upset my equilibrium. What was going on? Where was this place? Panicked, I grabbed for Dante.

His mouth came down on mine, and with his kiss I found I could breathe again. The roiling darkness inside me subsided in soft, lapping waves. Dante encircled me in his arms, holding me tight and safe in his embrace. I could hear his heart beating, and the sound helped calm my fraying nerves.

I don't know how long we stood together, locked in an

embrace, but eventually I started to feel stronger, more solid and stable. I could peek at the world from the corners of my eyes without feeling like I was going to throw up.

Dante spoke in short, clipped phrases. His voice sounded thin and flat and I noticed there was a strange echo to his words, almost as though I was hearing them two or three times.

"ABBY—Abby—*Abby*. How do you FEEL—feel—*feel?*"

I shook my head, trying to clear away the disconcerting echoes buzzing like insects around my ears. "I'm FINE—fine—*fine*. NOW—now—*now*."

His smile lit up his whole face. "GOOD—good—*good*." The echoes slowly faded until his voice resolved into his regular cadence, rich and full of emotion. "I'm sorry, Abby. I didn't think that would happen."

"What *did* happen?"

"I think you brought some of your time with you. I . . . I had to make it so you could survive in this environment."

He pulled back just a little, concern written large in his eyes, in the tightness of his jaw.

The dark black line I'd seen around him back at the park had returned, but this time it extended to include me as well. I could see a thin line of shimmering gold layered beneath the black armor that protected me in this place.

"Where are we?"

"We're on the bank of the river." Dante's voice had an odd catch to it. He gently turned me around so I could see the entirety of where we stood.

The sky, or what would have been the sky had there been

any depth to the world around us, was a horrible gray nothing-ness. No sun. No moon. My eyes hurt, like I had an eyelash stuck under my lid. I blinked and had to look away.

But that was even worse.

From horizon to horizon stretched a perfectly flat, utterly barren wasteland. Void of color. Void of movement. Void of sound.

Dante and I were the only things that disrupted the terrify-ing emptiness around us. His white shirt and black pants were a study in severe contrasts. My skirt was red as blood. The si-lence itched on my skin.

"We're outside of time," he said, his eyes the same flat gray as the non-sky above us. "Stepping out of the river and onto the bank is like sliding in between the moments of time. Come with me. Don't let go." Holding tight to my hand, he began walking swiftly to the left.

"Where are we going?" I asked.

"You wanted to see the river."

"But I thought we had just come from the river?" I frowned in confusion. My mind felt flattened; it was hard to think.

"The river has a connection, a presence, in this mirrored existence, too." Dante shrugged. "We're going to see the *other side* of the river."

"Ah, the back side of water," I chuckled.

Dante's eyebrows drew down in confusion.

"Sorry. Disneyland joke. Go on."

"Think of it like this: A tapestry takes threads of all differ-ent colors and creates something beautiful out of it. But turn the tapestry over, and you'll see all the knots underneath." He quickened his step a little. "It will make more sense when you see it. I promise."

It was eerie to walk next to him and not feel the air on my skin, not hear the sound of my footsteps, not see my shadow behind me. I could feel my mind splintering under the weight of the terrible void that had swallowed us whole.

And yet, something about this place seemed weirdly familiar. I closed my eyes and saw dark stars sparkling behind my lids. I could almost taste chocolate and pineapple on my tongue.

"I've been here before," I blurted out, my eyes flying open. "You brought me here before, didn't you? All those weeks ago when I was under all that stress."

Dante didn't break stride, but I saw the tension tighten the muscles along his shoulders. "It wasn't stress. You were feeling the pressure of too much time. I didn't know what else to do."

"Too much time?"

"It happened during breakfast at the café. I wasn't paying attention—I wasn't careful enough . . ." He shook his head. "I didn't realize it would hurt you. I didn't realize that you would have to make up for that lag in time somehow."

"What are you talking about?"

"You know how when you drop a stick in a river, how the water parts and flows around it? That's what happened at breakfast. Time split around us—two streams separating for a moment before joining again, but at a different pace than before."

I remembered how I had felt divided after breakfast, how I had two distinct memories of that event.

"Then I guess those glimpses of the future I saw were because of that disruption of time," I said eventually, amazed that I could say something so strange in such a strange place and have it make sense.

Dante stopped short. "What 'glimpses of the future'?"

I told him about the white flashes I'd experienced and how they'd gone away along with the pressure when he'd brought me to the bank the first time.

His eyes darkened.

"Is . . . is that bad?" I asked.

"I don't know," he said, his voice low and troubled. "Promise me you'll tell me if it happens again."

"O-okay. I promise."

He started walking again, his thoughts obviously far away.

The silence that fell between us was oppressive, suffocating. I hated the nothingness that was all around me. I wanted to hear the roar of a jet engine instead of the hollow hum deep in my inner ear, straining to detect even white noise. I wanted to see the setting sun flip the horizon from day into night instead of the glare of omnipresent, flat light. I wanted to smell the musty scent of Dante's wool coat instead of feeling the faint itch in my nose of empty air. I wanted my senses back. I interrupted his musings with another question.

"So, that day after breakfast, those matters of 'personal business' you had to attend to . . . ?"

He nodded, returning his attention me. "I had to come here to find my balance again. To take the twig out of the stream, so to speak."

"And the pressure I felt? That's the pressure you were talking about? The kind that can kill you?"

"Yes," he said quietly, and I shivered at the flatness of his voice. "If I hadn't seen you that day at lunch, hadn't recognized what was going on, the pressure would have grown and grown. It would have killed you. It's why I brought you here for just a flicker of time. You didn't need to stay long to find your own balance again. It's also why I had you keep your eyes closed. I didn't want you to see . . . this."

I remembered the sensation of an open vastness replacing the tight pressure strangling my heart. "And here I thought it was the chocolate that made me feel better."

Dante smiled, squeezing my hand softly. "I figured it couldn't hurt."

He tugged me with him, walking forward at a brisk pace, but it was hard to tell how fast we were moving since nothing changed around us.

I was having trouble focusing my thoughts. Talking seemed to help so I asked Dante another question: "What were those echoes I heard earlier? What was that all about?"

"Time doesn't flow on the bank, it just *is*. Everything is happening *now*, and everything has *already* happened, and everything has *yet* to happen in the future." Dante shrugged like he knew he wasn't making much sense. "Those were echoes from the past, the present, and the future."

"I don't understand," I complained.

Dante smiled a little. "It's best to think of something else while you're here. Something that will keep your mind focused on things that *do* make sense. Sometimes I recite *Inferno: 'Nel mezzo del cammin di nostra vita—'"*

"In English, please," I panted, trying to keep up with Dante's long strides in my heavy skirts. I mentally cursed Dave; if it weren't for his stupid performance superstitions, I'd be in jeans and sneakers and much more comfortable.

"'When I had journeyed half of our life's way, I found myself within a shadowed forest, for I had lost the path that does not stray. Ah, it is hard to speak of what it was, that savage forest, dense and difficult, which even in recall renews my fear: so bitter—death is hardly more severe!'"

"How uplifting," I drawled. "It fits right in with all this." I gestured with my free hand at the vastness pressing down on us like a fist.

"*Inferno* isn't all like that," Dante said, a flush staining his cheeks. "The language in some of the Cantos can be extremely beautiful. A few lines can sustain me for days here."

"Days? How can you tell?"

He glanced at me, an unreadable expression on his face. "I can tell."

I blanched as I realized what he was saying. Of course he could tell. Even in a place outside of time, he could tell because this barren hell was part of his permanent reality.

"Tell me one of those parts, then," I said softly. "One of the parts you love."

Dante thought for a moment, his steps slowing before stopping altogether. He reached out, cradling both of my hands in his grasp. He brushed the inside of my wrists with his thumbs. His changeling eyes glittered like falling snow. "'I was among those souls who are suspended; a lady called to me, so blessed, so lovely that I implored to serve at her command. Her eyes surpassed the splendor of the star's; and she began to speak to me—so gently and softly—with angelic voice.'"

I felt heat race through my cheeks, my throat, my wrists. A soft touch and some poetry and I melted. I was starting to understand what Dante saw in the writings of his namesake. "Who is she?" I asked. "The woman in the poem?"

"Her name is Beatrice. It is for love of Beatrice that Dante travels through the nine circles of Inferno and the nine tiers of Purgatory just to catch a glimpse of her in Paradise." He ran his fingertips along the curve of my cheek.

I closed my eyes under his tender caress, trembling. For just a moment, the vast emptiness around me was filled with a golden light.

He brushed his thumb over my lips. "You're my future, Abby. I don't want to lose you. I *can't* lose you."

I felt my breath catch in my throat and my heart speed up its rhythm.

He leaned down and kissed me again, his lips soft and gentle. I felt a warmth rising through my body from the soles of my feet, tingling in my fingers and toes. The kiss seemed to last forever—and, I reflected, in a place outside of time, perhaps it had.

I heard him draw a deep breath. "We're here."

Surprised, I opened my eyes. "Where—" I began, but my words were washed away at the sight before me.

The river.

I suppose I expected to see a traditional river—a huge

cataract of water rushing in white-water rapids along a deep ravine like the Colorado, or a wide, meandering highway of ripples and undertows like the Mississippi—but what I saw was unlike anything I could have imagined.

The vast, flat wasteland of the bank spread out before us like a pane of glass, but a few steps beyond where we stood, the glass seemed to ripple and shimmer, bend and convulse, creating a wide chasm of chaotic movement that shouldn't have existed in a place of such frozen and unchanging sameness.

Time flowed wild and fierce in that chasm. I could see it passing before my eyes while I stood just a few inches away, motionless on the bank. My mind struggled with the dichotomy.

"Impressive, isn't it?" Dante asked.

I nodded, unable to speak.

"I like to come here sometimes to see life in all its possibilities. What has been"—he gestured upstream at the ripples that constantly flowed—"and what might be." This time he pointed downstream, where the silver thread unspooled into the endless distance.

I looked across the shifting surface to where the ground seemed to return to its smooth, flat expanse. "What's over there?" I asked, pointing.

Dante hesitated. A hidden pain surfaced in the corners of his eyes. "It's where we came from. It's the past we left behind. We can never go there."

"Why not?"

"We've been exiled here—to this side of the bank. It's

impossible to cross to the other side. The moment we touch the river, we're pulled back into it. And even if there was some kind of bridge, we'd still need a door to take us home."

"Past and future . . ." I murmured. "'And never the twain shall meet.'"

"Shakespeare?"

"No, Kipling."

My eyes returned to the swirling sheet of glass at my feet. Images rose to the surface of the glittering chasm, jumbled and uneven. I wanted to look away, but I couldn't.

I saw a flash of me when I was eleven with my hair plaited in two tight braids down my back and a copy of *Lord of the Rings* tucked under my arm. I remembered that day. It had been my first solo trip to the library and I had been so sure of the way. I had wandered down unfamiliar streets for hours before I finally admitted the truth: I was lost. Desperate, I went into a grocery store and asked for the manager. He called my parents and gave me an ice cream and waited with me until they came to pick me up.

His name was Mr. Schroeder, I realized. *I thought I had forgotten that.*

I saw myself walking in a darkened hallway. I knew that someone or something dangerous waited for me at the end, yet I couldn't turn back.

I saw the day my parents married.

I saw Valerie talking to V at the Dungeon the night of the Zero Hour show. In one ripple, Valerie gave him her phone number. In another, she didn't.

I saw Natalie walking with someone in a splash of bright

sunshine under a blue sky. They were on a college campus and a diamond glittered on her left hand.

I saw Dante. His face was buried in his hands and I could almost hear the black chains on his wrists clanking as the ripples tore the image apart, fracturing and splintering into darkness.

I saw I saw I saw . . .

The images were too many. Too fast. I knew if I kept staring at the river, I'd drown.

I looked at Dante instead.

He wasn't looking at the river either. He was looking at me. His gray eyes had turned black. Sweat beaded on his forehead and the muscles along his jaw clenched. I felt the muscles in his wrist flex with tension as he squeezed his hand tight around mine.

"I have to send you back," he said. "You can't stay here. It's too dangerous. I didn't realize . . . I have to send you back."

"Okay." I was more than ready to go. I had a throbbing headache at the base of my skull. I felt years older and so exhausted I could barely stand up without Dante's arm supporting me. It was getting hard to breathe again. "Let's go."

"No," he said, shaking his head. "I have to send *you* back. I can't go with you right now."

I frowned. "Why not? I'm not leaving you here in this place alone."

I saw the muscles moving in his throat as he swallowed. "Bringing you here was a bad idea. I've upset the balance. I can't go back for a while. And you can't stay here. If you do . . . if you stay . . ." Dante shook his head. "I don't know what would happen, but I'm sure it would be bad. I promised you I would keep you safe."

Fear slid through my veins. "No, come with me, Dante. Please? I can't go back alone. I don't know how."

Dante took a step toward me, and for an instant I thought he was going to wrap his arms around me and everything would be fine—

He shoved me hard and I stumbled backward, tripping over the hem of my dress. "I'm sorry, Abby," Dante said, his voice seeming to come from miles away. The weird triple echo was back, but twisted somehow. "I'll come to you as soon— THEN—now—*never*—as I can."

I fell into the river. I tensed my body, thinking I would certainly shatter the glass chasm, but instead the waters of time closed over me without so much as a splash or a ripple to mark my passing. As I was swallowed up, I saw a dark shadow high above me, curving overhead, arching from bank to bank, bridging the gap between here and there, between now and then.

The transition was instantaneous.

I landed hard on my back, the breath knocked out of me. I looked for Dante—where was he? I needed his kiss to save me again. I didn't want to suffocate and die in that horrible nothing-place beside the river—but I was alone in Phillips Park, the same empty swings, the same flat picnic benches, the same prickly grass where we had parked in what seemed a lifetime ago.

I checked my watch. It had stopped at five minutes to midnight. *Zero hour,* I thought with a chill. I tapped the watch face and the second hand hiccupped into motion.

It's like I never left, I realized. *He's gone. And it's like I never left.*

I curled up in Dante's cloak, breathing in the familiar scent of his body, and surrendered myself to oblivion.

CHAPTER
19

My vision flashes white. The sight of it fills me with dread. Is this another glimpse of the future? I promised Dante I would tell him if it happened again. I turn, looking for him by my side, but he is gone. I am alone. Lost in the stark whiteness that surrounds me, fills me, leaves me cold.

Color slowly bleeds into the white. My eyes water at the sight of so much color, of so much white. My tongue and throat scratch as though I'd swallowed a cactus. A dull ringing sounds deep in my ear, muffled and distant. My skin is tight and loose all at the same time.

The world turns upside down around me. I am lifted. I am drifting. I am divided.

The dull ringing increases, becomes sharp, insistent. A voice. An almost familiar voice. An almost familiar name. If only my thoughts weren't drowning in memories. A tight vise squeezes my lungs. If only I could catch my breath again.

Then, like a clap, a shot, a shout—I sit up in my own bed, in my own house, in my own here and now. The dark pressure of the bank crackles off my skin like shattering glass. I gasp down a breath of cool, clear air, feeling the sweet release of time in my veins, feeling the heady rush of life returned, of balance restored.

I am whole again.

❽

"Can I get you anything else, sweetie?" my mom asked, setting the glass of juice on the table by the couch where I was snuggled up watching TV.

"No, I'm fine." A hint of exasperation crept into my voice. "Honest, Mom, I'm feeling fine. I really think I could go back to school tomorrow."

Mom pursed her lips, pressing the back of her wrist against my forehead even though we both knew I wasn't running a fever.

"Mom," I whined, wincing at how much I sounded like Hannah at her most petulant. How old was I again?

"Drink your juice." Mom patted my hand. "Someone's here to see you. Do you want some company?"

Dante. "Absolutely." I gulped down my juice and turned off the TV.

"Not so fast," Mom said, gently placing her hand on my shoulder and pushing me back into the pillows. "You still need to rest. I'll send him in."

I tucked my hands under the blankets to keep them from shaking. It felt like forever since I'd seen Dante and I had so many questions to ask him.

My memories of the last few days were still cracked and

incomplete. I remembered the park, but after that . . . I sighed deeply. After that was blankness, a white landscape, and the feeling of a wave lifting inside my chest.

I heard someone step into the family room.

But it wasn't Dante who had come to see me.

It was Leo.

He looked older somehow, the weariness carving deep lines around his eyes and mouth. His wrinkled shirt was open at the throat, and I saw the glint of a golden cross hanging against his skin.

"I hope I'm not intruding." He rocked his weight from his heels to his toes.

"No, it's fine," I said, surprised. Of all the people I thought would come visit me, Leo might have been at the bottom of the list. "Where's Dante?" I hadn't meant for the words to sound so blunt; I offered up a smile to help soften the tone.

Leo paused, an air of stillness settling around him. The sunlight reflected off his blue eyes, shading them silver, and for the first time I could see the similarity between Dante and Leo.

"Dante's fine," Leo said.

If I hadn't been listening for the hesitation, I would have missed it.

Leo nodded to the chair across from the couch. "May I?" He didn't wait for my reply but sat down, a serious look on his face. "We need to talk."

"About what?" I pulled the blankets up to my neck.

"About Dante. About what happened in the park two nights ago. About what happened afterward."

"Nothing happened," I managed before falling silent under the weight of Leo's gaze.

"Exactly," he said.

I blinked in surprise.

"The story for everyone else is that you and Dante left the play opening night and drove to the park. Shortly after midnight, you brought Dante back to the Dungeon and then returned home. You fell sick, but you're feeling much better now."

"But that *is* what happened," I said. "Isaac was sick at the play. Mom thinks I caught the same twenty-four-hour bug he had."

Leo shook his head. "No, what happened to you was more." He leaned forward in the chair, resting his forearms on his knees and clasping his hands together.

I glanced down and saw the pale, thin chains around his wrists. Chills ran from the back of my neck down my arms to my fingertips. A white shimmer surrounded my vision. *He knows,* I thought. *He knows Dante took me to the bank. He knows everything.* Dante's words crashed through my memory, making my ears ring—*time machine, treason, the river, the bank.*

I bit my lip, trapping the words behind my teeth. I didn't know what to say and I was afraid if I opened my mouth the words would spill out, unchecked and irretrievable.

"The story for you, *mia donna di luce,* is more complicated." Leo's smile stripped years from his face but failed to chase the shadow from his eyes.

I wondered about the Italian name he called me, what it

meant. I reminded myself to ask Dante. If I ever saw him again.

"The story begins the same way—young lovers taking a midnight trip to a park—but the ending is very different. Would you like to hear it?"

Numbly, I nodded, my mind churning with fragmented memories. I didn't want to go back to that place of empty air and shattered colors. The wave trapped in my chest rose to the back of my throat, threatening to overwhelm me.

"You saw the bank. And the river," Leo said. "I don't know how; it shouldn't have been possible, although . . ." He glanced at me, and something flickered in his shadowed eyes. He shook his head, finally murmuring, "although perhaps that is a story for another day." He took a deep breath and started again, "You saw the bank. And the river. And just as you brought some of your time with you to the bank, when you returned, you brought some of the bank's timelessness with you."

Dryness coated the inside of my mouth. I had a visceral memory of seeing my watch frozen in time, of the hands lurching into motion. A dark shadow looming overhead. A white wave cresting into color. I rubbed my hand over my arm, half expecting to feel the sharp edges of broken time still clinging to me.

"How did . . . ? What . . . ?" My questions jumbled together in my mouth. I didn't know what to ask first.

"When Dante didn't come home that night, I went looking for him."

"At the park?"

He shook his head. "On the bank."

"Oh." I tried to imagine the two men meeting in that time-less void, but even in my imagination they were pressed flat by the two-dimensional emptiness of the bank.

"Dante was . . . out of balance." The corners of Leo's eyes tightened. "He told me what had happened."

I looked down at my hands, strangely embarrassed, as though I'd been caught doing something wrong.

"He told me where you were and that you needed help. He wanted to come with me, to help you, but I told him he needed to stay where he was."

"Is he still there?"

Leo paused, then nodded. "And will be until the danger has passed."

I shivered. Why was he in danger? For me? Or because of me?

"It was almost dawn when I found you in the park, but in the spot where you were curled up on Dante's cloak, it was still midnight."

"What? How was that possible?"

"It is as I said—you brought some of the timelessness of the bank back with you. It was like you were trapped under glass. Frozen in time. I could see clearly the line where the ris-ing golden light hit the shell of lingering night."

"Then it was you who called my name," I murmured.

Leo paused again. I could see him swallowing once, then twice, before replying, "Yes."

"If I was frozen in time, then what happened? How did I get home?"

"I set you free. I was able to break the shell around you and absorb the extra time." He unclasped his hands, flexing his fingers before locking them together again.

"I'm sorry if helping me caused you pain," I said quietly, reaching out to cover his knotted fists with my open hand.

He looked up at me, the dark shadow back behind his eyes. "Helping you has never . . ." He swallowed and carefully moved his hands away from mine. "I mean, no, I wasn't in any pain."

If I hadn't been listening for the lie, I would have missed it.

"I burned off the extra time on the bank. Then I drove you home." Leo's tone was back to business.

"Where I've been asleep for a day and a half," I said. "Recovering from . . . what, exactly? Not the flu."

"No, though that is the story that everyone believes. Your body needed time to equalize, to return to a stable, normal equilibrium."

"And has it?"

"You're still alive." He shrugged. "If you hadn't found your balance again . . ."

The implications of Leo's unspoken words weighed me down. I looked down at my body, hidden under a mound of blankets. I felt like it belonged to someone else.

"So what do I do now? Will I have to go back to the bank, to keep my balance, like Dante does? Like you do?" I swallowed, trying to keep the tremors from my voice.

"Ah, no, *mia donna di luce,*" Leo murmured.

I hadn't realized I was crying until he reached out to hand

me a tissue from the box on the coffee table. His fingers felt rough and worn against mine.

"No, you are not bound by the bank as Dante is. As I am." He handed me another tissue. "You *are* a special young lady, Abby, but rest easy. You are still surrounded by the river just as you always have been."

"Thanks," I whispered, wiping at my eyes. "Dante's lucky to have you in his life."

"I think he's luckier to have you," Leo said.

"Is he going to be okay?"

"He's a good man. He'll find his own way through this life."

I bit my bottom lip. "Are you mad at him for telling me the truth?"

Leo hesitated, then smiled sadly. "I told you once that it was not my place to tell another man's secrets. It's also not my place to be angry when those secrets are told. Even if they are my same secrets."

"I won't tell anyone," I promised.

"I know." Then he laughed softly under his breath. "Dante told me you were dangerous, but I didn't realize how much."

I smiled at the memory. "He told me it was because I was brave enough to hear the truth."

"And that makes you easy to trust. But be careful—too much trust invites secrets, some of which you may not wish to know."

"I hope there aren't any more secrets I need to know about," I said. "The ones Dante told me about seem to be plenty."

A tight expression crossed Leo's face, then quickly

smoothed away as he ran a hand through his white hair. "I have some rules for you," Leo said.

I shook my head, frowning good-naturedly. "More rules? This is worse than school."

"Maybe, but there the worst that could happen is a bad grade. Failing to follow *these* rules could have dire consequences for more people than just you."

Properly chastened, I sat back, attentive and interested.

"Perhaps you know this already, but it is worth repeating— the time Dante spends here must be balanced against the time he spends on the bank. Keeping the balance is of paramount importance. That is rule number one."

"That sounds like a rule for Dante, not me."

"That brings us to rule number two." Leo hesitated, and I suddenly knew I wasn't going to like what he was about to say. "Physical contact—or even a strong emotional connection— can tip the balance farther, faster."

"What!" I sat up. "I can't touch him? Not even to hold his hand? Or hug him? Or . . . ?" I felt my face blush, remembering Dante's darkly sweet kiss. "That's not fair!"

Leo shrugged. "Nothing about this situation is fair. The truth remains, though—relationships complicate things."

I opened my mouth to protest, but Leo continued, overriding my voice.

"And yes, you *can* touch." Leo suited actions to words and squeezed my hand. "You can even kiss." His knowing smile meant he'd anticipated my thoughts. "But know that the more you do—the more time you spend together—the more time you must spend apart."

"Does Dante know about this?" I folded my arms in a huff.

"Of course," Leo said quietly. "Why do you think he's always so careful around people—including you?"

I thought back over the past month. I had lost count of all the times Dante had reached for me, only to pull away at the last moment. I could, however, probably count on one hand the times he *had* touched me, most notably when he had carried me to the car that first Saturday for breakfast. Then at lunch when he had helped heal me from that strange rip in time. And again at the Valentine's Dance when he had first tried to tell me the truth of his past.

I thought of all the times he'd avoided contact with other people.

"Wait," I said, "Dante spends all day at school and most nights at the Dungeon. He's always surrounded by people. Why is it so different when he's with me?"

"Because they are still wholly in the river. They haven't ever set foot on the bank—they don't even know it exists. You are different, Abby. You've seen the far shore and have returned." Leo's voice was soft. "You have been touched by time, and that makes you special."

"But you said I'm not like you. You said I wouldn't have to go back to the bank."

"And you won't. And you're not like us. I don't think you're like anyone else. As far as I know, no one has been able to travel to the bank without having first traveled through time's door. Make no mistake, Abby—you have been changed. It remains to be seen how that change will affect things to come."

I thought about that quietly for a moment. I didn't feel like

I'd been changed, but there was no denying strange things were happening around me. I knew one thing for sure, though.

"I don't want to hurt him. If me being with him puts him in danger . . ." I trailed off, knowing it was useless to continue. Having had a taste of togetherness with Dante, I knew I didn't want things to go back to the way they had been—the almost-touches, the fleeting looks, the cryptic comments. Dante had trusted me with his heart and soul. I didn't want to give them back now. I couldn't. They had already found a home in me.

"Dante can take care of himself," Leo said.

"So, rule number one," I summarized, "is to keep the balance. Rule number two: no touching." I frowned before I quickly amended it to "*Limited* touching. So what's rule number three?"

"Rule number three is that you must not ask Dante what he sees downstream."

"What does that mean?"

"Dante is unusually attuned to the river. Sometimes he is able to see events yet to come in the ripples and currents of time."

"He can see the future?" I thought about what I had seen in the river. Some of the images had definitely been of the past, but some of them might have been of future events. I wondered if I should mention it to Leo.

"At times."

"And I can't ask him about it because . . . ?"

"Because lately all he is seeing is you."

"Me?"

Leo nodded. "No one should know exactly what the future

holds for them. Knowing what he sees about you could influence your decisions and your choices; it could change your life irrevocably."

I swallowed.

"There is only one more rule, but it might be the most important one. You must never go back to the bank—I don't know if it is even possible for you to go back. However it happened, it's too dangerous to try to duplicate."

"Don't worry," I said. "That's one rule I won't have any trouble keeping. There's no way I want to go back to the bank." Just thinking about it made my ears feel like they were stuffed with cotton and my mouth taste like iron.

"That's a good girl," Leo said, patting the blanket covering my knee. He stood up to leave, but at the last minute, he leaned down and brushed a kiss on the crown of my head. "Sleep well, *mia donna di luce,* and don't worry—I will look after Dante, and Dante will look after you."

I thought about Leo's words long after he'd left. I hoped Dante would be coming back from the bank soon. We had a lot we needed to talk about.

CHAPTER
20

D ante stayed on the bank for three more days.

Three very long, very stressful days.

Mom let me go back to school, under strict orders to call her if I felt even the first inkling of a sniffle. I felt fine, though, which was good, since I had more important things to deal with. I still had to help with the play. Leo wrote a note for Dante's continued absence, which I dutifully delivered.

I apologized to Amanda for the fact that Dante had ruined Benedick's mask; I offered to help repair it, but after twenty minutes of my "help," Amanda took it away from me and said, "Thanks anyway."

I tried to talk to Valerie—but she turned away from me whenever I tried to approach her.

Natalie and Jason came to the play every night—which was both good and bad. Good, because it was nice that my friends wanted to support me. Bad, because they sat together in the audience, often paying more attention to each other than to the play.

Though, every time I saw them together, I realized maybe

it wasn't so much "bad" as it was "weird." I'd been with Jason for so long, it was still a little strange to see him with someone else—especially when that someone else was Natalie.

But deep down, I was able to wish them the best because deep down, all my thoughts were for Dante.

I missed him. I hadn't realized how much he'd woven himself into my life until he wasn't there. I counted the minutes in class until lunch, only to remember he wouldn't be there at our table. I counted the cast before each nightly performance, always coming up one short. I counted the number of times Leo answered my question, "When is he coming back?" with "When he can." It was more than I thought it should be.

I opened the door that night and grinned. Dante stood on the front step, his hands in his coat pockets, the collar turned up against the night wind.

"You're back!" I said, flinging my arms around him.

"It's good to see you too, Abby," Dante wheezed as I tightened my hug.

"Come inside, it's freezing out there." I closed the door behind him and we stood there for a moment in the foyer, just looking at each other. I felt like I hadn't seen him in forever and I traced his features with my eyes, relishing the familiar arch of his brows, the line of his jaw, the pool of shadow in the hollow of his throat.

"I'm sorry it's so late, but I had to see you. I couldn't wait until morning."

"I'm glad you came." I smiled warmly up at him. I led him into the front room. "My parents are out tonight, so I'm 'baby-sitting' Hannah, by which I mean she and her friends are downstairs watching a movie and don't need me at all. I was doing some homework, but I'd much rather spend my time with you."

Dante shrugged out of his coat, laying it over the back of the couch. I took a moment to appreciate the way his shirt stretched over his chest as he moved. Then he stripped off his gloves and set them down as well.

"I thought you didn't want anyone to see those marks," I said in surprise.

"I don't want other people to see them," he said. "I don't mind if you do. I feel like I'm finally able to be myself around you and I don't want to lose that. I don't want there to be any secrets between us, Abby."

"I don't think there are anymore," I said as he sat down on the couch next to me.

He gathered me up in his arms, cradling my head against his shoulder. I loved how we fit together.

"I didn't have the chance to tell you before," I said, gently tracing a fingertip around the scarred brands clasped around his wrist, "but yes, I believe you. About everything."

"I'm so sorry I put you in danger like that," he said quietly. "I didn't know it would get so bad so fast. All I did the entire time I was on the bank was worry about you. I am so glad to see that you are all right. I would never have forgiven myself if I'd let you come to harm."

"It's okay," I assured him. "I don't know that I'd want to go through that again, but I'm okay. Leo said you told him where I was, how to save me. You shouldn't have to apologize; I should be thanking you for saving my life."

Dante closed his arms around me tighter. I felt him rest his forehead on the crown of my head. His warm breath flowed down the side of my neck.

"You can ask me anything," he whispered. "And I will tell you the truth. Always."

He was so serious, like a genie offering up three wishes. I hesitated, wondering what, if anything, I should ask.

I thought about everything I'd experienced with him on the bank. "Do you ever wish you could go home?"

"No."

"That's it? No hesitation? No qualifications? Just a flat-out no?"

"Some wishes are too dangerous to even contemplate. I have enough trouble keeping my balance here in the present. I can't afford to divide my attention between wishing for the past and waiting for the future."

"Still—seems like it would be nice to go back, to see your family again."

"It's nice to be *here*, to see *you* again." He reached up, trailing his hand along my cheek. "Ask me another question."

It *was* nice to be in his arms, no barriers between us, no secrets, just the truth.

"What does *mia donna di luce* mean?"

"Where did you hear that?"

"Leo calls me that sometimes. Why? What does it mean?"

"It means 'my lady of light.' Why would he call you that?" he mused.

I shrugged, wiggling a little closer to Dante. "Maybe because I'm so beautiful—like an angel," I teased.

"But you are," Dante said, his voice serious. "You are exactly like an angel."

"I wish. Angels are free, unbound by any rules except to play their harps and keep their halos polished." I sighed. "Lucky angels. Which reminds me—" I slid my hand up and down his arm, relishing the shape of his muscles under his clothes. I didn't want to let him go, but I did anyway, untangling myself from his arms and leaning away from him.

Dante looked at me in confusion.

"Leo's rule number two," I said with a resigned shrug. "*Limited* touching."

Dante reached out defiantly and took my hand in his, twining our fingers together. I could feel the sweet sensation of his bare palm pressed against mine.

"I'm supposed to help you keep the balance," I said, though I didn't pull my hand away. I enjoyed the comfort of Dante's closeness too much. "Leo said *that* was rule number one."

"Leo is famous for his rules. What else did he say?"

"Let's see, rule three: I'm not supposed to ask you what you see about me in the river—even though I'm *dying* to know. And rule four: I'm not supposed to go to the bank."

"Ah. Those are good keeping-Abby-safe rules."

"So what are the keeping-Dante-safe rules? I'm sure Leo has some for you."

"He does. And there are more than four." A small, rueful smile crossed his face. Dante tugged on my hand, pulling me closer to him. I didn't resist. He slipped his free hand into the pocket of his jeans, withdrawing a small necklace. "This is for you." A heart-shaped locket lay in the hollow of his hand like a miniature moon, the chain spilling over his fingers like falling stars.

My fingers traced the intricate pattern carved on the face of the locket. The metal was warm under my touch. I felt the tiny hinges along one edge. My curiosity was piqued. "What's inside?"

"The key to my heart." He sat me up on the couch, gently brushing aside my hair so he could fasten the locket around my throat. He placed a kiss like a benediction on the back of my neck, right where the clasp rested against my skin. "And a wish."

"Can I open it?"

I felt Dante's lips smile against my neck. He turned me in his arms, so his face was close to mine. "Not yet. I'll tell you when you can open it."

He closed the distance between us, his lips touching mine softly, hesitantly, then, as the world around us slowed, more insistently, until the only thing I was aware of was the shape of his lips.

The kiss left me tingling and trembling.

"Where did you learn to kiss like that?" I murmured.

"From you."

"You flatter me." I blushed.

"It's the truth." He winked at me. "I remember the rules."

In the following weeks, we both remembered the rules. And we both hated having to follow them. We kept our physical contact to a minimum—holding hands, mostly—but a sparkling shiver seemed to have taken up residence underneath my skin. I felt it whenever Dante ran his fingertips over my arm or my hand or my face; I felt it in the absence of his touch, waiting, longing for him to return.

We spent as much time together as we could. He would come to my house for dinner one night; I'd spend the next Friday night dancing with him to whichever band was playing at the Dungeon. We became regulars at Helen's Café, sitting in the same booth by the window where we'd had our first breakfast together. Dante started teaching me Italian; I took him to the movies.

More often than not, we'd have to cut an evening short so he could go back to the bank. It was harder than I had thought it would be to find the right balance of time we could spend together and stick to it. The worst was when he'd have to be away for a whole day. I would try to keep busy with school, or spending time with Natalie, or, once, even hanging out with Hannah and her friends when they needed another player for A&B Clue.

As bad as the absences were, they somehow made our time together sweeter, more intense. I treasured every moment.

One Friday night, Dante and I went to the movies and then to dinner. Nothing Italian, though. Dante said what passed for Italian food here didn't taste the same way as he remembered it. We'd stopped for late-night Chinese instead. His fortune cookie said, "You are wise beyond your years," which I thought was less of a fortune and more of a comment about his character. Dante just laughed, pointing out that now he had proof that he had more than five hundred years of wisdom behind him.

My fortune cookie said, "Remember June 4th. Great things are in store for you."

"Now, *that's* a fortune," I said, holding up the slip of paper. "They never pin down a date. And I know this one will come true: June 4th is graduation."

Dante popped my cookie in his mouth. "Ah, omniscience is delicious."

I tucked the fortune into my purse and we laughed all the way home.

"See you tomorrow?" I asked Dante as he walked me to the door.

Dante paused. "Maybe Monday."

"You have to go back already?"

He leaned in to kiss my frown away. "I'll be back before you know it."

I watched until his lights vanished into the darkness before turning and going inside.

I lay in bed for a long time that night, thoughts and memories roiling through me in a slow boil. Fragments of moments floated to the surface and I turned them over in my mind, trying to see how they fit together, or even if they did. I felt sure all the ragged bits and pieces were connected, if I could only figure out how.

Dante's hands on my neck, tilting my face to meet his in a kiss that changed me from the inside out.

Zo, standing on stage at the Dungeon, drenched in light, casting a deep, impenetrable shadow.

V wrapping his strong arms around Valerie, turning her face to his, turning her body into his embrace, turning her away from me.

Leo's gentle smile at odds with his words warning me against kisses shared at midnight and wishes made at dawn.

Sighing, I slipped from my bed and sat on the edge of the window seat, dragging the quilt from my bed and wrapping it around my shoulders. Leaning against the wall, I looked out into the night sky. The moon seemed so close tonight. The thin skiff of clouds drifted slowly across the sky like encroaching blindness across a milky, white eye. I knew it was corny, but I couldn't help but wonder if Dante could see the same moon from where he was on the riverbank.

I smiled ruefully. Of course he couldn't see the moonlight. I'd been there. I'd seen the vast emptiness and the light that seemed to come from everywhere and nowhere. I wondered once more how long he would be gone. All I wanted to do was spend time with him, and it didn't seem fair that the more time we spent together now, the longer we had to stay apart in the future. If only there was a way I could reach him even while he was gone.

I opened my window. The cool night breeze breathed over

me, drew soft fingers through the curtains and over my face. I closed my eyes, remembering falling through the river, the tingling sensation on my skin as the waters of time closed over me. I breathed deeply, half asleep, half remembering, half wishing.

I heard the wind whisper with Dante's voice, so close he might have been outside my window or even inside my room. I smiled in my sleep—when had I fallen asleep?—and turned my face to the night.

"What are you doing here?" Dante asked, his voice drifting to me on the wings of a dream.

What was I doing where? I wondered. I was asleep in my room, dreaming, wasn't I?

A picture filled my mind: Dante, standing so still on the riverbank I thought at first he was a statue—a carving left behind to mark the way, or to warn away unwary travelers. The flat light of the bank fell in strange angles on his skin, making the lines of his body sharp. His whole body was on edge. Thin. Tapering off into shadow—shadows that encased his wrists in heavy black bands, weighing him down, anchoring him in place.

It hurt my eyes to look directly at the chains on his skin. It hurt my heart to see him trapped and miserable. I opened my mouth to call his name, but as the dream unfurled its wings in my mind and the images and pictures became clearer, more defined, I realized Dante wasn't speaking to me; he was addressing a dark figure who hovered at the edges of my vision.

"I didn't think you liked coming here." The words may have

been spoken in Italian, but I heard them in English in my mind. And Dante's contempt needed no translation.

"No one does." Zo's voice preceded his appearance in my dream. He strode into the scene like an actor commanding the stage. Heavy black shadows writhed around his wrists too, but, unlike Dante, Zo embraced his bands, wore them as a mark of honor and pride.

I felt a ripple of apprehension pass through me; I wasn't sure I wanted to be anywhere Zo was. But this was just a dream, right?

It certainly felt like a dream . . . but with the promise of something more. It was like I was standing on a ledge and one more step would push me over, set me on the bank for real. I felt the edges of my dream bend and flex—and I mentally took a step back, staying safely on this side of the dream.

"Why are you here?" Dante clenched his fists and I saw streaks of red shoot through the black shadows, arrows of anger seeking a target.

"I wanted to talk to you," Zo said. "You've been avoiding me."

"We have nothing to talk about."

Zo laughed, the sound cracking from his mouth and dying in the void between the two men. "That hurts, Dante. It's important that we trust each other. You of all people should know the importance of trust. And the power of secrets."

"What secrets?"

"A couple weeks ago, Tony was here when something unusual happened." Zo moved a few paces closer to Dante. I noticed he didn't leave any footprints behind him. "He saw you by the river."

Dante narrowed his eyes.

"With a girl." A sharp smile slashed across Zo's face. "And not just any girl. Tony saw you with Abby Edmunds."

Even safe in my dream, I felt a shiver when Zo said my name.

"Imagine that," he continued, circling around Dante. "Abby Edmunds. Here. Because the last time I looked, she didn't have a membership pass to our exclusive little club." He grabbed Dante's wrist, squeezing through the shadows to the skin beneath. Dante hissed in pain, the stark planes of his face pale and rigid.

"Let go of me."

Zo stepped back, baring his teeth in a feral grin. "When Tony told me what he had seen, I had to ask myself, Why would Dante want to bring someone *here*?" He spread his arms wide, turning in a circle to encompass the entire void around them. He pivoted on his heel and placed his hands on Dante's shoulders. "And then Tony told me the rest of what he saw." Zo leaned closer. "Tony said he saw you and Abby walk to the edge of the river. He saw you push her in. And when the river closed over her, he saw something we all thought was impossible, something Leo swore was impossible. Tony saw *a way back*."

A tick jumped in Dante's jaw. He chafed at his wrists as though they still hurt from Zo's touch. "I know what he saw. It has nothing to do with you."

"Nothing to do with me?" Zo repeated, letting go of Dante

in surprise. "A bridge appears, spanning the river—a bridge that leads to the past, to *home*—and you don't think it has anything to do with me—with all of us? How long did you think you could keep it a secret?"

"It's my secret to keep."

"Keeping secrets is a dangerous business."

"So is telling them."

Zo acknowledged the veiled threat with a nod of his head. "How many of your secrets have you told Abby, I wonder? What did you tell her to make her willing to trust you? Did you tell her you loved her?"

Dante looked away.

"I see. Then you haven't told her about Orlando? Or Sofia?"

He took a step toward Zo. "Don't."

"Interesting," Zo said, amused at Dante's reaction. "Secrets within secrets."

"I suppose *you* don't have any secrets."

Zo laughed again, a harsh sound, brittle and venomous. "I have as many as you do. Maybe more."

"Then you don't need any more of mine, do you?"

"That's where you're wrong. Tell me how you did it. Tell me how you brought Abby here."

Dante smiled and remained silent.

Zo frowned. "Did Leo teach you?"

"I think it's time for you to leave."

"What else has Leo taught you? What other secrets are the two of you keeping?"

Dante sighed, ignoring Zo. "I guess *I'll* have to leave then."

He turned on his heel and took three steps away from Zo. Between the third and the fourth step, Dante disappeared.

Zo howled in rage, the roar impossibly rising in volume, impossibly expanding to fill the edges of the emptiness of the bank.

Then suddenly he looked around, his senses alert, his eyes darting from side to side, before they abruptly snapped into focus. I could see the fury etched on his face, distorting his angelic features. As our eyes met across my dream, I heard his scream of rage transform into a roar of laughter.

I woke in a cold sweat, the predawn sky the same flat empty color as the sky over the bank. Shaking, I ran to my door and locked it, pressing my back against the wood. I slid down to the floor, my mind still in a fog. I knew my fear was irrational—Zo wasn't in the hallway, he wasn't anywhere close to my house—but I couldn't shake the feeling that when Zo's eyes had locked with mine, he had seen me. Really *seen* me.

I realized with a rising sense of dread that what may have started out as a dream had suddenly become something more dangerous.

CHAPTER
21

Monday morning, I saw Dante walking toward me in the hallway, his backpack slung over his shoulder, as though his life was as normal as the next person's.

My heart lifted at the sight of his tall frame parting the crowds. I'd been a wreck all weekend, barely sleeping for fear of having another dream that was more than a dream.

"We need to talk," I said, my voice clipped and low. "Now."

"All right. But first . . ." He brushed his fingers across my lips. "I've got a few moments to spare." He bent down and kissed me.

I felt the familiar sensation of time slowing down around us, of my senses heightening and mixing. I could taste the softness of his lips, hear the clarity of his clothes sliding over his skin. I ran my fingers through the curls at the nape of his neck into his hair at the same time he slid his hands down to lock at the small of my back. His fingers left tracks of heat in their wake. He pulled me closer to him, just the two of us in a stolen moment of time.

But now was not the time for kisses.

I broke away, pressing my lips together and letting the taste of him fill my mouth before swallowing hard. He tasted of exotic places and possibilities.

"I feel like I haven't seen you in ages, Abby."

"It's only been two days."

"Two days too long." Dante nuzzled at my earlobe.

I pushed him away, feeling myself blush. "Not at school," I said. The few people around us were oblivious to our embrace. "We only have so much time together. Let's not waste it."

I felt Dante's mouth curve in a smile against my neck. "I don't think this is a waste of time."

I managed to keep my eyes open despite Dante's focused attentions. "Who's Sofia?"

Dante's lips turned to ice. Time snapped back into motion. I felt a hard and fast lurch deep in my stomach and blinked at the sudden jolt in my surroundings.

He straightened up slowly, his face carefully composed to reveal nothing of his emotions. "Where did you hear that name?"

Now that the moment was here, I wasn't sure I had the courage to say the words to this sudden stranger who wore a mask of Dante's face. I looked around, even though I knew no one was listening to us in the crowded hallway. And even if someone was, no one would know what we were talking about. "I . . ." I cleared my throat. "Friday night I dreamed you and Zo were talking on the bank." I lowered my voice. "Zo said you were keeping secrets. He mentioned Sofia."

"You dreamed this." The mask remained in place. "Friday night."

"Well, I *thought* it was a dream. But weren't you . . . I mean, you *were* on the bank then, right? And . . ."

"You saw me—and Zo—in your dream." He spoke carefully, emphasizing each word as though he might have misheard me.

I nodded. "That's what I wanted to talk to you about. I don't think it was a dream exactly."

Dante grabbed my hand and pulled me behind him, heading for the main doors. He muttered a string of vicious-sounding Italian words under his breath.

"Where are we going?"

"Leo's."

"But what about class?"

"I'll have him write you a note." Dante crashed through the doors.

He didn't speak the entire drive to the Dungeon. I pulled into the parking lot and he opened the door and helped me out of the car. Once he had closed the car door, he grabbed my hand again and we quickly walked into the Dungeon.

"Leo!" Dante called as the door swung closed behind us.

I rubbed at my face with my free hand, waiting for my eyes to adjust to the dim light.

Dante muttered something under his breath. "Leo!" He turned abruptly and led me across the floor to the bar. He slammed open the door, but the back office was dark and quiet. Dante hit the doorjamb with his open palm. "Where is he?"

"Will you please tell me what's going on? Why do you need Leo?"

Dante reached out and grabbed a set of keys from a cubby-hole on the desk. He pushed me back through the door and toward the glass cabinet of Leo's curios. "You're in danger, Abby, and it's all my fault. I should never have taken you to the bank. I should never have told you the truth."

"Danger?" I looked around as though a monster lurked in the corners of the room, ready to leap out and devour me whole, but there was only Dante, his chest heaving with his uneven breathing. His gray eyes were chips of ice in his frozen face.

"If anything happens to you . . ." Dante stopped by the cabinet door, the keys jingling quietly in his trembling hand. He shook his head once as though making a difficult decision, or dispelling a bad memory. He jammed the key into the lock and wrenched open the cabinet door, shaking the contents in his haste. A set of teacups rattled in their saucers. A porcelain figurine of a ballerina teetered on her pointed toe and crashed to the shelf in a shower of pink-and-white shards.

Dante pushed aside an obelisk of carved jade that stood next to the brass machine on the top shelf. He grabbed the brass box and handed it to me.

"What's going on here?" Leo said, appearing suddenly in the doorway of the club, his arms full of groceries. "Dante? What are you doing? Put that back."

"Abby needs your help, *Papà*," Dante said, taking my free hand. "We both do."

Leo's forehead wrinkled as he frowned. He set the groceries down on the table nearest the door. He snapped the lock and flipped the sign to "Closed." When he turned back to us, I

was surprised to see the change that had come over him. Gone
was the benevolent bartender; the man striding across the floor
toward us was as regal and powerful as a lion.

In one swift motion, he took the keys from Dante's hands
and the brass machine from mine. He replaced the box on the
top shelf and locked the cabinet, clucking his tongue at the
disorder and destruction inside, and pocketed the keys. "Tell
me everything," he ordered, looking from me to Dante.

There was no question of disobeying that voice. Dante and
I sat down at a table. Leo towered over us, his hands wrapped
around the back of a chair. I didn't know where to begin. How
could I tell Leo I might have broken the most important rule
he'd laid down? Thankfully, Dante spoke first.

"When I told Abby the truth . . ." Dante was barely able to
meet Leo's steady gaze. "I didn't tell you everything that happened that night." He swallowed. "There was a bridge. It appeared when I took Abby to the bank."

Leo gripped the back of the chair so hard the wood splin-
tered in his hand.

"Tony saw what happened and he told Zo about the bridge.
This last time I was on the bank, Zo confronted me about it,
demanding that I tell him how I did it."

Leo's mouth dropped open and he sat heavily into the broken chair. "You . . . saw the bridge?" He grabbed Dante's arm.
"What about the door? Did you see the door?"

Dante continued as though Leo hadn't spoken. "I think
that when I took Abby to the bank something . . . I don't know,
broke through, opened up. Changed. Things changed." He

glanced at me and then back to Leo. "I think Abby might be able to access the bank by herself."

"What?" The color drained from Leo's face in one instant.

"I didn't mean to," I whispered. "I'm sorry."

Dante nudged me. "Tell him what you saw."

I told Leo about my dream, every detail I could remember, every scrap of conversation, everything.

Leo seemed to age before my eyes. "Tell me about the bridge," he said finally.

"It rose out of the river as soon as Abby passed through." Dante's face was grim. "And it led directly to the door."

Leo flinched as though he'd been struck. "How long did it last?"

Dante weighed his answer. "It's hard to tell. Long enough for someone to cross."

"And now Zo thinks he can go back."

"He *can* go back. If Zo opens the door and goes through . . ." His voice trailed off into ominous silence.

"Is that bad?" I asked. "Zo going back, I mean."

Dante and Leo exchanged a look.

"It can't be that bad, can it? I mean, wouldn't he just go back to the same time as when he left?"

"The machine doesn't work like that." Dante fidgeted with his gloves, finally stripping them off in agitation. "When we passed through it the first time—from past to future—we broke the bonds of time. We were placed beyond the reach of time. But we're still bound to the bank, to the balance." He rubbed at the dark chains around his wrists. "It was da Vinci's way of keeping us from permanently corrupting the river with our . . . *unnaturalness.*"

"But passing through it a second time—from future to past . . ." Leo shook his head, clearly unhappy. "If Zo travels through the door a second time, he'll break the binding of the bank."

"And that means . . . ?" I asked, glancing between Dante and Leo.

Dante looked at me, an unreadable expression in his eyes. "Without the necessity of balancing between the bank and the river, Zo could stay in the river without having to leave. Ever."

"And he'd still be immortal," Leo said bleakly.

"And invincible," Dante agreed.

"But without any danger of losing his mind." Leo slammed his fist onto the tabletop. "Going through the time machine once made him a prisoner . . ."

"Going through it a second time would make him a god," Dante finished.

"Once he figures out a way to bring someone to the bank so he can cross the bridge and go through the door," Leo said grimly.

Dante shook his head. "No. Once he figures out a way to bring *Abby* to the bank."

"What? Why me?" I hated to hear the crack in my voice, but I could scarcely believe the conversation flowing around me.

Dante brushed my hair behind my ear. "There's something special about you, Abby. I've always known that."

"I'm not special—" I protested weakly.

"It was your presence on the bank that summoned the bridge and the door," Dante reminded me.

"But Zo won't be able to take me to the bank, will he?" I asked Dante. "I mean, you're the only one who can do that, right?"

"I thought I had something to do with it," he said gently, reaching out to clasp my hand in his. "But if you can go alone . . ." He rubbed his thumb against my skin. "Maybe Zo doesn't need me. Maybe all Zo needs is you."

I swallowed down a dry throat. The image of Zo's face rose up in my memory. He may have looked like an angel, but I knew better. I opened my mouth to say something, anything, but Leo spoke first.

"He may need Abby to summon the door, but he can't open it if it's already broken."

Leo's chair scraped against the floor as he stood up from the table. Crossing to his glass cabinet, Leo unlocked the case and lifted out the brass object from the top shelf. Hefting it in his hand, he brought it back to the table and set it down in the center with a dull thud.

"I can't believe you keep it out in the open," Dante said flatly, shaking his head.

Leo shrugged. "I like to be able to keep an eye on it. Besides, no one but us even knows what it is."

"What *is* it?" I asked, reaching out to touch the symbols carved onto the three notches of the brass square: a spiral shell; a half-sun, half-moon circle; a musical staff. "It's beautiful."

"It's the hinge to the door of the time machine. Without it, the door won't open. Not for Zo. Not for anyone."

"Does Zo know what it is?" Dante asked.

"No—" Leo said at the same time I said "Yes."

They both looked at me.

The memory was clear in my mind. "The night of the Poetry Slam the three of them were standing next to the cabinet, arguing about something. They were looking at this." I brushed my finger over the hinge again. "I bet he's known for a while this was important. He just didn't know how important until he heard about the door."

The three of us were silent for a moment, contemplating the consequences we faced.

"Leo, we have to do something," Dante said, bleakly. "We have to protect Abby. We have to take her away from here."

Leo's face was grim. "You're right. We have to do something."

"What!" I protested. "I can't leave. What about my family? My friends? I'm going to college next year—"

Leo held up his hand, cutting off my words. "Dante, we've both known Zo a long time and we both know that if Zo wants Abby, he'll find a way to get her, wherever she is. Sending her away is not the answer."

"Thank you," I said.

Dante pushed back from the table, a wild look in his eyes. "I won't let him have her, Leo—"

Leo grabbed the hinge from the table and slammed it to the floor, shattering Dante's words into silence. One of the

delicate prongs broke off with a discordant clang. Cracks spi-
derwebbed across the top of the brass case.

Leo looked down at the fractured remains glittering on the
floor. When his eyes met mine, I recoiled from the darkness
that filled them like storm clouds. "Like I said, Zo can't open a
broken door."

Leo lifted his foot and brought his heel down hard on the
edge of the hinge. The second notch fractured with an audible
snap.

"No, don't!" Dante yelled. "Wait!"

He grabbed the broken notch and examined it closely.
Then he licked his thumb and brushed it over the half-moon,
half-sun symbol on the end. The dark paint smeared.

Leo's labored breathing was loud in the suddenly quiet
room.

Dante looked up with horror in his eyes. "This isn't the
hinge, *Papà*. It's a fake."

CHAPTER
22

L eo sank into the chair, an old man again.

"How do you know it's a fake?" I asked quietly.

"Because the real hinge was brass, the carvings were done by hand, and the machine was filled with gears and springs of da Vinci's best design." Dante spun the broken prong across the table. "*This* is simply painted yellow and brown and is hollow inside." Dante dropped his head in his hands. "It's a fake."

"So . . . where is the real one?"

Dante and I both looked to Leo, who looked away.

"Leo?" Dante asked. "Do you have it here? Somewhere in the back room, or in the apartment?"

"No. If this is a fake, then the real hinge is gone." Leo spoke mechanically, his face and lips the color of ash.

"Where is it?" Dark anger entered Dante's voice.

"My best guess? Zo has it."

A sharp zing raced through me, making my fingers and toes tingle. It felt like the room shifted around me, even though I knew I was on solid ground.

"How would he have gotten it?" Dante asked in carefully controlled tones.

Leo looked shaken. "The break-in."

"What break-in?"

"You said that Tony saw you and Abby on the bank and that he told Zo about seeing the door. That was the same night I came looking for you on the bank and then went to the park to take Abby home. When I returned here, the back door was unlocked. At the time, I wondered if it had been a burglar, but nothing had been taken. I didn't think something might have been *replaced*. I figured I must have left the door unlocked in my haste that night." Leo paused, thinking. "Zo must have seen his opportunity and taken it."

Dante was silent for a long time. I could see the cords in his neck tighten with the strain of biting back the words I hoped he wouldn't say. He swallowed once, shaking his head, and said them anyway.

"Just so we're clear—Zo knows where the door is *and* he has the hinge he needs to make it work."

Leo nodded. "But at least he can't summon the door by himself."

Dante looked grim, his gray eyes the black-blue shade of rage. "Then I guess Abby is the only key he needs."

I couldn't stay at the Dungeon. I had to get away from the bleak helplessness in Leo's eyes, from the even darker anger in Dante's.

I pushed through the door, stumbling a little on the steps. I blinked in the bright sunlight—how could it still be the same

day? I felt worn out. Wrung out. Washed away on a wave of
rising fear. I took a few deep breaths, but it wasn't enough to
quell the panic. Neither was Jason's counting trick.

I heard the door open and close behind me and I inhaled
Dante's unique scent the instant before he wrapped his arms
around me. He gently eased me back against his chest and
rested his chin on my shoulder.

"*Calmati*, Abby. *Sono qui, sono qui.*"

I didn't know what he said, but the tone of his voice
soothed my nerves.

"What's happening?" I asked. "I don't understand what's
going on. Or how I got involved—" I felt a sob in the back of
my throat and closed my mouth around it so it couldn't escape.

"I am so sorry," Dante said after a long moment. "I have
failed you."

"What are you talking about?"

"I made you promises—to keep you safe, to always tell you
the truth—promises I haven't been able to keep."

"When haven't you told me the truth?"

"It's what I haven't told you."

I half laughed. "You mean there's more? Being a time-
traveling criminal isn't enough?" I felt Dante tense behind me,
and I groaned. "I'm sorry. I didn't mean it to sound like that."

"It's all right," he said. "I understand."

I closed my eyes and sighed. "It's just so weird, you know?
When Leo broke the hinge and you said it was a fake—I swear
it felt like something inside of me died. And all that stuff about
Zo . . . I'm worried he'll find me and take me to the bank anyway. And if he already has what he needs—"

"I won't let him take you," Dante said. "I promise."

"How are you going to stop him?"

Dante tightened his arms around me, moving slightly so his forehead instead of his chin rested on my shoulder. I could feel his breath against the back of my neck, cold and trembling. "I don't know yet."

We stood together in silence for a while.

"Maybe . . . maybe it might not be so bad . . ." I said quietly.

"What?"

"Well, it's just that . . . would it really be so bad if Zo left? If he went back through the door? At least then we wouldn't have to worry about him anymore."

I felt a stillness fall over Dante's body.

"I would have done it for you," I said. "If you had asked me to."

"Done what?"

"I would have gone with you to the bank. Summoned the door. You know, so you could be free." I tried to turn in Dante's embrace, but he held me fast. "If Zo hadn't stolen the hinge, that is."

"If Zo hadn't stolen the hinge, I would have broken it myself," he said tightly. "I should have broken it long ago. No one should be able to go through the door a second time. Not even me."

"Why not? I don't understand why it would be such a bad thing. You said if Zo went through the door, then he'd be free of the chains that bound him to the bank. He could stay in the river. Wouldn't it be the same for you? Wouldn't you be able to stay in the river? With me?"

"Being able to stay with you would be my greatest wish," Dante said, desire warm in his voice.

"Then why wouldn't you want to go through the door again?"

"Because if Zo—or anyone—crossed that threshold for a second time, then the door would never be closed to them again. They would have access to any point in the river—to any time in history—and they would be able to actively participate in that time. Affect events. Change things. Know things."

"So?"

"So, what if Zo entered the river at just the exact moment to prevent your parents from ever meeting?"

Goose bumps rose up on my skin.

"Exactly," he said grimly. "It would be like dropping a rock into the river. The farther back you go, the more pivotal the event you change—the more events you change, period—the more rocks you leave in the river. And too many rocks in the river could redirect the river's flow . . ."

"Or stop it altogether," I finished. My mind shied away from the words even as I spoke them.

Dante nodded behind me. "That's what I meant when I said he'd be a god. So imagine if Zo returned to a point in time, say, before da Vinci built his time machine, and destroyed the door . . . or even its maker? Can you imagine the kind of destruction that would result from a rock of that size?"

"But if he destroyed the door, then he never would have gone through it originally—to go forward in time—so he never would have gone through it a second time—to go back in time—right?" My head hurt from trying to think through the paradox. "Why would da Vinci build a machine with that kind of flaw in it?"

"He didn't," Dante said quietly. "I did."

"What? *You* built the time machine?" I stumbled around the words, confused, feeling unspeakably grateful when Dante shook his head.

"No. I built the *flaw*." Dante sighed, whispering his story to me like a confession. "Da Vinci often inserted an impossibility into his plans as a kind of protection for his ideas. If anyone tried to copy the idea, they'd copy the problem and it wouldn't work."

I heard the catch in the back of his throat.

"I had been up for days working on the plans, copying his scattered notes into one cohesive blueprint. I was so tired that night, I didn't notice that I'd changed the hinge system so the door could be switched from a one-way door to a two-way door depending on which side you inserted the hinge mechanism. I accidentally corrected da Vinci's intentional flaw—turning an impossibility into a reality.

"Once I discovered what I'd done, I tried to fix it, but I couldn't exactly erase my mistake. I knew I'd have to redraw the entire set of plans—somehow do four days' worth of work in one night—or . . ."

"Or?"

"Or I'd have to insert a problem of my own. I figured that would be just as good. After all, I didn't really think the machine would ever be built. So many of da Vinci's ideas were just ideas. He didn't have the resources or the intention of building them all. I thought I was being helpful."

"What did you do? How did you fix it?"

"What's the best way of keeping someone from opening a door they shouldn't?"

"You lock it," I said. "And you throw away the key."

"Exactly," Dante said grimly. "Zo doesn't know the door is locked. Yes, he has the hinge, but without the key, it's useless."

Sudden relief filled me up from my toes and leaked out my eyes in a swell of happy tears. I leaned my head back against Dante's shoulder, drawing in a deep, cleansing breath. "Why didn't you say that in the first place? I wouldn't have worried so much." I even managed a small laugh. "Can you imagine the look on Zo's face when he gets to the door and realizes he needs a key?" I toyed with the locket around my neck. "It's in a safe place, right? Someplace where Zo can't get to it?"

Dante kissed me on the cheek. "My first priority is keeping you safe. The key doesn't matter as long as you stay safe." He turned me in his arms, holding me close for one more moment. "Come on," he said. "I'll take you home."

❽

I was grateful for every minute I could steal away to be with Dante. When I was with him, all my problems seemed smaller and more manageable. I wasn't fooling myself, though; I knew my main problem was still Zo. And thoughts of Zo were never far away, mainly because Zo himself was often close by, circling around us like a shark sensing blood.

He, Tony, and V roamed the streets, trailing Zero Hour groupies behind them like stardust. Always in the vanguard was Valerie, holding hands with V or laughing at something Tony said or singing the chorus of a song with Zo. I'd see her from across the street and it would feel like I was looking at her from across the world. There were plenty of reasons for me to despise Zo, but I added one more to the list: *stole my best friend.*

Zero Hour still played a few songs on occasion, but not at the Dungeon. After everything that had happened, Leo wasn't willing to let them back inside. One night we saw them at the park playing a simple set—V keeping time on a small hand drum, Tony strumming an acoustic guitar, Zo's voice rising so high and pure it felt like it was holding up the stars. Part of me wanted to stay and listen even as the rest of me knew how dangerous that would be, how easy it would be to fall under their spell and follow them wherever they went.

Dante tugged at my hand and we slipped away from the park, driving through the darkness with the windows rolled down and listening to the wind sing us home.

We figured as long as I avoided Zo, surrounded myself with people who could protect me, and stayed away from the riverbank, I'd be safe enough.

CHAPTER
23

A handful of cars dotted the parking lot at Phillips Park; I pulled into an empty spot closest to the swings. I sat for a moment in my car, listening to the ticking and hissing as the engine settled into inactivity. A couple of kids ran past, laughing and screaming. In the distance, a family spread out beneath the pavilion, grilling hamburgers and passing the potato salad. A typical spring evening at the neighborhood park.

For a moment I wished my life was as typical as the ones I saw before me instead of being filled with time-traveling criminals and mind-bending explanations of reality. But would I really give up Dante to go back to my life the way it had been before? I sighed. Of course not. I climbed out of my car and crossed the grassy hills toward the swings.

Lately, I'd been coming to the park more and more often whenever Dante had to spend time on the bank. After what had happened a few weeks ago when I'd somehow dreamed my way to the bank, Dante had forbidden me from being alone while he was gone. He hoped that if I was around other people, it might anchor me to the here and now and I wouldn't accidentally go wandering in places where I didn't belong.

It had worked so far—no more unscheduled trips to the bank for me—but I thought it was more because I was terrified of running into Zo there alone than anything else. Just thinking about Zo's glittering grin made me shiver.

I slouched into one of the empty swings and pushed myself up until I was standing on my tiptoes. Leaning back, I let go and felt the rush of air across my body, spreading my hair behind me like a fan. I watched the sky tilt upside down, the blood rushing to my head. Stretching my legs out as far as they would go, I pointed my toes and let my momentum slowly rock me back and forth. My thoughts drifted in rhythm, loose and aimless.

The sky . . . the grass . . . *the river* . . . the sky . . . the grass . . . *the bank* . . . the sky . . . the shoes—

Shoes?

A pair of sling-back faux-alligator shoes filled my upside-down vision.

I only knew one person who could pull off shoes like that.

"Hi, Abby," Valerie said brightly.

I twisted my body upright, struggling to sort out the swing's chains and keep my suddenly wobbly seat. The blood rushed out of my head, leaving me a little dizzy.

"I haven't seen you around much lately." Valerie sat on the swing next to me, crossing her ankles and smoothing her hands over her jeans.

I pulled my hair away from my eyes and into a tight twist,

using the time to study Valerie. She looked different. And not in a good way.

Yes, her hair was still perfectly styled, but she'd cut it short—a trimmed bob just above her ears—and the ends looked a little brittle, the color a little dull. The style didn't suit her, either; it made her face look too round, too soft, too elastic. At the same time, though, her eyes looked narrow and pinched.

Yes, she was still dressed to the nines in designer clothes, but her dark green shirt hung a little loose on her frame, and her blue jeans looked a little faded, the cuffs fraying along the edges. Her skin tone wasn't as bright as it used to be, and the bold colors she loved so much now made her look pale and washed out.

She looked old. Old and hard and used up.

"You're a hard woman to find when you want to be," she said with a playful smile, but I could see the shadow behind her lips.

"I don't know," I said carefully. "The people who are looking for me seem to be able to find me."

Valerie laughed as though I'd made a joke. "I know, darling, you are *so* popular these days."

I couldn't tell if she was kidding or not. I didn't laugh.

"Oh, honestly, Abby, lighten up." She kicked up her heels, setting her swing to swaying gently. She closed her eyes and leaned back.

The soft light smoothed the lines away from her face, brought a pink shade to her cheeks, made her look more like the Valerie I used to know. I watched her for a moment, carefree, and remembered all the times we had played on these same swings over the years. I felt a pang inside my chest. I hadn't wanted to lose my friend. Maybe it wasn't too late.

"Sorry if I've been hard to find," I said. "I've been a little busy."

"I totally understand. Can you believe our senior year is almost over?"

I shook my head.

"I heard you got accepted to that college *somewhere back East*." Her voice was light, teasing; she sounded like her old self. "You must be so excited. What was the name of it again? Emerson?"

"Emery College." I remembered the first conversation we'd had about Emery. It seemed like a lifetime ago.

"So much for our big plans, then," she said. "No boxer terriers for us after all."

"Guess not."

We swung for a moment before I mustered up the courage to say what was on my mind.

"So, I guess you're still going on tour with Zero Hour after graduation?"

Valerie dropped her feet to the ground, dragging her heels. "What are you talking about?"

I slowed my swing to a stop and turned to face her. "Last time we talked you said you were ditching college to go with V—"

Valerie shook her head. "I'm over V. Honestly, Abby, where have you been?"

"You haven't spoken to me since the play closed." I didn't try very hard to keep the bitter tone out of my voice.

She waved her hands as though my words were meaningless. "The play really stressed me out. I barely spoke to anyone. I just needed to take a break and regroup."

"Uh-huh," I said flatly. "So what happened between you and V?"

She rolled her eyes. "The same old story. The spark went out and we went our separate ways. I caught him cheating on me. He wanted to date another girl. Take your pick—they all end the same way. With me alone and heartbroken."

She pulled back on the swing, gaining air beneath her feet. She didn't look particularly broken.

"Anyway, I didn't come here to talk about my love life."

"Why *did* you come?" I interrupted before she could say anything else. She swung to a stop and looked at me with amazement.

"I came to apologize, darling."

"To apologize," I repeated.

"For the horrible way I've treated you lately. For ignoring my best friend in her time of need."

"My time of need."

"Of course. Everyone knows you've been dating Dante— and I mean *seriously* dating. You're probably bursting with great gossip to share but haven't had anyone to talk to."

"Actually, I've been talking to Natalie—" I lied, wondering if Valerie would take the bait.

"And Natalie was the one who told me I could find you here. She said you and Dante had had some fabulously romantic outing for your first date—way back after opening night of the play. Can you believe it's been that long since we've talked? Anyway, Natalie said Dante took you someplace out of this world. She said it was some great secret and that I'd have to ask you about it."

Oh, Valerie, I thought sadly.

"So, come on, Abby. Tell your best friend everything. Let's catch up, like old times."

Maybe it was the phrase *best friend* that did it. Maybe it was the false brightness in her eye. Maybe it was the months of watching her pull away from her old life and her old friends to submerge herself without resistance in a new life with new friends. Maybe it was all of it, but at that moment I felt the sharp bite of anger latch onto my chest, crushing my breath in its jaws.

"Cut the act," I snapped.

"What are you talking about?"

"Natalie didn't know I would be here, so she couldn't have told you anything. She couldn't have told you anything anyway, because I haven't told *her* anything secret about my relationship with Dante."

"So you *are* keeping secrets about Dante."

I didn't bother to reply. Instead, I hopped out of the swing and started to walk away. My flash of hot anger had burned away, leaving my chest cold and full of ashes.

"Is it about where he disappears to every so often? Do you know where he is right now?" she called after me.

I knew exactly where Dante was, but I wasn't about to tell Valerie.

"He's *there,* isn't he?"

My steps slowed, then stopped. I didn't dare turn around, afraid of what I would see on Valerie's face, more afraid of what would show on my own.

"Did Zo send you?" I closed my eyes against the truth I feared to hear.

I heard Valerie's shoes crunch on the gravel behind me. I felt her presence close against my back.

"Tell me how he did it, Abby," she whispered. "That's all Zo wants to know. Just tell me so I can go back to my own sweet Italian boyfriend."

"I thought you were through with V."

"I am. Hard to believe it, but you were right all along. It's not the drummer who controls the band—it's the lead singer. It's Zo. And I'm Zo's girl now." Valerie circled around to face me. "Just tell me what I want to know."

I looked her in the eyes, hoping I would see the old Valerie in them, the Valerie I'd known since forever. But she'd spent so much time with Zero Hour lately that I saw only Zo reflected in her eyes—his emotions, his desires, his wishes. She was right: She was Zo's girl now, through and through. She had become as dangerous to me as he was. I had to look away, my heart sore at losing my friend for the second time. I swallowed hard and summoned up my courage.

"No. I won't tell you anything."

I watched the change fall over Valerie's face like a mask. Gone were the soft, round curves of her face, replaced with harsh angles and shadows. The friendly false light in her eyes snuffed out in an instant. Her red lips thinned like a wound beginning to clot.

"He doesn't need you, you know. Whatever it is, *I* can help him. *I* can take him where he wants to go. Not you."

"You don't know what you're saying. You don't know what Zo is planning to do."

"I know he promised to take me with him."

"What?" I forced the word through numb lips.

A satisfied smile curved her mouth like a bow. "He said that when he left, he'd take me with him. That we'd be together forever. That he'd show me things I couldn't imagine." She bared her teeth at me. "So I hope you enjoy your time with Dante. You'll never have what I have with Zo."

Then she turned on her heel and walked away.

I heard the familiar sound of Valerie's Lexus roaring to life and then the high squeal of tires as she raced out of the parking lot.

She was in danger and she didn't even know it.

I jogged to my car and revved the engine. My thoughts raced faster than my car did on the way to the Dungeon.

Valerie's parting words simmered in my mind, which bubbled with questions and uncertainty. The bank was certainly an unimaginable destination, but somehow I didn't think that was Zo's intention. If he couldn't get what he wanted from me, would he try to take someone else to the bank? Would he try to take Valerie? If he did, and if the door appeared for her as it had for me, then what? Zo still wouldn't be able to open the door, so what would he do with Valerie? Zo wouldn't think twice about leaving her stranded on the bank. And if he did that . . . well, the consequences didn't bear thinking about.

I pulled into the Dungeon's parking lot, not bothering to straighten my car neatly between the painted lines, not bothering to lock my doors. I ran through the door and past the handful of couples scattered around the dance floor. I maneuvered my way around the pool tables toward the long bar where Leo was busy mixing one of his signature Tropical Treasures for Lily. I slid onto the bar stool next to her, tapping my fingers on the counter.

"Hi, Abby," Lily said.

"Hi," I answered absently. I tried to catch Leo's eye to let him know I needed to talk.

Leo took in my disheveled hair and flushed skin and nodded. "I'd be happy to help if you can wait a moment."

As I nodded, he handed Lily her drink. "Enjoy. There's a treasure just for you at the bottom of the glass." He smiled at her.

"Thanks," Lily said. Then she turned to me. "So, Abby, are you going to the Spring Fling with Dante this weekend?"

"Um, yeah, I guess so." With everything else on my mind, I hadn't given the dance much thought.

Lily looked around. "Where is he, anyway? I didn't see him here, so I assumed he was with you."

Leo and I exchanged a glance I hoped Lily missed.

"Oh, well—"

"If you see him, tell him I have those notes from math he asked to borrow."

"Sure thing."

Lily bounced off her seat, heading back to the table where Ethan was waiting.

I glanced around the room once, then turned immediately to Leo. "I need to talk to you."

"So I gathered. You're not very subtle—you know that, right?"

"It's about—"

"Zo and Valerie."

My jaw dropped open. "How did you know?"

"Dante." Leo flipped a towel over his shoulder. "He's been seeing some strange ripples in the river lately."

"And he didn't tell me?"

"I told him not to."

"Why would you do that?" Even if Valerie and I weren't friends anymore, I couldn't just abandon her to Zo's machinations.

"Because you're in some of the ripples," Leo said calmly. "And you remember the rules, don't you?"

"I know, I know, I'm not supposed to know because it'll interfere with my decisions, blah blah blah." I slammed my hand on the bar, earning myself some strange looks from the other customers and a frown from Leo. "What good is being able to see the future if you can't do anything about it?" I hissed.

"What would you do if you knew?" Leo asked.

"I don't know—something!"

"What if that something was the exact wrong thing to do?"

"What if it was the right thing to do?"

"How would you know the difference?"

I ground my teeth together. "How would *you?*"

"Abby, I know it's hard," Leo said, leaning over the bar. "But the river is too volatile right now to know anything for sure. Until it settles down, or until Dante or I can make sense of what he's seeing . . ." He shrugged.

"What am I supposed to do, then?" I felt tears of frustration well up. "Am I just supposed to let Zo have her? What if he hurts her worse than he already has? What if he tries to take her to the bank?"

"He can't."

"Oh, that's right," I snapped. "He needs me for that. Because I'm *special*."

Leo spread his white towel on the bar with a careful hand. "Don't discount yourself, Abby. You *are* special. And that's why we will protect you—"

I opened my mouth, but Leo overrode my words.

"*And* we'll protect Valerie to the best of our ability. I promise you, *mia donna di luce*. Please. Trust me. And if you can't do that—trust Dante."

I folded my arms on the bar and dropped my head on them. That was the clincher—I trusted Dante with all my heart—and I suspected Leo knew that.

"I'm just worried," I mumbled into the bar.

"I know. You are a good friend."

"I hope that's enough."

CHAPTER
24

Dante returned from the bank in time for the Spring Fling. Thankfully it wasn't a formal dance like Valentine's had been, so I didn't have to worry about wearing the wrong dress. In fact, I didn't have to wear a dress at all if I didn't want to. The theme was April Showers and May Flowers, and the boys were all supposed to come as something water-related (whatever that meant) and the girls were supposed to come as flowers.

"Costumes?" Dante had said when I told him about the dance.

"They're optional. But it's traditional. Formal dances are Christmas, Valentine's, and prom. Fun dances are the sock hop, Halloween, and the Spring Fling. Don't tell me you didn't go to dances back home."

"Not in costume," he said.

"Then think of this as an adventure." I kissed his cheek. "So which flower should I be?"

He curled me close to his chest, nuzzling his face into my hair. "Mmmm, can't you be all of them? My own bouquet of beauty? Like daisies opening their friendly petals." He brushed his fingertips over my eyelids. "Or marigolds that burn like the summer sun." He rubbed his hands over my back. "Or orchids—rare and exotic." He traced a finger across my collarbone down to rest lightly on the locket I wore all the time. "Roses for passion." He kissed me.

"You, sir, are too smooth for your own good," I remarked with a fluttering smile, leaning against his chest and closing my eyes in sweet bliss.

❇

I was remembering that kiss as we walked across the crowded dance floor looking for Jason and Natalie. Natalie had suggested we double-date, but that still felt a little weird for me, so I told her we'd just find them at the dance.

Dante, with his height, spotted them first. He squeezed my hand and then pointed to the far side of the gym, which was decorated with paper cutout storm clouds and raindrops and wallpapered with colorful flowers and green grasses. I stood on my toes, trying to see past a kid dressed as a shower—complete with curtain—and saw Jason's familiar golden curls. We pressed on through a garden of girls in flowered dresses, past Poseidon with his trident, and paused while two storm clouds rumbled by (boys in gray sweats covered with gray cotton balls—pretty creative, I thought).

"Abby, you look beautiful!" Natalie gushed when we reached her. She hugged me and then held me back to look at my outfit.

I had come as a white rose: a full skirt layered with white

lace, a pale pink silk cami underneath a sheer, short-sleeved blouse, Dante's silver locket resting in the hollow of my throat. Dante had also given me a single white rose to wear in my hair. He said I looked like an angel; I felt like I was surrounded by a cloud of light.

"Guess what flower I am?" Natalie asked. I started to shake my head, but she didn't wait for me. "A sunflower! Well, deconstructed, of course, I'm not tall enough to pull it off for real. See, here's my 'stalk'"—she brushed her green skirt—"and my beautiful petals"—a bright yellow shirt—"and the brown seeds on top"—she took off a dark brown hat that crowned her hair. "And here's my sun." She twined her arm around Jason's elbow.

Dressed in tan slacks and a muted brown shirt, the only sunshine things about him were his golden-blond curls and his dazzling smile. That was enough, though; he and Natalie were a perfectly matched pair.

"Did you decide not to come in costume, Dante?" Jason asked.

Dante looked stricken. He'd agreed to dress up as long as he got to pick what he was going to wear. "I'm Charon," he said. His dark pants and long-sleeved shirt didn't look that different from the clothes he usually wore. Tied to his belt, though, was a bag filled with coins. He hefted the bag in his hand. "Charon—the ferryman who takes souls across the river Styx?"

"Right, of course, Charon—" Natalie started.

"And the river Styx," finished Jason.

"It's okay," I told them. "I didn't know who he was either, the first time I saw him."

Dante shot me a dirty look and bumped my shoulder with his.

"Careful—you'll muss me." I pretended to pat my hair into place and we all laughed.

The music kicked up a notch, a wild beat that thankfully wasn't from a Zero Hour song. Jason pulled Natalie to the dance floor; Dante glanced at me.

"May I have this dance, fair lady?"

I gave him my answer in a grin and we spun onto the floor that was already filled with light and color.

We danced song after song, filled with endless energy and laughter. We switched partners at one point—me dancing with Jason; Dante with Natalie—and then back again. The music took a breath and then released the soft melody of "Time after Time."

"I love this song," I said as we slowed our steps to match the languid pace of the jazzy cover by J. J. O'Hare. Dante enfolded me in his arms and I rested my head against his chest, lulled by the steady beat of his heart next to my ear.

As we turned in a circle, I heard someone approaching.

I knew it was Zo even with my eyes closed because the world tightened around me. It was like when Dante kissed me, but instead of a close and comfortable cocoon, it was a sharp-edged trap poised to snap shut.

Dante, ever graceful, stumbled a little as we slowed to a stop.

"Ah, so sorry," Zo purred. "I've interrupted the lovebirds."

"You shouldn't be here," Dante said. He deftly turned so I was behind him, still keeping me close to him but keeping everyone else at bay.

"That's sweet," Zo said. "Still trying to protect the weak and the helpless." His eyes roamed over my face, intent and hungry.

"I'm not weak," I said, proud that my voice held firm. "And I'm not afraid of you."

Zo laughed, a vibrant roll of music. "There's no reason you should be. I'm no threat to you."

Dante narrowed his eyes. "I won't let you have her."

"I don't want her." He shrugged, a sly smile on his face. "She's useless to me. But please, Dante, if *you* have found some use for her, then by all means, *you* should enjoy her."

Dante, already on edge, tensed. I think he would have swung at Zo had I not been holding his arm.

Zo noticed. He leaned back on his heels, confident and strong, and folded his arms across his chest. The billowing sleeves of his crisp white shirt were folded back to display his chain tattoos. A bandanna covered his dark hair and a small gold hoop earring dangled from his left ear.

He must have seen me looking because he extended a bow in my direction. "The Pirate King, at your service. I just love costume parties, don't you?"

The effect would have been comical on most men, but Zo wasn't most men.

"Let me guess, Dante—you've come as Charon? Why am I not surprised that you stuck to the classics. I do find it rather appropriate, though. Charon was enslaved to the river, endlessly traveling back and forth on a meaningless, uninspired errand. While I am free to travel wherever—and whenever—I wish. Ah, the life of a pirate is truly liberating. I'd recommend you try it sometime, but unfortunately, there is only one key that can allow you passage to that life, and something tells me you don't have it anymore."

"Give it back," I blurted, feeling my anger rising. "It doesn't belong to you."

"Ah, the rose has thorns after all," Zo said, showing the points of his teeth in a feral grin.

"The door you seek won't open for you," Dante said quietly.

Zo's eyes lit on me and I shrank back against Dante's shoulder. "I don't need it to. I just need it to open for her." Zo turned, extending his hand, and pulled Valerie to his side. She squeaked a little as he tightened his hold and nuzzled against her neck. "My saucy little pirate wench," he said, nipping at her earlobe.

I hadn't seen Valerie standing behind him in his shadow, and I barely recognized her in the flickering light of the dance. She wore a black sheath dress, form-fitting and curving in all the right places. Elbow-length gloves encased her hands and forearms in black silk. She was a shadow in the night except for the sparkling necklace encircling her throat; I wondered if Zo could afford real diamonds.

"I'm not a wench," she pouted. "I'm your *belladonna*."

"That's right, love," Zo agreed. "My deadly nightshade."

Valerie wriggled closer to him, placing her gloved hands on either side of his face and kissing him passionately.

I turned away, feeling physically ill to see them together

like that. I wondered if she even knew I was there or if she only had eyes for Zo now.

"You wouldn't dare," Dante said. "You don't know how."

"Don't I?" Zo asked, caressing Valerie's arm draped around his neck. "Are you sure about that?"

"Don't do this, Zo. Please."

"What other choice do I have? You forced me into this, Dante. You and your accursed machine. I'll die before I let you take this from me as well."

"What if it's not you who dies?" he asked quietly.

"Zo's told me the risks and what might happen," Valerie said, running a finger along the side of his neck. "And I'm willing to do it. It's my choice."

I highly doubted she had made that choice on her own.

"Why else would I have done this?" she asked, stripping off her gloves. Her pale skin flowed smooth and unmarked to her wrists, where she was cuffed with matching black chain tattoos complete with red lines of fresh pain.

"Isn't it amazing what some focused attention and the right song can do to a person?" Zo said, a laugh bubbling underneath his words. He reached for Valerie's hands and kissed her wrists, right then left. "She is the best thing to come along in a long time. I don't know how I'd do this without her."

"Zo—" Dante started, but Zo's laughter cut him off.

The Pirate King gathered up his belladonna, turning on his heel. "I'd say I'll see you soon, Dante, but if I have my way, I'll never see you again."

The shifting crowd swallowed them up, leaving Dante and me isolated in a pocket of disbelief.

I managed to find my voice buried beneath a tumbling mountain of fear and uncertainty. "Why was Valerie like that? It's like she was someone else entirely. Like she was on drugs or something."

"An apt comparison," Dante said. "She's been spending months with Zo and his friends. I fear she's not the Valerie you once knew."

"When do you think he'll try it?"

"I don't know," Dante said. "It depends on if he really knows how to get her to the bank. If he does, then he won't wait long."

One song ended and another one started before I spoke again.

"Will she be okay?"

"I hope so." Dante quietly wrapped his arms around me as the music thundered around us like a storm. "I hope so."

CHAPTER
25

After seeing Zo at the dance, neither one of us felt like staying any longer. We said our good-byes to Jason and Natalie and bolted. The cool spring air felt like a soothing balm on my fevered skin. My mind kept repeating a dangerous couple of facts: Zo sounded like he knew how to take Valerie to the bank, and Valerie was willing to go despite the danger. The one fact I held onto was that Zo still needed the key. We could still stop him as long as he didn't get his hands on the key.

Dante suggested we stop at Helen's Café for a late-night breakfast, but I was too wound up to eat.

We drove home in silence, and he pulled Leo's Mustang into my driveway.

"Dante?" I asked, my anxiety tasting like copper. "What has Zo done to Valerie? What was all that stuff he said about 'the right song'?"

Dante rubbed his thumb against the back of my hand.

"They're breaking rule number one: They're deliberately upsetting the balance."

"How? Why—?"

Dante gently interrupted my questions. "Do you remember

what I told you about the pressure we feel? About how when there is too much, we have to go to the bank to burn it off? I've suspected for some time that Zo and his friends have found a way to . . . channel . . . some of that pressure so they don't have to go back to the bank as often." Dante's eyes were serious.

"How is that possible?"

"Time may be fluid, but it still follows rules. I think Zo has figured out a way to channel the pressure through something structured—like a poem or a song. I think it has something to do with the rhythm of the words, the cadence of the voice, the counting of the beats." Dante shrugged. "I wouldn't have thought it was possible, but there is a lot about this that seems impossible."

"Can you do it?" I asked, my mind tumbling with hope.

"I've only tried it once. At the Poetry Slam back in February. Just to see if I could. Just to see how Zo did it." He looked away. "In some ways, it was worse than just going to the bank. I don't know how he stands it."

"How could it be worse?" I asked. "I mean, wouldn't it be a good thing if you didn't have to go to the bank all the time?"

Dante shook his head. "The balance is set for a reason. It's to protect us as much as it is to protect the river. What Zo's doing . . . when he's redirecting the pressure—the time—back into the river, it's like he's creating a little whirlpool of emotion. The people who are caught up in the whirlpool feel a sense of heightened emotions—usually whatever emotion Zo is feeling at the time."

I felt like a living cliché as a light went off in my head. "So when Zero Hour played at the Dungeon, Zo was feeling excited and energized by being able to channel away the extra pressure through his songs—through Zero Hour's songs. And so we all felt excited and energized too, right?" I remembered so clearly that night when I'd first met Zo and what he'd said to me: "*I thank you for your acceptance of me tonight.*" Only now did I realize that what I'd accepted was a dose of his excess emotion. "And then on Valentine's Day, he was angry with you after your fight, so then the crowd was angry too." I shook my head. "No wonder everyone broke up that night."

It all seemed so clear to me now.

Dante looked at me with a strange expression on his face.

"What? Did I say something wrong?"

"No, you're exactly right. It's just . . . every time I think I have you figured out, you surprise me."

"I'm not that complicated," I said, blushing slightly.

"Yes, you are, Abby. It's one of the things I appreciate about you."

"So if you knew what Zo was doing with his music, why did you let them play that first night at the Dungeon?"

Dante grimaced. "We didn't know. Not until later. Not until it was too late."

"And now it's too late for Valerie," I murmured. "She's changed and it's all Zo's fault. He's been dumping his"—I frowned in distaste—"*leftovers* into her for months. It's no wonder she's completely in thrall to his wishes." I sighed. "He's not going to let her go, is he?"

"Maybe he will," Dante said, but he didn't sound entirely convinced.

"So tell me how it works," I said the next night as I sat with Dante at the bar of the Dungeon.

"How what works?" he asked, his attention focused on the papers in front of him. Leo was on the bank and the Dungeon had been closed all day. It was just the two of us at the bar— me munching on peanuts from a shallow bowl, Dante working on his history report: the inventions of da Vinci. I'd spent hours at the library researching for my report on Edison; he was writing his report from memory.

"It. You know—the time machine."

Dante's hand paused midword, the end of his "t" making a sharp line instead of its usual curved tail.

"Why do you want to know?" he asked quietly.

"Because you said you helped build it. I've never met anyone who's built a time machine before. I'm interested."

Dante set down his pen and closed his notebook. "You shouldn't be interested."

"Are you kidding me?" I dropped my handful of peanuts back into the bowl and shoved him hard on the shoulder. "The most important invention in the history of the world and the guy who worked on it is sitting right next to me and you tell me I'm not supposed to be interested?"

A grin stole across his face. "I don't know if it was the *most* important invention."

"It brought you to me," I said. "I think that's pretty important."

Dante's skin turned a dusky rose; he was even more hand-some when he blushed.

"Tell me what you miss most about home," I said propping my elbows on the bar, resting my head in the palm of my hand.

Dante shuffled the papers into a loose stack, his fingers fidgeting restlessly. The low glow of the Dungeon's lights ca-ressed his dark curls. He selected a blank sheet of plain white paper and rolled a pen between his fingers for a moment be-fore setting the tip to the paper and beginning to draw. "The quiet," he said finally. "It's so noisy here. So much rushing around. Everyone is in such a hurry. Back home . . ." He cleared his throat. "Back home, the pace was much slower. There was more time for quiet. For thinking."

"And what did you think about in all that quiet?"

"You," he said, grinning impishly, his attention still on the paper.

I rolled my eyes. "Liar. You didn't even know me. Tell me the truth this time."

"I thought about my future," he said. He kept his pen mov-ing, fast and precise, drawing and sketching. "Though I never thought it would be like this."

"Better? Or worse?"

He looked up at me then, laying his pen down on the bar. "Both," he said, sliding his hand behind my neck and pulling me close for a kiss.

His lips were unusually warm but I still shivered at their touch.

"What did you think your future would hold?" I asked

when he finally let me go. I settled down on my own bar stool, but I kept my fingers entwined with his.

He stroked my hair away from my forehead and I closed my eyes briefly under his gentle touch.

"Tell me about Jason," he said quietly, picking up his pen and resuming his drawing.

"Why?" I frowned. I didn't want to ruin the moment by talking about my ex-boyfriend. I tried to catch a glimpse of Dante's work, but he tilted it away from me so all I could see was a series of connecting lines, right angles, and wavy swirls.

"Because we hardly talked to him at the Spring Fling and I'm curious about the man who's known you almost your entire life."

"Then you should ask me to tell you about my dad. He *has* known me for my entire life."

Dante shifted next to me. "Eternity changes your perspective, Abby. Having been on both sides of the clock, I know how precious time is. How valuable. So what was it about Jason that made him worth so much of your time?"

Looking into those soft gray eyes I could see that Dante really wanted to know.

"Did you love him?" he asked me softly.

"Yes," I answered immediately. I saw a shadow cross Dante's face and hurried to explain. "Jason was—is—a great guy," I started, feeling my way through the awkwardness of articulating things that I'd never voiced before. "In the beginning, it was just . . . I don't know . . . easy to be friends with him. We grew up together. We liked all the same things." A thousand memories flooded through my mind. "It was easy to be his girlfriend, too. I think everyone assumed we were dating, so maybe it was one of those cases where the perception became the reality."

"Tell me what you loved about him."

"I'm not really comfortable talking about this—"

He pressed a finger to my lips. "It's all right. I can handle the truth. Tell me."

I sighed and closed my eyes, thinking. "He always had a Plan B," I said finally, opening my eyes.

Dante's eyebrows drew close together.

"When I was with Jason I always knew that, no matter what happened, he would have a Plan B in case something went wrong. If the movie we wanted to see was sold out, he'd suggest going bowling. If the bowling alley was full, he'd suggest a picnic in the park. If it was too cold for that, he'd challenge me to a game of Scrabble."

"I don't understand," Dante said. "You loved him because he had good social skills?"

"No, not exactly." I sighed. "I'm not explaining this very well. Jason had a . . . a certain quiet quality about him. A confidence that came because he was *prepared*. For anything. He planned ahead. He thought through every variable." I shrugged. "I liked the security. The stability. I never had to think about our relationship because I knew Jason had already done that. Like I said, it was easy being his girlfriend."

Dante was quiet for a long time. The only sound was the faint scratching of his pen on paper. "Why did you break up with him?"

"Technically, *he* broke up with *me*. Stupid Zo and his stupid band," I muttered ruefully.

"Zo's interference wouldn't have had any influence on your relationship if it wasn't already fragile and ready to break," Dante pointed out. "Why weren't you happy with Jason at the end?"

"Because he always had a Plan B," I said, shrugging again. "I know, it sounds all wrong, but it's the truth. You have to understand: Jason knew everything about me; I knew everything about him. There were no surprises with him. Ever. Jason wasn't a life-without-limits kind of guy. If something unexpected happened, he was right there to control it, organize it, classify it. The word *spontaneous* wasn't exactly in his working vocabulary. For a while, though, it was enough. And then . . ." I waited until Dante looked up from his work.

"And then?"

"And then it wasn't anymore." I reached up my hand and traced his strong jaw. He closed his eyes at my touch. "And then I met someone else."

"I can't offer you the same stability as Jason—"

My hand slipped from his jaw to cover his mouth. "I only have so much time, you know, and I want to spend it with someone who is ready, willing, and capable of living without limits. I want spontaneity. I want surprises. I want to spend my time with you."

Dante looked at me with those unfathomable gray eyes. I felt a smile curving his soft lips beneath my hand. He brushed his palm up my arm, curling his hand around mine. He gently pressed a kiss to the inside of my wrist, on the vein that pulsed with my heartbeat. His dark hair fell in soft waves over my skin.

"You are a gift, Abby. One I will treasure forever."

I felt a wave of emotion rise up in me because I knew that when Dante said *forever,* he meant it literally.

He kissed my wrist one more time before releasing my hand. Reaching for his paper, he folded the drawing into thirds and slipped it into an envelope and then slipped the envelope into his notebook.

Dante's low voice was a whisper. *"Grazie."*

"For what?"

"For being there when I needed you."

"Oh, well, in that case"—I smiled—*"Prego."*

His eyes lit up at my rough attempt at Italian.

"I've been practicing," I admitted with a shy smile.

"I've always thought Italian spoken by the lips of a beautiful woman sounds delicious." He leaned close to me, so close I could smell the sweetness of his skin.

I closed my eyes, my lips tingling in anticipation, when the dull thud of footsteps sounded from the apartment upstairs.

I felt the air change as Dante pulled away from me, the kiss suspended between us.

"Something's wrong." He frowned and took a step toward the door marked "Employees Only" just as the door swung open.

Leo stumbled out, his hair slicked back with sweat, his eyes haunted. Tremors shook his body. His skin looked paper-thin, stretched too tight over his frame.

"Papà? Papà!" Dante rushed to Leo's side, sliding under his

arm to help support him. Together they managed the few steps to the closest table. Leo was mumbling in Italian, his words pouring out so fast it sounded like one long, endless loop of panic.

"Slow down, *Papà,* slow down. I can't understand you." Dante knelt by Leo's side. "Tell me what's wrong. Tell me what has happened."

Leo took a deep breath and placed his hands on Dante's cheeks. He spoke three words slowly and clearly. And in Italian.

Dante's face paled beyond white. Even his lips turned the hard shade of marble.

I could feel his fear from where I sat at the bar. "What is it?" I managed to ask. "What did he say?"

Dante had to swallow twice before any words made their way out of his throat. "He said, 'He's taken her.'"

"Who?" I asked, though I already knew the answer. "Who's taken—?"

"Zo," Dante said quietly, his brittle voice on the edge. "Zo's taken Valerie to the bank." His words fell off the edge and broke in the silence that filled the Dungeon as the three of us looked at each other in stunned disbelief.

"You said he couldn't do that. You said you'd protect her. What's he going to do . . . ?" I didn't want to finish the question; I didn't want to hear the answer.

"He's going to try to summon the door," Leo said clearly, his voice sounding older than his age. "And when that fails, he's going to kill her."

CHAPTER
26

W e have to stop him," Dante said.

"I thought he'd stop himself. He doesn't have the key . . ." I said, confused.

"The lock will stop him from going through the door. It won't stop him from killing Valerie."

The fear I'd managed to avoid all day returned tenfold.

Dante was all business. "What happened, *Papà?* What did you see?"

"I was preparing to leave when I saw them," Leo said. "First Zo with Valerie, then Tony and V. They're all there. Together."

"What about the door? Did they find the door?"

Leo shook his head. "I followed them, trying to catch up to them, but you know how deceptive distances can be there. I stayed as long as I could—longer than I probably should have—but I didn't see the bridge or the door. Not before I had to leave. I'm sorry, Dante, I had to come back."

Dante nodded, gripping Leo's trembling hand with his own. "I understand, *Papà.* Be calm. You're all right now. You're safe." He stood up, pacing in front of the table, his head down, deep in thought.

"*I* don't understand," I said, crossing to Dante's side and matching his pace. "Why didn't he stop them? Why did he come back?"

"If Leo had stayed there any longer, we would have lost him," Dante said quietly to me. He glanced at Leo, who was hunched over the table, his body racked with spasms. "It was a close thing, even still."

My mouth went dry. "He's not"—I mouthed the word *crazy*—"is he?"

Dante shook his head. "No, but he can't go back to the bank for a while. It's too dangerous for him and I can't risk losing him."

"What about Valerie?"

"I'll go." Dante didn't hesitate. "I'll bring her back."

I gripped his arm, stopping him midstride. "Dante—" I hated myself for even thinking of asking him not to go. But I couldn't help myself. Two emotions warred in my heart, each demanding dominance: gratitude that Dante would be willing to risk himself; fear that he wouldn't come back.

"Someone has to go and it can't be Leo and it certainly can't be you." Dante smiled his small smile he reserved just for me. "Trust me, Abby."

"But it's not just Zo—Tony and V are with him too. It'll be three against one. And I don't know if Valerie will exactly be willing to come back with you . . ."

Dante cupped my cheek with his hand. "You know it has to be this way."

"I know, it's just . . . I don't want to lose you, either."

"You won't. I promise."

"How can you be so sure?"

Dante brought his other hand to my face, tilting my mouth to meet his. His kiss was sweet and tender, but banked with a hot passion that warmed his lips and left me melting.

"Stay with him, Abby. Please? I don't want either of you to be alone tonight."

"Of course," I said. "We'll both be right here when you get back. Which better be soon, you know."

"As soon as I can." He kissed me once more—just a brush and a breath—and when I opened my eyes, he was already gone.

❽

At Leo's request I turned off the lights in the main part of the Dungeon. The stage and dance floor were silent and still. It was weird to see the place so empty.

I left the lights on behind the bar, though. A pale yellow glow reflected off the large mirror on the back wall, sheening the bottles in a rainbow of colors. I glanced at the mirror, turning my face to the light like it was the sun. The shadows behind me were reflected too. It reminded me of a golden river of light flanked by banks of shadowed night. My own reflection was lost in the shadows and I suddenly wished I'd thought of a different metaphor.

"Is he back yet?" I asked.

"It's only been a few minutes." Leo had stopped shaking,

but his voice had lost its usual deep timbre. He sat at a table, his shirt collar unbuttoned and loose, his breathing slowly returning to normal.

"How long will it take?"

"As long as it does."

I was filled with too much restless energy.

I puttered—cleaning, sweeping—in order to keep my emotions at bay: the fretting, the worrying.

"Is he back—"

"No, Abby, he's not."

"Are you sure we can't help?"

"We can help by staying here." Leo squeezed his eyes shut, resting his head in his hands.

I grumbled, but I knew he was right. I wandered through the quiet Dungeon, absently flipping chairs onto tables, dragging my fingers over the multicolored names on the wall. I saw Jason's name. Natalie's. Valerie's. I traced my own name on the wall and remembered signing it the night Zero Hour had played. So much had changed since then. How much more would change before this night was over? Zero Hour's name and logo looked like a scar burned on the wall.

"Abby. Please. Come sit down. You're making me nervous." Leo paused. "Or would you rather go home to wait?"

"No!" That would be even worse. There, I had no one who would understand. Here, at least I had Leo. And I had promised Dante I would wait for him.

I made my way back to the pool of light splashing down on the bar and sat next to Leo at the table.

"Dante's been gone plenty of times and you've waited for him without complaint."

"All those other times, I knew he'd come back to me."

"And he will again this time."

"But this time he has to deal with Zo." I shook my head. "I only saw them together on the bank that one time, but it was scary how much stronger Zo was there. When he grabbed Dante by the wrist . . ."

"Dante can take care of himself."

But I could hear the worry in his voice.

I offered him some aspirin for his headache, but he said it wasn't that kind of pain. He said the only thing that would help was time.

"Has it ever been this bad before?" I asked quietly. Leo seemed to be feeling better, but I didn't know how long it would take for him to fully recover.

"A few times," Leo said. "Not for a long time, though. The last time the pain was this bad . . ." He shook his head.

"What happened then?"

"It was when I found Dante on the bank."

I sat up, interested. Here was a story I hadn't heard.

"I had gone to the bank. I was checking for newcomers. I never know when they're going to show up, of course, but they usually arrive in the same place, so I make it a point to go there as often as I can—just in case." Leo's voice took on the cadence of a storyteller.

"One day—about a year or so ago—I found him. Fresh through the door. The air around him still seemed to echo with the chimes of time travel. I couldn't believe it. When I approached him, his eyes were closed and I could hear him counting."

I remembered Dante telling me about his journey through time and how he'd counted the steps into the future.

"I introduced myself and explained briefly about the bank and the river, about what he could expect from his new life. And then I brought him home."

"Where he lived for a year before you let him come to school. Why so long?"

"Like anyone, it takes us time to acclimatize to new surroundings. Plus, I had to teach him the language, the customs. I had to arrange for his paperwork. Obtaining a driver's license isn't easy when you don't exactly have a valid birth certificate."

I smiled. "It sounds like a lot of work," I said. "Why do you do it?"

"The gates of heaven have Saint Peter to help usher souls into their new life. I thought the door to hell should have someone too."

"'Saint' Leo?"

He smiled faintly. "Something like that. I tell the newcomers that it's easier all around if they think of this as a kind of afterlife. Their old life is dead and they are here in . . . well, it's certainly not heaven. I like to think of it as a second chance—at life, at everything." He shrugged. "I try to help them adjust. Help them follow the rules. Sometimes it works. Sometimes it doesn't. Eventually, I let them go, hoping they will find some happiness."

I felt a knot of emotion rise up in my throat. "Thank you, Leo. Thank you for helping Dante." I brushed away the tears at the edge of my eyes. "I hope someone was able to help you the same way you helped him."

"You are kind, Abby. But I was the first one. And God willing, Dante will be the last." He said it so softly I wondered if he'd meant to say it at all.

"Dante told me a little of what it was like for him," I said carefully, trying to coax Leo into further conversation, not wanting to scare him into silence.

Leo shuddered, just a shifting of his shoulders, a tightening of his jaw, an unreadable expression on his face—a reflex of remembered pain.

"How long has it been for you?"

Glass fell over his eyes as he looked beyond me. "I was born in 1480. They closed the door behind me in 1500. I was only twenty years old then."

I did the math in my head but something didn't add up. "So, you've been here just a little longer than Dante?"

A ghost of a smile materialized. "Oh, no, I've been here much longer than Dante. He's only been here a year or so."

"But if you left in 1500 and came forward more than five hundred years—"

The smile hardened into flint. "I only came forward *one month*."

For the first time since Dante had left, my body stilled. I looked again at Leo, this time with clear eyes. He was old, yes—a mane of white hair, weary lines around his faded blue eyes—but now I could also see the ageless quality he carried about him as well. "You don't look like you're still twenty," I said.

"I'm not. I've aged a little over the years."

I could barely form the words. "So you didn't *skip* those years like Dante did—"

"I lived them." Leo nodded. "All five hundred and nine of them." He rubbed his wrist with his hand, chafing his faded chains that were so similar to Dante's and yet so different. "I've learned much and forgotten more. I've traveled the world. Seen things I'd never thought were possible. I've watched empires rise and fall. Survived war. Enjoyed peace." His eyes looked far away. "It's been so long since I've told the true story of my life."

"We've got time," I said.

Leo smiled sadly. "It seems all I have anymore is time and my memories."

"Tell *me* the story, then. You already know you can trust me."

Leo looked at me strangely, his eyes at once soft and scared. "I know, *mia donna di luce.*"

I recognized the endearment and I wanted to ask him why he called me that, but I didn't want to distract him from the story.

"I first saw the door in December 1500. It had never been opened yet, never been tried. I stood before the door and saw equal parts redemption and damnation.

"Redemption because if I did as they wished—if I tested the machine—they promised they'd protect my family and clear my name. Maybe I could still be the hero my mother thought I was.

"Damnation because I didn't really believe it would work—

I mean, a time machine? It was impossible. But if by some miracle I did survive the passage, if I did return alive, it would only be to face the friends I had named as traitors and betrayers. I had no illusions that I'd survive their revenge." He shook his head. "Sometimes I wonder if all this still isn't some part of my punishment.

"But I didn't have much choice. War and anger and fear make people do horrible things. I know. I've done my fair share of them.

"But, Abby, when I first met him . . . I thought he was an angel sent from God Himself to save us. He had a way about him, a charisma that was undeniable. And his voice . . . he'd say something and you'd just *know* it was true because how could something as foul as a lie come out of a face that fair?

"I learned too late how many lies he told.

"He said he believed in our war, but that we were on the wrong side. He said if we were true patriots—true sons of Italy—we'd do everything we could to end the war and bring victory to the other side.

"And I believed him. I believed *in* him. And so I—and others—followed him. We swore a pact, a bond of secrecy, a conspiracy of brotherhood.

"We met in dark back rooms, talking, plotting, planning. But it seemed like all we did was talk. Some of us were getting restless, wondering when our leader would channel his passion into action.

"I was perhaps the most vocal—demanding action, frustrated by our useless, childish talk. One evening I let my feelings be known, haranguing him endlessly.

"He cut my words off with a sharp smile and an envelope. Inside the envelope, he said, was secret intelligence he had obtained at great peril to himself. Intelligence that pinpointed the army's next major offensive, the next attack that would come.

"All he needed, he said, was a volunteer to deliver it to the other side.

"Of course, we all volunteered, but when his eyes never left mine, I knew he'd chosen me. When he handed me the envelope, I thought I'd die of pride.

"There have been many times over the years—many sleepless nights since—when I wished I *had* died that night. Then I might have spared myself and so many others . . ." His eyes flicked to me. "Other times . . . I think my fate is what I deserved."

I remained still, absorbed in the story.

"It doesn't matter of course, because I didn't die. I delivered the message—it was easier than I thought it would be—and returned to my brothers-in-arms, convinced I'd be hailed as a hero. And within our group, I was. We celebrated wildly that night, confident we had done the right thing.

"But when the battle was over and the dead were counted, I realized the people who'd died were people I'd grown up with. Neighbors, cousins, friends. People my parents knew. Boys as young as my brother. Boys who should have been playing at war, instead of dying in one.

"I realized I had done this. I had delivered the message that had doomed a generation of innocents. Their blood was on my hands. It didn't matter which side was right, or even which side *thought* it was right. The dead didn't care.

"Afterwards, I went to my brothers-in-arms and told them I was done—finished. He warned me I'd be killed as a deserter if I was caught. I shrugged. He said I'd be labeled a coward. I wavered. He said he'd kill my brother if I betrayed our conspiracy. I stayed.

"My brother was on the cusp of manhood but still very much an innocent. He was a thinker, a planner, a dreamer. He had been spared the soldier's life and I wanted more than anything to keep him safe, to protect him.

"So I stayed. I couldn't tell anyone anything without betraying the group and essentially killing my brother. I was trapped.

"When the next note needed to be delivered, there was no discussion, no debate, no volunteers. It was my task to do. My burden to prove my devotion to the cause. My chance to save my brother.

"But this time—for better or worse—I was discovered.

"I'll admit I felt a certain amount of relief, even as I knew the dire consequences facing me. I was prepared to die—I think I might have welcomed it—but it was not to be. I was offered a deal. A bribe. A way out.

"Reveal the names of my co-conspirators and the judge would be lenient with me. They wouldn't kill me outright but would instead give me an opportunity to redeem myself by testing a new and strange machine they had built.

"Refuse and not only would they kill me, but they would destroy the honor of my family. My father was a well-respected member of the community and my mother . . . how could I let my mother suffer dishonor for my mistakes? And how hard could the test be? It seemed like such an innocuous request.

"So, to save my family, I agreed. I told them the names. I was given my instructions. One month, they said. They would send me one month into the future. And then, after that month had passed, they would open the door again. If I was still alive, they'd let me go and declare me a hero. I'd be exiled, of course. It wouldn't do to have a supposedly dead war hero wandering around town. But if, after one month, I wasn't alive, well, at least they had their names—a list of traitors on whom they could continue to test the machine."

Leo stood up from the table and stumbled to the bar, pouring himself a glass of water.

My own mouth felt dry after listening to his story. "Then what happened?"

Leo drained his drink and pressed the empty glass against his forehead. "Then the time machine happened. Then five hundred years passed by." He refilled his water glass. "Then I found Dante on the bank. The one person I thought I'd never see again. Especially not there. Not then."

"You'd met him before?"

"You could say that." Leo closed his eyes and turned away from me.

"Dante never mentioned it. When did you meet him?"

"The last time I saw Dante di Alessandro Casella was the day I headed off to war. I told him to listen to our parents and to behave himself at da Vinci's studio."

The truth of Leo's words crashed over me, sending shivers through my body. I wondered if I was the one going crazy instead of Leo.

"Your parents?" My voice sounded faraway to my own ears,

drowned out by the echo of Dante's voice somehow telling me the other side of this same story: *My brother died in the war. He was a hero. I wanted to be just like him once.*

Leo turned to face me again. "Dante may have told you his secrets, but he doesn't know this one. This one is mine to tell." His voice cracked. "Long ago, in my other life, I was named Orlando di Alessandro Casella."

CHAPTER
27

"You're Dante's . . . brother?" My thoughts stalled on this one fact. The more I thought about it, the larger it grew in my mind until it was all I could think about, all I could say. "Why haven't you told him?"

"What good would it do? He believes the story that I died a hero in the war. Why would I want to take that away from him?" Leo looked down at his hands. "Why would I want him to know what I've done or to see what I've become?"

"He'd want to know," I insisted. "He deserves to know."

Leo shook his head. "Some secrets are best kept secret."

"And some secrets are more valuable when they're finally told," a melodic voice sang out of the darkness by the front door.

I whirled around, my heart in my throat, my palms slick with sweat. What was Zo doing here? I scanned the darkness, looking for Dante, but all I could see in the glow of golden light from above the bar were the frosted white tips of Zo's hair and the gleam of his teeth bared in a wicked grin.

"So the famous Leo is really just the coward Orlando. *That* is a useful bit of information to know."

"You're not welcome here, Lorenzo," Leo thundered, a spark of his old fire back in his voice. "Not after what you've done."

"You don't know the half of what I've done." Zo sauntered fully into the light. "But I didn't come to compare stories and battle for bragging rights." He held up a ring of small keys, jingling them in his hand. "You really shouldn't leave your doors unlocked. Why, just anyone could walk right in and steal a set of keys, replace them with copies, and you'd never know the difference."

I took a few steps into the shadows, still hoping to find Dante. If Zo was here, then where was Dante? Had he saved Valerie? Was he even now taking her home and to safety?

"Why did you come?" Leo demanded.

Zo tucked the keys into his pocket. "I seem to have run into a slight snag with my plans."

"And you honestly thought we'd help you?"

"Oh, no, of course not." Zo perched elegantly on a bar stool, leaning his back against the bar and propping one foot on his knee. "When Dante showed up on the bank, I was pretty sure he wasn't there to help me." His eyes froze me in place. "But that doesn't mean he hasn't proven to be very helpful after all."

"He would never help you—" I said fiercely.

"Yeah, see, here's the thing, Abby. Dante's no match for me on the bank. And when it came right down to it, he didn't have much choice. Just like you don't have much choice right now either."

"What do you mean?" He couldn't mean that Dante was dead, could he? I didn't breathe.

Zo dropped his foot to the floor, leaning forward to rest his forearms on his knees. "Shall I make this easy for you, Abby? Come with me back to the bank, or I'll destroy Dante. Completely. Utterly. Finally." He spread his hands and grinned at me. "It's your choice."

It was no choice and Zo knew it.

I told myself that Zo had to be lying. It wasn't possible that he could destroy Dante like he threatened. He couldn't have that much power. He was bluffing.

I walked up to him, my body trembling with an emotion I didn't dare name in case it was fear. I stopped in front of him, studying his hooded eyes, his self-satisfied grin, the black tattoos that marked him a criminal and a traitor. Dante had been marked the same way, but he was the innocent one. I decided my emotion couldn't possibly be fear.

"Dante was sent through the time machine because of *you*," I said, tasting the metallic tang of truth and anger on my tongue. "*You* said he was guilty when he wasn't."

I slapped Zo across the face. Hard. My hand flared red, tingling with my righteous anger.

Zo looked back at me, rubbing his cheek. His grin was still firmly in place.

I lifted my hand to hit him again, but he caught my wrist. I curled my fingers into a fist, struggling to break free.

He tightened his callused fingertips around the delicate

bones in my wrist. He brought his mouth close to my fist, his lips not quite touching my skin. "Such passion," he said. "How refreshing."

"Let her go," Leo said, pulling Zo's hand away while Zo laughed.

I glared at Zo, rubbing the circulation back into my hand.

Leo took my place in front of him. "Is that true? Dante is here because you told them he was one of us?"

"You told them my name. I told them Dante's," Zo said, shrugging as though it made perfect sense. "I warned you what would happen if you betrayed us, if you told our secrets." Zo's eyes glittered. "None of this would have happened if you had just followed the rules."

"That's not true," I snapped at him. "This is all *your* fault."

"Fault?" Zo jumped to his feet and trained his furious eyes on mine. "If you want to lay blame, look there, Abby. Look to Leo. We're all here because of his actions. We're all paying the price for his cowardice and his fear. I'm just trying to set right what he caused to go wrong."

"You lying—" I started, but Leo's soft voice covered my words.

"You're right, Zo. I made a mistake—more than one—but I have been trying to atone for them ever since."

"That's not good enough, old man," Zo barked, pushing Leo in the chest. "Your apology is way too little, way too late."

Leo stumbled back a step. I grabbed his arm to help steady him. "I helped you when you and your friends came through the door. I helped you even though I knew who you were and what you'd done."

"And you think that makes you some kind of hero? That we're somehow indebted to you?"

"No—" Leo started.

"Then stop interfering. If you were smart, you'd stay out of my way."

He shook his head. "I can't do that."

"I warned you," Zo said.

"Stop it! Both of you!"

Leo looked at me with confusion, Zo with anticipation.

It seemed like forever ago that Leo had spoken to me about the four rules: the rules to keep me safe. But how could I stay safe while people I loved were in danger?

I'd thought my way through a hundred different scenarios, trying to find a loophole in the choice Zo had presented me. But I couldn't see any way out. Valerie was likely still trapped on the bank. Zo was holding Dante hostage. Leo couldn't go without risking his own sanity. There was no one else but me. In truth, I didn't have any choice. I didn't want to make any other choice. Dante needed my help. I couldn't leave him, abandon him. I didn't want to. I was his Beatrice.

"I'll go," I said quietly.

"Abby—" Leo reached for my arm, but I stepped away from him. I had made my decision, but it was fragile and I couldn't risk Leo talking me out of it. My red-hot flare of anger had faded into an ember of weary resolve.

"I have to. It's the only way." I took a deep breath and took a step toward Zo.

Victory gleamed in his eyes.

Then Leo pushed me aside and swung his fist at Zo's jaw.

I heard the crack of bone against bone and Zo fell, hitting his head on the edge of the bar on his way to the ground.

Startled, I looked at Leo, my mouth open in surprise.

Leo cradled his right hand with his left, pain drawing deep lines on his face. "Go!" he barked. "I'll take care of Zo. Go, now, while there is still time."

"Go where?" I asked, looking over my shoulder at the door.

"To the bank. Go. Save Valerie. Save Dante." He placed his good hand on my shoulder and squeezed gently. "Set my brother free."

I nodded, my blood pounding with adrenaline. I felt the sharp flare of hope behind my heart and grinned.

Leo fished out the set of keys from Zo's pocket and nodded toward the "Employees Only" door. "Lock it behind you. And whatever happens, don't come downstairs. Don't open the door. Dante's room is on the left if you need a quiet place to concentrate." Leo pushed the keys into my hand. "You can do this, Abby. I trust you."

I took a last look at Zo, still on the floor, waiting to see if he would move; then I spun on my heel and ran for the door.

CHAPTER
28

I locked the door with hands that shook. My whole body shook. I could almost feel the passage of time flowing against my skin. Every heartbeat simply counted one more second of the head start that I was losing.

I took the stairs two at a time. I pushed into the first room on my left and slammed the door behind me. Pressing my back against the wood, I took in Dante's room with one glance.

A bed pushed into the far corner. A closet. A bookcase filled with papers, books, and odds and ends. I wanted to look at everything, examine every inch, riffle through his books, open his closet and breathe in the scent of him that surely lingered on his clothes.

But I didn't have time.

I closed my eyes and tried to remember what I had done before to make it to the bank. I thought back to that night in the clearing when Dante had held my hand and . . . and . . . What exactly had he done?

I tried to reconstruct the night in my mind but kept stumbling over the tactile memory of his hand around mine. How his long fingers twined with mine. How perfectly they fit together. How . . . it was no use.

I shook my head in frustration.

What about the night I had dreamed my way there? I laughed in despair. I wasn't exactly capable of falling asleep at the moment.

I felt tears prickling in my eyes. Time was running out. If I didn't figure something out—and soon—Zo would recover from Leo's knockout punch. And when he did, it would only take him an instant to make good on his promise, and Dante would be lost to me forever. I recognized the irony and grimaced. Dante was trapped in a place outside of time, and yet I still had only so much time to spare before it would be too late. Too late to save Valerie from certain death. Too late to save Dante from the insanity that threatened him every time he set foot on the bank of the river.

How could we have underestimated Zo so badly?

I paced Dante's room, prowling like a caged animal but feeling more like a mouse than a tiger or a lion.

Maybe that was it. Maybe I should be thinking of how to slide past, slide in, instead of barging in with a frontal assault.

What was it Dante had said once? That stepping out of the river and onto the bank was like sliding in between the moments of time.

That was the key. In between. After all, between the notes of song lived the melody. Between the particles of light shone the dawn. Between the words spoken breathed the creation of life.

Maybe I could slide *between* . . .

I lay down on his bed, forcing myself to relax. It was hard—my heart kept skipping beats, slowing down, only to speed up again.

I tried Jason's counting trick, then counting my heartbeats in between my breaths. Counting the pulse of blood in my fingers and toes. Counting the stars I could see from the curved window high on the wall. Counting the spaces between the stars.

So slowly, too slowly, I felt my surroundings start to fade.

I kept counting the spaces between, afraid I would lose my own focus, lose track of where I was, where I wanted to be. Afraid I'd lose Dante.

The silence deepened around me, thick and heavy. I heard a low ringing begin deep inside my inner ear, a straining to hear something. But there was nothing to hear. Not my breath, not my heartbeat, not the whispered numbers that fell from my lips like a prayer. Everything faded away.

I knew before I opened my eyes that it had worked.

I could feel the pressure clamping down on my lungs. The silence that had been soft as a winter snowfall turned sharp and painful. Still I hesitated opening my eyes. What if I'd made it, but not to where Dante was? I knew the answer before I even finished asking myself the question.

If I opened my eyes and Dante wasn't there, I'd die. I couldn't survive without him to protect me in this place. Burning fire blazed through my lungs, scorching what little breath remained in me.

I felt a kiss pressed to my mouth, rough and perfunctory. Dante never kissed me like that. His kisses were soft and

LISA MANGUM

sharing. I opened my eyes—and recoiled when I saw V leaning over me.

He pulled away from me but kept his hand clamped around my arm.

"So nice of you to join us, Abby," Tony said from behind him, a malicious twist to his lips.

I looked around quickly. The churning flood of the river surged close by us but there was no sign of Zo. Not yet.

No sign of Dante, either, but then I saw a shape a short ways in the distance next to the river. A lithe, willowy figure stepping lightly, bending low, reaching out, reaching up. It looked like she was picking nonexistent flowers, or perhaps dancing. The person turned and I saw her face clearly.

Valerie still wore her deadly nightshade dress, though without the gloves or her shoes. The darkness of her dress hurt my eyes. The bright emptiness in her face hurt my heart even worse.

When she saw me, she danced barefoot over the flat ground of the bank until she had reached V's side.

"You brought me a doll to play with!" she said, clapping her hands together like a small child. "Oh, she's pretty. I like her hair." She frowned. "I hope I have some dress-up clothes to fit her." She twirled, her arms extended high above her head. "I wonder what I should name her?"

She saw Tony standing nearby and ran to him, asking him if he had any ribbons in his pockets.

I locked eyes with Tony, horror clogging my thoughts, blurring the edges of my vision.

"What have you done to her?"

364

"Oh, it's not what we've done to her, it's what the *bank* has done to her." Tony shrugged. "It turns out not everyone is as well suited to visiting here as you are. Valerie's mind seems to have cracked under the pressure."

This must have been the "slight snag" Zo had mentioned so casually. I felt my hate for him flare up in a welcome pain. I would make him pay for this. For everything.

I shook free of V's grip and took a step toward Valerie, unsure of what I could do to help, but knowing I couldn't stand to see her like this.

A sharp report cracked behind me and I turned to see Zo standing on the bank. Fury surrounded him like a storm. Heat fairly crackled off his skin. He rubbed his jaw, and I suspected it had already healed from the blow Leo had given him.

My heart sank. I had almost made it. I'd beaten him to the bank, but not fast enough.

Without breaking his gaze from me, Zo barked something in Italian to V, who nodded and grabbed Valerie by her arm.

"Oh, are we going to a party?" she asked. "I like parties. Should I bring my dolly?"

V walked her to the edge of the river and shoved her in. She was gone midword.

I hoped she landed somewhere—some *when*—safe.

"There. That's done. Now we can get down to business." Zo stepped to the side.

I finally saw Dante. He was crouched on his knees, his hands covering his face, shaking with barely controlled emotion. Rage? Sorrow? Fear? It was hard to tell.

"Dante!" His name burst from my lips automatically. I took

a step toward him, but Tony grabbed me and held me back. His hand cut off the circulation to my fingers.

"He can't hear you, Abby." Zo walked toward me, a dark light in his eyes, his casual cruelty replaced with something more focused. "In fact, he can't do anything here. Not unless I say so."

"Let him go!" I demanded.

"We all have our little tricks here," Zo said, ignoring me. "Did you know Dante can see the future? It's too bad he didn't see this coming. V has an uncanny sense of direction here. And Tony swears he can hear echoes of the past." He smiled coldly at me. "My little talent here is that I can enhance emotions—grant pleasure or pain."

Zo pointed a finger at Dante and then flicked it upright. Dante's head snapped back as though it had been tied to a string. Zo curled his finger and Dante's neck bent backward, straining to obey Zo's command even though he couldn't move another inch.

I shivered to see Dante's throat so exposed, so vulnerable.

Zo dropped his hand, and Dante's head followed suit.

I tried to catch his eye, to make sure he knew I was there, but Dante wouldn't—or couldn't—look at me. He hid his face behind his hands, his black chains stark against his pale skin.

I gasped as I realized I'd seen Dante like this once before, when I had traveled to the bank and looked in the river for the first time. I had seen this exact moment. Was it possible? Had I really seen the future back then? I ground my teeth in frustration. If only I had looked a little further downstream, maybe I'd have seen how to stop Zo.

"What do you want?"

Zo grinned over sharp teeth. "I want my life back. And lucky for me, *you* are the one who can give it to me."

"I can't—" I started, but then stars sparked in my vision as Zo slapped me across the face. I felt my lips start to swell and tasted blood in the corner of my mouth. The ringing in my ears sounded even louder in the deafening silence around me.

"Don't be stupid. It's you. It's always been you." Zo trailed his fingertip down my cheek. "Because you, sweet Abby, are special." He shook his head sadly. "All that time wasted on your useless friend, when I should have been pursuing you."

I recoiled from his touch, turning my head away.

Zo glanced at Tony, who immediately stepped to flank V, who was guarding Dante at the edge of the riverbank behind us. Zo moved closer, intimate. "I'm surprised Dante didn't figure it out. Or maybe he did, but it was too late. You bring part of the river with you wherever you go. Even here. But of course, there's no time here on the bank, is there?" Zo spoke to me like I was a small child and I bristled at his tone. He saw my discomfort and grinned. "It's like oil and water—the river and the bank will never mix. But here you are, sweet Abby, with your special touch of time, and something's got to give."

A light bloomed in Zo's dark eyes, and I turned to see what had entranced him.

A slender bridge spanned the river. The path lacked railings or supports of any kind; I wondered if anyone could realistically cross that narrow walkway without falling off. The bridge arched high above the river, and I shuddered to think of falling from that height. I followed the curve to where it ended on the other side of the river and my breath froze in my body.

At the foot of the bridge was a flat black door, freestanding in the void. Even from here I could see the markings on the door: stars, a wave, a shell. An hourglass in the middle, the top bulb empty while a mound of sand completely filled the bottom bulb. Three narrow slots where the hinges would pivot, allowing the door to open to the past or the future.

The void shimmered along the edges of the door frame like water. I couldn't concentrate on it for long without my eyes starting to well up against the unnaturalness of it all.

My whole body flashed cold. My teeth started to chatter and I shook so hard I could feel myself vibrating in Zo's hand. I had seen this door somewhere before.

"Ah, Abby," Zo murmured, "it's perfect."

I shook my head and looked away. "It's horrible."

"It's the way home," he said.

Tony and V exchanged a hungry grin above Dante's head.

"You can't go back. You were sent through the time machine for a reason and you can't go back. Any of you." I knew I was babbling, mixing truth with lies, but I couldn't seem to stop the words from spilling out. Anything to keep from looking at the door.

"Leo may have said that, but we both know he has been keeping secrets."

I looked helplessly at Dante, wishing he would stand up and stop Zo, but if he knew the door was there and what Zo planned to do, he gave no sign.

"You can't open it," I blurted. "The door is missing a piece—"

Zo tightened his grip around my arm, a feral smile peeling back his lips. "You mean this piece?" He held out his hand, and Tony placed the three-pronged brass machine into his palm.

He gripped the two ends of the machine and pulled. The long side grew longer like a blade being unsheathed. Longer and longer the hinge unfolded until, instead of a compact letter E, the hinge had expanded to be tall enough to fit the empty notches carved into the door.

No one else seemed to hear the clear high note that shivered like a bell in the flat air of the bank. I heard the beginning of a quiet melody playing deep in my ear. It was a melody I almost recognized, a shiver just on the edge of my memory. I was sure I had heard it before. But where? When?

"Do you have any idea how special you are, my sweet Abby? You can come to the bank alone; you can summon the bridge; and I think *you* can open the door." Zo neatly telescoped the machine back into its small, portable size.

"No," I said, shaking my head and trying to take a step back. "I won't do it."

In a flash, Zo whipped me around, pinning me against his body, forcing me to look at the bridge and the horrible black door. "You will because I say you will. And here, you have to do what I say." He pushed the hinge into my hands and the music increased in tempo and volume.

I felt a jolt at the base of my spine, sharp and electric. All my joints felt loose, somehow disconnected from the rest of my body. Fire raced along my nerves, tingling in the pads of my fingertips, in the soles of my feet. A warm languor rose up inside me, then a calm fog that filled my mind with a sweet certainty.

Why wouldn't I want to open the door if Zo asked me to? He wouldn't ask me to do anything that would hurt me or Dante, would he? Of course not. All he was asking was for me to skip across the bridge and open a silly little door. That was all. It wouldn't take more than a minute. The melody of the door wound its way through my ears, soft as moonrise, gentle as a kiss.

Suddenly I wanted to see what was on the other side of the door. I took a step toward the bridge.

"Abby." Dante's voice was a husk, a shell, a fragment of a whisper, but it was enough to snare my attention.

"Be quiet, Dante," Zo said.

I felt his hand at the small of my back. The smallest pressure of his long fingers propelled me another step. I couldn't stop. I didn't want to.

"That's right, Abby. The door will open for you, won't it?"

As soon as he said it, I knew it was true. There wasn't a handle on the door, but I knew if I touched it, if I placed the hinge into the empty slots along the edge, the carved door would swing open, and then . . .

No. That was wrong. There was something else. Something missing before the door would open.

And if the door opened, something bad would happen. Wouldn't it?

"Abigail." Dante's voice buzzed in my ear. I waved it away. I didn't want to be interrupted. I was so close. Just a few more steps . . .

"I'm warning you." Zo's voice hardened. A strangled groan rumbled from Dante's throat before the sound was cut in two.

The vastness spread out around me like a blanket, an ocean that lifted me step after step, wave after wave, drawing me inexorably toward the door. I couldn't feel my breath in my lungs anymore. I couldn't even hear my own heart beating.

The bridge held firm under my steps; it was stronger than it looked. The river rushed in silver streaks beneath me, the flow of time spinning like stars in the night sky. I glided across the narrow path effortlessly. All that remained was to open the door. I reached out my hand. Almost. Almost.

"Abigail Beatrice Edmunds." Dante's voice rang in the void, loud and powerful—a clarion call I couldn't ignore. The hairs on the back of my neck stood up. I hesitated, the door singing in my head, my fingers almost brushing against the carved hourglass. Everything in me wanted to lean forward and marry the bright brass hinges with the dark black wood. Almost everything. Dante's voice echoed inside of me, a sibilant breath against the inside of my skin, a dark harmonic counterpart twining around the shimmering melody. Slowly I turned away from the door, the movement tearing at my soul, my mind.

The comfortable fog shrouding my mind evaporated. Zo's hold over me disappeared between one breath and the next.

"I warned you!" Zo barked. "You will not speak!" He pointed a long finger at Dante's forehead like a gun. Then he clenched his fist and twisted his wrist in a quick, violent motion like snapping a lock into place.

Dante screamed, clutching his head with his hands as though Zo had ripped something from him. His body tightened, quivering with tension and pain. Harsh lines delineated the angles of his face; shadows pooled under his eyes, in the hollow of his cheeks and his throat.

Zo was killing him, strangling him with pain.

"No!" I dropped the hinge at the base of the door. I set my foot back on the bridge, ready to dart across, but fear gripped me, freezing me in place. The bridge seemed to arch even higher than I remembered. How had I ever crossed this in the first place?

"Dante!" I screamed out desperately.

Zo's fist squeezed tighter and tighter, his knuckles white with pressure. The shadows painting Dante's face darkened to purple, then black.

"Do it, Abby!" Zo roared. "Open the door and I'll let him go."

I looked at the brass hinge and then at the door. I saw where the three prongs were supposed to go. All I had to do was pick up the brass hinge and slot it into place. But it wouldn't be enough. Dante said that the door was locked, that the lock required a key.

And without the key, I was as helpless as Zo.

Desperately, I looked from Zo to Dante, searching for a sign, a hint of what I should do.

Despite the agony etched on Dante's face, his eyes were clear and lucid.

"Open the locket, Abby," he whispered, and somehow I

heard him across the vastness of the river and the void. "It's time."

I closed my hand around the silver locket at my throat. Dante had said it held the key to his heart.

With trembling fingers, I reached up and opened the cover of the locket. A small silver key fell out into my hand. I stared at it in disbelief. All this time I had been wearing the key around my neck. I couldn't decide if it was the smartest thing Dante could have done or the most dangerous.

"Stop wasting time, Abby. Open the door!"

Frantic, I ran my eyes over the door, searching for the keyhole. There. There it was. A tiny keyhole in the center of a heart tucked into the wild patterns surrounding the hourglass carving.

"Please," I begged, the small, sharp teeth of the key biting into my hand. "Please don't kill him."

Zo lifted his fist and Dante jerked to his feet, standing on unsteady legs. "Don't worry, sweet Abby, I won't kill him—much as I'd like to. No, all you have to do is open the door and I'll let him go. Otherwise, he'll stay right where he is—on the bank. Forever." Zo spared a glance for me, pinning me with his dark eyes. "And you know what happens to us if we stay here for too long, don't you?"

Yes, I knew the blessings the bank bestowed—immortality and invincibility—as well as the curse it carried—insanity. Maybe he couldn't destroy Dante's body, but if Zo trapped him here, he would certainly destroy Dante's mind. I couldn't let that happen.

But with the door open, Zo would no longer be bound by

time and bound to the bank. Zo would be able to go anywhere, any *when*, he wanted to. He would truly be immortal and invincible. Able to go back and change the course of the river entirely. I couldn't let that happen, either.

My eyes met Dante's and I felt a stream of tears fall down my cheeks. Now what was I supposed to do?

Open the door and hand over control of time to Zo? Or keep it shut and condemn the man I loved to an eternity of insanity?

Be sure of your heart before you answer.

Set my brother free.

The ghost of a small smile appeared on Dante's mouth.

When I saw that smile, I knew what I had to do.

I closed my eyes and made my choice.

CHAPTER
29

I snatched up the brass hinge, pulling it open to its full length. The metal moved smoothly through my fingers. Quickly, I aligned the three notches with the spaces along the side of the door and pushed them home. They fit perfectly, and the melody that had been only a murmur suddenly rose into a wild crescendo.

I inserted the small silver key into the lock with a hand that only shook a little. As the key turned, I heard a high chime ring out.

The door swung open.

Darkness spilled out into the void.

Darkness and an icy cold breath of stale air.

I stepped back and turned away, my eyes immediately finding Dante.

He nodded ever so slightly and I sighed with relief. It was going to be all right.

Zo jerked his head, and Tony and V hauled Dante to his feet. The four men crossed the bridge to join me on the far side.

Tony and V dropped Dante at my feet and Zo walked directly to the door. He reached out his hand, gently caressing the dark wood. "It worked," he breathed. "It's open."

I crouched at Dante's side, my hands checking his forehead, his face, his body. I helped him to his feet. He leaned on me, his arm weighing heavily across my shoulders.

Zo wrenched the door back, forcing it open as wide as it would go, and then stepped back, embracing the darkness that flowed out like a fog.

I expected the hinges to protest, but they were as silent as if they'd been freshly oiled that morning. I saw that the brass hinges had locked into place, the wood fitting against the metal seamlessly. There would be no getting them out again without destroying the door. I glanced at the small silver key, the smooth knob protruding slightly from the wood. Quickly, I reached up and pulled it free, palming it into my pocket. Dante had given it to me; I wasn't going to leave it in this place if I could help it.

"It's beautiful," Zo said. "Last time, it happened so quickly I didn't have time to enjoy the artistry." He slid a glance at Dante from the corner of his eye. "I'll be sure to pass along my compliments to the artist when I see him again. His work is flawless—as usual."

"Thank you," Dante said, his voice rasping through his bruised throat. "I'm glad you appreciate my work."

"*Your* work?"

"I didn't just run messages for da Vinci. Sometimes he let me help."

Surprise filled Zo's face. "Everyone is just full of secrets today, aren't they?"

"Let's go already," V growled. Tony shuffled a step closer to the door.

Zo flung up his hand, stopping them where they stood. He fixed Dante with a dark look. "I know you're thinking of following us like some kind of hero. A friendly bit of advice—don't. If you do, I'll make sure you regret it all the days of your life. Keeping secrets is a dangerous business, Dante. And I have some secrets that are positively deadly." He parted his lips in a sharp grin.

I glanced at Dante, but he simply stood by my side, his gaze locked with Zo's dark eyes.

Zo dropped his hand and Tony slipped through the door. Then V.

The darkness of the door bulged slightly and I heard a low rumbling like footsteps running in the distance.

Zo paused, his hand curled around the door frame. "Thank you to you both. I couldn't have done this without you." He laughed, then, and the sound felt like insects crawling on my skin.

He was still laughing as he vanished into the darkness as completely as if he'd been swallowed whole.

I rounded on Dante. "Why did you let them go?" I demanded. "I thought you were going to stop them."

His eyes traced the carvings on the door, his attention far away.

"What about all that talk about not letting Zo control time? Now he's gone and—"

Dante took a step toward the door, his hungry eyes distant and angry. His pale skin was luminescent in the flat, harsh light. He looked like a lost ghost—or an avenging angel. "I can still catch him as long as the door is open. When it closes, though, the door will be destroyed." His smile was grim. "A final, fail-safe feature of da Vinci's design."

The door still gaped wide open, a toothless maw of unending blackness. My skin was unaccountably cold.

"Dante!" I called out, terrified that he would walk through the door and leave me alone. "Dante, don't. Please."

He stopped and slowly turned his back to the door. The edges flickered, softening and melting. It couldn't last much longer. And when it shut, Zo would be gone. Out of reach forever.

Dante looked from me to the door, anguish etched into his silver, gray-shadowed eyes, aging him even as I watched. I could see an echo of Leo's features in his face.

"Abby." His mouth caressed my name, but all I heard was *good-bye.*

Tears welled up and spilled over my cheeks. I brushed them away roughly with the flat of my hand. My tears were the only flowing water besides the river in this hellish, barren place. I wasn't going to sacrifice them here.

Dante caught my tear-stained hand and brought my fingers to his lips. As he kissed the tears from my skin, I felt the rough texture of his lips an instant before they met mine.

He pulled me to him, wrapping his long arms behind my back, sliding his strong hands up to cup the back of my head. His face was wet with tears too.

He finally released me, but I could still feel the weight of his body encircling mine, I could still smell the scent of his skin on my own, I could still breathe the sweetness of his breath inside my lungs.

"You still owe me two questions, you know," Dante said with a rueful half-smile. He leaned down until our foreheads touched. "Two getting-to-know-Abby questions. Do you remember?"

"I remember," I whispered, closing my eyes, dreading what questions he might ask at a time like this.

"Do you remember the rules?"

I nodded against his cheek. Total honesty. It's what we had always asked of each other, even when the questions were hard, even when the answers were harder.

"So, Abigail Beatrice Edmunds, here is my first question." Dante swallowed hard. He trembled in body and in voice. "Do you love me?"

My eyes flew open as a wave of fresh tears spilled down my face. I suspected he would ask me hard questions, but not this one. Not here. Not now. I opened my mouth but he quickly pressed his finger to my lips. "Be sure of your heart before you answer."

"I *am* sure," I said without hesitating. "I've been sure for so long, sometimes it seems like it's the only thing I'm sure of anymore. Yes, Dante, yes, of course I love you."

It was as though my words revived him, resurrected him from the brink where Zo had trapped him. His smile lit up his whole face. Warm color rushed into his skin, replacing the pale, waxy hue with soft pinks and golden browns. He sighed with relief.

I buried my face into his chest, nestling into his embrace. Here, finally, was the Dante I had come to save.

"*Grazie,* Abby," he whispered as he pressed a kiss to the crown of my head and brushed my hair with his fingers. "You don't know how much it means to hear you say you love me. How much more it means to know it is the truth."

"Of course it's the truth," I mumbled.

"I know. Which is why I have to ask my second question."

I leaned back and looked up into his face. "Don't," I said, suddenly sure he was going to ask the impossible. "I don't want to answer any more questions. Ask me later. Please? Let's just go back right now. Zo's gone—they're all gone—" I choked off my words as Dante glanced over his shoulder at the door standing halfway open behind us.

He overrode my words with a single whisper. "If you love me, Abby—then will you let me go?"

A thousand *no*s filled my mouth, but not a single one emerged. How could I say no? How could I deny him this one chance to follow Zo through the black door? When the door closed, it would be closed for good—destroyed. I couldn't take that chance. I couldn't force Dante to take that chance.

I tried for a smile, but it felt wobbly on my face and I let it go rather than forcing it. I slid my hands down Dante's arms, my fingers tracing his taut, corded muscles one last time. I twined my fingers with his and looked past Dante to the door. It had almost closed.

"*Because* I love you," I said, proud that my voice hardly

cracked at all, "you don't have to ask." I let go of his hands and took a step backward. I clasped my hands tightly together behind my back to prevent myself from reaching out for him again. Tears slipped down my cheeks, but this time I let them fall to the barren ground.

Understanding illuminated Dante's eyes, lining them in silver. He swept me into his arms, lifting me off the ground, and kissed me, his lips at once hard and fierce and yet still gentle and insistent. I wanted the moment to never end.

But all too soon Dante lowered me back to the ground. He reached out and touched the silver locket around my throat. "No matter what happens, you still hold the key to my heart," he murmured.

I curled my fingers around the locket, not wanting to miss these last few moments with Dante. The door was almost closed. Almost gone. There was only a sliver of an opening left, but it was enough for Dante to slip his fingers through and wrench the door back open. The hinges screamed like a dying creature and I shivered at the unwelcome comparison.

Countless words rose to my lips, but I stayed silent. I had to let him go, knowing he would take my heart with him.

Dante looked back once, one last glance, one last look. His eyes found mine without even trying. The darkness haloed around him like a jagged cloud. "I love you," he called out. The words shot to me like an arrow. "I LOVE YOU—I love you—*I love you.*" The strange triple echo was back, this time repeating Dante's declaration to me through all the days of the past, the present, and the future.

A supernova of white light flared from the center of the

door, so bright I had to look away, blinded. The music I'd heard cut short midchime and the familiar silence of the void enveloped me again. I felt the heat of the flare blister against my skin, scorching the locket around my throat, searing the pattern of the chain around my neck.

I screamed in pain, falling to my knees.

I don't know how long I stayed there, blinking back tears, but when my vision cleared, I saw that the door had been incinerated. No lump of melted brass, no charred door frame—nothing remained.

Dante was gone. And the door was destroyed.

CHAPTER
30

The floor of Dante's room was cold. Bitter cold.

I could still hear his parting words: *I love you.* It was the first time he'd said those words to me. I feared I would never hear him say them again. I pulled my body even tighter into a ball, trying to hold on to the last memory, the last moment I'd shared with Dante.

A flash of light painted my eyelids red. I opened my eyes and vibrant colors burned across my vision. After the desolation of the flat bank, any color seemed painful, but these reds and oranges and yellows felt like needles in my tired and swollen eyes. I tried to focus, blinking and squinting, but the colors flickered and danced, bouncing close to me and springing away again. I couldn't see anything clearly except for the wildly shifting light around me.

What was going on?

I placed my hands on the floor beneath me, hissing at the ice cold that burned my skin. Pushing myself up, I hit my head against something low that curved over me. Dropping to the floor again, I rolled onto my back and looked up at the thin shell that arched over me, completely encasing me like a butterfly in a glass jar. The realization of what had happened dawned in my tired mind. Just like the last time I'd fallen through the river, I'd brought some of the bank's timelessness back with me.

But unlike last time, I wasn't trapped in a flicker of midnight while the day dawned around me. This time I was frozen in a breath of ice while the Dungeon burned around me in an inferno of fire.

❽

Panic shot through me. I could see the flames flickering next to me, but I couldn't hear the crackling sound or feel the burning heat as they raced across the floor. I could see the black smoke billowing up, blocking out the ceiling like a thunderhead on a stormy day, but the air inside my shell was clean and crisp.

I pulled my knees to my chest, afraid to touch the edges of my cocoon in case it shattered and left me vulnerable to the fire's hungry touch. I didn't dare breathe.

I watched helplessly as the flames ransacked the room like destructive animals. They devoured Dante's small collection of books. They jumped on his bed, burning holes in his blankets and his pillow. They darted beneath the closet door, eager to rip through his clothes.

It wasn't enough that Dante was lost to me forever; now I had to lose what he'd left behind as well? It wasn't fair. A wave of hurt and anger and sorrow built up inside me. I kicked out against the shell that protected me, hoping it would shatter and set me free, but I didn't so much as smudge the clear curve. The panic I had originally felt deepened into something approaching terror. How was I supposed to get out? Leo knew I was upstairs, but was he trapped in the fire too? Or had he already looked for me and left while I was still on the bank? It was bad enough to be alone, trapped in a burning building. It was worse to be alone, frozen in time, and trapped in a burning building.

I kicked again, this time with both feet, but the recoil shook my ankles and knees.

I couldn't hear anything but my frantic breathing, my racing blood. How long could I survive? Would the building burn to the ground and leave me still alive and well in the wreckage? I had a sudden vision of a group of firefighters swinging their axes against the shell of time, trying to save me, only to see the axe heads bounce off the seemingly empty air around me. A hysterical giggle burst out, and I clamped my hands over my mouth to keep the rest of them inside.

I felt tears trickling over my hands and I closed my eyes. I heard a low tone rumbling through the shell and groaned. If this was the end, I wasn't sure I wanted to see it happening up close and personal.

"Abby!"

My eyes flew open and I saw Leo crouching on the floor next to me.

"Stay still!"

He reached out and touched the shell. His face tightened. I could see the muscles in his arms quivering with strain.

The cold began melting away, replaced with a blistering heat. I could hear the hissing and spitting of the flames.

Leo clamped down on his jaw, the veins in his neck popping under his skin.

A crack sounded close to my ear. I looked up at the shell. Thin lines arched above me, branching out from Leo's touch like tiny rivers of darkness. I watched them zigzag in random patterns, racing each other from one side to the other. When a crack touched the floor, the entire shell quivered. The space inside shook like a struck bell.

Leo's groan turned into a roar. He compressed his outstretched hand into a fist, and, in an instant, the shell around me vanished as completely as if it had never been.

Leo fell to his hands and knees, his head hanging down as he gasped for breath.

I could see a bright blue shimmer arc around him like heat lightning. It flashed hot, then disappeared. The heat remained in his eyes, though, turning them electric blue.

The fire increased in light and heat, circling ever closer to us now that the final barrier was gone. I felt the heat singe my hair, the prickling of impending pain on my scalp.

Grabbing my hand, Leo hauled me into his arms. He got to his feet, bending over to shield my body, and bolted for the door, kicking through the burning wood into the hallway beyond.

The fire was even hotter outside Dante's room. I coughed, the smoke burning trails in my lungs. I couldn't see anything but red. The color of destruction.

Tears ran down my face, evaporating in the blistering inferno around us.

I clung to Leo as he tripped down the stairs, ran through the common room of the Dungeon, and crashed through the door to the outside.

The cold air hit me like a fist, reaching into my body to pull out my breath. A wave of dizziness washed over me. Flashing lights rotated in my vision—redyellowred. I heard voices calling out, screaming orders. Distantly I registered the outline of a firefighter in a yellow coat running past us, heading for the burning red mouth of the Dungeon's door.

Even though we stood in the middle of the parking lot, surrounded by cars, trucks, and people, it felt like we were invisible to outside eyes.

"The Dungeon," I croaked. My mind felt sluggish, mesmerized by the hungry flames I could see over Leo's shoulder.

Leo didn't bother turning around. "Zo's work. He—"

I felt my eyelids flutter, blinking to keep out the darkness that brushed at the edges of my mind like wings. My head lolled back on my neck.

"Abby? Stay with me, Abby," Leo said, gently patting my face. He stood me on my own feet, wrapping his large hands around my shoulders. "Hold on for just one more minute, please. You'll be safe, but I need you to stay with me."

I clutched at Leo's forearms, swaying with the effort of keeping my balance. I could feel my body twisting into knots, trying to regain its equilibrium. The darkness pushed closer; I could almost feel the black wind breathing inside my head. My stomach churned as though I could vomit up the timelessness

I'd brought back with me from the bank. I had to sit down. I had to lie down.

But Leo wouldn't let me.

"Tell me what happened, Abby. What happened to Dante?"

His name ripped through me like a cry. "He's gone," I said numbly.

"Did he go through the door?"

I nodded. My tears slid down my cheeks and into my mouth. The salt tasted like loss. Bitter, endless loss.

Leo relaxed, the worry in his eyes melting away. "Good," he breathed. He pulled me into a tight hug. *"Grazie, mia donna di luce. Grazie."*

I closed my eyes, inhaling the charred, bitter smell of smoke that embraced us both. My nose itched with the scent of blackness.

"Leo, I'm tired," I mumbled into his shirt. "Can I go home now?"

"Of course, of course," he said, stroking my hair. "Go home and sleep. You'll need to find your balance again."

"Will you be there when I wake up?" I asked, ready to welcome the oblivion the darkness promised, but not wanting to let go of Leo. He was my last link to Dante.

The darkness didn't care what I wanted.

I heard Leo say, "No, but I'll see you soon," and then my vision flashed to white. But instead of seeing a glimpse of the future, all I saw was blackness, like the smoke from a burnt home, like the hourglass door freestanding in a barren void.

When I thought of the door, a brittle sharpness cut

through my mind and I thought I heard the sound of shattering glass.

And then I didn't hear anything anymore.

❸

When I woke, it was to the sight of white. White walls, white sheets, white tiles. A white machine sat next to my hospital bed, keeping careful count of my heartbeat, my breathing. An IV tube ran into my arm, slowly dripping clear fluids into my veins.

My mouth felt like it had been coated with cotton. I blinked the grit from my eyes. I felt scoured to the bone. My throat hurt inside and out. I reached up weakly and felt cotton gauze bandages taped over my collarbone and around the back of my neck.

A figure was sitting in a chair next to my bed. I squinted in the hospital half-light.

"Mom?" I croaked through a dry throat.

"Abby?" Hope sounded bright in Mom's voice. She stood up from her chair and pressed my hand with both of hers. "Abby, you're awake! Are you okay? How are you feeling?" She brushed back my hair and kissed my forehead.

"M'ok," I mumbled, still trying to find my bearings. "How long have I been asleep?"

"Four days," Mom said, wiping away tears from her cheeks.

I felt my breath hiccup in my chest. *That long?* No wonder I was in the hospital. I couldn't pass this off as a twenty-four-hour flu bug. I wondered if the effects of my adventures with time had shown up on any of the doctors' tests. Hopefully not. Hopefully they had just chalked it up to exhaustion from almost dying in a burning building and the effects of smoke inhalation.

Which reminded me.

"What about Leo? Is he okay?"

"Abby, you don't need to worry about anything right now. Let's just concentrate on getting you better."

"He saved me from the Dungeon. I want to know what happened."

Mom sighed. "Leo is fine. The firefighters said he was a hero, bringing you out of the fire like that. But the Dungeon was a total loss."

"Can I see him?" I wondered how Leo felt about being called a hero again.

"No, honey, I'm sorry. He stopped by yesterday morning to drop off a package for you and to say good-bye." Mom gestured to a thick, sealed envelope resting on the bedside table.

Leo's gone? Just like that?

"He said he'd been planning to travel, and with the Dungeon gone, he said he didn't have any reason to stay."

What about me? I thought, closing my eyes. *I'm not a good enough reason?*

Mom hesitated. "He said he and Dante would miss you."

Hearing his name forced the tears from beneath my closed lids.

"Oh, Abby, I'm so sorry. I know you and Dante were pretty serious. I didn't realize you'd broken up."

My heart ripped in my chest. How could I tell my mom I

hadn't broken up with Dante, that in truth he'd gone back in time to stop Zo? And that having crossed the door a second time, he had become like Zo was—a master of time. It sounded unbelievable to me, and I'd been there. My memory kept replaying that last moment, that last declaration of love. I held on to that memory, tucking the hope that we would see each other again deep inside my heart.

I kept my mouth shut, turning my face to the window, letting the tears flow unchecked.

Mom stroked my hair for a while in silence.

I finally pushed past my emotions, locking out the diamond-hard pain of loss and doing my best to throw away the key. Someone else had been there on the bank. Someone else I hoped was okay.

"Have you heard from Valerie?" I asked quietly.

Mom's hand stopped moving.

I turned my head, sure I didn't want to hear the answer, knowing I had to. I saw it in Mom's eyes.

"She's not okay, is she?"

Mom shook her head.

I only heard part of what she said. *Mental institution. Undergoing treatment.*

"I was talking to her mother and she said Valerie had gone out with that boy—from the band you like—one night, and then . . ." Mom shook her head. "It was just so fast. The doctors can't explain it. The police are looking for him and his friends, but they seemed to have skipped town."

They've skipped more than that, I thought bitterly. I asked Mom if I could be alone for a while. I knew she didn't want to leave me, but in the end she placed one more kiss on my forehead and left, saying she was going to call Dad to tell him I'd woken up.

As the door closed behind her, I dropped my head back onto my pillows. Everything was so messed up. Dante was gone. Leo was gone. Even Zo and his band mates were gone.

I ground my teeth thinking about that last one. They deserved to pay for what they'd done to Valerie. I closed my eyes and wished Dante success in his hunt through time.

I wondered how soon it would be before problems with the river would start to show up. Would there be any warning, or would things just change? Would I even notice?

My eyes fell on the package Leo had left for me. I reached over and could just snag the envelope with my fingers. Pulling it toward me, I saw my name written on the outside. Not Dante's hand; Leo's. Beneath my name were the words: "Dante asked me to give this to you."

Opening the flap, I extracted a stack of papers clipped together at the top. The first page was a letter.

Abby,

If you are reading this, then it means I am gone.

I wish I could be there to explain in person, but hopefully Leo will be there to answer your questions. I trust him like a brother and I know you can trust him too.

My heart constricted a little at that. There hadn't been time to tell Dante the truth about Leo. Now I feared the chance was gone for good.

You know that I can see events in the river—events that are to come. For a long time, all the ripples led to the same point: a confrontation at the door. But then the images stopped and I didn't know what would happen. I was blind. Everything hinged on your choice. Would you open the door? Would you let me go through the door?

If you are reading this, then you chose to open the door, chose to let me go. And I know this, you made the right choice.

I know you are worried about Zo and his friends. I know you want to protect the integrity of the river. And I know it seems crazy—that the only way to stop Zo is to let him go—but trust me, your choice is the only thing that will give us a chance for success against him.

I knew you had to make this choice on your own. It's why I couldn't tell you what I was seeing in the river. It's why I gave you the key as early as I did. So that, when the time came, you would have everything you needed to make the choice. And I knew I could trust you to do the right thing—no matter the cost.

I hope I was able to return Valerie to you. The ripples around her are murky and complicated. I hope she survived this intact.

I hope you survived intact as well—your heart, I mean. I know how painful it is to lose someone you love, to let someone go, to leave someone behind. Hold on to me, Abby, to my memory, to the time we spent together and the dreams of the future we shared. That way, a part of me will still be alive with you wherever—and whenever—we are.

I promise you, Abby, I will stop Zo. I'll protect you. And I know we'll be together again. I promise.

I take comfort knowing that in all the variations I saw, one thing remained constant—my love for you.

I do love you, Abigail Beatrice Edmunds. I love you through all the twists and turns of the river. I love you beyond the borders of the bank and back.

Do you remember when I told you about the poet Dante and how he survived the circles of hell and the tiers of purgatory and ascended to heaven to catch a glimpse of his Beatrice? When it was time for them to part, he offered one last prayer to his beloved. A prayer that rings true for me as well.

> *O lady, you in whom my hope gains strength,*
> *you who, for my salvation, have allowed*
> *your footsteps to be left in Hell, in all*
>   *the things that I have seen, I recognize*
> *the grace and benefit that I, depending*
> *upon your power and goodness, have received.*
>   *You drew me out from slavery to freedom*
> *by all those paths, by all those means that were*
> *within your power. Do, in me, preserve*
>   *your generosity, so that my soul,*
> *which you have healed, when it is set loose from*
> *my body, be a soul that you will welcome.*

I don't know exactly what the river holds for me now, but if this letter is a list of things-Dante-knows, then this much I know for sure: It was worth it to catch a glimpse of you.

All my love,
Forever,
Dante

I read the letter again. And again. The tears flowed faster each time. I could hear Dante's voice in my head, quiet and confident, and I missed him to my core. I may have made the right choice, but that didn't mean I felt good about it.

Eventually, I set the letter aside to look at the other papers Dante had left for me in the envelope.

I gasped.

My tears stopped instantly.

The rest of the pages were drawings. I recognized Dante's strong hand in the delicate lines that covered the paper. My eyes flew over the straight lines, the curved lines. Arrows pointing in all directions. Labels next to everything.

Page after page of illustrated gears, wires, springs.

Page after page of detailed instructions.

Blueprints for a door—one that could be freestanding in its frame.

Patterns to trace—a spiral shell; a half-sun, half-moon circle; a musical staff. A wave, a maze, an hourglass. A heart with a tiny keyhole in the center.

Plans for a brass, three-pronged hinge—three carved notches jutting out from a solid back like a capital letter *E*.

I set the papers down on my lap, the pages fluttering around me like angel wings, whispering like wishes.

Here was da Vinci's greatest and most terrible invention.

I read everything. Every label, every note, every instruction. Hardly any of it made sense. I'd never been good with measurements or visualizing three-dimensional objects from a two-dimensional drawing, but I couldn't stop looking at the blueprints. I savored every word Dante had written, every line he'd drawn, imagining the pen in his hand, flowing, dancing over the blank pages until they were filled to the edges with his memories.

It must have taken him days to draw these, I realized. Weeks, even. He must have known he wouldn't have much time to finish them once Zo set his own plans into action. I remembered too that Dante had been working on something the night of the fire—something he'd tucked into an envelope—before he went to the bank to stop Zo.

At the time, I'd thought it was his report on da Vinci's inventions. I was almost right. I smiled, wondering what Ms. McGreevey would have said if Dante had turned this in as his final paper.

I was running my fingers over the papers, laughing at the idea, when I saw my name in a small note on the last page.

Abby: Are you still willing to live without limits? Will you join me?

I looked up at my empty room in a daze, my heart already answering, not waiting for my mind to catch up.

I had to get out of the hospital.

Now.

❷

Mom didn't want me to go alone. She offered to go herself. She suggested that Dad drive me, even though it was just next door. She threatened to send Hannah with me.

"Mom," I said, "it's not that far. I'll be fine."

"You're not strong enough. You just got out of the hospital."

"I'm fine," I said for the thousandth time. "It's only seventy-nine steps."

"You counted?"

"Childhood game." I shrugged and walked out the door.

The sun was bright, the sky clear. It was a perfect spring day. I breathed deeply, enjoying the smell of the flowers. Ever since my return from the bank, I'd noticed my senses were heightened, as though time away from the world had made me appreciate it all the more when I'd returned. I wondered if it was a temporary thing or if it would last.

As I walked the seventy-nine steps, I was filled with memories. Some good—like all those birthday parties bowling with Jason or the time we got lost in the woods and he held my hand for the first time. Some not so good—like the time I thought Jason had told a lie about me and I'd given him the silent treatment for a month.

I even remembered our first kiss. Maybe not a sweet memory, but certainly not sour anymore.

I carried the papers in my hands carefully, almost reverently.

I wondered if Jason would be able to help. If he'd even be willing to help. I didn't know what I'd do if he said no.

I knocked on the door and waited, my heart in my throat—and in my hands.

Jason opened the door, and the sunlight turned him golden from head to toe. I blinked in the increased brightness and looked up at my good friend, hoping he would have the power to save me.

"Hi, Abby," he said, surprise in his voice.

I held out the papers Dante had left for me—the blueprint to his past, the doorway to our future—and smiled my best smile for my childhood hero.

"Hi, Jason. I have a favor to ask. I need you to help me build this."

ACKNOWLEDGMENTS

I remember when I was a sophomore in high school, I had to write a little paragraph for my creative writing class about my goals and dreams. It was easy: I was going to write a book and be published. And now, here it is. Here I am. And what I didn't know back in high school—what I couldn't have known—is how sweet a dream realized can taste. It's delicious. And addicting.

So I would love to take this chance to thank the people who helped me realize this very important dream of mine.

First, my husband, Tracy. It's funny—I wrote a hundred thousand words and yet I struggle to find even a few words to express how much I love him. I don't think I could say everything I want to say to Tracy even if I had a hundred million words. That's okay. He's always been able to understand the language of my heart.

Thanks to my family—the Gaunts, the Mangums, the Bailies, and the Cookes—a girl couldn't ask to be loved by a better family.

And thanks, Mom, for always being willing to talk shop

with me—including the pros and cons of paper clips and file folders and the proper placement of a semicolon.

And a very special thank you to my niece, Amanda, a talented author in her own right who read my manuscript three times and gave me excellent insight and suggestions I otherwise would have missed. She may be only thirteen, but she is wise beyond her years. I love you, Mandy!

Thanks to my darling friend, Valerie, who has made me laugh since elementary school. She'll always be Queen of the Prom in my book.

Thanks to all my friends at Shadow Mountain who worked so hard and believed in me from the beginning, including but certainly not limited to Chris Schoebinger, Emily Watts, Tonya Facemyer, and Richard Erickson.

And last, but not least, a heartfelt thanks to my fabulous writing group for the years of Saturday morning breakfasts, good books, and valuable advice: Tony and Rachel, Pam, Crystal, and Heidi. Meet me at the Lamborghini dealership, guys—I'm buyin' the yellow one!